D0295646

Kiss Me, Kill Me

Kiss Me, Kill Me

Maggie Shayne

WHEELER
CHIVERS

This Large Print edition is published by Wheeler Publishing, Waterville, Maine, USA and by AudioGO Ltd, Bath, England.

A Secrets of Shadow Falls Novel #3.
Wheeler Publishing, a part of Gale, Cengage Learning.

The text of this Large Print edition is unabridged.
Other aspects of the book may vary from the original edition.
Set in 16 pt. Plantin.

LIBRARY OF CONGRESS CATALOGING-IN-PUBLICATION DATA

Shayne, Maggie.
Kiss me, kill me / by Maggie Shayne.
p. cm. — (A secrets of Shadow Falls novel ; no. 3)
ISBN-13: 978-1-4104-3169-1 (hardcover)
ISBN-10: 1-4104-3169-X (hardcover)
1. Single mothers—Fiction. 2. Children—Crimes against—Fiction. 3. Large type books. I. Title.
PS3619.H399K57 2010
813'.6—dc22 2010034592

BRITISH LIBRARY CATALOGUING-IN-PUBLICATION DATA AVAILABLE

Published in 2010 in the U.S. by arrangement with Harlequin Books S.A.
Published in 2011 in the U.K. by arrangement with Harlequin Enterprises II B.V.

U.K. Hardcover: 978 1 408 49367 0 (Chivers Large Print)
U.K. Softcover: 978 1 408 49368 7 (Camden Large Print)

Printed in the United States of America
1 2 3 4 5 6 7 14 13 12 11 10

This book is lovingly dedicated to the readers who've been with me from the beginning, always breathlessly waiting for the next installment, and to the new ones we've picked up together along the way. Every word I write, I write with you in mind, wondering what you'll think, if you'll like it, if something I toss in for you will make you smile, if you'll get our inside jokes, if I'll scare you, if you'll cry at the end like I did. Every word. Thank you isn't nearly enough, but I thank you all the same.

Prologue

Sixteen Years Ago

Carrie Overton had known her life was about to change forever. She just hadn't known how *drastically.* But when her headlights picked out the shape of a lone woman standing beside her car on the roadside, she knew something was wrong. It was the dead of night in the middle of nowhere. The woman was leaning on her rusty, lopsided car, one arm braced on the hood, the other, cradling her swollen belly. Her face bore a grimace of pain and no small amount of fear. And, in fact, when Carrie flipped on her signal light — though there was no one other than an army of raccoons to see it, she thought — some of that fear changed to visible, almost palpable, relief. The woman — no, she was really little more than a girl, Carrie saw as she drove closer — held up a hand, as if to signal her to stop, though Carrie had already decided there was little else she could do.

She pulled over behind the girl's car, a primer-colored breakdown-waiting-to-happen, shut her own engine off and got out. The silence of the night struck her as she walked quickly over to the girl. Her shoes crunched on gravel, crickets chirped as if nothing was wrong, and night birds called out noisily every fourth step or so.

"Car broken down?" she asked, almost hoping it was as simple as that, even though every instinct in her body was telling her otherwise. And her instincts were probably better than most, seeing as how she was a doctor. A new one, yes, but a doctor all the same.

The girl met her eyes, and Carrie saw that they were wet. "No. I think I might be in labor."

Carrie felt her own quick gasp, but just as quickly she grabbed hold of her nerves and replaced them with the quiet calm she had learned patients needed from their MDs. "Lucky for you I came along, then. I'm a doctor."

"Are you kidding me?"

"Nope. I'm on my way to start a new job at Shadow Falls General Hospital."

"That's where I'm going, too!" the girl said, but then she whimpered, and closed her eyes and hugged her middle. "God, that *hurts.*"

"Okay, breathe through it," Carrie told her. "Like this." And then she demonstrated, puffing short bursts of air from pursed lips.

The girl obeyed, and in a moment, as the pain eased, Carrie opened the rear door of the girl's car and helped her in. "Come on, lie down on the backseat, where you can be more comfortable until I get us some help."

"I think comfortable is impossible at this point." But the girl moved anyway. Not far, though. She took two steps, then bent double once more, almost falling to her knees this time. She began puffing those short breaths again, and for the first time Carrie felt a real sense of alarm.

Hunkering down to be at eye level with the now-crouching mother-to-be, Carrie asked, "How far apart are the pains?"

"Almost constant," the girl whispered between puffs.

"Okay. Okay," Carrie said soothingly. She waited for the pain to pass, and then quickly moved the girl into the backseat. Clearly she was about to deliver a baby. Another birth pang came and went before she got the girl even half-undressed. Then Carrie had to leave just long enough to race to her own car and grab her bag. In seconds she was back, kneeling on the pavement beside the open car door.

"The pains only started an hour ago. I thought I'd have time to get to Shadow Falls."

"Most women would have," Carrie told her. "You're being an exception to the rule today. But don't worry. I can deliver your baby right here just fine. There's nothing to be afraid of."

"Then why am I scared shitless?" the girl asked. "Unhh! Oh, God."

Carrie tried to project confidence and hide her own nervousness — she'd delivered babies before, after all. Not on deserted country roads in the backseats of barely roadworthy cars, but she didn't imagine many doctors had. She laid a calming hand on the girl's bulging belly and felt the baby move inside. It instigated a wave of sadness, but she tamped it down. "It's a miracle, you know. It's a miracle you're experiencing right now."

"Miracles *hurt!*" Pant, pant, pant. "Have you ever — oh, hell! — delivered a baby before?"

"Dozens of them," Carrie lied. She'd delivered three — exactly three — during her residency, but she'd never had to fly solo, without a nurse or sterile tools or gloves, not to mention a backup neonatal team standing by.

"I'd give anything not to have to do this," the girl moaned.

"I'd give anything to trade places with you right now," Carrie told her.

"You must be nuts, then — oh, hell, oh, hell, oh, *hell!*"

"Not nuts, just broken. I . . . I'll never be a mom." Maybe telling her that would make her realize what a blessing this event was. How important. How special.

The contraction passed, and the girl's expression eased. She studied Carrie's face. "You can't have kids?" she asked.

Carrie met her eyes. "Nope. I was born with defective fallopian tubes and —"

"Oh, *shit!* Something's happening. I have to push. I have to —"

"Go ahead, push." Carrie got low and flattened her hands against the bottoms of the girl's feet so she would have something to brace against. The contraction eased, and the girl fell back, heaving a sigh.

"Relax until the next contraction," Carrie told her. "Then we'll push again."

"It's odd, me meeting you out here like this," the girl said.

"We haven't officially met, though, have we?" Carrie pointed out. "I'm Carrie Overton. Doctor Carrie Overton. And you are . . . ?"

The girl didn't answer. She was gripped by another contraction, and then another, and the opportunity for conversation was gone, aside from the necessary bits. *Breathe through it. Push harder.*

It wasn't long before the baby's head came into sight. And with the next push, the shoulders began to emerge. "You're so strong," Carrie said. "This is going to be over in no time, hon. Two more pushes, maybe three."

"I want it to be over with *now!*" the girl cried.

"I don't blame you. Come on, push with me now."

The girl pushed, and Carrie talked and comforted, and in short order she was holding a tiny, wriggling baby boy in her arms. He released a series of congested bleats, making her laugh softly. "A boy," Carrie said. "And he's got a great set of lungs on him, too."

"Is he okay?" the girl asked. "I want him to be okay."

"He's fine. He's absolutely . . . beautiful. God, look at him. He's perfect." Carrie sniffled, then tied off the cord, cut it and wiped the baby down as best she could with gauze and sterile water. She suctioned his nose and mouth with a small blue aspirator, wrapped him in her own jacket, and for just a moment held him in her arms, smiling down at his tiny face. When tears burned in her eyes, she blinked them away and gently placed the baby in his mother's arms.

"You should try to nurse him," Carrie whispered. She couldn't speak any louder than that for the tightness in her throat. The idea of never being able to have a baby of her own . . . it was a constant twisting blade in her heart. She knew she would be a far better mother than her own volatile, passionate, hot-tempered mother had been. "I can hardly wait to see what he weighs," she added, mentally trying to change the subject.

She helped the new mother clean herself up, got her sitting upright, watched her trying to nurse and then nodded. "Okay, listen. I passed a house a few miles back. I'm going to drive back there, see if I can use their phone to get an ambulance out here for you, and we'll get you and your little guy to a nice clean hospital where you can recover properly. Okay?"

The girl lifted her face, her expression oddly detached. "I thought doctors all had those car phones nowadays."

"Not this one. Not yet. Anyway, I doubt it would work out here even if I did. But I'll be quick."

"And you'll come right back here?" the girl asked.

"*Right* back. I won't be more than ten or fifteen minutes. And you'll be fine, I promise."

"And the baby, too? He'll be fine, too, alone for that long?"

Carrie tilted her head. "He won't be alone, honey. He has you."

"I could fall asleep, or —"

"He'll be fine. I promise." Carrie started to back away, but the girl reached out and gripped her hand.

"This was supposed to happen. You finding me here. It was meant to be. I know it was."

"Maybe so."

"For sure. I knew a man once. He always said everything happens for a reason. And that if you want something bad enough, it can happen."

"Well, I'll bet you wanted help pretty badly. Maybe he was right."

The girl nodded slowly, her gaze turned inward. "Please hurry back."

"I promise. I'll be just as fast as I can."

"Thank you," the girl whispered, and she

squeezed Carrie's hand before she let her go.

Back in her own car, Carrie held her tears in check until she got the vehicle turned around and was headed in the direction she'd come from. But then the dam broke, and the insistent tears spilled over. She knew it was stupid, because there were other ways to have children besides giving birth to them. There were lots more babies in the world than there were suitable homes or deserving families.

She drove through the darkness, her eyes peeled for the house she'd passed, squinting to see better through the stupid tears. She was starting a new life, a new job — no, a fabulous career — in an idyllic New England town. She was buying the cutest little house she'd ever seen, and she had every intention of raising kids there someday. The adoption process was slow, slower yet for a single parent with a demanding job — so it would take a long time. But someday . . . Someday she would have a child, and she would give it the kind of solid, stable home she'd never had. No way was her child going to be uprooted and moved from place to place every time its father got itchy feet. The Overton home would be a permanent one, a solid one, and it would always be calm and quiet. No loud screaming matches. No physical altercations with the neighbors. No temper tantrums from people old enough to know better. None of the drama she'd grown up with.

No. Her child would have a quiet, loving, peaceful existence, and a hometown. She'd always wanted a hometown.

And she was on her way to the one she'd chosen, she reminded herself. Part One of her dream, all but complete. And even though the waiting lists were long, and even though adoption agencies tended to give preference to married couples over single women, she would get her baby someday. She would.

There! There was the house she'd passed.

She flipped on her signal and prayed the place was entirely dark only because it was 2:00 a.m. But there was no car in the driveway, and after at least five minutes' worth of pounding on the door and jabbing the doorbell repeatedly, she realized no one was home.

Well, all right. She would just bundle the mother and baby into her car, and take them with her until she found a phone. Or maybe she would just drive them the rest of the way to Shadow Falls herself. It couldn't be more than two hours away.

Returning to her car, she reversed out of the empty driveway and headed back to where she'd left the young woman and her son.

When she got to the spot, however, the primer-colored sedan was gone.

A jolt of alarm shot through her as she drove nearer, wondering if she had the right spot, but she was sure she did. There was her jacket, the one she'd wrapped the baby in, lying in the grass along the roadside, right near where she was sure the other car had been parked. Her headlights picked out the pale green fabric. Carrie pulled over and stopped. Surely that young woman couldn't intend to drive the rest of the way on her own, could she? She'd just given birth, for heaven's sake. She needed rest, and the baby needed —

The jacket was *moving.*

"No," Carrie whispered. "No. Tell me she didn't —" She wrenched open her door and hurried out, hopping the slight ditch to where her jacket lay, still wriggling.

Almost afraid to look, she bent and unwrapped the fabric. The tiny newborn lay inside, pink and healthy and squirming.

"Oh, God, she left you. How could she — how could *anyone?*"

Carrie gathered the baby, jacket and all,

into her arms, then felt the rustle of paper as she rose.

A note, written on the back of an old envelope with the address torn off, was stuffed in a pocket of the jacket.

Carrie,

His name is Sam. I hope you'll let him keep it.

We were supposed to meet so I could give him to you. That's what I meant by what I said before. You've been wanting a baby — and you got one. I've been wanting a solution, and you were it for me. This was meant to be. That man I knew was right. I always knew he was special. My Sam is all yours now. And don't worry. I won't change my mind about this.

Ever.

The note was unsigned. Carrie folded it and tucked it into her jeans pocket.

Then, snuggling the baby close to her chest, she walked back to her car. She looked up and down the deserted stretch of pavement, but she didn't see any sign of the girl or her car. No headlights approached, announcing that the new mother had come to her senses.

And then she looked up at the sky, silently asking the stars overhead what she was supposed to do next. As she stood there in the night, a star shot in an arcing path right over her head.

Like an answer. Like a wish.

He cried softly, and Carrie stared down into the open, unfocused blue, blue eyes of a newborn baby boy. She smiled.

"Hi, Sam," she said softly. "I think maybe . . . I think maybe I'm going to be your mommy. What do you think about that?" She was almost trying out the notion, testing the words as she said them. But they felt so good, she could barely believe it.

She didn't know how she would pull this off — find the mother and make it legal, she supposed. Somehow she would find a way. Somehow she could make this work. Somehow . . .

Somehow, in one night on her way to her new life, her dream had come true. Whoever that man was who'd told the girl that if you wanted something badly enough, it could happen, he must have been wise. A guru or a holy man or something. Because this felt like a gift. Like it really *was* meant to be.

Bending, she pressed her lips to Sam's forehead as tears, happy ones this time, rolled down her cheeks. "I'll find a way to make this work, Sam. I promise. And I will be the best mother you could ever wish for."

1

Present Day

"Go, Sam! Woohoo!" Carrie pumped her fist in the air when her lanky teenage son nailed the soccer ball with the inside of his size-ten foot, sending it like a bullet past the goalie and into the net. He glanced her way, gave her a half smile that didn't reach his eyes, then tapped the yellow band on his arm to remind everyone watching who that goal was for.

As she sat down again, Carrie was embarrassed by her outburst. It was inappropriate, given the circumstances.

The game continued, and she looked around at the other spectators. Parents and other locals, mostly, lining the bleachers at the edge of an extensive and well-groomed field behind Shadow Falls Central High. School hadn't yet started — even though preseason games and practices had begun for soccer, track and cheerleading.

September in Shadow Falls had a definite scent to it, and a distinct feeling to it, as well. You'd know autumn was coming even if you couldn't see or hear a thing. The leaves were beginning to turn, though they were nowhere near their peak just yet. The sun was just as bright as it had been all summer long, but not as hot anymore, and the breeze had a brisk snap that was missing in the summer months. Fall was rolling in. You could feel it, taste it in the air.

But there was something besides autumn hanging in the air around Shadow Falls. There was a pall that was hard to miss. A lingering darkness that hadn't let up for five days. It only grew, in fact. Every day that Kyle Becker didn't come home, Shadow Falls got a little grimmer, a little grayer.

Even the tourists must know the reason for the town's unusual melancholy mood by now. It was hard to miss, with the Teen Runaway posters stapled to every telephone pole, fence post and unsuspecting maple tree, and the thrice-daily gathering and dispatching of volunteer search parties in front of the old firehouse, just in case something had happened to him, a possibility no one wanted to contemplate too intently.

Every player on both soccer teams, the

Blackberry Chiefs as well as the Shadow Falls Vikings, wore a yellow armband to show unity in hoping the missing sixteen-year-old would come home soon. Five days. Carrie didn't know what the kid was thinking.

"Nice boot," someone said nearby.

Carrie looked up to see local cop Bryan Kendall, in uniform, sitting four feet to her right. "It was, wasn't it?" she said. "How are you, Bryan?"

He shrugged. "Been better."

"I imagine you're over your head in wedding plans about now, aren't you? What have you got, six weeks to go?"

"Just under. But it's not the wedding plans weighing me down. Though I gotta tell you, I'd just as soon elope and get straight to the honeymoon."

"I'll bet."

"It's this Kyle Becker thing," he said.

She nodded, sighing. "The timing couldn't be much worse, could it?"

"Not much. Tough checking out every stranger in town at the kickoff of leaf-peeper season."

She nodded in sympathy as she scanned the bleachers, spotting a few unfamiliar faces among the locals, even here. Not many. The tourists preferred winery tours and foliage photo-ops to high school sporting events. But a few of them had discovered the soccer match and settled in to watch. One in particular caught her eye. He sat a few rows down and off to the left, and he was immersed in a supermarket tabloid with Shadow Falls' latest scandal splashed on its front page.

Dead Woman Misidentified for More Than Sixteen Years.

Anonymous Source Puts Up Half-Million-Dollar Reward for Her Missing Baby.

Carrie closed her eyes, shook her head, wishing the story of her son's birth mother would just go away already. But it was everywhere. And the idiot offering the reward wasn't helping.

All those years ago, the dead woman had been identified as one Sarah Quinlan. It was only in the past few weeks that her true identity, Olivia Dupree, had been revealed. That had renewed interest in the case, and the additional information that the dead woman had given birth only weeks prior to her murder had given the story legs.

No one in Shadow Falls had known Olivia

was pregnant or heard anything about a baby, but now everyone in the U.S. of A. suddenly seemed to be interested in speculating on what had become of it. *Especially* with the huge reward thrown into the mix.

Carrie hadn't known the dead woman's name when her body had been trundled into her hospital's morgue for autopsy. But she'd recognized her face. It had been only six weeks since she'd last seen it, after all. She'd been searching Shadow Falls for the young woman, hoping to get her to sign the adoption papers that would officially make Sam Carrie's own. On that horrible day, she'd realized it would never happen.

She alone knew what had become of the murder victim's missing baby. He'd just scored a goal on the soccer field, and he didn't even know he was adopted.

"You know that guy?" Bryan asked.

Carrie blinked and realized that her eyes were still glued to the tourist with the tabloid. He had long, honey and caramel hair, pulled back and held with a black rubber band. He had whiskers, too. Not a beard, exactly. Just a neatly trimmed layer of bristles that was probably supposed to be sexy.

Okay, it *was* sexy. Just not to her.

He wore jeans, and a T-shirt with several

guitars on the front of it and some words underneath, but she was too far away to read them clearly.

"Carrie?" Bryan nudged.

"No, no, I don't know him. I was just thinking he looks like a hippie."

"Nah, they usually travel in groups." He was being funny.

She wasn't laughing. "So maybe he's a lone hippie. Can't say I approve of his choice of reading material."

"He probably doesn't care." Bryan nodded in a direction slightly farther left. "That one's reading the same thing, but since he's wearing a buttoned-up suit, you probably don't find it as offensive."

She looked beyond the long-haired man to where Bryan had indicated. Another man sat there, light brown hair in a neat cut that seemed a little too short and too severe for his face. It was a nice face, though. He had a deep tan that stood in sharp contrast to his pale brows and even paler blue eyes, giving him a striking appearance. And his suit was impeccable, not to mention expensive.

"It's just as offensive. Though I'm more surprised to see an intelligent-looking guy like that reading it."

"I think he looks like an Oompa-Loompa."

She elbowed Bryan in the rib cage but had to laugh, and it broke a little of the tension. "You're just not used to seeing sun-worshippers at the peak of their color."

"The man is orange."

"He's not orange. He's deeply tanned. And he looks harmless. The hippie, on the other hand . . ."

"Doesn't look the least bit suspicious to me," Bryan said.

"Never trust a guy in a ponytail," she told him. "If you're still checking out tourists, I'd suggest you move that guy to the top of the list."

Bryan rolled his eyes. "I don't seriously think we're looking at a stranger abduction here, Carrie. Do you?"

"Of course not. Kyle's sixteen. Same as Sam. God, it's hard to believe they're only two years from legal, isn't it?" She sighed. "Anyway, it was a bonehead move on Kyle's part to leave without a word, though . . . Sammy insists Kyle would never run off without telling him."

"You think he's right about that?" Bryan asked.

She looked across the soccer field at her son. "You know how kids are at this age — it's all about the drama. And my son's second favorite activity is drama club."

"I don't blame him. He kicked ass in 'The Wizard of Oz.' "

She smiled, remembering. "He's a natural. I think he could be a professional actor if he wanted to."

"I agree. I also think he watches too much CSI."

"I hope that's it," Carrie said. "I just don't want to believe child abduction is something that can happen here in Shadow Falls." She watched Bryan's face as she spoke, hoping for some confirmation of her theories.

He looked away as he said, "I just wish we'd get a lead on Kyle so we would know one way or the other."

Her heart skipped a little. "Bryan, are you saying . . . are you saying there's a chance Sam's right? That Kyle *didn't* run away?"

He shrugged. "There's no evidence that anything happened to him. Every indication is that he just took it into his head to run off. I just wish he'd call his family and fess up already. It's cruel, putting them through this. They're good people."

"I never thought of Kyle as a cruel kid," she said.

Bryan averted his eyes. "Yeah, I know. It does seem out of character, and that's what's bothering me about all this."

It sounded to Carrie as if Bryan might be

rethinking the current popular theory about Kyle's disappearance, and that realization sent a chill up her spine. But before she could question him further, she saw his eyes widen and followed his gaze to the field just in time to witness a teeth-jarring impact between a player and the ground. There was no one near the kid, so obviously no one had hit him. He was clutching his chest, and his mouth was open wide.

"Gotta go, Bry!" Carrie grabbed her medical bag, always nearby at sporting events, and bounded between spectators to get to the field.

The crowd was on its feet but parted to let her through. She wasn't in a panic — this happened on a fairly regular basis, and it was usually nothing. As she cleared the knot of players and parents being held at bay by the coaches and refs, she saw the boy.

The kid on his back was Marty Sheffield, and he had a full-blown asthma attack going on. She could tell that his pulse was skyrocketing; his eyes were rolling back already, and his lips were blue.

"Okay, Marty, easy now. Easy." She yanked an inhaler from her bag. She also kept one in her glove compartment and two at her house. The number of asthmatic teens was ridiculous and seemed to be growing all the time. Not just in Shadow Falls, but nationwide, and she blamed air pollution, though she couldn't prove it.

"You're gonna be fine," she said automatically as she knelt beside the fallen boy, held the inhaler to his lips and gave him two short bursts. He tried to suck the medicine into his lungs, but she didn't think he'd gotten very much.

"Are you sure?"

That was a new voice. Male, and not local, because she knew all the locals.

"I know CPR if —"

"He's breathing," Carrie lifted her eyes and damn near gasped aloud when she saw the hippie from the bleachers kneeling on the opposite side of the prone player. His eyes were an interesting mingling of green and brown, and they were filled with concern as they bored into hers. He was far better looking than he'd seemed at first glance. Not that she had time to think about that right now.

"What are you doing down here? Do you know this kid?"

"No, but I —"

"Then you should get back to your seat with the rest of the spectators."

He lifted his brows as if mildly offended.

"Happy to. I just thought you might need an extra pair of hands, with every firefighter and EMT in town out searching for that missing boy."

He *was* paying attention to local news, wasn't he? she thought, as she fished a premeasured dose of epinephrine from her bag, tore off the cellophane wrap and jabbed the needle into Marty's arm.

The man with the perfect jawline and cheekbones started to rise, but she said, "Hey, hold up a sec. You're right. I might need you." And then she looked past him, her entire focus on her son, who was hurrying toward her. Sweat had smeared the black smudges underneath his eyes, making him look even more menacing to the opposing team, she supposed. If a kid like Sammy could ever look menacing, anyway. She saw his massive red SUV sitting nearby and realized he must have run to the parking lot to get it, then driven it out onto the field to transport his teammate if a trip to the E.R. turned out to be necessary. Now he held up the keys.

"Can you drive, so I can tend to Marty?" she asked the stranger.

"Sure."

She ran a hand over Marty's forehead, lifting the sweat-damp hair away. He was semiconscious, and breathing a little easier, though his airway sounds were still terrible. He was whistling louder than the referees had been. She waved the coach over. "Get him into the back of Sammy's Beast," she said, using their nickname for the Ford Expedition Funkmaster Flex Edition that was Sammy's pride and joy. The coach and the stranger worked together to lift Marty and then ease him into the cargo area.

"I can't believe this," Sam said, standing at the rear of the vehicle, looking in at his friend. "First Kyle goes missing, and now Marty —"

"Marty's had asthma attacks before, and he'll have them again, hon, but I guarantee you, he's going to be fine."

"I've never seen him this bad."

She peered under Marty's eyelids as she spoke, "He'll be fine — really — but I'll be at least an hour. Finish the game, okay?"

"Yeah. Yeah, okay," Sam promised. By that time, Sadie, his blue-eyed blonde cheerleader girlfriend, was at his side, looking worriedly into the back of the car.

"Mom says he'll be okay," Sam told her.

"Thank God." She sent Carrie a hopeful look. "Take good care of him, Doc-O."

"You bet I will. His parents are over there," she said, pointing. They'd been on their way to the refreshment stand when they got the word that something had happened to their son, and they were still making their way to the field. Carrie gave the worried pair an encouraging wave. "Tell them to follow us to the hospital, and that I'm just taking precautions, okay?"

"Sure, Carrie," Sadie replied.

Carrie spotted the hippie, still standing nearby. "Give that guy the keys, Sam. He's driving."

Sam nodded, then tossed the stranger the keys. He caught them easily.

"Go easy on my wheels, bro," Sam said, and then made a fist and gave the stranger a knuckle bump.

The man looked a little puzzled, not by the knuckle bump, but by Sam's words. Still, he closed the back hatch after Carrie climbed inside, then moved around to get behind the wheel.

Gabe felt as if he'd stepped into some kind of alternate dimension. He was driving a forty-thousand-dollar vehicle that apparently belonged to a teenage kid. There was a beautiful woman in the back who was, by all appearances, exactly the opposite of his type in every imaginable way, and yet he was attracted to her. How could he not be?

She was confident, capable — if a bit bossy — and completely comfortable with herself.

He had come to this small New England town in search of a sixteen-year-old who might be his own child — only to immediately learn that just such a kid was missing and a presumed runaway, and now another one was having a serious medical crisis right before his eyes.

Not that the posters of Kyle Becker bore any resemblance to anyone in his family. If you could call it a family. Nor did the kid in the back. Hell, the gorgeous lady doctor's apparently spoiled son looked more like him than any teenager he'd glimpsed so far.

Yeah, right, and was he going to get all worked up over every sixteen-year-old kid in Shadow Falls, male or female, who bore a slight resemblance to himself? That would be useless. He'd come to this town to talk to the professor who'd been living as Livvy — scratch that, as Olivia Dupree — all this time. *His* Livvy had almost never used her full first name. He was here to see what the professor knew, not to stalk teenagers. Since the good professor was out of town, he would just have to wait and bide his time.

Gabe lived his life by a certain code, and while it wasn't one that most people would agree with or even understand, it worked for him. He believed thinking positively would bring positive experiences. He believed being kind to others would bring kindness into his own life. He believed that what was meant to happen tended to happen — if you didn't go around trying to force it. Trying to force things to happen usually only managed to get in their way instead. Pushing too hard would prevent the very thing you were pushing for. He'd seen it happen time and time again.

If he was meant to find Livvy's baby — her teenager now, and maybe his own son or daughter — then all he needed to do was relax about it, and keep his eyes and ears open.

And yet he couldn't help but feel an inordinate amount of worry for the injured kid, and even more for the missing one. More than he would have a few weeks ago, before he'd read the news that had convinced him he might have a child around here somewhere.

He could imagine how those parents must feel about now. He knew how he had felt, after learning that the girl he'd lived with for eight months more than sixteen years ago had been killed only six months after she'd left him. And that she'd given birth not long before her own life had ended. And that no one knew what had become of the baby.

It was like grieving for the loss of something he'd never had.

Or crying, he thought. Yeah, *crying over something he never knew he had.* Damn, that was a good line. He needed to write that down.

"When you hit Main Street, take a left," the lady doctor called.

Gabe looked back at her. She had a cell phone to her ear and was muttering stuff about "the patient" to whoever was on the other end. Someone at the hospital, he presumed. Looking at her, he got that tight feeling in his belly that always made him nervous as hell. He didn't like being nervous. It wasn't his natural state. "Got it," he said. He took the left, then said, "How far to the hospital?"

"Ten minutes if the traffic's bad. Five if it's good. And by traffic, I mean kids on bikes, tourists on foot and the occasional misbehaving bovine. It's actually only 3.1 miles, but that's as the crow flies. Still, it would have taken longer to wait for one of the volunteer firefighters to get back to town and drive the ambulance out there than to drive him ourselves, so —"

"Do you always answer a four-word question with a forty-word reply?"

She frowned, lifting her head to meet his eyes in the rearview mirror. "It was a five-word question."

"I stand corrected. Still —" He broke off when he heard motion, and glanced back to see the boy twisting and thrashing.

"Should I pull over? You need a hand?"

"I'll let you know." She leaned over the boy, and her hair, which was pulled back in a long, red and curly ponytail, leaned over with her. "Take it easy, Marty," she said. "You're okay. You just had a particularly stubborn asthma attack, but you're just fine. You have to try to relax, though. Relax and breathe slowly."

Her voice was like silk, Gabe thought. Soft and comforting, while still managing to be firm and strong. A patient wouldn't be likely to argue with a voice like that.

"Right at the next light," she said.

"What?" He was totally off track. "Oh. Got it. I see the signs now, anyway."

"Good. When you see the hospital on the right, go to the second driveway. That takes you right to the E.R."

"Okay."

"Easy, Marty. We're almost there."

"Doc?" The kid's voice was slurred. "Doc-O?"

"Yeah, it's me."

"Am I real bad, then? I am, ain't I?"

"Your grammar is in critical condition, but your body is fine."

"It is? I think I hit my head."

"I'll take a look, but your head is the hardest part of you, kid."

The young man laughed softly, and Gabe found himself smiling behind the wheel even as he turned and drove around to the E.R., stopping right in front of the double doors.

The doors opened, and two men with a gurney between them came straight to the back of the SUV. They didn't do a double take when they saw the huge limited edition Ford, so Gabe assumed they were used to seeing it.

He didn't like flashy cars. He didn't usually like the people who drove them, either. And yet he found himself enjoying both this car and the woman inside it.

She got out, and started to follow the gurney and her patient inside, but at the last minute she glanced over her shoulder at him. "You can park it and wait, or take it back to the soccer match. Thanks for the help."

"You're welcome." She was gone before he could add, "I'm Gabe, by the way."

Not that she probably gave two hoots what his name was.

However, it occurred to him that if anyone knew about the population of Shadow Falls, teenagers included, it would be the local doctor. And depending on how long she'd been there, she might know even more than that.

Carrie emerged from the treatment room and was met in the doorway by Marty's parents. "He's fine. I promise," she said.

Janine Sheffield sagged in visible relief. Gary, her husband, closed his eyes briefly. "Can we see him?"

"Absolutely. And you can take him home, too. He has a mild concussion, from hitting his head when he went down. Keep an eye on him overnight. Give him another nebulizer treatment tonight, and one in the morning. I don't expect any problems, though." She took a step back and held the door open for them.

They headed in, and Carrie let the door fall closed behind them, then spotted the handsome stranger sitting in the waiting room, caught his eyes and lifted her brows. "You waited."

"I didn't want to leave you stranded. The kid's okay, I take it?"

"Yeah, he'll be fine."

"I'm really glad to hear that."

He meant it, she thought. Okay, so he was a hippie, but that didn't mean he couldn't like kids. Carrie frowned. And he was a stranger in town and there was a kid missing. Was that anything to worry about? She had to wonder. But no, she was not going to start buying into the kids' dramatic theories. Kyle had run away, end of story. The searchers wouldn't find anything in the woods. Kyle would turn up sooner or later, and Carrie would be near the front of the line to give him a good lecture about the needless scare he'd given the entire town, to say nothing of his poor parents. She hoped he would be grounded for a year, frankly.

Meanwhile, the good-looking stranger was still waiting there, and looking better by the minute, in fact. The more she looked at him, the handsomer he got. What was up with *that?*

"If you're all set here, come on," he said, "we should get back to the game."

"Match."

"Sorry?"

"In soccer it's a match, not a game."

He lifted his brows.

She closed her eyes and shook her head. "Sorry. I'm irritating that way. Come on."

She turned and started for the exit doors. "Where did you park The Beast?"

"I took a chance and put it in a reserved spot," he said. "I figured with wheels like that, everyone would know they were yours."

"Not mine." She held the door open until he joined her outside, then fell into step beside him. "My son's. It's his pride and joy."

"I'll bet. Not too many kids can afford to drive around in something like that." He extracted the keys from his pocket, aimed the key ring at the shiny red SUV and hit the unlock button, then held them out to her.

"Oh, he can't afford it, either, believe me. It was a gift."

He held out the keys, but she shook her head. "Do you mind driving? I'm not real comfortable maneuvering something that size just yet. We — he hasn't had it all that long."

He shrugged. "So it was a *recent* gift, then."

She nodded, then got in the passenger side and fastened her seat belt. The stranger got behind the wheel, stuck the keys in the ignition, and then paused and turned to face her. "I'm Gabriel Cain, by the way."

She smiled, because it was so ludicrous

that they hadn't even exchanged names until now. "Carrie Overton." She clasped his hand, and it was warm as it closed around hers. Big, too. And strong, his grip firm and sort of lingering. "Thanks again for the help today."

"You're more than welcome." He looked at their clasped hands for a moment, a frown creasing his brow, and she felt uncomfortable enough to break the contact. There had been a little hint of attraction just then, she thought. And this guy was not even close to her type.

He started the engine and backed out of the parking spot.

"Gabriel Cain," she said as he drove. "Why does that name sound familiar?"

He shrugged. "So how does a kid your son's age — what is he, seventeen?"

"Sixteen," she said.

"Sixteen." He nodded. "So how does a kid of sixteen rate a gift like this? You're quite a generous mom."

"No way did I buy this for him. It's worth three of what I drive."

He looked surprised. "His father, then? Let me guess. He's trying to earn brownie points to make up for the divorce."

She frowned at him.

He shot her a sheepish look. "Sorry. Too

personal, huh? I just noticed you aren't wearing a ring, so I figured —"

"You figured wrong. And if you're thinking my son is a spoiled rich kid, then you've got that wrong, too. He's a great kid. *Exceptional.* And believe me, he earned this baby, or I wouldn't have let him accept it."

He swallowed hard. Then he said, "Sorry if I hit a nerve. You're right, that was what I was assuming. I, of all people, should know better than to judge anyone by appearances. You have my apologies."

She blinked, realizing she'd been judging *him* by his appearance from her first glimpse of him. "I didn't mean to snap. It's been a long week. The truth is, he saved a woman's life. She gave him the SUV to thank him."

"That sounds like a fascinating story."

"It is. Olivia — God, I'll never get used to not calling her that. Sarah was probably a little too generous. But she really wanted him to have it, and I couldn't say no."

He paused for a long moment, then cleared his throat and said, "You're talking about Sarah Quinlan, aren't you? The professor who's been living as Olivia Dupree for the past sixteen years."

She shot him a quick sideways glance.

"Sorry. It was all over the news. Pretty hard to miss."

"Probably."

"So you know her, then? The professor?"

"I know her pretty well, yes."

He compressed his lips as if in thought, and then said, "I don't suppose you could introduce me? I'd really like to talk to her."

She lifted her brows. "God, don't tell me you're another reporter!"

"No, I —"

"Do you actually *write* for that rag I saw you reading at the soccer match?"

"No! No. That's not it at all."

"No? Then why do you want to meet her?"

He shrugged. "It's personal."

She narrowed her eyes at him. "Well, it's impossible, anyway. She's on her honey-moon. Sam and I are keeping an eye on her place while she's away. She took her horse-sized dog with her, thank goodness."

He blinked twice, then looked at her. "Sam?"

"My son."

"Oh." He cleared his throat. "Is that a . . . family name?"

"It's just a name." She lowered her eyes. "You know, the tabloids have it all wrong. Oliv— Sarah is a terrific person. She had a good reason for using a dead woman's identity all that time. Her own life was in danger."

"Yeah, but the dead woman whose identity she stole had left a baby behind, somewhere. Didn't she even consider she might be robbing some family of all they had left of a loved one?"

"She didn't know about the baby until a few weeks ago. All she knew was that the real Olivia was alone in the world."

"I see."

She drew a breath and tried to calm her racing nerves. God, if anyone ever found out that her Sam was the long-dead woman's missing child, she would lose him. She would lose the most precious thing in her world, and no doubt her job and probably her medical license along with him. Not that those things mattered. Without Sam, she wouldn't have anything, anyway. He was everything to her.

And this man seemed far too curious about local gossip for her peace of mind. He pulled into the school parking lot, which was abandoned by then, with the exception of a VW Bus with an insane paint job. The soccer match had long since ended, and she didn't even know which team had won.

She looked at the bus, with its wild swirls and crazy colors, and said, "I take it that's yours?"

"Mmm-hmm. You like it?"

"Is Scooby-Doo waiting inside?"

He smiled at her, a genuine smile that made her catch her breath as the dimples in his cheeks deepened. "I haven't found a dog yet that likes to travel as much as I do."

"So you're a drifter."

"If you want to call it that."

She looked at him curiously. "Just what do you do, Gabriel Cain?"

"I'm a songwriter," he told her. And then he got out of the SUV and walked toward his bus. When he opened the driver's door she glimpsed a guitar resting on the passenger seat and a GPS on the dashboard. He lifted a hand to her just before getting in. "I'll see you around, Carrie Overton."

She paused, then got out and went over to his van. He'd closed the door, but the window was down. "Folks have been gathering at the old firehouse three times a day to go out searching for Kyle Becker, the missing boy. Next shift gathers at four. I'm sure they'd welcome another volunteer."

He nodded. "I'll be there."

"Good."

He started his motor and put the bus into gear as music spilled from its speakers. James Taylor. Good stuff. Then he drove away and left her wondering why she'd delivered the spontaneous invitation.

A kind, intelligent, kid-loving hippie drifter who listened to James Taylor and drove the Mystery Machine.

He might not be her type, but she had to admit, the man was interesting. And damn good-looking. If you were into that long-haired, unshaven, bad boy look, anyway. Which she, she reminded herself sternly, definitely was *not.*

2

Carrie drove her son's ridiculously ostentatious car away from the high school, and thought about Gabriel Cain and why his name sounded so familiar. He obviously wasn't well-off, driving an old VW Bus around the way he did. A drifter, by his own admission. She'd always wondered what drove men like that. Her own father had suffered from what her mother had called itchy feet. She'd grown up hating it. *Hating* it. Just when she would get used to one school district and begin to make a few friends, her father would yank up stakes and make them move again. It had been traumatic to her as a child and even more so as a teen. But her mother had always put her father first, ahead of her own child. And she'd hated that, too.

She'd never understood the wanderlust.

And she was irritated that she was thinking about painful elements of her childhood just because some stranger had wandered into her E.R. To hell with that. She reached for the MP3 player's controls, found the playlist titled Just for Mom and, smiling a little at her son's thoughtfulness, hit the Play button.

Then, as the smooth, soothing guitar and deep, rugged vocals of country music legend Sammy Gold filled the car, she relaxed and enjoyed the rest of her drive.

Her modified A-frame was waiting, as peaceful as always. Sam and the ever-present Sadie sat on the broad front porch. As Carrie pulled the SUV up to the oversize garage, she saw that Sam had his legs extended, feet on a wicker footstool and an ice pack on his knee.

Frowning, she parked the SUV, hit the button to close the garage door, then hurried outside, across the drive and up the steps to the first level of her two-story wraparound deck.

"What happened?" Carrie dropped her medical bag and purse on the glass-topped wicker table, and crouched in front of her son to remove the cold pack.

"Nothing, Mom. It's just a little swollen and sore from overuse. Coach said to ice it."

"Coach didn't go to medical school." She

poked and prodded at his swollen knee, then flexed it a few times, one hand over the kneecap to feel for any problems.

"So what's the diagnosis, Doc?" Sam asked.

She tried not to smile and said, "It's strained from overuse. Ice it."

"Thank God for med school, huh?"

"Watch it, pal." She smiled at his teasing, though, and finally turned to Sadie. "Hi, hon. How's your day going?"

"Better now that you're here. You wouldn't believe how he's been whining about the game."

"Lost, huh?" Carrie asked her son.

"By one. *One.* On a penalty shot based on a bad call. You wouldn't even *believe* —"

She held up a hand. "Yes, I would."

Sam gave them both the stink-eye and tried to change the subject. "How's Marty?"

"He's fine, hon. No side effects. Just a nasty bout of asthma and a bump on the head to boot."

"Good thing Marty's got a thick skull," Sadie put in.

"That's what I told him." Carrie sighed as she looked at her watch. "It's almost time for the afternoon round of searching for Kyle. But maybe you ought to take tonight off, Sam. Rest your knee."

"No way. I'm not going to stop looking until we find him."

She thinned her lips but didn't argue. "It's your call, hon. But I really don't think we're going to find Kyle by trekking through the woods."

"I know what you think," he said. "And you know I think you're wrong. Dead wrong. Kyle didn't run away. He *wouldn't* run away. Something happened to him — something bad."

"I know you believe that —"

"And no one's taking it seriously. Everyone's assuming he just ran off, that he isn't out there somewhere, needing help."

"Regardless of what anyone believes, Sam, everyone is out looking. Bryan Kendall swears that he and everyone else in the police department are treating this like a missing person case, not like a runaway, just in case. So all the bases are covered."

"Right," Sadie said. "And we appreciate how much time you've been putting into the search, Carrie. Even though you don't think it's going to get us any results."

"Thanks for saying so," Carrie said. And she gave the girl a smile, thinking again how much she liked Sadie. She was tough and smart and not afraid to say her piece. Girls were growing up strong these days. She liked that, too.

Sam was still frowning, no doubt frustrated. Carrie wished she could make this better for him, but only bringing his friend back home would do that. Damn Kyle for worrying everyone like this.

"It's three," Sadie said. "If we're going to be at the firehouse by four, we'd better grab a bite and get ready."

"I'm not hungry," Sam muttered.

Sadie met Carrie's eyes, rolled her own. "The average halfback runs eight miles per match," the girl said, "burning off a few thousand calories in the process. There's no possibility that you are not hungry. So it's obvious you're saying that just to make sure we know how miserable you are. But honestly, Sammy, it doesn't help Kyle one bit to play stubborn and refuse to eat. It only hurts you. So do what you want. Your mom and I are going to get some food."

And with that she got to her feet and sauntered through the wide entry door into the house.

Carrie smiled. "I swear, son, you've got yourself a keeper there."

He smiled back. "I know I do." Then he tossed the blue cold pack to her and leaped off the chair to his feet, forcing Carrie to bite back a squeak of protest.

In a moment her son was through the door, catching up to Sadie and sliding his arms around her waist from behind.

Carrie sighed, glad Sadie was around to help pull Sam through this tough time, and started forward herself, then stopped when she heard a vehicle in the driveway.

Turning, she saw an unfamiliar old-school station wagon with wood-grain sides. She hadn't seen one like it since she was a kid, she thought. It pulled to a stop, and a smiling woman got out, her head of snow-white hair like a soft, fluffy cloud. Twinkling eyes, crinkled at the corners, gazed her way as the woman waved a hand.

"Hello," she called. "Dr. Overton?"

Carrie nodded and, since the woman was hurrying toward her, trotted down the steps and met her in the driveway.

"I'm Rose. Rose McQueen. I know it's terribly presumptuous of me to come by in person like this, but I just had to try."

Rose McQueen. Carrie's rapid-fire brain ran the name through its files and found a match. If only she could be so efficient in figuring out where she'd heard the name Gabriel Cain before.

Now what was *he* still doing on her mind?

"Yes, I remember," she said, tugging herself back into the moment. "You phoned me last week about the room over the garage."

The woman nodded. "Yes, and you said you weren't going to be renting it out this year."

Carrie nodded, catching a whiff of the woman's perfume, which reminded her of her grandmother's flowery favorite scent. "It's just with the circumstances —"

"The missing boy. I know. I've seen the flyers. And you have a son of your own, so I completely understand why you wouldn't want a stranger around right now."

"Exactly," Carrie said. She didn't add that she wasn't all that worried about strangers, since she didn't think Kyle had met with any sort of foul play. No, she was more concerned about the gossip-seeking tabloid junkies and money-seeking amateur sleuths, all sniffing around for information on the missing baby from sixteen years ago.

"But still, I wanted to come by. Partly because most people just *love* me once they meet me," Rose said, exaggeratedly batting her eyelashes and offering a coy smile that had Carrie smiling right back. "And partly because I figured you could tell at a glance that I'm no menacing kidnapper type."

"I can see that you're not at all menacing." The older woman wore a long floral print jacket that floated when she moved, over a plain white button-down top and dressy brown trousers. The jacket gave the outfit flash, color, style and motion, and it looked expensive.

"Oh, wait, I almost forgot." The woman opened the very large quilted shoulder bag she carried and tugged out a plastic container with a tight-fitting lid. "These are for you and your family. A blatant attempt at bribery, I admit. But you get to keep them even if you don't change your mind."

Carrie took the container, which was semitransparent. "Brownies?"

"The best brownies in the universe. Even if you say no now, you'll be saying yes after you eat your first bite just in hopes you might get another batch."

Carrie laughed out loud that time. She *liked* this lady.

"Now, I promise I won't make a pest of myself by asking again after today. This is my last-ditch effort. But I haven't been able to find a vacancy anywhere else in town, and the woman at the store said you usually rent out that garage apartment to tourists in the fall, and I really want to be here as the leaves begin to change this year. I've missed it *so* much."

Carrie lifted her brows. "You've been here

before, then?"

"I grew up here," Rose said. "Well, until I was ten and my family moved west. I told myself I'd have one more autumn in Shadow Falls before I died. And I'm not one to complain, but it looks like I might not have too many more autumns in me."

Carrie blinked and knew the woman had her. How could she say no to a plea like that? And it was true; she usually did rent out that room, more as a favor to the town than out of any real need for the extra cash. Shadow Falls encouraged its year-round residents to make use of extra space that way, because it was good for tourism. The regular rooms booked up a year in advance, but the town hated to turn away anyone who wanted to visit. Especially lately, when times had been tough. The ski resort owners were having more trouble than anyone. Poor Nate Kelly was talking about selling his Sugar Tree Lodge. The winters just hadn't been producing the snow they used to, and making it was expensive. But while the ski business was the one in crisis, things were tightening up for everyone in the tourist industry, so providing a room for overflow visitors was Carrie's little bit of public service for her adopted hometown. But she hadn't intended to do it this year.

Until now. "Well, I don't know," she said, teasing the woman back a little. "Maybe I'd better taste one of these brownies first."

Rose smiled, knowing she'd won her case. "I think I like you, Dr. Overton."

"Call me Carrie." She pointed to a spot beside the garage. "You can pull the car up right there. I'll run in and get the key, and then I'll show you the room."

Rose beamed. "Oh, thank you, Carrie. Thank you so, *so* much. You can't possibly know what this means to me."

"Sam Overton, right?" Gabe had seen the familiar giant red SUV pull up in front of the old firehouse, watched the boy get out, and felt a surprising letdown when he noted that the female with him was the cute little blonde girlfriend and not his redheaded mother. He'd been looking for her amid the crowd of volunteers since he'd arrived fifteen minutes ago.

The firehouse was like something out of a forty- or fifty-year-old snapshot, a small wooden structure with a giant bell on top that would have to be rung by hand. Hand-painted lettering spelled out Shadow Falls Fire Station. Gabe figured there was probably an old-fashioned pole inside, too.

Behind and to the right, there was a big

modern fire station with three bays, overhead doors and speakers mounted on the roof. But the town had the good sense, in Gabe's opinion, to keep the old one. And not only to keep it, but use it. It fit here, nestled amid the maple- and pine-covered hills that were just beginning to come alive with color.

Sam glanced at Gabe then looked again. "Right, you're the guy who helped out with Marty at the game earlier." He extended a hand as he added, "Thanks for that."

"No problem. How's he doing?"

"Fine. Great. So you're joining in the search, then?"

"Yeah, your mom told me about it. I, uh — I thought she was going to be here."

"She's gonna be late. We got a boarder at the last minute, and she had to get her settled in."

"A boarder?"

"We rent the little apartment over the garage when there's overflow at the local inns and stuff." Sam winced, partly due to the elbow in his rib cage. "Sorry," he said to the girl who'd thrown it. "This is my girlfriend, Sadie."

Gabe extended a hand to the pretty cheerleader, remembering her from the soccer game — *match*. "Gabriel Cain," he said.

"Good to meet you."

She opened her mouth to reply, but was cut off by Sam, who gaped and said, "Not *the* Gabriel Cain? The songwriter?"

Gabe lowered his eyes. "Yeah, but I'm kinda keeping that to myself for the moment."

"Why? I'd be wearing a T-shirt with my platinum records all over it!" Sam looked at Sadie, who was wearing a puzzled frown. "It's Gabriel Cain. You know. 'Birds in the Wind,' 'Silent Song,' 'Sunbeam' . . ."

Her brows went up as Sam said, his voice growing louder with every word, "He *wrote* them. And tons more. He's freakin' famous."

"Again," Gabe said, "keeping a low profile here."

"Sure, sure, I got that. But damn, Gabriel Cain, right here in Shadow Falls. Hey, I play a little, you know. We should jam or something. How long are you going to be in town?"

Gabe smiled, loving the kid's enthusiasm. "I don't know yet. I tend to go where the wind takes me."

"Dude, that must be amazing."

"It's an honor to meet you, Mr. Cain," Sadie said. "A real honor. I'm sorry I didn't recognize your name, but 'Silent Song' is one of my favorites. It's on my iPod."

"Thanks." He shifted his focus to the boy again. "I'd love to jam with you, Sam. I've got my guitar in the bus, so we can get together whenever you have time."

"The bus? You brought a bus? How are you gonna keep a low profile with a —"

Gabe cut him off with a nod toward his vehicle. "Not a tour bus. A VW Bus," he said.

Sam looked at it and grinned. "You call that low-profile? What is it, a sixty-four?"

"Sixty-five. I call her Livvy."

"Livvy? Old girlfriend?"

He nodded. "Yeah. She was as much of a wreck when I found her as the bus was. I managed to do for the bus what I couldn't do for the girl."

"What's that?" Sadie asked.

Gabe shrugged. "Save her, I guess."

Sadie looked sad and lowered her head, but the sentimental moment was completely lost on Sam, who was moving closer to the bus with the other two left to follow in his wake. He ran a hand over the paint, the giant flowers and psychedelic swirls of yellow and green, and shook his head. "You restored her yourself?"

"I had help from friends here and there, but mostly, yeah, she was my project."

"What's under the hood?"

Gabe smiled. "Nothing like what's under yours, kid. I heard you earned that Ford the hard way."

It was Sam's turn to look embarrassed. "It wasn't as big a deal as the professor made it out to be."

"I kinda doubt that."

The kid looked up into Gabe's eyes, and Gabe had a moment of stark revelation. There was something about the boy's eyes — something painfully familiar. Or maybe he was just getting way too into wishful thinking.

"Looks like something's happening," Gabe said, nodding at the uniformed men now moving through the crowd, urging people to break into groups of ten or so.

"Yeah, time to go. I'd love to see the inside of the bus sometime, though."

"I'll let you drive her later, if you want."

"Really?" Sam beamed, but then his smile faded as he heard a cop on a megaphone begin the routine speech about how the search would unfold this evening, what areas would be covered, and what someone should do if they found anything.

Anything, Gabe knew, meant Kyle Becker, Sam's missing friend. And, more than likely, it meant his body. Because finding him in the woods alive didn't seem a very likely scenario. He could only hope the kid wasn't in the woods at all but had run away, as the curly-maned doctor theorized. He clapped a hand to the boy's shoulder. "Hang in there. I know this is a rough time for you."

Sam met Gabe's eyes and shook his head. "I don't think we're gonna find him, Gabe. Not . . . not alive, anyway."

Sadie gasped. "Don't say that, Sammy!"

"Sorry, I just — I know Kyle. He wouldn't run away without saying something, you know? He'd have told me if he was thinking about something like that. And it's not like he's got any reason, you know? Not like you do, Sadie. If anyone was going to run away, it would be you. But not Kyle. He had it good. Great family, no issues. He had no reason in the world to take off."

Gabe looked at Sadie, wondering just what her home life must be like if her boyfriend felt she had reason to run away. But she misread the look and seemed to think he was looking for her to confirm Sam's words.

"He's right, Gabe. Kyle wouldn't just leave. Hell, even I wouldn't do that. Not without telling someone."

"Not without telling me," Sam said, sliding an arm around her shoulders and pulling her closer to his side.

"You know it, Sammy." She leaned her head on his shoulder. "Come on, Gabe. We'll all get in the same group."

"Thanks. I was kinda hoping you'd ask. I don't know anybody else in town."

"Other than Carrie, right?" Sadie said. And she had a little twinkle of speculation in her eyes as she said it.

"Other than Carrie. Right."

They walked together, the teens arm in arm, melding into a group that looked a few searchers short. Another man came hurrying along with them, apparently looking for fellow stragglers to join up with.

Gabe recognized him. He had brown hair, closely cut, styled with the help of too much gel. His skin was startlingly tanned in contrast to his light brown hair and brows, and his dress shoes were totally unsuited to hiking through the mountains. Gabe had seen him at the soccer game — er, match, he thought with a little smile. He'd only noticed the guy because they'd been reading the same issue of the same tabloid. And because he'd been the only guy at the game wearing a suit and tie. This afternoon he'd chosen dress pants that were probably thin enough to let stray briars stick through, and a sporty black and yellow jacket he'd probably picked up in town. It looked brand-new.

"Mind if I join up with your group?" the man asked, addressing the kids, not Gabe, which Gabe found a little off-putting.

"It's not our group," Sam said. "But sure, come on."

"I didn't think I was going to make it on time," the stranger added with an exaggeratedly heavy breath. "Just heard about this."

"Are you from out of town, too?" Gabe asked.

The man looked at him as if he'd only just noticed his presence but sent him what seemed to be a genuine smile. "Yes, I am. Ambrose Arthur Peck," he said, extending a hand.

"I'm Gabe." Gabe shook hands with the newcomer. "Where are you from, Ambrose?"

"Milwaukee. I'm CEO of an investment firm there. Manlin, Taylor & Strauss. Have you heard of it?"

"No," Gabe said. "But don't think of that as a bad thing. I only tend to hear about the ones under investigation by the FCC."

Sadie pretended to cough, but only to disguise a snort of laughter. Gabe felt a little bad for sort of dissing the guy. Just because he himself didn't like trying to impress people by sharing his résumé upon meeting them, that didn't mean he ought to judge those who did. To each his own.

"I'll have to get one of your cards," Gabe said, to try to make up for it. "An honest firm that manages to be successful in this economy is a real find."

The man looked at him as if doubting he had any money to invest, but he smiled and said, "I don't have them on me, but I'll make sure I do the next time we meet."

"Great." Gabe turned his attention to the people in the group they had joined. The rest were all locals, he thought. He caught a few names, tried to commit them to memory. Marie was the plump lady with the bad haircut who looked forty but was more than likely in her twenties, and she was a baker. Made pies and cakes for the local eateries, she said. The tall skinny guy who looked like an undertaker was Nate Kelly, and he owned one of the local ski lodges. There were others, but the names and faces blurred together. They chatted comfortably until a white-haired man with a face like a road map and wearing a police uniform stepped onto some sort of platform in front of the old fire station. Gabe couldn't see what the platform was, due to all the legs around it, but he could see the cop clearly now that he stood a foot above everyone else, especially since the man was tall to begin with.

"Okay, pipe down," the man said, and his voice was like gravel. "For those who are new, I'm Chief MacNamara, Shadow Falls P.D. Thanks for helping us out on this. We wish to hell we didn't need it. You're each going to get a copy of a map with your area marked in red. There's a grid pattern on your maps, to make it easier for you to make sure you cover all the ground. You'll each be given a whistle. If you find anything suspicious, blow the whistle. Don't go near what you find, don't touch anything. Just blow the whistle. The only exception to that is if you find a person who is alive but injured, and in need of your immediate assistance. Other than that, just blow the whistle. Is that understood?"

The crowd nodded and murmured.

"I mean it. Now, this is the boy we're looking for." He held up a poster with Kyle's face on it. "Don't worry. You'll each get a copy. He was last seen five days ago, so if he's lost in those woods, he's going to be hungry. You're all getting a protein bar and a bottle of water to give to him if you find him and he's able to eat it." He looked to the side, where firefighters and cops were already beginning to hand out supplies to the searchers. The items were all packed into plastic drawstring bags made to be worn backpack-style, and one was being handed out to each searcher.

"We quit at dark," the chief went on. "You'll each have a team leader from the police or fire department, and I expect you to do what they tell you. If you don't like that, go home. When the search ends and you return here, please put the supplies you've been given into one of these boxes up front, so we can use them again when we resume in the morning. Any questions?"

He paused for about a second and a half, then said, "Good. Now, Paul and Diana Becker have a word or two for you."

Sam leaned close to Gabe. "Kyle's parents," he whispered. "They start off this way every shift, every day."

"She looks exhausted," Sadie said softly. "God, I think she's aged ten years this past week."

"No wonder," Gabe said.

"Those poor people," Ambrose muttered. "What they must be going through."

Gabe nodded in agreement, then they fell silent as Paul Becker, a lumberjack-sized torso on a five-foot-six frame, took the chief's place on the platform. Despite his bulk, Kyle's father looked as if a stiff wind would blow him over.

"Diana and I want to thank you all for coming out. Our friends and neighbors — you've been here every step and we're grateful. You out-of-towners — I don't even know what to say. Takin' time out of your vacations to help us, well, it's pretty amazing. Thank you."

He looked at his wife, who stood in the circle of his powerful arm. She had a raccoon look to her, but not from running makeup. The dark circles beneath her eyes were purely stress induced. She was a little stooped, too, but not, Gabe suspected, from osteoporosis.

She said, "We want you to know you're in our prayers, every last one of you. God bless you."

Her voice was weak. The group applauded as the couple stepped off their makeshift podium, people touching them, patting them on the arm or shoulder, as they made their way inside the old firehouse, which seemed to have become a command post of sorts.

It was a photographer's dream of a building, that little old-fashioned firehouse, Gabe noted again, even as his heart went out to the couple who had just entered. He had an eye for beautiful things. Usually it was natural beauty that appealed to him, but not exclusively. He loved beautiful places, and Shadow Falls certainly qualified. But the old-fashioned charm of its buildings and the respect with which they'd been preserved made the place even more attractive to him.

His admiration of the idyllic scenery came to a halt as his group began moving and he heard air brakes hissing from the road behind him. He looked around to see a line of school buses pulling up along the roadside. Gabe stuck close to Sam and Sadie as a grim feeling settled over him. The realization hit him that this search might end with something none of them wanted to find.

Once their bus was fully loaded and its door closed, a firefighter stood up in the front.

"Here we go," Sam muttered.

Gabe glanced over to where Sam sat with Sadie in the seat beside the one he and Ambrose were sharing, and saw him fitting a set of earbuds into place and fiddling with his iPod.

"You should probably pay attention," Ambrose said.

"He's heard it a dozen times already," Sadie told him. "Really. Trust me, it's okay."

Ambrose lifted his brows but returned his attention to the man up front, as did Gabe.

"Now that we're in private, I need to give you the part of the speech I wish I didn't have to. Kyle's been gone five days. Now, the weather's been good, so if he's out here somewhere and hurt, he might very well still be alive. But we can't ignore the possibility that we're looking for a body out there. So you need to make sure you keep that in mind and poke around in the underbrush. Use a branch to prod small bodies of water. Keep an eye out for drop-offs and cliff faces, and check out the bottoms of those. And while it's unlikely, I also have to advise you to note the location of and report any earth that looks freshly turned. Much as I hate to even think along those lines." He lowered his head. "Hope for the best but prepare for the worst, as they say. Now let's go find Kyle and bring him home."

The bus rumbled into motion, and Gabe understood why Sam hadn't wanted to listen to that particular speech. It must be hard to be reminded of the worst-case scenario when the subject of the speculation was a friend. Maybe a best friend.

No kid should have to go through this. Not ever.

Gabe settled back in his seat and thought

about how the importance of his own search paled in comparison to this one. He pulled out the flyer he'd been given, taking a good long look at Kyle's smiling face, reading the stats printed below it, including his birthday.

And that reminded him, painfully, that the boy had been born at the right time to be the kid he'd come here to find. Had Kyle actually been missing for a whole lot longer than the last five days?

3

Rose argued over who would carry her luggage up the outside staircase to the garage apartment but conceded when Carrie jokingly said it was a deal-breaker.

She only had three bags anyway. A large suitcase, a smaller overnight bag that matched it, and her giant quilted handbag. Carrie took the suitcase and the overnight bag, noted the Prada tags dangling from the handles and thought the woman must be loaded. And yet her car was a relic. Sam would know the make, model and what kind of engine powered the thing, but Carrie's knowledge extended only to recognizing an old car when she saw one. Maybe it was a classic or something.

Not that she cared how much the woman was worth.

Carrie set the luggage on the floor just inside the door and, turning, handed the key to Rose. "It's all yours. You should have a good cell signal up here, and if you brought a laptop with wireless, it should pick up the signal from the house. Use it all you want."

"My goodness, free Internet? This room is a real bargain." Rose smiled, then extracted a notepad and pen from her oversize handbag, quickly scribbled on the top sheet, tore it off and handed it to Carrie. "Here's my cell number . . . oh, and I'll pay in advance for the first week, too — that is, if cash is okay. I can't believe I remembered everything but my checkbook when I changed handbags for the trip." She rolled her eyes. "Age does odd things to one's memory, dear. You'll see someday."

"It's not a problem. I don't know anyone who would object to cash."

Smiling, Rose handed her a stack of twenties.

She seemed as delighted with the garage apartment as if it were a room in a five-star hotel. Then again, Carrie had taken pains to make it as homey and comfortable as possible. The cabinets were old-fashioned, slate-blue-painted wood with antique white china knobs. The walls were eggshell, with slate-blue trim to match the cupboards, and the table was fashionably retro red Formica, with vinyl-padded chairs on metal frames.

There was a small living area, complete with satellite TV and a floral print love seat, chair and antique-looking coffee table. The bedroom was tiny but had everything it needed, and the adjoining bathroom had been recently modernized.

Carrie scribbled down her cell number for Rose, then looked around, trying to think of anything she might have forgotten, but she was pretty sure she'd covered everything. "If you think you're all set, then, I'll head out," she said.

"I'll be fine here. I'm a little tired, anyway, so by the time I unpack and get settled in, I'm sure I'll be ready for a nap. Go on, enjoy your evening."

"It's not that kind of an evening," Carrie said softly.

Rose frowned, her face sincere. "Oh?"

"I'm joining with other volunteers to search the woods for the miss— the runaway boy."

"You knew the boy, then?"

"Know him. I know him," Carrie said. "He's one of my son's best friends. They met in day care."

"You've lived here that long?"

Carrie nodded. "More than sixteen years now."

"I'm so sorry, dear. I hope you find him

safe and sound. Is there any way I can help?"

"Not tonight, Rose. You're tired, and I don't think traipsing through the mountains is what you need tonight."

The older woman nodded. "Or any night, for that matter." She rubbed her back. "Arthritis, you know. Still, there must be some way I can help. You've been so kind about letting me stay here when you didn't intend to." She tilted her head. "I'll think on it. Maybe by tomorrow I'll have come up with an idea."

"That's sweet of you," Carrie told her. "I hope to God that by tomorrow it won't be needed."

"I hope so, too. With all my heart." Then, to Carrie's surprise, Rose hugged her. "Stay strong, dear. Keep on hoping."

"Thanks, Rose. Call me if you need anything. If I'm out of cell phone range, just leave a voice mail. I'll call you back as soon as I get a signal again."

"Oh, I'm sure I'll be fine. Good luck, dear."

"Good night, Rose."

Carrie Overton left at last, and Rose parted the curtain and watched her as she walked down the exterior stairs. A moment later she heard the garage door opening below her, and seconds after that Carrie's minivan backed out, then rolled smoothly down the paved driveway and out of sight.

Sighing, Rose dug in her quilted bag and pulled out a copy of the most recent edition of the Shadow Falls high school yearbook, opened it to the sophomores' page and gazed at the faces she had circled after her perusal of the birth records from the summer of sixteen years ago — the year the good Dr. Overton had arrived here, interestingly enough.

Running her fingers over the three young people whose faces were encircled in red ink, she whispered, "Don't worry, baby. I'll find you soon. I promise." And then, digging further, she pulled out a red pen and drew an X across the already-circled face of Kyle Becker.

By the time Carrie had turned on the propane for the garage apartment's kitchen range, thrown the switch to engage the electricity, shown Rose around and explained how everything worked, testing everything as she went just to make sure it *did,* then headed out to the firehouse, three hours had passed. The searchers would have begun at four and would search until dusk. And it was nearly dusk now. With such a long head start, though, her odds of catching up to them in the woods before they were well on their way back to the road were slim.

The best she could do would be to wait at the firehouse for them to return. It was hard on Sam, going through this nightly ritual. And being Sam, he joined in the searches during the day, too, when he didn't have soccer practice or a game. The first two days, he'd even skipped practice to search for Kyle, but Carrie had finally insisted he try to keep to a routine, to achieve some kind of normalcy in the midst of all the chaos and worry and fear.

She wished with everything in her that she could take his pain away, make this all better for him. He was suffering, and she hated seeing her son suffer. God, she would give just about anything to see Kyle walking up to her front door, a towel over his shoulder, asking to use the pool out back.

Her stomach knotted. She told it to stop. Kyle was fine. He was going to show up any time now.

She pulled into the firehouse's sprawling, black-topped, vehicle-filled lot, spotting Gabriel Cain's VW Bus and automatically steering into the serendipitously empty spot right beside it. By then the sun was setting.

Another twenty minutes, she thought, and the buses would be lining up, opening their doors so the streams of volunteers could come pouring out.

But maybe this time there would be good news. Maybe this time . . .

She knew better, though. If they'd found Kyle, she would have received a phone call by now. Sighing, she got out of her car and walked over to the Volkswagen, peering curiously through its windows.

A guitar case lay on the floor between the front seats. An air freshener in the shape of an eighth note dangled from the mirror. The GPS system was a new one, high-end, and was mounted to the dash. She tried the door and wasn't surprised to find it unlocked. Then she slid it open and stuck her head inside. She was curious, just dying to climb in and do a little snooping. That would be completely inappropriate, she told herself. Totally out of line. And besides, she had no business being so curious about the man. He was just another tourist, not to mention a drifter and a starving artist and a dozen other things that made him all wrong for her.

And yet she couldn't seem to stop thinking about him, being curious about him. Why? What was it about Gabriel Cain that so fascinated her?

There was a rolled-up sleeping bag in the back, she noted. Or at least it looked like a sleeping bag. And a green canvas duffel, like the kind they gave to military personnel. The duffel was stuffed full, but she wasn't about to look inside.

There were stacks of magazines and books, and she *couldn't* resist flipping through those, wondering what a man like him might read.

Nature magazines, travel magazines, magazines about hiking and kayaking. But there were also things like *Newsweek, Time, Mother Jones* and the *Onion.*

She wasn't surprised he was a lefty. Or a nature nut. She wished some of the publications gave insight into his character that she *hadn't* already guessed. Okay, she turned to the books. There were several in a netted basket he'd rigged up on one side of the van. Without climbing in, she couldn't see all the titles, but she saw a few. One caught her eye. *Turning to Gold: The Life and Times of a Country Music Legend.*

She recognized the title. It was about her favorite singer, Sammy Gold. The aging star had recently made a huge comeback, after recording his own version of a famous heavy metal ballad. Gold's take on the song had outsold the original, and earned him the respect and dollars of a whole new generation of fans.

She, of course, had loved him long before that.

Carrie backed out of the VW and slid the door closed, feeling a little guilty for snooping, but not overly so. She hadn't done more than peek. But her timing turned out to be impeccable, because she heard the distinctive sounds of bus engines in the distance even as she stepped an innocent-looking distance away from the VW and tried to act as if she hadn't been snooping. The buses, three of them, pulled up along the side of the road in front of the firehouse, air brakes hissing. Their doors folded open, and the volunteers began streaming out, heading to their cars. It was clear there'd been no sign of Kyle today. The searchers had the usual hanging heads and disappointed faces that were somehow relieved at the same time. At least they hadn't found a body.

She spotted Gabe the minute he stepped off the bus, and his eyes were on her almost as fast. The smile that appeared on his face the minute he saw her told her he was absurdly glad to see her, and then he turned to speak to someone behind him, pointing in her direction as he did.

The person behind him turned out to be her son, followed closely by Sadie, and the two met her eyes and waved. She frowned. What were they doing, hanging out with the stranger?

Even more oddly, Sadie turned to speak to the man right behind her, another total stranger. And he, too, glanced her way and lifted a hand in greeting.

Wait, wasn't that the suit-wearing tourist she'd spotted at the soccer match? It was. Good Lord, had Sam and Sadie appointed themselves the unofficial Shadow Falls welcoming committee?

Before she had time to think more on that, all four came toward her, arriving in mid conversation as Sam was telling Gabe about how the falls here were nearly always in the shadow of the surrounding mountains, giving them — and the town — their names.

"Hey, Mom. You know Gabe. And this is Ambrose."

"Ambrose Arthur Peck," the man put in. "Of Manlin, Taylor & Strauss."

"Oh. Of course, sure, I've heard of your firm." Albeit, only because the financial advisors' TV commercials ran on her favorite twenty-four-hour news station every hour, on the hour. "It's a pleasure to meet you." She extended a hand, her brain telling her that Ambrose was the one she ought to have her eyes on, not Gabe. But his handshake was wimpy, his skin damp, and his eyes never bored into hers in the way that Gabe's did. Instead they met, then dodged, then met and dodged again. Jerky eyes, in constant staccato motion.

"The pleasure is all mine, Dr. Overton. I've heard wonderful things about you."

"I'm afraid my son's opinion of me might be slightly biased," she said.

He smiled. "Oh, but it wasn't just your son. The lovely Sadie and Mr. Cain joined him in singing your praises, as has anyone else I've asked about you."

Her smile died. "You've asked about me?"

"Um. . . ." He lowered his eyes. "I — I suppose a more suave sort of man wouldn't have let on."

She lifted her brows.

"I saw you at the game. Noticed the lack of a ring and thought I might ask you to dinner while I was in town."

"Oh." Carrie was a little embarrassed on his behalf, but flattered, too. Her gut reaction was to say no way, but her practical brain told her that he was far more likely to be a suitable date than a starving artist would. "Well, I haven't eaten yet tonight," she said.

"Oh, tonight. Yes, well, tonight. I um —"

"We're having Gabe over tonight, Mom," Sam said.

"Whoa, hold up now," Gabe said, raising both hands, traffic-cop style. "You and I made those plans, Sam. Your mom didn't." Then he nodded at Carrie. "You do what you like. We can get together without you. Or, just pick another night to jam if you'd feel better not having a stranger in your house when you're not home."

The guy was considerate. And polite. And gorgeous, in that free bird, drifter sort of way.

Sam moved forward, gently closing a hand on Carrie's forearm and tugging her off to one side, out of earshot of the two men. Leaning close, he whispered, "Please, Mom? That Ambrose guy is a dork, anyway."

"Sammy!"

"I know, I know. You prefer dorks. I get that. But you get lots of chances to have dinner with guys like him. How many times am I gonna have a chance to play guitar with Gabriel Cain?"

She blinked and tipped her head to one side. "You say that as if he's somebody important."

Her son blinked at her in a way that only a son could. His expression was one she might use if she were standing in front of the *Mona Lisa* and someone suggested it would make nice refrigerator art.

"What?"

"Mom, he's famous. *Way* more famous than Manlin, Taylor and Mozart."

"Strauss," she corrected. Then realized he'd been making a joke and acknowledged it with, "But that was good."

"Gabe's songs have been recorded by some of the biggest stars in the biz. Six of them have gone platinum."

She lifted her brows, unable to stop herself from looking over her shoulder at the apparently unemployed hippie in the distance. Watching her, he smiled with one side of his mouth and lifted a hand just slightly.

She looked back at her son. "You're kidding, right?"

"I bet everyone in town has at least one of his songs on their favorites list."

"Everyone but me," she said. "But then again, I prefer country music. So it's safe to say he's *not* a starving artist, then?"

Her son's eyes had moved away from her and widened, and then he smacked his forehead and said, "Jeez, Mom."

"What?"

She turned at the sound of a male voice behind her saying, "Not starving, anyway."

She spun and had to tip her head back to meet Gabe's eyes because he was significantly taller than she was. "That was probably rude."

"Not at all. I *was* a starving artist for a long time. I don't consider it an insult. And I like to think success hasn't changed me much. Your assumption assures me that I haven't. Frankly, I appreciate it."

She lifted her brows. "I just assumed . . ." She shook her head. "I was making judgments based on your appearance. Something I've tried hard to teach Sam to never do. And I'm frankly ashamed of myself for it."

"Don't be. I promise, it's my deliberate intent to look the way I do, to convey the image that look conveys. It's who I am."

"Yeah. He doesn't start every sentence by saying, 'Hi, I'm famous. Have you heard of me?' the way that other guy does."

"There's nothing wrong with being proud of your success, pal," Gabe said, even as Carrie was opening her mouth to correct her son.

"Then why don't you act like *you* are?" Sam asked.

"My values, my choice," Gabe replied easily. "Doesn't mean I get to force them on anyone else, much less judge them for their own. Shoot, I don't believe in big, flashy vehicles, either. For me, they just don't fit. But I wouldn't even think about telling you to sell yours and buy an old VW. Because for you, *that* wouldn't fit."

Sam nodded. "I got you."

"Good." Gabe turned to Carrie. "Have your dinner with Ambrose if you want. My feelings won't be hurt in the least."

She met his eyes. "Really?"

"Really."

She blinked, and felt right down to her toes that she would far rather spend the evening getting to know Gabe. And yet that practical part of her mind whispered that Ambrose was a whole lot closer to what she wanted. And that Gabe was the epitome of everything she didn't want.

"I think," she said slowly, "that *his* feelings *would* be hurt."

"I think I agree with you."

She held his gaze, and something tingled along the back of her neck. "You do?"

"Yeah. He seems to put a lot of stock in ego. And being turned down *would* be a blow to his."

She nodded, glancing at Ambrose, who was in an apparently fascinating conversation with Sadie. The girl was clearly wise enough to know that he was the topic of discussion and that she should keep him distracted until they had finished.

God, she loved that girl.

"You're welcome to go back to the house with the kids, Gabe," she said. "If I let Sam miss the opportunity to, uh, jam with his hero, I'll lose out on that mother-of-the-year nomination yet again."

Sam rolled his eyes at her corny joke, but there was love and appreciation in them, too.

"I'll try to get home early," she said. "Maybe if you guys can hold off on dessert, we could all have it together when I get back."

Gabe lifted his brows. "Really?"

She shrugged. "It's not every day a girl has a rock star in her house."

"Just a songwriter," he said. "I only play for pleasure."

"Even better."

"Yeah?"

She nodded. "Even though you should know I prefer country music myself."

"Sammy Gold. I know."

"Oh, my son *has* been talking, hasn't he?"

Gabe nodded. "Ambrose is getting antsy," he said. "Come on, Sam, let's collect that girl of yours, and you can guide me back to the hacienda."

"Sam, check on Rose for me when you get home, will you?" Carrie interjected, even as Gabe and Sam began to walk away.

"Sure."

And then Gabe said, "Rose?" and Sam leaned closer, and began to tell him who she was as they moved on. Sam waved a hand at Sadie, never breaking his stream of words, and she smiled, said goodbye to Ambrose and headed to join them. Gabe got into his bus, Sadie and Sam got into the Sam's treasured Expedition, and Carrie moved up to stand beside Ambrose.

"Sorry about the delay," she said. "But yes, I'd love to have dinner with you. I just had to work out some logistics first."

"That's wonderful. I'm so glad," Ambrose said. "I saw a lovely restaurant with a view of the falls the other day. God, what was the name?"

"Fallsview," she said with a smile.

"Oh. Now how did I forget that?"

She shrugged. "Doesn't matter. I'll just let you know in advance that it'll have to be an early night for me."

"Those *logistics,* hmm?" he asked.

"I'm afraid they can only be shuffled so far."

"That's fine. Honestly. I'll be grateful for the company. But, um, since you have to leave early, why don't we take separate vehicles to the restaurant and just meet there?"

"That is an eminently practical suggestion," Carrie said. "I like the way you think."

"Thank you," he said, and then he stood there, silent for a moment, shifting from one foot to the other, until he finally said, "Well, I guess I'll see you there, then?"

"Perfect. I'll see you there."

He took out his keys, looked at them, looked at her, looked at his car, then turned and walked away.

Being awkward with women, she told herself, was not a character flaw. It was actually endearing in a way.

And yet it wasn't the upcoming dinner on her mind as Carrie drove through the tiny, quiet town toward the falls and the restaurant. It was Gabriel Cain. The quiet, unpretentious, apparently famous songwriter was not at all what he had first seemed. Not at all.

And she wondered what other facets of his personality remained as yet unrevealed. She was dying to talk to him, to listen to him talk back.

Not to mention use Google to see what came up.

She wished to the gods that Ambrose Peck

was as appealing to her as the songwriter. But sex appeal wasn't everything. She knew that. And in every other way, Ambrose was exactly her type.

Just like the last respectable, solid, intellectual she'd dated had seemed to be, she told herself, though she tried not to listen. She'd wasted a couple of months on that jackass.

Oh, well. Live and learn.

4

Ambrose didn't wait for her in the parking lot. She found that a little odd but shrugged it off as she got out of her car and looked around. The building was made of darkly stained, rough-hewn barn beams and glass, and not much else. It made for the best view in town. Not seeing Ambrose anywhere, she went on inside.

She spotted him at a table near the back, perusing the menu. She noticed his hands and the ring he wore, a figure eight lying on its side — the sign for infinity, she thought. Interesting choice. Nodding her intention to the hostess, Carrie wound her way between tables to join him.

He must have heard her footsteps, because he lowered the menu and rose to his feet. "Ah, there you are."

"I was only a minute or two behind you," she said.

"Oh, I know. I just thought I'd go ahead

and get us a table. You did say you were short on time tonight."

Carrie pasted a smile over her momentary irritation and nodded. "That was . . . thoughtful. Thanks." She pulled out her chair and sat down. Ambrose sat, as well, and picked up his menu again.

"Do you have any idea what's good here?" he asked.

"Oh, everything's pretty good. I like the broiled haddock a lot. Their tartar sauce is —"

"That would be an option if I were in the mood for mercury poisoning."

"— homemade." She blinked twice. Had he just criticized her for saying she liked haddock?

"As a doctor, I would think you would be aware of the damage heavy metal contamination can do."

"Oh, I am. I think fish is fine in moderation."

"I prefer not to take that chance." He never took his eyes off the menu. "How is the pasta?"

"Good. Better if you let them grate some fresh lead over it."

"Excuse me?" He lowered the menu, looking over the top of it at her.

"Lead. Heavy metal." She shrugged. "It

was a joke."

"Oh?" His brows rose. Then he smiled. "Oh! I see now. I'm afraid I don't have a very highly developed sense of humor," he confessed, shaking his head.

"No!" She pressed a hand to her chest. "I never would have guessed."

He blinked at her. "Now you're being sarcastic."

"See? You do so have a sense of humor," she said with a smile.

He shrugged. "Pasta, then," he announced, and, setting the menu on the edge of the table, he looked around in search of the waitress. When he spotted one, wobbling toward another table bearing a huge tray full of food, he held his hand up in the air as if hailing a taxi.

"She's busy, Ambrose. Besides, I haven't decided what I'm having yet."

"I took it you were having the haddock," he said.

"I said I liked it, not that I was having it tonight."

He frowned at her. "You sound upset. Have I done something to irritate you, Carrie?"

She met his eyes, saw that they were concerned and softened her tone. "Impatience irritates me. I see a lot of it at the hospital."

"I see. I was only trying to speed things along. You said you were short on time, so —"

"Why don't you let me worry about managing my time, Ambrose? You can relax and enjoy the meal. Okay?"

He tipped his head to one side, seemingly puzzled, but said, "Okay."

"Good."

By then a different waitress had come over to their table, and Carrie could tell by the look on her face that she'd seen Ambrose's insistent signal.

"Are you ready to order?"

"No, as it turns out," Ambrose said.

The waitress lifted her brows, and Carrie said, "Yes, we are. I'll have the haddock." She closed her menu and handed it to the girl, certain she knew her from somewhere. She'd probably treated her at the hospital or seen her at a soccer game or some other school function.

"How is the pasta sauce made?" Ambrose asked, reopening his menu.

"From scratch," the girl — Wendi, according to her name tag — said. "Tomatoes, peppers, onions, garlic, rosemary, basil — the usual stuff."

"MSG?" he asked.

The girl sent Carrie a look. Carrie shrugged helplessly, and then Ambrose looked her way, and she went still and tried to look innocent.

"I'll have to go ask the chef," Wendi said finally, and then she hurried away. Moments later she was back. "No MSG," she reported.

"Hmm. That's good to know." Ambrose held the menu open a bit longer, then closed it and said, "And what about the pork loin? How is that prepared?"

The girl pointed at the paragraph beside the entrée on the menu and read aloud. "Made with an apple-mint sauce, and served piping hot and brimming with flavor."

"That much I already knew. But how is it *cooked?* Baked, broiled, sautéed?"

"Nuclear fusion, I believe."

Carrie choked on a laugh, then quickly pressed the cloth napkin to her mouth as if she really had been choking.

Ambrose blinked up at the waitress, not so much as cracking a smile. "Pardon?"

"I'll go ask." She hurried away again.

Ambrose shook his head and muttered about the quality of service these days. Carrie was beginning to wish she'd done what she wanted to do and stayed home tonight.

Wendi returned. "The pork is broiled, sir. No MSG, either. I asked. There's no MSG in anything we serve."

"Fine." Ambrose perused the menu some more. For a guy who'd been set on the pasta and waving impatiently a few minutes earlier, he certainly was taking his time now.

Finally, as the girl stood there noticing that her other tables were in need of attention, Ambrose snapped the menu closed and said, "I'll have the veal."

The girl scribbled. "Is that it?"

"I think you'd better bring me a diet cola," Carrie said. "And put a shot of rum in it, will you?"

Wendi smiled for the first time and nodded. "Got it."

And then she was gone.

"My goodness, you would never know the girl is paid by the hour, the way she rushed us," Ambrose said. Then he placed both palms on the table and looked at her. "But that's neither here nor there, is it? Now that the unpleasant part of the evening is out of the way, Carrie, tell me about yourself."

She lifted her brows, because he was smiling and, she thought, trying to be friendly now. "Oh, there's not much to tell."

"Of course there is. You're a doctor. That's fascinating in and of itself. And a single mother, too. Tell me, how did that come about?"

Mentally, she raised a steel wall between them. "By choice," she said, her tone chilly.

"I'm sorry. Did I ask too personal a question?"

"Yes, you did."

"I'll try not to do that again."

"No worries. I won't answer anything that's out of bounds."

He met her eyes, and she looked away. "What about you," she asked after a moment of strained silence. "What are you doing in Shadow Falls, Ambrose?"

"Just a much-needed vacation. We've been working particularly hard at the firm for the past year, trying to keep a handle on our clients' finances in this volatile economy. It's not for the meek, that much is for sure."

"I see."

"I doubt it."

She wondered why she'd thought this guy might be interesting. Smart, she decided, did not equal interesting. "So you decided to get away to relieve some stress, then?" she asked.

"Just a brief respite to refresh my mind," he said. "And I've heard the foliage here is something to be seen, so . . ."

"It really is," she said. "But it won't peak

for another three or four weeks yet."

"I might very well still be here."

"Oh, your stay is open-ended, then?"

He nodded.

"Must be a very liberal investment firm you work for."

"Financial planning firm," he corrected. "I'm a partner. I pretty much do what I want."

"I see."

Wendi returned with Carrie's drink, set it down in front of her and placed a basket of warm rolls in the center of the table.

"Excuse me, but I have to make a quick call." Ambrose got up and moved away from the table into a quiet corner, bringing his cell phone to his ear.

Carrie took the opportunity to say, "I'm really sorry he's so rude."

"Oh, don't be silly. It's not your fault."

"Believe me, I had no idea."

"Blind date?" Wendi asked.

"All but. Listen, I want two more drinks — rum and Coke — but he doesn't need to know what they are. I'm only telling you so you can tally up the check in advance. We won't be ordering dessert. Bring the check the minute we finish eating."

Wendi smiled hugely. "I'm more than happy to help you out, Dr. Overton."

"I *knew* I knew you," Carrie said.

The girl smiled. "You put three stitches in my head last year." The girl lifted her hair off her forehead. "Softball bat."

"Yeeouch. Listen, if I promise to slip you a really good tip, will you do me one more favor?"

"No tip necessary," the girl said. "Name it."

"I'd better not be driving, so would you call my house and tell my son I'm going to need a ride home, and to be here in one hour and just wait for me in the parking lot?"

"Sure, I'll tell Sam. I don't have your number, though."

"Twenty-four, sixty-one," Carrie said. She didn't need to give the girl the exchange or the area code. They were the same for everyone in town.

"You've got it." Then Wendi looked over at Ambrose again. "It really wasn't a blind date?"

"No."

"Hmm." Wendi shrugged and turned to go back to her other duties.

Twenty minutes later the food was served and Carrie was draining her second rum and Coke, feigning interest in Ambrose's diatribe on 401ks versus IRAs, and recent income tax code changes.

Fascinating stuff.

Not.

She dug into her haddock with relish, mentally willing molecules of mercury to ride the airsteam across the table and rain down onto his veal. It was difficult not to shovel the food into her mouth as fast as humanly possible, but she didn't want to be obvious.

"Refill on that Coke for you," Wendi said, placing the third and final drink in front of Carrie. "How's the fish?"

"Perfect," Carrie said.

"And your veal, sir?"

"It's a bit dry, but I didn't expect five-star cuisine, after all."

Carrie gulped the last bit of liquid from drink number two and handed the empty to the long-suffering Wendi, who took it with her back to the kitchen. She must have been sharing the date from hell tale with the rest of the staff, though, because even though the alcohol was washing over her brain at this point, Carrie was aware of the sympathetic looks she was getting from the other employees.

Ambrose, thankfully, was oblivious.

Nearly an hour later, finally, the meal was

over, and Wendi was right on the spot, asking if they would like to order dessert. Carrie spoke before Ambrose, saying, "No, thank you."

"Oh, I don't know," Ambrose said. "Maybe we should see what they have to offer before making a hasty decision. Can you bring the cart around for us, miss?"

Wendy looked at Carrie helplessly.

"There's no cart, sir. Just a dessert menu."

Carrie sighed and turned her attention back to Wendi. "Bring us the menu." While she held the girl's eye, she tapped her glass. "And another *Coke*."

"Sure. I'll be back in two shakes."

She was true to her word.

Carrie sipped her drink while Ambrose worked his way through a slice of apple pie, after complaining about the selection and quality of desserts the establishment offered. And finally, finally, *finally,* the check was delivered to the table. It included four "Diet Cokes" at five bucks a pop.

"That's outrageous! Twenty dollars for a few sodas?"

Before he could say more, Carrie yanked the bill from his hand, slapped her credit card on top of it and handed both to Wendi.

He looked at her as if she'd grown a set of antlers.

"I insist," she said. "Consider it a welcome to Shadow Falls and a thank-you for helping out with the search today."

"It's completely unnecessary," he said.

"I won't take no for an answer."

Wendi took the card away, returning in short order with the final receipt. Carrie added a twenty-dollar tip, signed the bottom and handed it back to her. Then she pocketed her card and got to her feet. She swayed just a little and had to grab hold of the edge of the table. She shot Ambrose a quick look and hoped he hadn't noticed.

He hadn't. He came around the table and, taking her elbow, walked with her to the front door, opened it for her and looked genuinely sorry the evening was over. "I hope you had a pleasant time," he said.

"It was very nice," she lied.

"Next time perhaps you'll allow me to treat you."

"If you're still here the next time I have a hole in my schedule, it's a deal," she said. Had *schedule* sounded like *shedule* just then? Good God, the rum was hitting harder than she'd thought. She was glad she'd taken the precaution of having Wendi phone Sam to take her home.

"I see." He said it as if perhaps he did.

"Good night, Ambrose." She tried to

make it sound friendly and kind, but she thought she had probably already hurt the man's feelings. And while he'd been irritating all evening, she thought her dislike of him and eagerness to get the meal over with might have some other cause.

Another cause with long hair, an unshaven face and a guitar over his shoulder.

"Good night," Ambrose said, and then walked toward his car.

Just for show, Carrie walked toward her own, but as she did, she scanned the parking lot in search of her son's Funkmaster, which ought to stick out like the proverbial sore thumb. And she didn't see it.

Upon reaching her own understated, ordinary minivan, she noticed someone leaning on it. The very guy she'd just been thinking about. Just? No, she'd been thinking about him all evening.

Glancing behind her, she saw Ambrose's car pulling away in the distance. Good, he probably hadn't seen. No point in hurting his feelings even more. And then she looked at Gabe again. He was coming around the car now, moving toward her.

"Surprised to see me?" he asked.

She nodded, mute, trying to think of something to say. "I thought Sam was coming."

"Sam dropped me off. I asked him to."

"Why?"

He shrugged. "It sounded to me like you were having a miserable time with our pal Ambrose. I figured the timing was perfect. I'll look great by comparison, and you'll be impressed in spite of your dislike of, uh, hippie drifters."

She smiled a little crookedly. "Drifter hippies," she corrected, then looked away. "Sam told you I said that, huh?"

He nodded, held out a hand. "Keys?"

She fished them from her purse and placed them into his open hand. As she did, her own hand skimmed his palm, and she felt it right to her toes.

Their eyes met, then slid away. He walked around to the passenger side, opened her door for her and stood back to wave a gallant arm toward the car.

She got in, and he closed the door. A moment later he was behind the wheel, adjusting the seat to accommodate his long legs. He started the engine, turned on the headlights, fastened his seat belt.

She turned his way, her head resting on the seat, and found herself just staring at his profile for a long moment.

He glanced at her. "Feeling good, are you?"

"Mmm-hmm. Totally relaxed. And relieved. Thanks for rescuing me."

"Anytime," he said.

"And for being so good to Sam."

He smiled. "You don't need to thank me for that, Carrie. He's a great kid."

"He really is," she agreed.

Gabe nodded. "Yeah. And that Sadie . . . she's quite the firecracker."

"You've got that right." She inhaled slowly, then let out her breath. "So I guess I just have one question."

"Shoot," he said.

"Why is it you care whether or not I'm impressed with you?"

He met her eyes, but only briefly. "Well, because you're smart and gorgeous and fascinating, and because I'm male."

She smiled slowly. "Are you always this direct and honest?"

"I really do strive to be."

"That's . . . refreshing."

"Glad you think so."

"I do. And I think I owe you an apology for misjudging you. My son says you're rich and famous." She made a face. "Not that *that* makes any difference. There are plenty of rich and famous people who are total jerks, I'm sure."

"Rich is a relative term. And open to a

wide variety of interpretations."

"Yes, it is," she said. "So do you consider yourself rich?"

"Beyond my wildest dreams," he admitted. "But not because I have a mansion or a fancy car or gold-plated faucets in my bathrooms."

"Do you?" she asked, a bit wide-eyed.

"I don't even own a house. And you've seen what I drive. No. I'm rich because I get to do what I love most for a living. I'm rich because I get to live anywhere I want in this beautiful country of ours. I'm rich because I'm free. I go where I want, stay as long as I want, do what I want, work when I feel like it, and I'm happy most of the time. That's my definition of being rich."

She nodded slowly. "I think that's a damn good definition."

Gabe could tell she was tipsy. Not drunk. He doubted the respectable doctor would ever allow herself to get beyond control. But he was glad to see that she was relaxed enough for an honest conversation. As he drove her back to her house, he said, "Sam tells me you took in a boarder."

She nodded, her head resting on the seat back. "I end up with a couple every fall. Didn't want any this year, but —"

"Why not?"

She slid him a sideways look. "Between Kyle being missing and all the reporters who've been in town until recently, digging for any secrets they could find, I thought it best not to talk to strangers."

He nodded as if he understood. "You have secrets you're worried about them digging up?"

She swung her head toward him so fast he thought she must have wrenched her neck. "No! Why would you think that?"

He looked at her. "I didn't think that." *Until now,* he thought in silence. "I was just responding to what you said — the press in town digging for secrets, yada, yada."

She blinked as if her mind were having trouble processing his words. He decided to cut her a little slack, though he wouldn't forget the clue she'd dropped here tonight. She had a secret. She didn't like the press digging around town. And he knew what the press had been digging for. Information about Livvy, dead all these years. Information about her baby, the one that might be his. Now why would the local medico be nervous about questions like those?

"So what made you rent out the room when you'd already decided not to?" he asked.

She shrugged. "This lady was a lot easier to turn down on the phone than she was in person."

"She came to your house?"

Carrie nodded. A red curl dropped onto her nose, and she brushed it away with the back of one hand. "Yeah, just as we were getting ready to meet you at the firehouse. That's why I didn't make it." She shook her head. "She's really sweet, and all alone, and it just would have been mean to say no."

"Besides, she doesn't look like a reporter, right?"

"Right."

"Then again, who does, huh?"

She shrugged.

"I mean, you accused me of being a reporter when we first met. Do I look like one?"

"No. I mean, not an airbrushed, suit-wearing, hair-styled, talking head sort of reporter, anyway. You look more like an embedded, in the line of fire, risk-taking, rogue type."

"I do?"

She nodded. "It's the hair."

"The hair?" He ran a hand over his head, from the front to the ponytail in the back.

"This hair, too," she said, and then he felt her palm on his whiskered cheek and experienced an electrical storm in his pants. Holy shit.

He cleared his throat, sought ways to change the subject, to distract himself, if not her. "Your son is great. You've done an incredible job raising him."

She lifted her brows. "Thank you. I agree completely. Sam's amazing."

"Have you done it all on your own?"

"Mmm-hmm."

"So then, you were never married . . . ? To his father, I mean."

She slanted him a look. "I've never been married to anyone."

He studied her face briefly. "So Sam's father isn't in your life. Is he in Sam's?"

"No."

"Do you even know who he is?"

She widened her eyes. "Are you suggesting I sleep with so many men I can't keep track?"

"I didn't mean it like that at all. I just — I mean, do you think you have the right to keep Sam from getting to know his father?"

"You don't know that I'm keeping Sam from doing anything."

"That's true, I *don't* know. Are you?"

She looked at him. "I would never do anything to hurt my son. If he wants to know about his father, all he has to do is ask. And he will, when he's ready. And then I'll tell him everything I know. But I don't have to tell you any of it."

"Everything you know?" he repeated. "That's an odd way to put it."

"Why are you asking so many questions about my son?"

He felt a rush of guilt for taking advantage of her slightly inebriated state. Sam looked a little like him, maybe a lot like him, and he had the right birthday, and damn, he sure did have a gorgeous mother, to boot. But that didn't prove anything. And he thought again that maybe this thing he'd been calling a gut feeling was nothing more than a serious case of wishful thinking gone awry.

Still, her evasiveness made him more suspicious than before. He would definitely be looking into Sam Overton's records — the public ones, anyway. Sadie's and Kyle's, too. The problem was, adoption records weren't public, so he wasn't sure his search would tell him much.

He wasn't worried, though. Nor was he in any big hurry. He was here to find the truth, and he had no doubt he would. He'd waited sixteen years — admittedly without knowing he was waiting — so a few more days or even weeks wouldn't hurt anything. Impatience wasn't a trait he much liked. He was relaxed, laid-back, easy. He trusted that things would work out the way they were supposed to. That he'd been led here, that he'd learned about Livvy's baby at all, seemed to him to be proof of that. He had time. Time to find his child. And time to do so without alienating the most fascinating woman he'd met in years.

"I'm sorry. I didn't mean to pry. I really like Sam, and that's the truth." He met her eyes, trying to gauge whether or not she believed him. But he couldn't tell. "How about some music?" he asked.

She nodded and reached up to hit the button on the CD player. And the minute she did, the smooth, down-home country stylings he had come to detest wafted from the speakers. It was enough to send a ripple of irritation through his calm waters.

He looked at her as the gravel-voiced legend launched into a song about life on the farm. "You really like this stuff?" he asked.

She frowned. "What do you mean? It's Sammy Gold. Everybody loves Sammy Gold."

"No, not everybody."

She blinked and tipped her head to one side. "You don't like him?"

"I actively hate the man."

"But why?"

He shook his head as he hit the Stop button to make the music die. The car refilled with tense silence.

"Wait a minute. You're in the music business. And you actively hate country's biggest star. There has to be something more to this story."

"There's not." It was, he knew, a bald-faced lie.

"There has to be. Do you *know* Sammy Gold?"

"No."

"Ever met him?"

"No."

"Ever written a song for him?"

"No."

She drew her brows tightly together, tilting her head to one side. "But you must have a reason. You don't seem like the kind of guy who would resent someone for their success."

"No, I'm definitely not that kind of guy."

"So did you try to sell a song to him, and did he reject it and maybe insult your skill as a writer?"

He made a face and looked at her. "You're weaving together some pretty far-fetched scenarios, but I guess it's understandable, you being a woman who's had several drinks."

"Four. Four is not several."

"Four. And what kind of drinks were these?"

"Rum and Coke. Diet Coke, that is."

"Well, that shouldn't render you too sloppy, then."

"I'm not sloppy at all."

She reached out and pressed the button again, and once more Sammy Gold's voice and simple handful of guitar chords filled the car.

The more he sang about home and family, about values and morality and being a one-woman man, the more Gabe hated him. The man was a liar, was what he was. He didn't value family at all.

He certainly didn't value his own son.

Gabe knew that for a fact. Because in his entire life the man had never once even bothered to come out and meet him. Or even spoken to him by phone. His checks came like clockwork — and they were big checks, sent on the condition that no one ever breathe a word about the fact that Sammy Gold had fathered a bastard son with a gold digger.

Gabe's mom had been living high on Sammy Gold's dime for as long as he could remember. In contrast, since reaching the age of eighteen, Gabe had never spent a nickel of the man's money. Nor did he intend to.

No, he had no use for Sammy Gold.

Reaching up, he hit the button again.

Carrie looked at him, thinned her lips and said, "I was really starting to like you."

"Yeah?"

She nodded. "But now I don't know. You're all nosy about my love life, and you detest my favorite singer. So . . ."

"Maybe I'm all nosy about your love life because I'm starting to like you, too. You ever think of that?"

"No." She widened her eyes and blinked at the air in front of her face. "No, I haven't. Is that true?"

He pulled the car into the driveway and shut it off, then turned in his seat to meet her eyes. "That I'm starting to like you? Yeah, it's true."

"Well then . . . maybe I can forgive your taste in music."

"I hope so."

"If you'll tell me why."

"Let's see how this goes. And then maybe I'll tell you why."

"Then there *is* a reason why you hate him! I knew it!"

He nodded, then leaned closer and kissed her on the lips, lightly, slightly, but their mouths clung for a suspended moment, and she tasted damn good and a little bit like rum.

He pulled back.

She stayed where she was, eyes closed, and whispered, "Wow."

"That good, huh?" he asked.

"No. I mean, yes. It's just that I never thought —"

"Never thought what?"

She opened her eyes. "I never thought I'd kiss a hippie drifter." Then she smiled broadly and, turning, opened her door and got out.

He got out, too, and came around the car to hand her the keys. "Drifter hippie," he corrected.

She laughed, and it was beautiful to his ears. Looking up at him, she said, "Don't you dare tell Sammy we kissed."

"Okay."

"Even if we do it again," she added softly.

"Oh. Are we going to do it again?"

She lifted her brows. "I think we might."

"Then I'm looking forward to it."

"Me, too."

"We could do it right now, if you want."

"No way. Sam would see and read too

much into it, and —"

"I know. You're right."

She nodded, but he could see the confusion in her face, in her eyes. "I'm gonna head out then," he said.

"Oh, you're not coming inside? I thought we were having dessert."

He met her eyes. "It's late. I think it's best if I leave."

She nodded but clearly didn't understand. He thought about telling her that if he didn't leave now, he wasn't going to want to leave at all. But then he decided it would be counterproductive. He had to find out the truth about Sam.

And it probably wouldn't be a good idea to let the tender feelings starting to germinate way down deep take root.

She was still standing there, still staring at him. Everything in him wanted to bend down and kiss her good-night. It would be long, and slow, and it would be potent. He knew it. Just thinking about it was potent. But it would also be a roadblock to his goals.

His number one priority here was to find out if Samuel Overton might possibly, by some wild trick of fate, be his son. And the more time he spent with the kid, not to mention his bewitching mother, the more he found himself beginning to hope he was.

Carrie lowered her eyes at the same time, and her disappointment was palpable.

Gabe felt a knot in his stomach. "I'm sorry," he said. "You really had your heart set on dessert, didn't you?"

She lifted her head. "Don't be silly. Besides, I had dessert — a dessert drink, anyway — with Ambrose."

"He was that charming, was he?"

"He was that insistent," she said. "Go on, go. It's fine."

The door above them opened, and Sam shouted down, "Hey, Gabe, you're coming back up, aren't you? I need you to show me that transition again."

Gabe looked from Sam to his mom, met her eyes, saw the hope she was trying to conceal. "Yeah, pal. I'll be right up," he called without looking away.

And then he watched Carrie's beautiful face turn from hopeful to delighted, and was a little bit puzzled by it. Or maybe he was just reading the reflection of his own feelings in her eyes.

5

She'd heard her son's soft strumming as she'd ascended the steps, gripping the rail on her way, due to the rum swimming around in her brain. Gabe stuck close, one hand on her elbow, and she found she liked the feel of a man so close to her side. She liked the smell of him, too. Clean and masculine, with a hint of musky cologne. It was heady, with the stars overhead and the bullfrogs croaking in the distance. Good thing they were going inside.

Rum and this guy and a late-summer Shadow Falls night were not a safe combination for her.

Sam stopped strumming when she came in through the front door, Gabe following close behind her.

"Hey, Mom. So how was the *date?*" He was sitting on the oversize brown sofa with his guitar, a Fender brand electric-acoustic she'd bought him for Christmas two years ago. The gleaming light wood finish was as spotless today as it had been when he'd first taken it out of its case. He treated the thing as tenderly as he treated his truck.

"Pretty bad, actually."

"Yeah, I figured, when you had the waitress phone in for rescue. You have a few drinks?"

"I had four. Precisely four. And I'm feeling them."

Sam grinned, then spotted Gabe's confused look and explained to him. "Four is one more than her limit. And she *never* exceeds her limit. So it must have been a really bad date. Then again, I could have predicted that."

She closed her eyes. "So you know more than I do about men," she said. "Big deal. Being one, you shouldn't be so proud of that."

"Don't need to know much to know you could do better."

She shrugged. "So you keep saying. No matter who I date. So where's Sadie? I feel outnumbered here."

"She headed home after Gabe left to pick you up."

She looked at her watch. "But it's only a little after nine."

"Yeah. Her mother called. She exceeded

her limit, too." He sighed heavily, and added for Gabe's benefit, "Her limit, unfortunately, is three *bottles*."

"Ah, hell," Gabe said. "I'm sorry. Is Sadie okay?"

"Sadie's always okay." Sam set his guitar down. "I ought to call her, make sure things are copacetic. I'll be back, though. We're having dessert, right?"

"You bet we are." Carrie hung her handbag on the little hook beside the door and waved at Gabe to follow her into the kitchen, looking around her home as she did, trying to see it through his eyes. The living room was nearly all done in wood, the floors, the walls, the mantel. All were rich, knotty red-fox-colored hardwoods. The exception was the fieldstone fireplace that burned real logs. The prints on the walls were of wildlife and nature scenes. The giant window that reached up to the peak was undressed, because of the beauty of the view beyond it.

In the kitchen, there was a section of real brick wall with a double oven built into it. The range top was part of the counter, which was black granite. Everything was black — the sink, the side-by-side refrigerator-freezer, the range hood, even the toaster and coffeemaker. To set it off, the walls were white, and the floor a black-and-white checkerboard of marble tiles.

"Damn," Gabe said. "The kitchen is as gorgeous as the living room. You've got great taste, Carrie."

"I like it. I want this place to be a haven. Home is important to me."

He nodded. "You've made a beautiful one here. And there's a peaceful energy to it that's like — it feels like it shuts out all the trouble outside. Sort of washes over you as soon as you walk in."

She leaned back against the counter and looked at him, touched. "You really feel that? Because that's just how it feels to me." He nodded, and she went on. "It's important to me. I never had a home, growing up. Not a real one, anyway."

"No?"

She shook her head, turning to open the fridge and stare blankly inside, mostly just to break eye contact. "We moved almost every year of my childhood, town to town, state to state."

Gabe frowned. "Was your father in the military?"

"No. He was a drifter. Like you." She licked her lips. "I hated it."

"Ouch."

She shrugged. "Just getting that out of the way."

"So you never want to leave here at all?"

"I didn't say that. We travel from time to time, and I'll do a lot more of that once Sam is out on his own. But this is my home. It will always be my home. I like having it here, knowing my haven is waiting for me when I'm ready to return."

She tilted her head to one side. "Don't you have anyplace like that? A home base?"

He shook his head. "The closest thing to home for me is my mother's place, and my mother and I — well, her idea of home is a pretentious, hollow mansion outside L.A. It's like the polar opposite of what you have here. Cold. False, somehow."

"So what's stopping you from making a haven of your own?" she asked.

He shrugged. "I've never thought I wanted or needed one yet. I always figured someday I might, but that day just hasn't come."

"I see."

"So what's the deal with Sadie's family?" he asked after a long moment of comfortable silence.

She closed the fridge and opened the freezer, spotting a tub of caramel crunch ice cream, and taking it out. "Her dad died six years ago. Ice fishing accident."

"He drowned?"

She nodded. "Her mom wasn't entirely stable, even before, and she pretty much hasn't stopped drinking since. Holds down a minimum wage job, but just barely. And she's totally dependent on Sadie. Sadie keeps the trailer clean, takes care of the money, pays what bills she can, brings home groceries when possible."

He sighed, lowering his head. "Does she realize she's not really helping her mother at all?"

"We've had that talk," Carrie said with a nod. "She knows she's enabling her mom to some extent. But at the same time, she's making her home life bearable for herself."

"And making her mother dependent."

"I know. I know. But at what point does walking away help Sadie, rather than hurting her? She's got two more years till she graduates high school. She can get into a good college. She has the grades, and she'll qualify for hardship grants as well as scholarships. Meanwhile, she's just making her life as tolerable as she can, and spending all the time she can away from home."

"I already got that she was tough. Smart. And way too wise for her age. Now I know why."

Carrie nodded. "I just hope she'll have it

in her to leave when the time comes. You know that woman's going to heap as much guilt on the poor kid as she can."

"That kind always do."

"You sound like you know whereof you speak."

"Yep." He didn't say more, and instead opened a cupboard and located ice-cream bowls, taking three of them down. "But Sadie's got a great role model in you. You'll help her know how to make the right call, when the time comes."

"I hope so." She scooped ice cream into the three tulip-shaped dessert bowls, then returned the carton to the freezer, opened the fridge and pulled out chocolate-, caramel- and strawberry-flavored sundae sauces, handing them all to Gabe. "Here. Take off the lids and give them thirty seconds each in the microwave."

"Okay."

He went about the task, while Carrie opened another cupboard and located crushed walnuts, pecans and M&M's.

He watched her as she sprinkled liberal portions of each onto the ice cream.

"Wow. You really know how to make a sundae."

"We take our ice cream very seriously around here." She handed him a tablespoon-sized ladle. "A little of each, please. I'll get the whipped cream and cherries."

"How do you keep so trim, when you eat like this?"

She smiled at him. "By getting lots of exercise and limiting ice-cream sundaes to one night a week. And thank you for the compliment."

"It was nothing but the truth."

She nodded at him to get moving, and he drizzled the now-warm syrups over the bowls of ice cream. She followed by spraying swirls of whipped cream, and then she dropped a cherry on top of each one.

"Beautiful," he said. She looked up and saw that his eyes were on her, not the sundaes. And then she shivered, because this . . . this attraction between them had come out of nowhere. She hadn't expected it or been ready for it. And now that it was here, she didn't know what to do with it.

She managed to smile, and then snatched two of the sundaes and hurried into the living room, thanking her lucky stars when Sam came running back down the stairs.

"Sadie's fine. Her mom locked herself out of the trailer again and had passed out on the front lawn by the time Sadie got there. But Sadie got her inside and into bed." He met Gabe's eyes. "The woman's a real basket case."

"Your mom was telling me. Sorry to hear it, Sam."

"Sadie deserves better," Sam said.

"She wouldn't be who she is if she had it better."

Sam frowned at that comment, but took his sundae from his mom and sank onto the sofa beside his guitar. "I never thought about it that way before."

"It's the only way you should think about it. Look for the positive. There's always something somewhere, even if it's sometimes tough to find it. Sometimes it's not apparent until years down the road, even."

"Yeah?"

Gabe nodded.

Sam took a spoonful of ice cream. "I've heard that philosophy before, Gabe, but I have to tell you, I'm not real sure I buy into it. If everything has a positive side, what's the positive to Kyle being missing?"

"I don't know, pal. Kyle's path is his own to walk. We can't figure out anyone's issues but our own. We can try, but we'd only be off base. When things happen where you can't see any good side, it's usually best to focus on things where you can. Hold on to the good."

"That's tough to do right now."

"The bad stuff is there. Shit happens, as they say. The question is, do you focus on it and feel bad, or try to find reasons to feel good in spite of it?"

Sam nodded thoughtfully. "Doesn't it seem . . . callous to try to feel good when someone you care about is in trouble?"

"Does your wallowing in misery make his situation any better?" Gabe asked.

"No."

"So what's the point of being miserable, then?"

Carrie listened to the conversation and tipped her head to one side. "That's got to be the most unique perspective I've ever heard."

"Well, it's just the way I see things. Doesn't mean anyone else has to agree. But if it helps a little, you're welcome to it."

Sam met his mom's eyes and gave a slow, deep nod, as if to say, *I told you this guy was awesome.* Then he set his bowl aside and picked up his guitar. "That riff you showed me, Gabe. Was it —" He played a series of chords as Gabe nodded.

"You dropped the G, right at the end there."

Sam did it again, and this time Gabe nodded in approval while Carrie beamed. "That was really great, Sam!" she said.

"Gabe taught me more in a couple of hours than all my lessons combined."

"You had a good foundation to begin with. That's important," Gabe said. "Maybe we can do this again soon."

"I'd love that."

"Me, too," Gabe said, sliding a meaningful but subtle glance Carrie's way. "But I think we'd better call it a night for now."

Carrie was surprised to see that her bowl was empty, as was Gabe's. Sam's was nearly so. How had dessert passed so fast?

"If we have to, I guess," Sam said, but he kept right on playing.

Carrie got to her feet and followed Gabe to the door. He paused there, turning, staring down at her, making her feel butterflies in her stomach. "So the search resumes at 8:00 a.m., then?"

"Yeah, and it's my day off from the hospital, so I'll be there."

"Sam, too?"

She smiled. "Sam, too. And probably Sadie, as well, if her mother's not too incapacitated."

"I'll see you there, then."

"Okay. Good night."

"Night." He looked at her for a long moment, then his gaze shifted to her son, behind her on the sofa. The strumming had stopped, so Carrie presumed Sam must be watching with undisguised interest. The brat.

Meeting her eyes again, Gabe held them for an intense moment that was almost as intimate as a good-night kiss would have been. Then he backed away, turned and moved across the deck and down the steps to the driveway beyond. She closed the door after he left and was watching out the window as he made his way to his VW Bus. Just as it started up and pulled away, she noticed Rose, standing in the window of the garage apartment looking out at the driveway. Even as Carrie looked up at her, the curtain fell closed and the silhouette behind the glass moved away.

"I think he likes you, Mom."

She turned sharply, sending her son a *don't-be-ridiculous* look, while inside a little voice was saying, *Do you really think so?* She bit her tongue and didn't ask the question aloud. It was, she told herself, the kind of thing a sophomore girl with a crush would say. No, not even that. Sadie wouldn't be caught dead acting so . . . stupid.

"He's totally not your type, is he?" Sam asked. "I mean, he's just the opposite of the kind of guy you're looking for."

"I'm not looking for anyone."

"You know what I mean."

She nodded, sighed and walked to the sofa to sit down on the far end while her son continued strumming. "So what do you think I usually look for in a guy?"

He shrugged. "Definitely not good looks. You tend to go for pretty homely types. And boring is definitely on your wish list."

"Bad-looking and boring. That's what you think I want in a man?"

"And smart, I guess. And employed. And ordinary. You like conformists."

"I *am* a conformist. Or hadn't you noticed?"

He smiled at her. "Not as much as you like to think you are."

"Oh? So you think there's a wild streak in your old mom, just waiting to be let loose?"

"Mmm-hmm. And I think it's starting to tug at its leash a little now that Gabe has appeared on the scene." He strummed another chord with a sweeping flourish. "But I'm just a kid. What do I know?"

"Yeah," she muttered, and her gaze shifted to the door again. "What do you know?"

The searchers gathered again at 8:00 a.m. and boarded the bus, Gabe, Sadie, Sam and Carrie taking adjoining seats. The door began to close, then opened again to admit a latecomer.

Ambrose Peck hurried up the steps, looking harried. He wore khaki trousers, with an off-white button-down shirt and a brown windbreaker. His hair was neatly glued to his head. He wasn't tousled or disheveled, but he still managed to look harried. It was his expression, Carrie thought.

He quickly made his way up the aisle, pausing beside Carrie. "I swear, I'm never late for anything. Can't believe I overslept."

She smiled back, though she was groaning inwardly. "It's all right. You made it. That's all that counts."

"Yes, I guess so." He met the eye of the man in the seat ahead of Carrie and Gabe's, and the man slid over to make room.

He sat on the edge as the bus rumbled into motion. "I was too late to be assigned to a group, though. Is there room in yours?"

Gabe offered a friendly smile from his window seat beside her and said, "There's always room for one more." He ignored Carrie's kick in the ankle and kept on talking. "We've got Nate with us again today, too," he added, with a nod toward the man sitting in the seat beside Ambrose.

Ambrose looked sideways, noting his seatmate for the first time. "Oh, yes! Hello again, Mr. Kelly."

"Mr. Peck." Nate, who usually looked depressed, actually offered a half smile when he greeted Ambrose. Highly unusual for him.

"You two know each other?" Carrie asked.

"Mr. Kelly and I had a fascinating talk about the state of the ski business here in town yesterday," Ambrose explained. "I offered a few suggestions that might ease his —"

Nate cleared his throat heavily and meaningfully. And Carrie wasn't sure, but she thought he might have thrown a little elbow, too.

Ambrose flinched and shot him a quick look, then smiled, though it looked more like he had a bad case of indigestion. But it always looked that way, she thought. Smiling was not a natural expression for him.

"I'm sorry. Of course any financial discussions I have with someone are confidential. Client or not."

"Besides, nothing's likely to help much at this point," Nate added.

It was the longest sentence Carrie had ever heard the man utter. He was notoriously grumpy, gruff and mostly silent. And the worse his business went, the less he spoke. His face reminded her of the fisherman on the boxes of fish sticks in the market. Thin and chiseled, as if it had been carved into Mount Rushmore. Gaunt and grim, too.

"We're all hoping for a long snowy winter, Nate," she told him. "Things are certainly starting out nicely. The inns are booked up already."

"Yeah, because it's warm."

"Well, that's true."

"And dry," Nate added. "Warm and dry." He shook his head slowly, sadly.

"Maybe the cold and the moisture are saving themselves up for huge snowfalls later on," she offered in a cheerful tone.

"Hmmph."

Ambrose stepped in and tried to engage the grumpy old ski lodge owner in small talk as they made the short drive to the areas they were to search this morning. Nate Kelly responded more than Carrie had seen him respond to anyone. It seemed he actually liked the irritating financial wizard.

And maybe Ambrose wasn't really all that irritating. Maybe he was perfectly fine, and she was just too smitten with Gabe to notice it.

In short order their teams were marching into the woods, maps in hand, beating the undergrowth in search of Kyle.

She and Gabe paired up to walk together. Sam and Sadie did the same. Ambrose and Nate were far to the left and seemed to move faster than the others, and they were soon far ahead.

The moment distance allowed it, Carrie said, "Thanks, by the way, for inviting my date from hell along."

Gabe smiled at her. "Hey, he's not such a bad guy."

"And how do you know that?"

He shrugged. "He's here, isn't he?"

She lifted her brows in question but kept her eyes on the ground, bending to move aside clumps of brush and look underneath.

"He's on vacation," Gabe went on. "But he's donating time to search for a missing kid he doesn't even know. That, in my estimation, earns him the benefit of the doubt."

She sighed. "I suppose that's true."

"And just because he's a lousy date, that doesn't mean he's a lousy person," he added.

She nodded. "True. But being rude to the waitress begs to differ."

He lifted his brows. "I really don't like people who are rude to waitstaff." Then he shrugged. "Then again, anyone can have a bad day."

"Do you actually *like* the guy?"

"I just don't *dis*like him. He seemed like a pretty okay character when he was on our search team. Friendly. Talked to Sam and Sadie like grown-ups, and I like that. I get irritated with people who talk down to kids." He glanced her way as they traipsed along through the thick growth of ferns and reeds.

The forest smelled like life, lush and green and moist, with a subtle hint of approaching autumn, decay and black soil.

"He's made friends with the guy I peg as the most crotchety man in town, too. Even seems to be trying to help him out — and I think it's at no charge. You can't fault that, can you?"

"No, you can't. And I got that feeling, too. You're right about Nate, by the way. He *is* the town grump."

Gabe nodded. "Besides," he said, "I figure since you had such a lousy time on that date with him, I should keep him close. Makes me look better by comparison."

She made a face at him, and he made one back, one so funny she found herself laughing out loud. And then she caught herself and stopped. The sounds of the forest filled the silence. She said, "How could I laugh, here of all places? Out here searching the woods for —"

A whistle pierced the air, and Carrie went dead silent, her eyes meeting Gabe's. His were just as wide, just as stunned. And then there was a voice, shouting, "Here! Here! Hurry!"

"Is that *Ambrose?*" she asked, looking in the direction from which the voice had come.

"Come on!" Gabe gripped her arm, and together they raced ahead through the forest, nimbly jumping roots and dodging low-hanging branches that would have whipped them bloody.

On the way, Nate Kelly's gruff voice came to them, as well. "This way!" he shouted. "Hurry!"

And finally, after what seemed like forever, they spotted Ambrose standing with one hand on a tree, his head bent low. A few feet from him, Nate Kelly sat on a giant boulder, head in his hands.

They rushed to the pair, both Carrie and Gabe speaking at once, asking half questions. "What . . . ? Where . . . ?"

But Ambrose, shuddering, only lifted his other hand to point, then brought it back to cover his forehead and eyes.

Carrie looked and saw Kyle Becker sitting on the ground, his back against a tree trunk, his legs stretched out in front of him, his head tipped to one side. His eyes were closed, and his skin was unnaturally pale. But aside from that, he looked as if he'd just sat down to take a nap.

"Oh, God." She started forward.

Gabe's hand fell to her shoulder as he stepped up beside her. "I'll go."

She met his eyes, shook her head. "No, you stay back. You'll contaminate the scene."

"But —"

"You're a stranger in town, Gabe. You don't want your hairs or handprints or DNA on that boy. Believe me."

"But he's —"

"Dead," she whispered. "He's dead, Gabe."

Thrashing and crashing came from behind then, and Carrie looked back and saw Sam and Sadie burst through the trees. Sam's eyes shot to hers, then to Kyle on the ground not far ahead.

"Kyle!" He lunged forward.

Gabe cut him off, catching his shoulders, holding on to him, speaking low and soft, as Carrie hurried ahead. She crouched beside Kyle and had to force herself to press a hand to his neck in search of a pulse. But she'd known from her first glimpse of him that she wouldn't find one. It was partly his color, but mostly something else. Something unidentifiable. There was a palpable difference between a living person and a dead one, a difference that wasn't only physical. She'd seen it, *felt* it, enough times to recognize it instantly. Death gave off a very different energy than life did. There was no life in the body where Kyle Becker used to live. None whatsoever.

Still, she checked for a pulse, then started to cry before she got any further. His skin was already cold. She'd hoped, just this once, to be wrong. Tears blurred her eyes, and she withdrew her hand, rose and swallowed hard. Then she turned to face Sam, and when she met his eyes, she shook her head sadly.

"No. No, Mom, *no!*"

Carrie walked slowly to her son and tried to fold him into her arms, but he pulled free of her. "No, do CPR on him or something. God, you have to *do* something!"

"I'm sorry, baby. He's been gone for several hours now. There's nothing I can do for him. I'm sorry. I'm so, so sorry."

"No! Dammit, no!"

Sam turned and ran headlong back through the woods. Carrie lurched as if to go after him, but Gabe caught her arm. "I'll go. You're needed here." He nodded at Ambrose, who was doubled over, gagging into a stand of bushy little princess pine and sweet fern. And then at Nate, who hadn't moved from his spot on the boulder and seemed to have turned to stone himself.

"Sadie?" Gabe asked.

"I'll stay with Carrie," she said. She was standing still with her arms folded over her chest, her eyes glued to the dead boy's passive, peaceful face. "Sam won't want me seeing him like this. Just tell him I'm here for him."

Gabe nodded and met Carrie's eyes. "I'm so sorry."

"I know you are. So am I."

Nodding, he turned and jogged off in the direction Sam had gone. Sadie gave her a slight nod and then went over to Nate, kneeling in front of him and speaking softly. Comforting him, when it was one of *her* peer group, one of her friends, a kid she'd grown up with from the time she was born, only a week after him, in the same hospital.

Ambrose was still bent double, holding on to a tree for dear life, so Carrie went to him, putting a hand on his back. "Are you all right?"

"I'm . . . I don't know. God, I never — I just — I didn't prepare myself for this."

"I don't think anyone *can* prepare for

something like this."

He straightened, wiping his mouth with the back of his hand, the other still pressed to the papery bark of a poplar tree. Carrie tugged her backpack off and unzipped it. As a doctor, she always brought extra supplies: a first aid kit, cold packs, gauze, an EpiPen and plenty of inhalers, among other things. She handed Ambrose enough gauze pads to wipe his mouth, then smacked a cold pack between her palms, rubbed it vigorously and laid it across the back of his neck. "That'll help."

"Thank you." He lifted his eyes toward the body. "What happened to him?"

Carrie looked back at the boy, *really* looked at him for the first time. Frowning, she tugged the missing poster from her backpack and skimmed the detailed information at the bottom of the page. Last seen wearing jeans, a T-shirt with a cartoon cat on it and a plaid flannel button-down shirt.

Those were the same clothes he was wearing now. "Something's wrong here," she said softly.

"What?" Ambrose looked at her, then at the body, then at her again. "What is it?"

She shook her head. "Ambrose, keep blowing your whistle. Sadie, Nate, when people get here, I'm going to need your help keeping them away from the body. A good ten, fifteen feet on all sides. Only until the cops get here to handle that job. Okay? Can you handle that?"

Sadie lifted her chin and nodded. Nate brought his head up for the first time, set his jaw and nodded as well, rising to his feet. Ambrose watched them and then imitated their determination, though he looked less certain. Both men, she thought, were grateful to have something to do. Sadie would have stepped in regardless, without being asked. Not to help her cope, not because it felt better, but just because it was what needed to be done.

Carrie knew that her son was devastated. But no more so than Sadie was. And she wished Sam had a little less drama club and a little more steadfast, solid strength in him. Gabe had been right. Sadie's tough life had made her the strong, capable young woman she had become. And thank God she was here for Sam right now, Carrie thought.

She shook those thoughts away and returned her attention to the body, trying now to stop thinking of it as Kyle. Kyle was gone. She moved closer but stopped a good three yards out, standing in one spot and looking, closely at the ground around it. And then at the body again.

Someone came through the brush. She heard them long before they arrived, and so she was looking his way when Bryan Kendall, in uniform, broke through the undergrowth. He saw her, then Kyle, and the sight brought him up short. He shot a look at Carrie.

"He's been dead for several hours."

Bryan sighed deeply, his head falling forward. But he picked it right back up again. "Who found him?"

Carrie nodded at Ambrose and Nate.

"We did," Nate said, facing Bryan and holding on to a sapling for balance, as if his knees were weak. "Me and Mr. Peck here."

Ambrose nodded, stepping forward. "I'm Ambrose Peck."

"You're a tourist, Mr. Peck?" Bryan asked.

"Yes. I helped out last night and wanted to do so again today — but I never expected —"

"Your help is deeply appreciated, sir. I'm going to need to talk to you later. Just standard stuff. Will you stick around?"

"Of course I will. I'll do anything you need me to do. Absolutely anything."

"Okay." Bryan Kendall pulled a walkie-talkie from his belt, moving slightly away from the others and speaking softly into it. Then he reclipped it in place, came back and turned to Carrie. "I'll need you here, of course, but everyone else —"

Too late. Volunteers who'd been close by were already appearing like ghosts from amid the dense growth of trees and underbrush. Silent, wide-eyed, every one of them staring at the dead boy. Every cheek was wet with tears.

"Damn. We've got to notify his parents before they hear it from someone else," Bryan said softly. "Not a job I'm looking forward to, I can tell you that. I so didn't want it to end like this."

"I know. I know," Carrie whispered. "But no one's going anywhere until you make them. So focus on the body for just a second, will you? Look at his clothes."

Bryan looked, and his eyes narrowed. "They match the description of what he was wearing the day he disappeared."

"Right. But do those clothes look to you like they've been worn for six straight days? Much less six days lost in the forest? Those clothes are *clean,* Bryan. Why are they clean?"

He nodded. "Looks as if he just left the house, doesn't he?" He frowned, moving a little closer, kneeling, looking. She came up behind him. "His hands aren't even dirty."

"Where the hell has he *been* all this time?"

Carrie asked softly.

"And what the hell killed him?"

She shook her head slowly and wondered if she was going to be the one who had to make that determination. For the life of her, she didn't know if she had it in her to perform an autopsy on a boy she'd known since he was a baby.

6

"Hey," Gabe said softly.

Leaning against a sapling in the middle of the woods, Sam lifted his head but didn't turn around. Gabe knew that was probably due to the tears he didn't want to show. "I can't go back there."

"I wouldn't ask you to. Or to go home or to calm down, or to hang in there or to talk to me. And I'm not going to tell you Kyle's in a better place or any of that crap, either. This sucks. You're supposed to be pissed off and messed up. He was your friend. You're allowed to act like a complete asshole if you want to. No one's gonna question it."

It would attract attention, though, if Gabe let his own wrenching emotions spill over. So he contained them, tried to focus on Sam's grief rather than his own.

Sam nodded slowly, rubbed his eyes, turned around. "I need to be alone."

God, the kid looked like hell. His eyes

were red, his face pale and gleaming with tear tracks. "That's understandable, too. You want solitude, you got it. I have to make a small request, though."

Sam sighed heavily. "What?"

"Could you get that solitude you need at your place — or my place, if you want? Just so your mom can focus on — what she has to do instead of worrying about you being alone in the woods somewhere."

Sam sniffed hard, knuckled his nose roughly. "I don't want to think about what she has to do."

"Then don't. She probably doesn't want to think about it, either. Just focus on the end results. You have a lot of questions. Kyle's parents will, too. Maybe she can help answer them."

Sam nodded in small jerky motions. "She has to." He lowered his head, shook it slowly. "He looked like he was sleeping, you know? Just like he was sleeping."

"I know."

"What the hell happened to him, Gabe?"

Gabe shook his head slowly. "I wish I knew. Maybe we will soon."

"So what's the silver lining on this one, huh? Can you tell me that?"

"I didn't say everything had a silver lining. Some things just plain suck, and this is one of them. What I said was, you have a choice about what gets your attention. You can let this eat you up inside, let it become the defining moment of your life and go downhill from there. Or you can grieve and rage, and then start to get past it. But I don't expect you to do anything but grieve and rage right now. No one does. You wouldn't be normal if you did otherwise."

"I never cared much about being normal." Sam's face twisted, and fresh tears sprang free. "Dammit, Kyle, how can you be dead?"

"Ah, hell." Gabe clapped the kid in a hard hug and was surprised that Sam allowed it. His own eyes were wet when they stepped apart. "Come on. Let's get the hell out of here. We'll phone your mom from my place."

"I don't even know where your place is. If it's one of the inns or —"

"No way. I rented a cabin up in the woods above the falls. Big place, lake out back, dock —"

"I know the one. It's kind of notorious, you know."

"So I've heard. Doesn't bother me in the least. Will it bother you?"

"I don't have room for much to bother me right now, Gabe. Everything's busy, just . . ."

"Grieving and raging. I know, kid. I know."

Carrie got out of Bryan Kendall's car at the firehouse. She'd stayed at the scene, observing and making notes while the crime scene team took photographs and measurements, and gathered trace evidence. She'd supervised as Kyle's body had been moved at last, zipped into a body bag and carried to the nearest spot an ambulance could reach.

She stayed, feeling like Kyle's guardian, until the doors closed and the ambulance drove away, taking him to the hospital morgue.

"Thanks for the ride," she told Bryan.

He nodded. "You're welcome."

"Off to talk to Kyle's parents now?"

"The chief broke the news in person. Figured it was best to get it done before those volunteers came down off the mountain and set fire to the Shadow Falls grapevine."

Carrie nodded, looking at the nearly empty firehouse parking lot. Then she spotted Sadie, who'd been bused back with all the other volunteers. She was sitting alone near Carrie's minivan. She tried to wave, but Sadie's gaze was turned inward, her face very still.

"What do you make of that Ambrose Peck

character?" Bryan asked.

Carrie tugged her attention away from Sadie and focused on Bryan again. "Why ask me?"

Bryan shrugged. "He said you two had dinner together last night. What's he like?"

"Anyone of us could have found Kyle this morning, Bryan."

"You said he was quite a ways ahead of everyone else, though."

Nodding slowly, she thought before speaking. "Yes, but then again, so was Nate Kelly. And you're not asking questions about him."

"I don't need to ask questions about him. He's a local. I know him. So what about Peck?"

She shrugged. "He's a nervous little man. Kind of . . . quirky."

"In what way?"

"I don't know. Awkward, uncomfortable around strangers. Fussy. Boring as hell." Blinking, she met Bryan's eyes. "He doesn't seem like a boogeyman, though. He was a lousy date, impatient, and rude to the waitress, but that doesn't mean he's capable of —" She couldn't say the rest, so she shifted gears. "Besides, given what we saw out there, it's way too soon to assume —"

"We won't make *any* assumptions until

the autopsy's done."

"It's hard not to speculate. Hard not to go down to the morgue and start looking for answers myself."

"It's out of your hands, Carrie, and that's a blessing, really. You're too close. Thank God the state police want their own guy on this."

She nodded, but remained torn about the decision by the state police to bring in their own team, including a forensic pathologist who would perform the autopsy. Then again, she didn't have any say in it, so she didn't suppose her opinion mattered.

"Good night, Carrie. Tell Sam I'm really sorry."

"I will. Good night."

Bryan made a loop around the parking lot and headed back out. Carrie walked over to where Sadie sat. She felt as if her legs were made of lead, as if she'd walked a hundred miles.

"Have you been here all this time?" she asked the girl.

Sadie nodded. Her eyes were puffy and red, but dry. She'd probably cried herself out by now. "I didn't want to go home. And Sam needs some space right now, so . . ."

"And you need the opposite. One of the many differences between men and women.

When bad things happen, we want someone to hug, to talk to, to comfort and be comforted by, to cry with. They want to lock themselves in a dark room and work it through inside themselves."

"I thought it was just him."

"No, it's pretty universal, from what I've seen. Not that I'm the voice of experience or anything. Still, I hate to think of you sitting here alone all this time. It's been what, four hours?" She looked at her watch.

"I went for a long walk, stopped at the library for a while, cried a lot." She lowered her head. "I thought Sam would call sooner or later."

"He hasn't called me, either. But Gabe did. Left a message on my cell. I got it as soon as we got back within signal range. He took Sam to the cabin he's renting. Says Sam's been sitting on the deck looking at the lake and not saying a word. Gabe's been staying out of his way."

"He's nice. Gabe, I mean."

Carrie nodded. "I think he really is."

"So do you think it's okay if we go out there now?"

"I think we have to do whatever we have to do to get through this, just like Sam is. If that means going out there, then we're going. And frankly, I think I need to hug my son right now about as badly as you probably do."

Sadie blinked. "Don't you have to go to the hospital? To . . . you know."

"Nope."

"But . . . ?"

"I'll explain on the way. Come on, let's go."

Sadie rose to her feet and picked up the stack of library books that were sitting beside her. They were all about the grieving process, one specifically aimed at the survivors of those who die young. Carrie wondered if they would help and supposed they couldn't hurt. Sadie had made good use of her time alone, at least.

"You know, no matter what the shrinks tell you, everybody grieves in their own way," she told the girl. "You have to give yourself permission to do that."

"Oh, I didn't get the books for me. I just thought . . . maybe I could help Sam through it if I understood a little more."

Carrie frowned. "I hope my son knows what a special young woman you are."

Sadie smiled, but her heart wasn't in it. "I try to remind him on a regular basis."

Taking her hand and pulling her to her feet, Carrie hugged the girl gently, stroking her hair as Sadie's head rested on her shoulder.

After a long moment, they walked arm in arm to Carrie's car and got in.

The cabin Gabe had rented was as beautiful and isolated as it was notorious, its previous owner having been a serial killer who'd died before the state had a chance to try him. Now it was in the hands of a gaggle of lawyers while various civil suits worked their way through the courts. In the meantime it was rented out, the money going to upkeep and taxes, which was lucky for Gabe. He thought the place was incredible, and it didn't have any creep factor at all — not for him, anyway.

He had to admit that the day had messed with his emotions. Seeing Sam so devastated had shaken him almost as much as seeing that other poor boy's body in the woods had done. A boy who could have been his own.

Okay, he admitted he didn't have any reason to think Kyle had been Livvy's missing baby. Just a birthdate that fit the right timeline. And yet, it was possible. And it twisted his gut into knots to think he might have missed the chance to know his son.

Besides, the death of any sixteen-year-old

— blood relative or not — was cause to grieve.

But a lot of Gabe's angst seemed to fall away when he heard a car in the driveway and looked out the window to see that it was Carrie. It felt as if the two-ton weight that had been on his shoulders throughout most of this day suddenly began to dissolve at the sight of her.

He didn't allow a lot of stress in his life. Didn't tolerate bad feelings. And he knew a lot of methods for getting rid of them on those rare occasions when they showed up. Long walks and gazing out at natural beauty usually did it for him. This, though — this bit about bad feelings melting away at the sight of another human being — was a new experience entirely.

Then again, it was also very similar. Natural beauty was natural beauty, after all.

Carrie got out of her car, and he saw that Sadie was with her. Good. It was about time for Sam to let someone in. He walked through to the kitchen, opened the back door onto the deck. Sam sat there, staring down at the lake, dead silent, just as he'd been all afternoon.

"Your mom and Sadie are here, Sam."

Sam sighed. "I need more time."

"I get that. And I'm not telling you what

to do. But when you care about people, sometimes you need to give a little thought to what *they* need. And I think they need you right now."

He lifted his head, met Gabe's eyes and blinked. "Sadie's probably been alone all day."

"Probably."

"I'm an idiot."

"You're sixteen."

Sam reached up a hand. Gabe took it and pulled the younger man to his feet. Then they went back through the house, entering the living room together just as the front door opened and the two women walked in.

Sam opened his arms, and Sadie rushed into them. They held each other hard, and Gabe thought they were both crying again. He turned from the couple to Carrie. She looked exhausted.

"I don't know what you need," he said softly. "But if you tell me, you've got it."

She looked at the kids and then back at him. "That," she said.

She didn't have to say it twice. Gabe moved closer and folded her into his arms. Hers wrapped around his waist, her head beneath his chin. And he didn't know about her, but it felt like relief to him. God, it felt . . . like relief where none should have been possible.

He held her for a long time and hoped it felt as healing to her as it did to him. Finally, she lifted her head. “Thank you. I needed that.”

“I did, too.” He put a casual arm around her shoulders. “I’m making dinner. Care to keep me company in the kitchen while I finish up?”

“You didn’t have to do that.”

“People need to eat.”

“It’s very much appreciated.”

“Don’t be so sure until you taste it.” Gabe walked with Carrie into the kitchen, leaving Sam and Sadie to talk. “He’s going to have a hundred questions.”

“And I won’t be able to answer most of them. I have more questions than I did before you two left, to be honest.”

“Why?”

She swallowed hard. “Kyle’s clothes were clean. *He* was clean. In the woods six days, and as clean as if he’d just showered this morning. Dead only a matter of hours. Way too close to town to be lost. And . . .”

“And?”

She looked into his eyes. “I don’t know why I trust you, Gabe, but I do. I need you to keep this to yourself for now, all right?”

She trusted him. He heard that and almost

winced. He was keeping a huge secret from her. That was a mistake, and one he needed to correct at the first opportunity. But now was not the time.

"I promise I won't breathe a word. Ever, if necessary."

"Okay." She drew a breath, glanced into the next room to be sure Sam and Sadie were still out of earshot, and said, "Gabe, there were needle tracks in Kyle's arms. Several of them."

"You think he OD'd?"

"I don't know. I mean, that's what it looks like, but it makes no sense. I'm a doctor. I was around that kid all the time, and I never saw any sign that he was using." She shook her head. "How could I have missed it?"

"Don't be too hard on yourself. Wait until the autopsy is done."

"Yeah, if I can even get access to the results."

"What do you mean? I thought you were the M.E. around here."

"I am, but this just became a State Police investigation. They're bringing in their own forensic pathologist, and frankly, I think that might be for the best. They have expertise and experience I can't match."

"But they couldn't possibly care more," Gabe said. "Still, I can't help but think you're right. It's for the best. For you, anyway."

She lifted her eyes to meet his. "If I had to make a Y-incision in the body of my son's best friend, I seriously doubt I'd ever stop having nightmares. But I'm a doctor. I should be able to put my personal feelings aside."

"You're a human being." He looked at her and got lost in her eyes. "You're a beautiful, caring, feeling human being. And one of the most devoted mothers I've ever met."

Her brows rose, and she looked at him.

"I mean that. Sam . . . Sam's lucky to have you."

"Sam is my miracle, Gabe. He's my miracle, and I'm the lucky one."

"Voilà!" Gabe said as he carried the food out to the deck and set it down on the patio table with a grand flourish. "Chicken nuggets and curly fries."

Sadie sent him a look. "You want us to *eat* that stuff, or should we put it out for bear bait?" It was one of several attempts she had made to lighten the dire mood. Most had been met with stony silence by Sam, but Carrie and Gabe tried to play along.

"Keep that up and I'll put *you* out for bear

bait," Gabe told her.

Sadie faked a smile. "Well, then, I guess I'll force myself."

"No worries, Sadie." Carrie plunked the large bowl she was carrying onto the table, as well. "I insisted on making a salad to go with, so we women wouldn't be forced to indulge in the junk food."

Sam looked up. "Don't let them fool you, Gabe. They *love* junk food."

It was the first time he'd taken part in any of their conversation, and Carrie went almost limp in relief. She suspected it was doing him a world of good, sitting out here. Though he seemed to be brooding, mourning in silence, he was surrounded by towering pines and blue, blue sky above, turning slowly into purple twilight now. In the distance, a serene lake, as still and silent as the sky, seemed to absorb pain and reflect back healing. And the roar of the falls, not far away, could be heard in the distance.

Sam sat up straighter in his chair and reached for the nuggets, then the honey-mustard sauce, putting some of both on his plate. Then he added a much smaller than normal portion of the fries and proceeded to drown them in ketchup. Finally he looked up at Carrie, who quickly shifted her eyes elsewhere.

"You can stop pretending not to be noticing how much I'm eating," he told her. "I know your brain is calculating the nutritional value of every crumb on this plate."

She smiled. "I gave up on counting up nutritional values long ago, when I realized that kids are somehow gifted with the supernatural ability to extract exactly what they need from whatever refuse they devour. I ought to propose a study to prove it."

"That would make you famous," Gabe said. "But it wouldn't take a study to convince me."

"Or anyone else," she replied. "I mean, if it wasn't true, they wouldn't live to see twenty-one." She closed her eyes as soon as the words were out. "Oh, shit. I'm sorry. That was an idiotic thing to say."

Sadie dropped her fork, and it clattered to her plate. She was staring at Carrie with huge eyes. "I never heard you swear before."

"I've never been this lousy a mother before." Carrie looked across the table at Sam. "I'm at a loss. I just don't know how to make this better for you, and I feel like I'm supposed to. I'm sorry."

Sighing, Sam reached across the table and covered her hand with his. "It's okay, Mom. I'm gonna be all right. I mean, I'm gonna feel like crap for a while, but I'll get through it. And really, it's no one else's job to make me feel better. Not even yours. It's mine. And I've got this. I promise."

His eyes shifted to Gabe's very briefly, and Carrie saw the nearly imperceptible nod that was Gabe's response. She'd always thought Sam was exceedingly mature for his age, but this was above and beyond. She suspected it was Gabe's influence taking root in the fertile soil of Sam's sharp mind.

"I wasn't going to bring it up," Sam said, and he spoke slowly, as if choosing his words carefully. "But it's what we're all thinking about, anyway. Mom, when will you know what happened to Kyle?"

She really didn't want to discuss the autopsy with Sam. She didn't think he needed that kind of image on his mind. All she said was, "I don't know."

"Well, aren't you — you know — ?"

"No, hon, I'm not. The State Police have their own doctor for that. He — or she — will be in town tonight and take a look at Kyle in the morning."

"But they'll let you be there. I mean, it's your hospital and your job. They can't deny you access, can they?"

She smiled at his innocence. "*They* can do pretty much whatever they want, Sam."

"It's just . . . this isn't dinner conversation. Sorry."

Gabe said, "The subject is sitting here like an elephant on the table, Sam. Pretending it's not isn't going to make it go away."

Sam nodded. "I just want to know what happened to him, that's all. I mean, he didn't look like there was anything *wrong* with him."

"I've been wondering that, too," Sadie said softly. "I mean, how many things could kill a guy his age without leaving a mark on him?"

They both looked to Carrie, expecting her to be the one to give them the answers they so desperately wanted — and probably just as desperately needed. She met Gabe's eyes briefly and took a sip of water to give herself time to gather her thoughts. "There are a few things that come to mind. He may have had a condition that was never diagnosed, I suppose. A heart issue or diabetes, or even asthma or a severe allergy we didn't know about. He might have taken a minor fall and hit his head in a place not immediately obvious, maybe suffered an internal bleed afterward. He might have . . . taken something. Something he thought would be harmless that turned out to be —"

"Wait a minute, wait a minute." Sam held up a hand and stared at her as if she'd grown another head. "You're talking about *drugs,* aren't you?"

"You asked what could cause death without leaving a mark. I'm just telling you — drugs are one of the leading causes of death among teens his age."

"Not Kyle," Sam said, and he said it with conviction. "No way, not ever."

"Then it was something else. But I'm confident whatever caused Kyle's death, the state's doctor will find out."

Sam took a long breath, blew it out slowly, and finally nodded. "I'd just feel better if you were doing it."

"But how would *she* feel, Sam?" Gabe asked.

Sam looked up, met his mother's eyes and then lowered his head. "I'm sorry. You're right, that would be too much. I just —" He looked at Gabe. "She's good at her job. She's *really good.*"

Carrie blinked rapidly and felt her heart go soft. "I've never heard you say that before."

"I figured you knew," he said.

"I know I'm a competent doctor. I just didn't know *you* knew it."

"I've always known it, Mom. And you're way beyond competent." He looked at Gabe. "It's no bull — she's amazing."

"Stop it already." Carrie was going to burst into mom-tears if he didn't stop praising her. "Eat your dinner."

He ate a nugget, but he looked as if he was forcing himself to eat sawdust. Then he said, "When do you think they'll have the funeral?"

"That will depend on . . . well, a lot of other things, hon," she said. "Right now it's impossible to say."

"What are you going to do about the camping trip you guys have been planning?" Sadie asked him.

He shook his head. "I'll talk to the guys. I really doubt anyone's going to feel like going. Not without Kyle."

"But you've been talking about it for so long," Sadie said. "I think Kyle would have wanted you to go."

"I don't know." Sam swallowed hard, then looked across the table. "What do you think, Gabe?"

Gabe put his napkin down, leaned back in his chair. "It's probably too soon to decide. Give yourselves time to process everything first."

"Yeah. That makes sense, I guess," Sam said. But he didn't look satisfied.

Carrie saw Gabe noticing that, too, and then he spoke again.

"I was in a similar situation once. I was older than you, but a few friends and I were planning to hike down the Grand Canyon. One of them, Ronny Dean, died just before we were supposed to go. Heart attack. No one saw it coming."

"So what did you do?" Sam asked.

"Well, just like you, we were torn. We were grieving, you know, but yet we thought he would have wanted us to go. So we made it a trip in his honor. We told stories about him all weekend long. And it . . . it helped. I mean, at first, we had trouble getting the words out, but by Sunday, we were remembering some of the wild things we did and laughing. Actually laughing."

"Wow."

"Yeah. We drank a toast to him before we broke camp. And I gotta tell you, it felt like he was right there with us."

Sam nodded slowly. Then again, a little harder. "Thanks, Gabe. When things calm down a little, I'm going to run that past the guys, see what they think."

"You're welcome. Now why don't you take your girlfriend for a walk down by the lake while your mom and I clean this mess up?"

"You guys cooked. We can clean up," Sadie said.

"No." Gabe pointed toward the water. "Go on. Nature . . . heals. Go on."

"All right, but not for long." Sadie looked at her watch. "I have cheer practice tonight, and they won't cancel, not even with this. We have a tournament next week."

"I'll drive you back whenever you're ready, Sadie," Carrie told her.

Then Sam and Sadie, hand in hand, walked down the steps to the grassy slope and the lake beyond.

Carrie watched them go, then turned to Gabe. "Ronny Dean? A toast at the bottom of the Grand Canyon? Really?"

"You doubt me?" he asked, feigning hurt.

"Well, unless you wrote the Sammy Gold song, 'Ode to Jimmy Bean,' you're a big fat liar."

"I am not fat."

She smiled slightly. "No. You're not."

He started clearing up the dishes, stacking plates and heading inside with them. She gathered things, too, and followed. "So why the fabrication?" she asked.

"I wanted to make him feel better, and it was the first thing that popped into my head that fit." He shrugged. "And I'll tell him the truth later on, when he's past the roughest parts of all this."

After setting the dishes in the sink, she

turned, leaned back against the counter and gazed at him. "I think it was just what he needed to hear, Gabe. It was a good idea, even if it was a fib."

"It's one of Sammy Gold's most obscure songs. I really didn't think you'd pick up on it."

She tipped her head to one side. "I have everything he's ever recorded. Even the obscure stuff. The question is, why would you know it? I thought you hated him."

His face changed then. It went from open and warm to almost blank. "I'm in the business, remember?"

Frowning, she said, "You *really* don't like him, do you?"

"No. I really don't."

"Then you must have a good reason."

His brows went up. "How can you be so sure? Maybe I'm just a music snob."

She laughed very softly. "You're not any kind of a snob. You're a warm, caring, intelligent man. Shoot, you even defended Ambrose Peck. You don't seem to dislike anybody."

"I mostly don't."

"So then there must be a reason why you hate Sammy Gold." Turning to face the sink again, she cranked on the faucets and added a squirt of detergent, then watched the sudsy water rise. "I confess, I'm burning with curiosity."

"At least you're burning with something."

She shot him a narrow-eyed look over her shoulder. "You said you might tell me sometime."

"Yes, I did."

"So are you going to tell me now?"

He stared at her, saying nothing.

She tilted her head to one side. "It would distract me from the dark cloud stuck over my head right now, maybe."

He nodded slowly. "I suppose it might."

"So?" She held his eyes and waited, and she knew the minute he decided to give in. There was some sort of shield over his eyes, invisible, but there, and she could have sworn she saw it dissolve.

"I can't believe I'm saying this, but yeah. I'm going to tell you." He moved up beside her as she began washing dishes and took on the drying portion of the task. "But you probably aren't going to believe me. The truth of the matter is that Sammy Gold is my father."

7

She looked at him as if she thought he was joking, a small smile on her face. But when Gabe didn't return it, her eyes slowly went wider, and her smile vanished like morning dew from a sunbathed blade of grass.

God, she was beautiful.

"Your . . . father?"

He nodded. "My mother was — is — a gold-digging groupie."

"Gabe!"

"What?"

"That's a terrible thing to say about your mother."

"It's a terrible thing to *know* about my mother. But it's the truth, nonetheless. She managed to lure Sammy Gold into the sack just as he was starting his meteoric rise, and she ended up pregnant. She's never admitted it, but I'm convinced she planned it that way. When I was born, she hired a lawyer, had a blood test done, and notified Gold's handlers that there was about to be a very expensive and very public paternity suit filed."

"She didn't . . . go to him? Talk to him face-to-face?"

"Not the way she tells it, no. Obviously I only have her story to go on. Though if she were going to lie to me, it seems like she would have made herself a little bit more sympathetic."

"So what happened?" she asked him as she pulled the sink stopper to let the water drain.

Gabe dried his hands on the towel, then handed it to her. "Mom was offered a hell of a settlement in exchange for signing a confidentiality agreement. As long as she keeps her mouth shut about who fathered me, she gets a big fat check in the mail every month. And every year of my life, the amount has gone up a bit, just to keep her motivated."

He was watching Carrie's face as he told her the story he'd never told anyone else, ever. She seemed fascinated by it, but she was watching *his* face, too, as if trying to hear what he wasn't saying out loud.

"I suppose it's understandable that he would pay to keep it quiet," she said slowly, thoughtfully. "I mean, his trademark is home and family. All his songs are about loyalty and fidelity and trust. Being a good man, finding a good woman, staying true."

Gabe wandered to the door, glanced out at the kids down on the shore. "That was probably true then. Now, though, it wouldn't hurt him a bit. He's practically a deity to country music fans. Besides, it happened a long time ago, in his youth."

"I imagine it would still shake up his marriage, though," she said.

"Are you . . . defending him?"

"No." She put a hand on his arm. "It probably sounded that way, but no, Gabe, I'm not. I'm really not. I'm just trying to understand what would possess someone to do what he's done, what could drive a man to disavow his own son. That's all. It's . . . it's unimaginable to me."

The hackles that had risen in response to her comments settled down again. "I can imagine it would seem unimaginable to you, as much as you love Sam. Your Sam, I mean."

"I would die for my son," she said simply.

He nodded. "I don't doubt that for a minute."

"So tell me more."

He sighed, but he talked. As he did, he poured the coffee he'd brewed into two cups, handed one to her, then nodded at the cream and sugar on the counter. "Part of the agreement was that neither my mother nor I would ever try to approach or contact Sammy Gold by any means whatsoever."

Carrie frowned then, studying his face as she sipped her coffee, black. "That's even more abhorrent."

"Ah, now you're getting it."

"But why would he do that? Why wouldn't he even want to *know* his own son?"

The question was so poignant, coming from her, that Gabe was rendered momentarily speechless. It didn't help that he was growing more suspicious that Carrie's Sam might be his own son every time he saw him. So much about him, from his expressions to his moods, not to mention his hair and his eyes, reminded Gabe of himself. And every now and then, in an instant that was there and then gone quicker than the twinkle of a firefly, Gabe was sure he saw his father's face in Sam's.

"Gabe?"

He brought his attention back to Carrie and realized he was beginning to like her. No, that was wrong. He *already* liked her. He was beginning to feel . . . more. And to regret not telling her who he was from the very start. Then again, at the very start, he hadn't even *suspected* that Sam could be his own offspring. And now he'd painted himself into a corner. If he told Carrie, she would hate him. If he didn't, then he was compounding his crime by continuing to commit it.

He had to make sure. He had to make sure *first,* because if he told her now and it turned out not to be true, then he would have alienated her for nothing.

Carrie snapped her fingers under his chin, and he met her eyes.

"Gosh, this really does eat away at you, doesn't it?"

"What does?"

"Your father. Him never acknowledging you, never wanting to meet you. Paying your mother to keep you a secret. It hurts. I can see that."

Gabe blinked himself back to the topic at hand. His father. Not his son. "Actually, I was thinking of something else entirely. I think I got over feeling betrayed or hurt by my father a long time ago."

"That's bull. How do you ever get over something like that?"

"By not thinking about it. Whenever it hits me, I sort of acknowledge it, then let it go. I spend my time on things that make me feel good, not on things that make me feel bad."

She frowned at him. "What kind of a philosophy is that? You just ignore bad things and figure they'll go away?"

"It's not about making anything go away. It's about getting onto the same wavelength as the good stuff in life. It comes to you easier that way. But if you stay on the wavelength with the bad stuff, you get more of that, instead."

"Fascinating," she whispered. "And you actually believe this."

"I know this."

"And how's it working out for you so far?"

He shrugged. "Up to now, only so-so. Couple of gold records, a few platinum ones. Living exactly the way I decide to live, doing what I want, when I want. Making more money than I could ever need. But now I think it's really kicking in."

"Really." She didn't hide the sarcasm in her voice.

"Mmm-hmm. I met you."

She sucked in a soft little gasp, barely noticeable, but he noticed it. And it was followed by three rapid blinks and a quick averting of her eyes. *Score,* he thought silently. It had touched her, what he'd said just then. It had gotten to her, and that had to mean she was feeling something, too.

She lifted her eyes, met his again and smiled softly. "I'm really glad I met you, too. But maybe this is a good time to point out the obvious."

"Which is?"

"You're here on vacation. You'll be gone when it's over. So let's not let ourselves start thinking this . . . this attraction between us is anything more than — well, than what it is."

He blinked. "Oh."

"Doesn't that make sense to you?"

"No."

She frowned. "Why not?"

Shrugging he said, "Because I believe in living in the moment. Doing what makes me happy in the moment. Always."

"And I believe in doing what's best for my son, what's best for my patients and what's best for my friends."

"So when do you do what's best for you?" he asked. "Just where does *your* happiness fit in?"

"Taking care of others is what makes me happy. It's what I do. What I don't do is wander, or drift from place to place, or pack up and move whenever the mood strikes me. I have roots here. I've planted them here, and I intend to stay here."

He frowned slightly. He'd been planning

to kiss her, but he was having second thoughts. "You almost sound angry at me," he said. "Have I done something to make you angry, Carrie?"

She blinked and looked away. "You're making me wish there was a crumb of a chance for this to be . . . something."

"Then wish it. And stop being so sure it's impossible."

He put a hand on her shoulder and turned her to face him. "Please? Just try it my way for a few days. Start thinking only things that make you smile." He pushed her hair behind one ear. "You're so damn beautiful when you smile."

"Gabe," she whispered, but he was already moving in for that kiss. And she melted into him, opened her mouth when he nudged her to, pressed her body closer when he tightened his arms around her waist. He cupped the back of her head and bent over her, and he traced the edges of her lips with his tongue. Just that, and he knew she wanted more.

The sound of the door opening, then quickly closing again, broke them apart, and he looked over her head to see the kids on the deck, their backs pointedly to them.

"They're pretending they didn't see us," Gabe said. "And they're not very convincing — especially given Sam's drama club experience."

"Oh, hell."

"Stop it." He looked down into Carrie's eyes, stroked her hair. "Just stop being negative, will you? There's no harm in them knowing we kissed."

"Of course there is. Sam worships you already. He'll get his hopes up, think this is going to be something, and then get his heart broken when it ends."

He bent his brows together and clasped her shoulders. "You really need to get a dictionary, because your idea of being positive really needs some work."

She rolled her eyes.

"Just try. For me?"

"How, Gabe? How, when I have to go to the hospital tomorrow and try to get them to let me observe Kyle's autopsy?"

"Don't do that," he said. "Don't subject yourself to it. It will be painful and sad, and it'll make you a magnet for more of the same. The job will be done. It doesn't have to be you."

"You heard Sam, though. He's counting on me. I have to be there for him."

He lowered his head. "It's a bad idea, Carrie. I wish you'd trust me on this."

"I'm a doctor. This is the sort of thing I do."

"You don't have to."

"I choose to. I'll be in that room in the morning, no matter what I have to do to make that happen." Averting her eyes, she added, "I'm just not as good as you are at taking life lightly, I guess."

"Okay. Okay. I get it." He heaved a sigh, then said, "I'm not taking *you* lightly, Carrie. Don't think that's what's happening here."

She studied his face for a minute. "You're not easy to figure out, you know that?"

"There's nothing to figure out, Carrie. I'm just what I seem. For the most part."

"For the most part?"

He nodded. She looked at him for another long moment, then turned away and went to open the patio doors. "Time to go," she called. "And I don't want to hear any snickering, whispering or comments on the way. Got it?"

"What are you even talking about?" Sam asked. "C'mon, Sadie." He took her by the hand, and the two came in. As they crossed the kitchen past Gabe, Sam held up a hand. Gabe reciprocated the high five, grinning.

"Brat," Carrie muttered. But the two teens just kept walking, straight through the log cabin and out the front door. She glanced at Gabe and sighed. "I'm sorry if things got . . . tense. I don't mean to be that way. I just. . . . I'm cautious, I guess."

"If you can kick that up just one notch to 'cautiously optimistic,' you'll feel better. That's a term you doctors use a lot, right?"

She nodded. "I'll think about it," she said.

"Really?" He was surprised.

"Yeah. Not because it makes any sort of sense whatsoever, but just because . . ." She lowered her eyes and even her voice. "Just because . . . I really *like* kissing you."

Oh, hell, she'd nailed him right between the eyes with that one. He reached for her, but she dodged gracefully.

"Oh, no. I'm not giving those two any more ammunition. They're going to torture me no end as it is."

"It'll do them a world of good," he said. "And you know it."

"Yeah, I do. I'll . . . see you tomorrow, Gabe."

"I can't wait."

He watched her walk the same path her son had, through the living room and out the front door, and he had a self-satisfied smile on his face the whole time. She liked him. And he liked her.

And then his smile died, as he realized

how angry she was going to be when she found out that he'd been keeping a huge secret from her from the very first day they'd met. A secret that could affect her son, who meant more to her than anything in the world.

"Yeah, and I'd better take a dose of my own advice here, huh?" he said aloud, then heaved a heavy sigh and tried to think positively. He was going to find just the right time to tell her in just the right way, and she was going to understand.

Right. She was probably going to punch him squarely in the nose.

The next morning Carrie Overton stood beside a table in the hospital's morgue. She hadn't slept the previous night. She might have, with the help of a tranquilizer, but she'd wanted to be sharp for this morning. She'd given Sam a mild sedative before bed and convinced him to take it. Sadie had gone home earlier, insisting she would be fine. And somehow, Carrie didn't doubt it. The girl was as tough as they came.

The morgue was equipped to hold up to eight cadavers at a time in cold storage drawers, but she'd never seen more than three in there at once, and that had been a rare occasion. Most of the time the morgue was empty.

This morning, it was not. The disrobed body of Kyle Becker lay on a table, beneath a sheet, awaiting autopsy. His clothes had been removed with extreme care in the presence of police. They'd been brushed, and every particle that fell from them had been collected and would be examined.

A camera sat near to hand, in case it was needed, and a digital recorder hung suspended from the ceiling. It was running now, as the unfortunately named Dr. Carson Butcher, an overweight forensic pathologist with shaggy blond hair and a pockmarked face, began to sweat his way through the external exam, saying aloud, "No remarkable bruises or signs of trauma. However, there are clear needle tracks in the left arm, crook of the elbow."

Leaning over, Carrie pointed to the additional needle mark in the upper left forearm, this one bruised.

Dr. Butcher nodded. "In addition, there's another puncture and bruise in the upper left forearm. This one appears to have been made by a larger needle."

"It looks almost as if he's had blood drawn, doesn't it?" Carrie asked.

"I was thinking the same thing. Get a

good clear photo of that, will you, Dr. Overton?"

She nodded, lifted the camera and took a series of shots. "The police took some, as well."

"Good. All right, let's get to the internal. Though I strongly suspect the cause of death is going to have to wait for the toxicology results. Two weeks minimum from the state lab."

Carrie reached up and shut off the recorder.

Carson lifted his head. "What?"

"There's a lab in Burlington. Small, nowhere near as high-tech as the state crime lab, but they could handle a tox screen. The police might want to run some blood and tissue samples through there, to speed up the process."

He frowned. "Then the police are going to have to be the ones to order it."

"And they might. I'm only suggesting we take extra samples. In case they do."

Dr. Butcher set the scalpel down and met Carrie's eyes. "I know this is your town, and that you knew this kid, but I'm not willing to jeopardize my career because you have a stake in this. It's just another case to me. I'm doing exactly what I'm ordered to do on this, nothing more."

He eyed her skeptically, then pushed the shock of straw-colored hair off his sweat-slick forehead. She knew his type. He was officious and occasionally a bully because he felt insignificant. His career was the only part of his life where he could exert control. He probably had no personal life, no love life and few friends.

"We need to release this boy to his family as soon as we can, Dr. Butcher. They need to bury him — they need to get some closure."

He nodded. "I understand that. But you should be telling it to the police." He reached up to turn the recorder on again. "Moving on to the internal exam, beginning with the standard Y incision."

He moved his scalpel to Kyle's chest, and Carrie stared at the pale, pale skin and still, dead face of her son's best friend, and thought she was going to vomit.

Carson Butcher looked up at her, his blade poised above the sternum. Then he stopped what he was doing, straightened and switched the recorder off again. "I'm sorry, Dr. Overton. I know I gave the okay for you to observe, but I'm no longer comfortable with that."

"Just because I asked about taking extra samples?"

"Just because you look like you might faint. And that would interrupt the flow of my work."

"Maybe if we could cover his face first . . . ?" she said.

He shook his head slowly. "I'll see you on my way out, let you know what I've found. All right?"

Lowering her head, knowing he was right, she said, "Okay." And then she turned and left the room.

She felt horrible, as if she'd failed Sam — and maybe Kyle, too — by not being there to observe the autopsy. And yet she felt relieved not to have to watch a child the same age as her son being opened up, his organs removed and weighed, the top of his skull removed.

Yes, she was relieved.

God knew she had plenty to keep her busy at the hospital. Patients to check in on, test results to review, new admissions to evaluate. She broke at lunchtime and went down to check on Dr. Butcher, but he was deep in conversation with Chief MacNamara and another man. Both the chief and the stranger wore street clothes — suits, ties. She suspected the other man was from the state police. As she stood outside the morgue, looking through the mesh-lined window in the door, Dr. Butcher looked up, spotted her and said something to the other men, who both looked in her direction.

She nodded hello, but when the men all turned back to their discussion, rather than waving her inside, she knew better than to hang around. Her plans for later on dictated that she act with the utmost discretion now.

She walked away and took the elevator back to the floor where she had her office. Her phone beeped as soon as she stepped into the corridor, and she frowned at the screen, then clicked the little notepad icon to read the text message. It was from Dr. Butcher.

Nothing definitive. Waiting 4 tox results.

That was all. She was grateful he'd at least gotten in touch and texted back a simple Thx, even while making a mental note to thank him in person when she got the chance. She would have asked him to e-mail her a copy of his report, but she knew he would refuse. The guy was too by-the-book. And coming from her, that was saying something.

Flipping her phone closed again, she rounded the corner that brought her to her office door and found it open, and Sam sitting at her desk inside.

He met her eyes. She thinned her lips, and lowered hers.

"Is it done?"

She lifted her gaze again and nodded twice. "It's done."

"And?" he asked.

"And there was nothing definitive, Sam. We're going to have to wait for the lab results before we'll know anything."

He held her eyes for a long moment, searching them, and she knew why. "I'm not lying to you, Sam. I wouldn't. You know that."

"Not even for a police investigation?"

"No. Not even. I'd tell you if I knew anything, but I don't. I really don't."

He closed his eyes, lowered his head. "How long?" he asked.

"Until we know?" He nodded, and Carrie sighed. "Around two weeks," she said, being brutally honest, even though she knew he would hate hearing it.

Sam rose from the chair in a rush. "Two weeks!"

"I know it's a long time, but —"

"Do you think his mom can wait two weeks? Could *you,* if it were me down there in the morgue?"

"Don't say that. Don't even *think* that."

He turned his back to her. "I'm sorry. That was crude. I know it's not your fault."

"I'm doing all I can. I promise. If there's a way to move things along any faster, I will. Okay?"

"Is there?" He faced her again, his eyes narrowing as she averted her own. "Wait, there is, isn't there? You wouldn't have said that if there wasn't."

"I have . . . an idea or two."

His frown grew. "You're not . . . you're not doing something that could mess up your job or anything like that, are you?"

She tipped her head to one side. "You know me better than that. I'm a conformist, remember? You said so just the other day."

"What I said was that you're not as much of one as you'd like to think you are."

"Doesn't matter." She looked at her watch. "My lunch break's just about over, Sam."

"All right."

"You have anything planned?"

He shook his head. "Kyle's mom asked me to look for any photos of him. Said she was doing a collage of them for the services. I told her to let me and the guys do it for her."

Carrie almost choked up but managed to hold it together. "That's incredibly thoughtful of you."

"It didn't seem like something she ought to be doing. I don't know. I'm running around today picking up photos from everyone who has one they want included, including a bunch from Mrs. Becker."

"Will you be home in time for dinner?"

He nodded. "You?"

"A little on the late side. But I should make it by seven-thirty, quarter of eight."

"I'll see you then." He started for the door, then paused and turned. "Sorry I lost it before."

"It's understandable. All's forgiven."

"See you tonight, Mom."

"Love you, Sam," she called. And heard his obligatory but heartfelt, "Love you, too" as the office door closed behind him.

She waited until nearly seven, when the morgue was less likely to see any action. For some reason, any business needing to be done down there tended to get done during the day. No one liked it there in the dark. It wasn't something anyone admitted aloud, it was just the pattern. Everyone noticed, but no one commented.

She made it seem as if she were leaving for the day, locked up her office, put on her jacket, said her goodbyes. And then she took the elevator an extra level down and went into the morgue. No one was around, and the place was as dark as a dungeon, but she made her way through the outer rooms without turning on a light, only pausing when she reached the interior room known as the meat locker.

Then she flipped on the overhead lights, which seemed blinding at first, and went to the drawer where Kyle — no, not Kyle, Kyle's body — lay. She gripped the handle, giving it a twist, and then pulling the heavy drawer open. It was noisy, clattering and even squeaking all the way, and she cringed, as if someone were close enough to hear.

But no one was.

The echoes of the sounds died away, and she ordered herself to relax. It wasn't easy. She wasn't a rule breaker. But what she was doing wasn't all *that* illegal, anyway. Kyle's body would be released to his family first thing tomorrow morning — that was as soon as the funeral director could come and pick it up. It could have been released this afternoon, but hadn't been. Gabe would probably say that was a sign. Or something.

Wouldn't he?

Hell, she didn't know. She only knew that if there was a way to get answers sooner, she had to take it. Maybe not answers that would hold up in court or convict a killer. But answers that would give peace to Kyle's mother, to his father. Answers that might help keep the other teens of Shadow Falls safe.

And if that was against the rules, then so be it.

Carrie pulled up a clean instrument tray and gently removed the sheet from Kyle's lifeless body, trying not to see the fresh stitches holding his chest cavity together, or the ones keeping the top of his skull attached.

And then she got to work.

8

Carrie was bone tired when she dragged herself home at the end of that long day. Long? Hell, it had felt like the longest of her life. And she knew Sam and Sadie would be there waiting, probably still expecting answers she wasn't yet able to give them. She hoped, ridiculously, that Gabe would be there, too, and was disappointed not to see his van sitting in her driveway.

She caught hold of herself, reminded herself that whatever was happening between her and Gabe, it was still new, far too new for her to feel as much as she seemed to be feeling. It must be the powerful emotional drama happening all around her, making everything within her seem more . . . intense. More powerful.

When she opened the front door and walked inside, she smelled a mingling of delicious aromas that warred with the queasiness of her utterly empty stomach.

Someone had been cooking up a storm. Frowning, she looked around. "Sam?"

"In here, Mom."

His voice came from the kitchen, so she kept on heading the way her nose had already been sending her. Rose was just pulling a large roasting pan from the oven, an oversize mitt on each hand.

"Welcome home, dear," the older woman said with a beaming bright smile. "We've made dinner."

Carrie raised her brows. "You didn't have to do —"

"Of course I did," Rose said. "You poor thing, what you've been through today. What all of you have been through," she corrected, with a sympathy-laden look at Sam, who stood nearby taking plates from the cupboard. "Naturally the last thing you're up to is cooking, and I doubt you've eaten a morsel all day."

"Well, you've got me on that one," Carrie admitted.

"I'm so terribly sorry about your young friend."

"Thank you. That's sweet of you."

"When there's nothing else to do, offer food. That's what I always say." Rose shrugged, setting the pot roast onto the granite counter. "Now, there are potatoes, baby peas and carrots, and an apple pie to go with it. Enjoy."

"Thank you so much. Gosh, it looks and smells wonderful."

"You're welcome. And now I'll leave you to it." Rose tugged off the oven mitts, set them beside the pot roast and hurried out of the kitchen.

Carrie sent Sam a puzzled frown and hurried after her. Sam followed.

"Rose, wait. You can't just leave. After all that hard work, you should stay and enjoy dinner with us."

"I wouldn't hear of it."

Sam said, "I already tried, Mom. She thinks she'd be intruding."

"That's nonsense," Carrie said. "We'd love to have you."

"Yeah," Sam said. "And like I already told you, Gabe is coming, too. And so is Sadie."

"Gabe's coming?" Carrie asked, looking at her son, completely distracted from the topic at hand.

"What, you thought he wouldn't? He'd have to be an idiot."

Carrie felt her lips pull into a self-satisfied smile. "Was that a compliment?"

He rolled his eyes. "We won't notice one more at the table," he told Rose. "Besides, how are we gonna make a big gooey fuss over how good it is if you aren't even here to hear us?"

"Oh, you're such a polite young man. And it's sweet of you to ask, but no. I really do have my own plans for the evening. Enjoy the meal. Good night."

"Good night. And thanks again, Rose," Carrie told her."

"You're welcome." Rose hurried out the door, and Carrie watched her quickstep her way across the driveway.

"Isn't she just the oddest woman?" Carrie asked.

"I think she's campaigning for us to adopt her."

Laughing softly, Carrie started to lower the curtain and turn away, but then she saw that crazy van of Gabe's come bouncing into the driveway.

"Wow," Sam said.

Carrie dragged her eyes from the van to her son. "What?"

"You really like him." She opened her mouth, but her son held up a forefinger. "No, don't even start. You do, I can tell. If you could see the look on your face right now, you wouldn't even try to deny it. You like him."

"I like him," she confessed. "But he's so . . . different from what I thought I wanted in a man."

"Yeah. You wanted a geek. We covered that. But, Mom, you got a genius instead. That's a definite upgrade."

"Is it?"

"It is."

"Well, just don't read too much into it. He's a drifter, Sam. He probably won't hang around here very long."

"I think he will."

"Why do you say that?"

" 'Cause I got to see *his* face when you arrived at his place last night. Even with everything going on, it was pretty obvious." He went to the door and opened it before Gabe even got a chance to knock. "Hey, Gabe. Come on and help me set the table. Sadie will be here any minute."

Gabe walked in, and Carrie hoped her feelings weren't as obvious to him as they had been to Sam. She tried to school her face into a neutral expression, but it wasn't easy. She was as tense as she could be, the memory of the day still hanging like a black cloud in her mind. And she'd done something that was unethical, if not illegal, to boot, by taking those samples. She would compound the sin by taking them to the private lab herself, and quietly asking her friend, Marcus Kenyon, to run them through the mass spectrometer without a word to anyone anywhere.

She'd never done anything so outrageous before.

Okay, she had. She'd forged a birth certificate and raised Sam as her own without a word to anyone. And that far outweighed this on the bad-ass scale, she supposed.

All of that tension curled into a tight little knot in her belly as she said hello to Gabe. He looked into her eyes, then moved forward with his arms open and folded her into them.

She was instantly overcome by a feeling of relief. Her taut nerves seemed to relax, her muscles unclenched, and she felt warm right to her core. She leaned against him and closed her eyes, and, just for one moment, let the hurt and angst of the day flow out of her. It was as if he were siphoning it off, taking it into himself instead.

"God, I needed that," she whispered very softly in his ear.

She felt him nod against her cheek, and then he eased his grip on her and stepped back without quite losing touch. "It smells delicious in here."

"You can thank Rose for that," she said, stepping out of his embrace, to turn and walk beside him into the kitchen.

"Your boarder?" As Carrie nodded he went on. "Good, I finally get to meet her."

Carrie shook her head. "She made us dinner but declined to stay and enjoy it with us."

He frowned. "That's too bad."

"Well, she said she had other plans, but I have to wonder. She seems to be a rather odd woman."

"Here comes Sadie," Sam said, looking out the still-open front door.

Carrie looked, too, and saw Sadie wheeling up on her bicycle. She parked it in front of the door and then climbed off, a bulging green backpack over her shoulder.

"Hey, guys."

"What, are you moving in?" Carrie asked her.

She shook her head. "Cheer practice later. Dress rehearsal for the dance routine before the competition. So I needed to bring the works."

"Pom-poms and all?" Sam asked, patting his chest as if the thought were too much for his heart to handle.

She rolled her eyes at him and looked away. But Carrie knew she was relieved to see Sam even trying to make a joke, given the circumstances. She felt the same way.

"Hey, Carrie." Sadie came closer and gave

Carrie a gentle hug. "How are you holding up?"

"Better, now that I'm surrounded by my favorite people," Carrie replied, hugging the girl back.

Sadie tipped her head sideways and smiled, clearly touched by Carrie's words. Then she sniffed and looked around in search of the source. "Man, something smells good."

"That would be our dinner," Sam said. "Which reminds me, Gabe, you want to give me a hand?"

Gabe nodded, and he and Sam headed into the kitchen. Within a few minutes the two males had finished setting the table, and then the four of them sat down to try their best to do justice to Rose's generous offering. It wasn't easy, however. No one had an appetite, given the main topic of nonconversation.

Finally Sam broke through the uncomfortable silence. "Did you find out anything more today?"

Carrie lowered her eyes. "I'm sorry, hon. There really isn't anything more to tell you than what I said when I saw you earlier. There was no obvious cause of death. The answer won't come until we get all the lab work back."

Sam thinned his lips. "So what are they testing for?"

"It's a wide range, hon. I'm not even sure of the full list." She shook her head, still in a state of slight disbelief that they were discussing the autopsy of the kid who'd once posed her garden gnomes in pornographic positions on April Fools' Day. It was surreal. "The important thing is that it's done. They're going to release him to his family first thing in the morning. And I got a call on the way home. The funeral is scheduled for tomorrow afternoon. I know it seems awfully soon, but a lot of the relatives have been in town since he first went missing. That family needs closure."

"I know," Sam said softly. "Mrs. Becker told me when I stopped to pick up the pictures she wanted in the collage."

"I brought some, too," Sadie said. "Remind me to leave them with you before I go."

They ate Rose's delicious meal but barely tasted it, and even Sadie's and Gabe's attempts to inject lighter topics into the conversation fell flat. It was just a sad night. There was nothing to be done about that.

When the meal was over, Gabe carried the remnants of the pot roast into the kitchen, where Sam had taken the dirty plates. He set the roast on the counter as Sam handed the plates to Carrie, who was running water into the sink.

"My guitar is out in the bus," Gabe told Sam. "You want to jam for a while tonight?"

"I don't think I'm really up to it."

"Your call. No pressure. I don't know, but for me it's a release. I pour all my angst into my music."

"Yeah, but I'll bet you do it alone."

"I have to admit, I usually do."

Sam nodded as if he'd already known that and said, "Thanks for the offer, Gabe. Rain check, okay?"

"Sure."

Sam left the kitchen. Carrie watched him go with worry in her eyes. "I don't like it when he's this morose," she said.

"You can't blame him. He's lost his best friend."

"I didn't say I didn't understand it. I just don't like it."

Gabe moved up behind her at the sink, slid his hands over her shoulders, squeezed them gently and spoke a little closer to her ear. "And how about you? Are you okay?"

She turned to face him, curled her arms around his neck and stepped closer. And as he held her, she felt more of the day's tension fading away. "I did something I probably shouldn't have done today."

"What?" he asked, looking down into her face.

"I snuck down to the morgue after the state's pathologist finished up, and I took extra blood and tissue samples from Kyle's body. I'm planning to take them to a private lab owned by a friend of mine for analysis. Tox screening, mainly."

"Is that *legal?*" Gabe was looking at her as if he'd never seen her before.

She'd managed to surprise him, she guessed.

"I'm sure it's not. And I know any results I get won't hold up in court. But it might tell the police something they need to know a little bit sooner. And it would give his parents answers they're on pins and needles waiting for."

Gabe stepped back a little, almost as if he needed to get a better angle to stare at her in disbelief. "It's not like you to buck the system, is it?"

"What do you mean by that?"

"I mean, I've been thinking you're mostly a rule follower. Not a rogue."

She shrugged. "You sound just like my son."

"And he knows you better than anyone. We couldn't both be reading you wrong, could we?"

"Depends on the situation, I guess."

"Couldn't you be risking your medical license by doing something like this?"

"If it's necessary, should that really matter?" She pursed her lips. "It's the right thing to do, Gabe. Besides, it won't be the first thing I've done that could get me booted out of medicine forever."

"Really?" His brows rose, and he seemed deeply interested. "Now you've got my attention. Not that you didn't already."

"Never mind," she told him. "Forget I said it."

"Not likely. Will you tell me about it, this deep dark sin you committed somewhere in your shadowy past?"

Her heart quickened in her chest, because she found herself really *wanting* to tell him the secret she had never told another soul. And that scared her. "I don't know yet," she said. "I've never told anyone, so —"

"So you'll have to trust me first."

"I'll have to trust you *completely* first."

"It's that big?"

"The biggest."

He sighed, searching her face. "You just had to whet my curiosity, didn't you?"

She shrugged. "Figured it would give you a reason to keep coming around."

"I already have a reason to keep coming around." His smile faded, and his eyes intensified. "And it feels like a pretty powerful one, to be honest."

She averted her gaze. "Really?"

"I don't lie, Carrie."

Inhaling deeply, she said, "This is feeling pretty powerful to me, too." And then she lifted her head to read his reaction to that.

But instead of giving her the chance to glimpse whatever was happening in the depths of his eyes, he closed the distance between them and kissed her. It was a long, tender kiss that grew quickly deep and passionate, the kind of a kiss that should have been a preamble to something more. She dug her fingers into his hair, wishing she could tug the band away and see it loose and wild. She might have, if not for the circumstances. But as it was, the kiss ended with both of them craving more, needing more, wanting more, and with both of them knowing it wasn't the right time. Not tonight.

Eventually they pulled apart, but only slightly. He rested his forehead against hers, and she wondered if his heart was pounding as rapidly as hers.

"I'm gonna go," he told her.

"Already?"

"I think we both know it's . . . necessary."

She sighed, but nodded against his forehead.

"Besides, I'm working on something new, and I think it's going to be good."

"A new song?"

He nodded, then ran a hand over her hair. "You're a great muse."

She rolled her eyes, secretly touched to the core. "I'll bet that line works every time you use it."

"I'll let you know, since this is the first and only time I've tried it out." He kissed her again, briefly this time.

"I'll walk you out," she said.

On the way they passed Sam, who was sitting on the sofa looking through a box of photos. He'd started a stack of them beside the box, and Carrie saw that the one on top was a shot of him and Kyle, arm in arm, at the age of nine, wearing their baseball uniforms.

Her heart twisted tight at the memory. She caught Gabe looking, too, and thought he was choking up a bit, as well.

"Sadie said to say goodbye for her," Sam said, barely looking up from his job. "She had that dress rehearsal tonight. It's only an hour, but she'll head home after that."

"She went on her bike?" Carrie asked.

"Alone?"

"She wouldn't take no for an answer," he said. "Said it was good exercise and got pissed when I got pushy about it. She's as stubborn as you are, Mom."

"Still . . ."

"It's only a couple of miles. It wasn't even dark yet."

Kids. One minute insisting Kyle's death was the result of some big bad boogeyman, as unlikely as that theory seemed — especially given those needle tracks in his arms. The next minute, taking off alone on a twisting country road.

"I'll look for her on my way down," Gabe said.

"Oh, she'll be there by now. It's a ten-minute ride, and she's been gone twenty already."

Gabe nodded and sent Carrie a reassuring look in exchange for her worried one.

"If this is the dress rehearsal, when is the competition?" Gabe asked, probably just to change the subject. "Tomorrow?"

"A week from Saturday. She's already informed the coach that technically, a dress rehearsal is the last one before the real performance. But the coach sees it differently."

"As in, it's any rehearsal where they're

dressed?" Carrie asked.

Sam smiled, but not with his eyes, and shot Gabe an apologetic look. "It's a small town. Not every job opening has a dozen applicants. Sometimes you just take what you can get, and the cheerleading coach's main qualification is that she was a cheerleader herself."

"Hey, I'd be the last guy to judge." Gabe continued on to the door, and Carrie walked with him, then held it open as he said goodbye. She wished he would kiss her again, then wished he wouldn't. Not with Sam watching. Gabe took her hand, squeezed it and walked backward until distance forced him to let go. He waved once more halfway down the steps, and Carrie ached inside. She watched him get into the bus and saw it rolling away moments later, its perfectly round headlights painting a path ahead of it. As he left, she noticed that Rose's old station wagon was no longer in the driveway and wondered where the little old lady had gone.

Sighing, she turned and sat down beside her son. "Can I help?"

He smiled a little, and held up a recent photo of him and Kyle mugging for the camera in their soccer uniforms. They were muddy, wet and smiling broadly. "Remember Coach Walsh and the year of the horrible soccer weather?"

"That's a great one," Carrie said. "That's frame-worthy."

"Yeah, I know. Do you remember that game? It was last season, near the end."

"I remember it, all right. I was freezing my butt off in the bleachers. Had a blanket around me and spent five bucks at the hot cocoa stand. It rained. It snowed. And you scored the only goal of the game, saving us from heading into a 0-0 overtime. A feat for which I was immensely grateful."

He smiled sadly and set the photo on the pile he'd started. Then he and Carrie continued sorting. Nearly two hours later the box was empty and they were arranging their favorite photos on a large poster board when the phone rang.

Carrie picked it up. "Hello?"

"Hi, is this Dr. Overton, Sam's mom?"

"Yes, it is." Carrie frowned a little, glancing toward Sam.

"Carrie, this is Donna Damien, the cheerleading coach. Is Sam there with you?"

"Yes. Is anything wrong?" As she asked the question, Sam's eyes focused on her with a frown.

"Well, I don't know," the coach said. "That's the thing."

"What is it, Mom?" Sam asked, frowning harder.

"It's Sadie's coach. Pick up the extension."

Sam was off the sofa and had the other phone within seconds. "This is Sam. What's going on?"

"I just wondered if you might know where Sadie is? I've tried her mother, but that woman is about as useless as — I'm sorry. That wasn't nice, but —"

"Screw nice!" Sam burst out. "What do you mean, where's Sadie?"

"Sam!" Carrie warned, but she didn't blame him. Alarm bells were going off in her own head, as well.

"That's just it," the woman on the phone said. "She didn't show up for practice, and this was really important. The first of our final four dress rehearsals, and —"

"She didn't show up?" Sam sent his mother a helpless look. "She didn't *show up?*"

"All right, okay, don't panic," Carrie said. "Donna, listen to me. Sadie left our house two hours ago. She was on her bike. It's only a couple of miles to school. You're saying she never made it there?"

"No. God, you don't think . . . ?"

"No. No I don't think that at all. Have

you called the police, Donna?"

"I thought I'd check with you first."

"Call them right now, all right?"

"I'm driving to school," Sam said.

"Wait for me!"

"I'm not waiting for anything." Sam slammed out of the house.

Carrie choked down the bile she felt rising in her throat, but she couldn't quell the chills racing up and down her spine, or the panic taking root in her heart. "I've gotta run, Donna. Call the police. I'll be in touch."

She hung up without waiting for the other woman to answer and ran in search of her purse.

9

Carrie raced outside and dove into the passenger side of Sam's SUV, her cell phone already in her hand. She dialed as he drove, but they were moving in and out of range, and she had to stop and start over three times before she finally got Gabe on the other end.

The sound of his voice made her close her eyes in the tiniest bit of relief. "Gabe, thank God you answered."

"Carrie? What's wrong? Is Sam all right?"

"Fine. He's with me. Gabe, we can't find Sadie."

"What do you mean, you can't find her?"

She drew a breath, forced herself to say the words she wished to God she didn't have to. "Her coach called. She said Sadie never made it to practice. She's not at home, either." She moved the phone slightly away from her mouth. "Sammy, slow down, hon. We won't see a thing going this fast."

He slowed down measurably, but the SUV still raised a cloud of dust in its wake as he steered it down the winding dirt road toward the village and the school.

Gabe said, "You're driving the route she took, I gather."

"Yes, but so far, nothing."

"God, I never should have let her ride her bike," Sam muttered under his breath. "If anything's happened to her —"

"Nothing's happened to her," Carrie said.

"If she made it this far, someone would have seen her," Sam said. "Look, there's the diner, the general store, the barber shop. Someone would have seen her."

"Maybe not. It was almost dark when she left."

"She said she'd make it before dark. That's why she left when she did. Damn, why didn't I make her let me drive her?" Sam shoved a hand through his hair.

"Someone should walk the route," Gabe said into the phone. "I'm on my way right now. We'll walk it together, all right?"

"Sam's not going to wait, Gabe."

"I don't blame him. Fine, you'll be starting in town and heading back toward your place, then?"

"Yes."

"I'll catch up with you. Has someone

called the police?"

"Yes, the coach."

"I'm on my way, Carrie. Hang in there. Look in the ditches and over any drop-offs. Maybe she had an accident and needs help."

"God, I hope she's all right."

"Me, too," Gabe said. "Me, too."

She disconnected and dropped the cell phone into her pocket. "Park right there — by the school. We should walk back to the house. We can do a better job searching on foot."

"I was thinking the same thing. God."

"She's okay. She's okay, Sam. This is just us panicking because of all that's happened. There's some simple, logical reason for all this."

"Yeah. Yeah, there has to be."

"You have any flashlights in here?"

He nodded, pulling the car into an empty spot in front of the school building. Then he got out and walked around to the back, where he opened the rear hatch to retrieve a pair of flashlights from one of the storage compartments.

He flipped one on and handed her the other. "Let's go."

They started up the main road, one of them on each side, walking quickly and shining their lights into the bushes and ditches along the way, calling Sadie's name over and over into the empty silence of the night.

As they left the village behind and started up the twisting, narrow road out of town, Carrie looked into the thick woods on either side of the road, and a deeper dread built up inside her. The leaves hadn't yet fallen, or even changed much so far, but the smell was that of decay, rich and ripe and damp. It was a cool night, not yet cold. She couldn't see her breath. If Sadie were outside, injured or stranded, she wouldn't be freezing.

God, they had to find her.

She walked along one side of the road, while Sam took the other. He'd leaped the ditch and was walking along the very edge of the tree line, swinging his flashlight from side to side, and the sound of his voice calling Sadie's name brought tears to Carrie's eyes. Please, she thought, please, not Sadie. What if they'd been wrong? What if Kyle's death hadn't been a self-inflicted accident? What if someone . . .

Flashing lights approached slowly from behind, cutting off her terrifying thoughts. Carrie turned, shielding her eyes to see the police issue SUV moving slowly closer. There was a spotlight mounted to its roof, turning slowly to probe the brush just as Carrie and Sam were doing with their flashlights.

It pulled up between them and stopped. The window was already down, and Bryan Kendall was behind the wheel, looking as worried as Carrie felt. "Have you found anything yet?" he asked.

"No," Carrie said. "God, Bryan, where could she be?"

"I wish I knew. But we'll find her. We will, dammit."

She nodded emphatically. "Did you go out to her place?"

"Yeah, for what good it did. Her mother was so drunk she still doesn't get what's happening. Couldn't say a thing about Sadie except that the girl has no respect for her own mother and ought to be shipped off to reform school."

"She's the one who ought to be shipped off, and to someplace a lot worse," Carrie said, feeling guilty for saying it, but not guilty enough to stop herself.

"Tell me about it."

"Bryan, do you think —"

"It's too soon to think anything. Let's try not to jump to any —"

His words were cut off by Sam's heartbreaking shout. It was nothing but a single word. “No!” And yet it held all the pain and anguish a sixteen-year-old heart could possibly contain, and it brought fresh tears to Carrie’s eyes.

“Sam!” She ran to her son, only vaguely aware of headlights approaching, another vehicle pulling over, a door slamming, footsteps running closer.

“Sam?”

She saw him kneeling a few feet off the dirt road, the flashlight on the ground beside him, its beam aimed at nothing. As she moved closer, shining her light around him to illuminate the weeds and brush, something gleamed.

Sadie’s bicycle, lying on its side without a rider.

Gabe didn’t even know how to make sense of what was happening to the teenagers of Shadow Falls. But it seemed pretty clear now that something was. Kyle hadn’t just wandered off into the woods for some teenage, drug-induced outing. He hadn’t just decided to shoot up alone in the forest and then died of an overdose.

He did know that Sam needed him right now, and he thought briefly of the serendipity that had brought him here, to this town, to this young man who might be his son, now of all times.

"Get him away from there. This might be a crime scene," Bryan Kendall said, even as he ran back to his vehicle. He pulled it up closer and aimed the spotlight at the bicycle, so that it illuminated the ground for several feet around it. Then he got out again.

Gabe put his arm around Sam's shoulders. "Get up, son. Come on, take a few steps back."

"I can't. . . . I just can't."

Gabe tightened his grip, hauling Sam to his feet and back to the edge of the road, where Carrie quickly ran to his other side and slid an arm around his waist. Sam turned into his mother's arms. "God, Mom, what happened out here?"

"Watch where you walk!" Kendall called. "There may be tire tracks or footprints or . . . something." He was already stringing yellow tape from tree to tree to mark the area where no one was to go.

"What if someone hit her?" Sam asked. "What if they hit her and just drove away — or what if they didn't even know it? She could be hurt."

"I've got men coming," Bryan said. "Believe me, Sam, we'll search the area. But the bike doesn't look banged up. I don't think this was a hit-and-run."

"Then what was it? What the hell happened to her?" Sam demanded. He pulled free of his mother's grasp and strode up to the cop, gripping him by the shoulder and forcing him to meet his eyes. "Bryan, what's really going on? Tell me."

"I'd tell you if I knew, kid. I swear I would." Bryan looked at Carrie. "Get down to the firehouse. We'll reopen the search center, activate the telephone tree and get the volunteers organized. The sooner we start, the better. And it'll give you and Sam something to do while we process the scene and search the immediate area. Okay?"

She nodded and gripped Sam, tugging him back toward where the VW Bus waited, but he yanked free. "I can't leave."

"Sam, we have to."

"She might need me."

Gabe went to Sam, laid a hand on his shoulder. "I feel the same way, pal, but listen, any traipsing around we do up here is as likely do her harm as good. We could trample evidence — evidence that might tell the cops where she is. They know what they're doing. They're trained for this. We can be more help to Sadie by doing what Officer Kendall asks. For now. Just for now, okay?"

Staring into Gabe's eyes, tears falling unashamedly from his own, Sam nodded. It broke Gabe's heart to see the boy in this much agony. At least Kendall was already searching the woods around the bike.

"I'm gonna help you get through this, Sam. I'll be here every step of the way. I promise."

Swallowing hard, Sam nodded. "Okay, let's go."

"I'll have the chief meet you there. I imagine within the hour, half the town will be there," Kendall said.

Bryan Kendall's prediction proved true.

Most of the town's residents showed up at the firehouse as word of a second teenager gone missing spread faster than any fire Shadow Falls had ever seen. The emergency alert siren wailed to let people know something was happening. It hadn't been used since a freak twister had moved through three years ago, demolishing a handful of barns and some trailer homes in the outlying areas, but sparing Shadow Falls itself, thanks to the mountains guarding it.

Many of the residents came out to the firehouse as soon as they heard the sound, while others phoned one another to learn the reason for the alarm. The news spread, and the old firehouse was jammed full of people when Chief MacNamara took the podium in the front. Carrie and Gabe looked up from directly in front of him, Sam standing in between them.

The chief looked around the room, his grim face grimmer than ever. "It's my sad duty to report to you that we have another young person missing. Sadie Gray."

There was muttering in the crowd, though most present already knew the reason for the gathering.

"Is it the same person who killed Kyle Becker?" someone shouted.

"Is there a child killer on the loose?"

"Why aren't we out there looking for her?"

Carrie even heard one person mutter, "That girl's drunken whore of a mother is the one they ought to be looking at."

Chief Mac held up his hands for quiet. "First, let me assure you that we already have teams out combing the woods. Second, I must admonish you not to speculate or jump to conclusions. We still don't know what caused Kyle Becker's death. We don't know it was anything but accidental."

"What do you need, Chief, a note from the killer?" someone called out.

"Yeah! Why are we standing around here, when we should be out searching?"

The questioning grew louder, but the chief

held up his hands and made a "settle down" motion. "Trust me," he said, "we're doing everything we would be doing either way. But we're trying to keep an open mind. What you need to know is that Sadie Gray was last seen about seven-thirty at Dr. Overton's house. That's up on Black Bear Hill, about a mile above town. She left on her bicycle, heading for the school and cheerleading practice, a ten-minute ride, but she never arrived. We've found her bicycle in the ditch, along with her backpack containing her uniform, pom-poms and billfold." He picked up a sheet of paper, slid his glasses onto his nose and began to read. "Sadie Gray is sixteen years old. She's five feet six inches tall, and weighs a hundred and fifteen pounds. She has straight blond, shoulder-length hair and blue eyes. She was last seen wearing a ponytail, a pair of blue jeans, a purple T-shirt and a denim jacket."

"Were there signs of a struggle, Chief?" someone shouted. "Where you found the bike, were there signs of —"

"I can't comment on that. The state police are treating this case as a stranger abduction, just in case. An Amber Alert is going out as we speak."

"What about the mother?" someone asked. "Has anyone questioned her?"

"Mrs. Gray is at the station now, and she is cooperating fully. She is not a suspect."

"Can we help with the search, Chief?" someone else shouted.

"Not until morning. And I mean it. I want no civilians in the woods until daybreak, and then only under our supervision. We can't risk some well-meaning volunteer contaminating or destroying evidence. For now, just go home, and keep your eyes and ears open. If you notice anything suspicious, report it. Even if it seems minor, report it. We have posters being printed. We'll have them up before morning, and we'll have a supply for you all to put up, as well. But for now, there's nothing more any of you can do."

As Carrie and Gabe flanked Sam, all but holding him upright, he said, "This can't be happening."

"It's going to be all right."

"How can you say that?" Sam stared at his mother, his eyes wet. "What if it's the same person who had Kyle? What if he's going to do the same thing to Sadie? God, I never even told her how much she means to me. Do you realize that? I didn't tell her —"

He lowered his head, and his tears fell freely once again. "They can't expect us to just go home and wait. I can't do that, Mom."

She bit her lower lip and, still holding Sam, met Gabe's eyes over her son's head. "There *is* something we can do. Come with me."

Sam lifted his head, frowned through his tears at her.

"We have to go to the hospital first, then to Burlington, to a lab. And we have to keep it quiet."

"You're going to run the tox-screen yourself tonight, aren't you?" Gabe asked.

"Better than waiting two weeks for the state crime lab's report to come in. And if it *is* the same guy, it might help."

Sam nodded hard. "But I don't feel like I ought to leave town. Even just to drive to Burlington. I mean, what if she's close? What if she needs my help and I'm not there?"

"Baby, you don't even know where to begin looking."

A hand on his shoulder made him turn, and Bryan Kendall stood behind the three of them. Carrie stiffened, wondering if he'd overheard them. He gave no indication that he had. People were shuffling toward the doors, but Bryan led the three of them farther inside, to an empty spot in the large space. "I just want you to know, we *are* searching tonight. Not just outside, like we did with Kyle, though. We're working on checking out every building, barn or house where someone might be able to hide out with a kid and go unnoticed. With permission from the owners where possible, with search warrants from a judge where it's not, though that will take longer."

"You can get a judge to agree to that this late?" Gabe asked.

"We can try."

Sam shook his head in frustration. "There are *dozens* of hunting cabins and shacks in those woods."

"Not to mention all the winter businesses that haven't opened yet for the season," Bryan said. "I know. It's a lot. But we're covering them. We're looking for her, Sam. We are."

"But will you find her? In time?"

Bryan lowered his eyes. "If it's humanly possible, Sam, we will. And I hope to God we do."

Sam looked at Carrie. "Let's go."

She nodded. "Thank you, Bryan. We know everyone is doing all they can."

"We really are."

Nodding, the three of them started to turn and head out, but Bryan said, "Um, before you go, I just need one more thing."

"What is it?" Carrie asked.

Bryan shifted his weight from his left foot to his right, and his gaze locked onto Gabe's. "I need to ask you where you were when the girl disappeared, Mr. Cain."

Gabe's face went blank, and then, as understanding dawned, his expression turned to slightly offended and a little bit worried. "I was at Carrie's for dinner. Sadie left the house a little while before I did."

"That's right," Carrie said. "We did the dishes, and when we returned to the living room, she had already gone. But, Bryan, you don't seriously think —"

"I had to ask. You were the last three people to see her. I need to account for your whereabouts for that entire time. So again, what time did she leave the house, and what time did you follow, Mr. Cain?"

"Gabe had nothing to do with it," Sam snapped. "He's a friend. I thought *you* were, too."

Carrie put a hand on her son's shoulder. "The sooner we answer his questions, the sooner we can get out of here." She looked at Bryan. "It was about seven forty-five when Gabe left our place."

"And what time did Sadie leave?" Bryan asked.

They all looked at Sam, and he shrugged. "Around twenty minutes before Gabe did."

"All right. And after that, what did you and your mother do?"

"Sat on the sofa, sorting through old photos," Sam said.

"We were making a collage for Kyle's funeral," Carrie said. "We were still working on it when the cheerleading coach phoned a couple of hours later to ask if we knew where Sadie was."

Nodding, Bryan made a note and turned his gaze to Gabe again. "And what did you do when you left the house?"

"I drove back to the place I'm renting. Which means I took the same road Sadie took. But I didn't expect to see her along the way. Sam said she would have been at school by then."

"And you went where?"

"Straight to the cabin, up Falls Road."

Bryan frowned. "You're renting the Di Marco cabin?"

Gabe nodded.

"Okay. And what did you do next, Mr. Cain?"

"I worked on a new song for the next couple of hours."

"Song?"

"That's what I do. I'm a songwriter."

"A famous one," Sam put in.

Bryan looked surprised but kept his focus. "So you went to the cabin and worked on a song."

"Yeah. I sat on the deck, looking out at the lake and playing guitar and making notes. And no, I didn't see or talk to anyone. I didn't hear a thing from anyone until Carrie called to tell me Sadie was missing. And then I headed here to help look for her. However, you're welcome to search the cabin, if you want. My van, too. It's right outside."

Bryan nodded. "Okay. Listen, I just need to know you won't leave town until I give you the okay."

"I won't leave town until we find Sadie safe and sound," Gabe said. Then he looked at Carrie and added, "If then."

She met his eyes, acknowledged his words with a tender look. Then she shifted her gaze. "Really, Bryan, is the third degree really necessary?"

"I wouldn't be doing it if it wasn't," he said. "But now I'll leave you three alone. If you think of anything else, call me. Or if you hear from her or —"

"Of course we will," Carrie said.

"You'd better catch this guy before I do," Sam said softly, " 'cuz if he hurts Sadie, I'm gonna do some damage."

Bryan stiffened, then licked his lips. "I'm going to pretend I didn't hear that, Sam. But be careful what you say. You don't want the kind of trouble comments like that can lead to." Then he nodded to Carrie. "I'll keep you posted."

Sadie remembered rounding a corner on her bike when she felt a bee sting her shoulder and jerked in surprise. Her hand had flashed out to swat the insect away as she swung her gaze toward it. That was when she saw it was a fuzzy-tipped dart of some kind in her arm, not a bee, and her hand, already in motion, knocked it away before she could change her plan and simply pluck it out instead. By the time she'd started wondering where the dart had come from, her head was swimming and her bike was toppling sideways.

She'd caught herself, managed to bring the ten-speed to a halt, and then been unable to swing her leg high enough to dismount. Her vision went dark, and she fell over, bike and all. She dragged her leg out from under it and managed to sit upright on the ground, holding her head and swaying.

She'd vaguely seen a dark form pick up

her bike and roll it into the woods along the roadside. Just a shove, and it bounded away until it hit a bush and toppled over again.

The thought of Kyle had popped into her head then, and with it, fear. "Who are you?" she'd tried to say, though the words came out slurred and blended together. "Whaddyou want . . . with me?"

There was no reply. Instead, the dark hazy shadow of a shape bent over her, wrapped a blindfold around her face, and then pulled her hands together in front of her and bound them there with what felt like tape. She tried to struggle, to fight, but she was nearly out cold.

And then she was out for real, and only darkness remained.

Now she was awake again, barely, though she was dizzy, and everything felt distorted. Bringing her taped hands upward, she pushed the blindfold off her face and took a look around, even while tearing at the duct tape with her teeth. Finally getting hold of an edge, she tugged, until at last she was ripping the bottom layer, and all the hairs on her forearms, off at once.

Good.

She was in a small, dingy, dark room that smelled like an old basement and felt like one, as well. Stacked stone walls and a dirt floor.

She realized she was sitting on a bed, or maybe a cot. Narrow and small, twin size at best. There were clean-smelling blankets and a plump pillow. Panicking, she rose to her feet and heard clanking and rattling, all the while willing her eyes to adjust to the pitch darkness around her.

"Where are you? Why did you bring me here?" she cried.

But only darkness answered.

She stretched her arms out, palms forward, and began moving in search of a wall or a door, only to feel a tug at her ankle after a few steps. Only then did she realize she was chained. She'd heard the rattle of the links but hadn't put the pieces together in her drug-dulled brain. Now she reached down and touched the metal shackle that encircled her ankle, then traced the chain that led from it until it vanished behind the bed.

Sadie was scared. God, she'd never been so scared. She sat on the bed again, hugged her knees, lowered her head and wept. This had to be what had happened to Kyle. It had to be. And now it was her turn.

She should have listened to Sam and let him drive her down to practice. She should never have gone alone.

How was Sam going to bear it if *she* died, too? Who was going to take care of her mother, for God's sake?

"I don't want to die," she whispered. "People need me. And there are so many things I still have to do." She lifted her head and stared into the darkness around her. "Don't kill me," she shouted. "Whoever you are, don't kill me! Please."

She cried, and after a while, when she'd cried herself out, she started to feel something besides fear and sorrow. She started to get mad. What right did this asshole have to chain her up like this? To kill Kyle? What had he ever done to deserve dying alone in the woods?

She lifted her head again, and she shouted as loud as she could, "I'm not gonna just let you kill me, you sonofabitch! Do you hear me? I'm gonna fight. I'm gonna fight you with everything I've got. You'll wish you'd picked an easier target before long! I'll make you sorry you ever set eyes on Kyle or on me or on this entire town!"

She grabbed hold of the chain that held her ankle and yanked, then yanked again. It didn't give at all. But it did generate another idea, and she used her hands to follow it to where it was anchored to a round eyebolt sunk into the stone wall.

This sick bastard was going to have a challenge on his hands, she promised herself. She wasn't stupid, and she wasn't the kind to sit and whimper and cry, and wait for rescue.

She'd learned how to be strong, to be independent, to be resourceful. Gabe said everything happened for a reason. Well, maybe this was the reason for her entire life. Maybe this was why she'd had to grow up tough.

Maybe, just maybe . . . her mother's horrendous parenting skills had given her something of value after all.

10

Sam emerged from his staredown with the passing darkness long enough to say, "Thanks for driving, Gabe."

"What're you? Kidding? I love driving this thing." Sam had insisted on taking "The Beast," but he'd apparently known better than to think he could drive it himself tonight.

From the passenger seat, Carrie sent Gabe a surprised look. "I wouldn't have taken you for a fan of oversize, gas-guzzling phallic symbols."

"Hey, I'm a supporter of hybrids and all, but I'm still a *guy.*"

She made a face, as if in disapproval, but he knew it wasn't real. The look behind her eyes was grateful, thanking him without saying it aloud, for being there, for trying to help her kid. Maybe . . . his kid.

And damn, but he knew the look in her eyes was going to change when she finally found that out. It wouldn't be soft or tender or wanting or grateful. No, it would become feral. The look of a lioness protecting her cub. And he would become the enemy.

"Gabe? Are you all right?" Carrie asked softly after a quick peek back at her son, who'd returned to gazing out the window at the passing night in anguished, stony silence.

Gabe snapped himself out of the grim place his mind had taken him and tried hard to focus on the here and now. Here and now she liked him. A lot. Right now she needed him. And that was going to have to be enough.

"Fine, I'm fine. Worried, just like we all are." He looked at Carrie beside him, then at Sam in the backseat, and he ached for them. And that was when he knew he was starting to feel a whole hell of a lot more than simple affection for them. He was starting to fit into this intimate picture a little too well. As if he belonged there, somehow. And it was way too soon to feel that way. He didn't even know for sure that —

But something inside him did. Sam had the same jawline. The same eyes. The same dimples in his cheek when he smiled. But he wasn't smiling now.

"I've phoned Marcus at home," Carrie said. "He'll meet us at the lab."

"That's the owner? Marcus?" Gabe asked.

She nodded. "He's a friend."

"That's some friend."

"It's not like that. He trusts me, that's all. He's worked with me enough to know how . . . anal I am."

It was self-deprecating, that last bit, and he wasn't going to let her get away with that. "You're thorough. You're a perfectionist. And you're brilliant. Those are not bad qualities, particularly in one's doctor, Doctor."

"I wasn't fishing for a compliment," she said.

"I know you weren't." That wasn't who she was, he thought. And then he wondered how he knew her so well, so soon.

"Take this exit," she said, and he did, following her directions from there, until the big SUV's headlights were illuminating a one-story brick office in a suburban village sprinkled with them.

Carrie opened her door. Gabe stayed where he was, but she poked her head back in. "I need you with me," she said. As if it should have been obvious to him.

He nodded and told himself this was idiocy. Insanity. Stress, maybe, or his old habit of being drawn to needy women. She hadn't fit that mold — until now. She was strong and confident and capable. But she needed him right now. And that made his heart go soft.

Maybe, too, this surge of protective instinct was some kind of testosterone-related reaction to being this close to his son. *Maybe* his son. God, he needed to know for sure.

Swallowing, he got out and, with Sam trailing silently behind, walked with her to the back door. As they did, a tall man with a shaved head got out of his car on the other side of the lot and walked over to meet them.

"I owe you big for this, Marcus. Thank you."

"Don't worry. I'll collect. This is on the Q.T., I take it?"

"Oh, I intend to tell the police what I know, just not how I know it. At least they won't be hog-tied waiting for results from the state crime lab."

"You could get into trouble." Marcus frowned at her. "That's not like you, Carrie." Then he looked at Gabe, and his eyes were suspicious. "Is somebody *making* you do this?"

"No." But Marcus was still looking at Gabe. Carrie snapped her fingers under his chin. "Hey, Marcus. No. This was my idea."

Marcus looked her in the eyes somewhere between "hey" and "no," and his expression finally eased.

"I'm Gabriel Cain," Gabe said, kind of liking the guy's caution. And his guts. He must've had twenty pounds on the guy.

"Marcus Kenyon." He shot a glance at Carrie that was intended to be furtive.

"He's a friend, Marcus."

Marcus eyed Gabe again. "Sorry. You're just — you're not her type, man. It threw me."

"Oh, really?" Gabe pretended that was news to him, then shrugged it off.

"Here are the samples, Marcus. I want you to look for everything you can think of. I need to know what killed him."

Marcus took the small picnic cooler with the samples inside from Carrie's hands. "I'm not gonna ask. I think I know anyway, but I'm not gonna ask."

"How fast can you do it?"

"For you? Three hours."

She nodded hard. "Three hours, then."

She turned to leave, and Gabe and Sam were turning to follow, like loyal soldiers, when Carrie stopped so abruptly that they nearly bumped into her. Whirling, holding up a forefinger, she said, "Marcus, wait!"

He stopped with his hand on the door, tipping his head skyward, as if he knew something unpleasant was coming.

"I have reason to suspect there was blood drawn from . . . from this person before his death."

"You found a puncture wound?"

"Lots of them. But one was bigger and right here." She pressed a finger to her forearm. "It looks like someone either started an IV or drew blood."

"And?"

"If they drew blood, what would they be drawing it for? And I'm thinking that if it were for any reason other than the killer thinking he's a vampire, then that blood might have ended up here."

Gabe swung his gaze to Carrie, stunned by how easily she'd figured that out.

"You're the only private lab around, Marcus."

"That doesn't mean —"

"You might have a killer's name and credit card number in your files, for God's sake."

Marcus shook his shiny head, then lowered it. "We guarantee confidentiality."

"A kid was killed, Marcus," Gabe said.

"And now my girlfriend is missing," Sam added, stepping forward.

"Sadie?" Marcus looked horrified when Sam nodded. "When? I haven't heard anything about that."

"Tonight. A few hours ago," Sam said softly. Then he turned away, choking up again.

Marcus sighed, then nodded. "All right. I'll get your samples running, and then I'll look through the files. Okay?"

"Any blood work from a new client in the past seven days where the sample was O Negative," Carrie told him.

"That won't be very many." Marcus tilted his head to one side. "In fact, I do recall one, about a week ago. O Negative isn't all that common. I should be able to pull it right up. Hold this and follow me."

He handed Carrie the cooler, unlocked the door and strode into the back hall, flipped on a light switch and bent to unlock an office door. Then he pushed it open and froze.

Gabe noticed right away that the file drawers were open, a few files lying on the floor beside them. Next he realized that there was probably supposed to be a CPU somewhere on that desk, where a high-end flat-screen monitor and an ergonomic keyboard sat alone, attached to nothing, unplugged cables lying in a tangle around them.

Marcus spun around, shocked. “What the hell?”

“Carrie must have been right,” Gabe said. “Whoever took that kid drew blood and sent it here for testing. Then they came in to clear out any evidence they left behind — your file on them, the test results. Everything.”

“But —” Marcus took a single step forward.

Gabe caught his arm, stopping him. “They could still be here. Carrie, Sam, wait here.” He met Marcus’s eyes. “Let’s you and me take a look around, huh?”

Marcus looked reluctant, but he nodded. Carrie clasped Sam’s arm to hold him by her side, and Gabe and Marcus moved slowly into the lab.

It was a mess, papers strewn everywhere, but nothing seemed to be broken, Gabe moved amid machines and equipment whose purposes he couldn’t have begun to guess, along with more familiar test tubes and microscopes. They searched the entire place, but whoever had broken in was apparently long gone.

They returned to the rear exit door and pushed it open, scanning the lot. “There’s no one inside,” Gabe said. “But we’d better not traipse around in there any more than necessary."

She nodded. "Marcus, what was his name?" Carrie asked. "What was the name of the person who brought you that sample?"

Marcus shook his head slowly. "Something really common. John Brown or something like that. But he didn't bring it to me. It came in the mail, so I never met the guy. If it even was a guy. Anyone could use a fake name. How would I know?"

"Did you keep the envelope?"

Marcus crossed his arms and looked at her as if she were crazy.

"Well then — do you remember what tests he had you run?"

"If I'm remembering right, it was a simple type and cross-match."

"Where did you send the results?"

"I don't remember the address! Jeez, Carrie, what do you think I am? A walking computer?"

"Marcus, just try!" she pleaded.

He shook his head rapidly. "I don't know. I think it was a PO box somewhere. But I don't remember." He looked behind him toward the lab and the mess inside. "I've got to report this to the police. And I can't be running these samples of yours when they get here."

"Then run them first," Carrie said.

He walked away, shaking his head. "No, no way, Carrie. I can't —"

"Marcus, you have to. Please. He's got Sadie."

The bald man shook his head again. Then he looked at Sam, rolled his eyes and sighed his surrender. "Come back in three hours. Because you're taking *this* —" he took the cooler from Carrie's hands once again "— straight back with you."

"Three hours," Carrie agreed with a nod. "Thank you, Marcus."

"I never saw you tonight. You understand? You never told me shit about any of this. Got that?"

She agreed, and Marcus was still muttering to himself as Carrie, Gabe and Sam walked back to the SUV.

"I don't like this," Carrie said, as she reached the car. "I don't like this at all."

She looked scared, Gabe thought. More scared than she'd already been. And he didn't know why. He felt as if she were in on something he wasn't, and he didn't like that feeling.

"Is there something I'm not getting?" he asked, searching her face.

"I don't know yet."

"And you don't want to tell me."

"I don't know what to tell. Something's . . . niggling at me. I just don't know what."

He frowned at her. "That's more like something *I* would say."

She shrugged. "Maybe you're rubbing off on me."

"I want to get back," Sam said. "What if Sadie calls?"

"We've got reception," Carrie told him, holding up her cell phone. "You've got yours?"

He nodded.

"And I set the home number to Call Forwarding before we left to look for her. So if she calls home, it will ring on my cell. We won't miss a call. And we need to know how Kyle died. It's the best thing we can do for Sadie right now."

Sam nodded slowly. "I hate this."

"I know."

"Three freaking hours when we could be out searching."

"The police said not tonight."

"Do you think I care?" Sam barked the words as they all climbed into the SUV.

Carrie looked wounded, and Sam muttered an apology. It sounded sincere.

"Look, what are we going to do for the next three hours? That's what I'd like to know," Gabe said, trying to change the subject.

"It's 3:00 a.m.," Carrie said. "We can probably find a twenty-four-hour fast-food restaurant if we drive out toward the highway." She shrugged. "Sit, eat, talk. Trade stories. I don't know."

"I need to eat," Sam said. " 'Cause once we get back, I'm not coming out of those woods until I find her."

Gabe patted his shoulder, and they went to find an early breakfast. He could use the boost.

They ate with surprising gusto, given the circumstances. But, Carrie thought, each of them felt the way her wise-beyond-his-years son did: that they needed to stay as strong as possible for Sadie's sake. Because that son of a bitch who had taken Kyle's life was *not* going to take Sadie's.

She wouldn't let that happen.

They killed two hours between finding a Denny's, eating and stopping to gas up The Beast before driving back toward the lab.

Carrie kept an eye on Sam in the backseat, and within a few minutes Gabe apparently grew curious to see why and peeked at the boy himself.

Sam's head was sinking slowly to one side,

then bouncing up again, as he fought to hold off sleep. And again, and then finally, his head stayed down as he sank deep and fast.

Gabe glanced at Carrie. "You put something in his decaf, didn't you?"

"Just the tiniest bit. Let him sleep now, while he can. It'll wear off by the time we get home."

"You love him a lot," Gabe said, and it wasn't a question.

Carrie gazed back at her son, and her heart went soft and warm. "He's the best thing that ever happened to me. My miracle, that's what he is."

"Your miracle. You've said that before."

She brought her gaze around, realized she'd probably said too much, but reminded herself that this was Gabe she was talking to. This man could be trusted; she sensed that to her core. And that was an odd thing for her to feel about a man like him. A drifter, like her father. But for once she was going with her heart and not her head.

"I was told I couldn't have children. I'd just about given up hope. And then he just . . . happened."

"He . . . happened?" He frowned at her. "You mean you got pregnant or you adopted him?"

She shifted her eyes away from his, unable to look him in the eye and lie to him, yet telling the lie automatically. "Got pregnant, of course." And then she added her long-practiced elaboration. "You mean you can't tell? Most people think he looks like me."

He lifted his brows. "I don't think he looks *anything* like you," he said.

She met his eyes, then looked away again. Okay, so the power of suggestion didn't work on him. "I don't, either," she said with a false laugh. "But other people are always seeing something I don't."

He seemed . . . almost disappointed. As if he were waiting for her to tell him something more, something real. As if he knew, somehow, that she had just lied to him. But that was ridiculous. That was her own guilty conscience playing with her mind. He didn't know. How *could* he?

She thought about changing the subject, gave up, and turned on the radio to fill the silence for the remainder of the drive back to the lab. And then she and Gabe were getting out, leaving Sam to sleep off his "decaf" in the backseat.

Marcus came out the back door, handed the cooler to Carrie and said, "Good, I can call the police now."

"Why didn't your alarm system do that?"

Gabe asked, for the first time noticing the sticker advertising a security monitoring system in the window.

"It went down yesterday," Marcus said. "Repairman couldn't make it until tomorrow." He glanced at the sky. "Today, that is. I doubt it's a coincidence."

He shifted his attention to Carrie. "There was Benterol in the blood sample."

She blinked. "Benterol?"

"That's all I found. Benterol. I don't have to tell you, it's a powerful tranquilizer. There wasn't a lot left, but it's been a while. Traces fade over time. But by my calculations, he must have had enough in his system to kill him."

She nodded. "Thanks, Marcus. I'll tell the cops."

"Oh, I'm not done. I forgot before, but I still had a frozen sample of that O Negative that came in a week ago. I always use what's needed and freeze any extra, just in case a test fails for some reason. I only clean out the freezer once a month, so it was still there. And it matches the samples you brought in."

She stared at him. "Matches?"

"Same source. The blood you brought me tonight is the same type as the blood that came in a week ago. I checked. It had traces of Benterol, too. Now, I haven't had time to run DNA, of course, but I'd stake my life on it. Your hunch was right. Someone took the kid's blood and sent it here for typing. That same someone fucked my alarm system and broke in here tonight to remove every trace he'd ever been here. But he didn't know I still had this." He held up a frozen vial. "Now get out of here so I can report all this, will you?"

Carrie hugged him, then she turned and ran back to the SUV. "I need to see Bryan," she said. "Drive fast, okay?"

"You bet," Gabe said. Once they were underway and her impatience and worry were increasing exponentially and visibly with every mile, he said, "You know something, don't you?"

"I hope I'm wrong. God, I hope I'm wrong."

"Are you ready to let me in on it yet?"

"I don't even know if there's anything to let you in on, Gabe. But . . . when we get home . . . I'll show you when we get home."

So he drove. And she felt a little badly for keeping her thoughts to herself, but they weren't even fully formed yet, and she wasn't sure where they were going. She had a feeling in the pit of her stomach — mother's intuition? Or was she projecting her own deepest fears onto this situation when they didn't really fit?

Whatever. She had to follow through on her hunch. Better safe than sorry and all that. She dialed the cell phone.

"You calling Kendall?" Gabe asked.

She nodded as she waited for the connection to take hold. "I don't want to wait any longer."

"It's indecent to wake anyone at this hour," Gabe said, but he didn't say it was unnecessary. "Still, I suppose that's what he took on when he chose the job."

"I think he chose the job back when Shadow Falls was a nowhere town where nothing ever happened. He didn't sign on for this. Hell, it probably didn't even seem like a possibility."

"Probably not."

She listened to the phone ring, heard Bryan's voice answer, felt a little guilty, but knew she was only doing what she had to.

"Sorry to wake you. It's Carrie."

"I was up. Dawn and I just got back from our morning run, actually."

"You're sickeningly healthy."

"It was more to vent the frustration of all of this than anything else. What's up, Carrie?"

She drew a breath. "I can't tell you how I

know. But your state crime lab's report will say that Kyle Becker died from an overdose of Benterol."

"Uh-huh. And would this have anything to do with the break-in at Bloodworks, Inc, in Burlington?"

"There was a break-in at Bloodworks?" she asked, sending Gabe a guilty look.

"Right. And you know nothing about it."

"Why would I?"

Bryan sighed. "Marcus Kenyon called the chief. *He* wasn't already awake, by the way. He says Marcus thinks there's a connection to the missing kid and wants me to follow up. You want to tell me what that connection is, or are you going to make me wait?"

"I don't have any way of knowing, Bryan."

"Right. I'm heading out there now to talk to Marcus, assuming I can get to him past the Burlington cops."

"You love the Burlington cops."

"Off duty, yeah. On duty, they're bulldogs."

She sighed. "But you won't stop trying."

"You know I won't."

Nodding, she said, "Thanks for letting me know."

"Thanks for the . . . anonymous tip."

"Yeah. Anytime." She rang off, and that was when she noticed they were nearly home. Soon Gabe was steering The Beast into the driveway, ignoring the garage entirely and stopping near the house. She looked out at the sun rising slowly over the forested mountains. She loved the view from her home — it had been the major selling point, all those years ago.

Now, though, the view seemed more ominous than beautiful. Somewhere out there, Sadie was in the hands of a maniac. A maniac capable of murder and who knew what else? Not that she could think of anything worse than what the bastard had already done.

And worse even than her fear for Sadie was her growing worry that her own son would be this madman's next target.

11

Sadie had pulled the bed away from the wall and found the bolt that held the chain in place. It was sunk into the concrete, but the cellar was old, the concrete crumbling in places. Weak, maybe. She knelt behind the cot and, gripping the eyebolt with both hands, began alternately pushing and pulling. At first she felt no give whatsoever, but after an hour or so the bolt seemed to wiggle a bit, so slightly that she wasn't sure whether she was imagining it.

But she kept working, and she kept feeling movement, and she thought it might be increasing by the end of the second hour.

Her hands ached. Her knees hurt, and she was tired. She needed a break, but she didn't dare take one. Kyle was dead. She might be, too, pretty soon, if she didn't find a way to get out of here.

She ignored the pain in her hands, though they were blistering and raw from the constant friction of the rusty bolt. Her arms and shoulders and neck ached, too, from her hunched position on the floor. She ignored that, as well. But she didn't — *couldn't* — ignore the sounds of the lock turning in her prison door. He was back!

Scrambling up onto her feet, she quickly pushed the cot back up against the wall, got onto the mattress and hugged her knees to her chest. She was shaking, and she hated it. She hated being so afraid, feeling so powerless. Knowing she might die at any moment. Was her captor going to kill her now?

The room stayed black as pitch when the door opened, and the form, all swathed in black from head to feet, seemed no more than a darker shadow in its midst. The shadow bent, and Sadie heard rattling as it lowered something to the floor and slid it forward. Then she smelled food — wonderful aromas that made her stomach growl. God, she was hungry!

The shadow straightened up again and began backing out, pulling the door closed.

"No!" Sadie cried. "No, wait! At least tell me what you want with me!

"Please, I need to know! If I'm going to die here, I deserve to know why!"

The form hesitated only momentarily,

then quickly backed out and closed the door, even as Sadie leaped off the cot and lunged forward, forgetting the chain, which yanked her left leg right out from under her. She hit the floor facedown and lay there sobbing.

But eventually she sat up and wiped her eyes, wincing as the back of her hand crossed her forehead and brought fresh pain. She moved her fingers gingerly, feeling a bump already rising, but no gash and no blood. She supposed that was a good thing.

Sitting on the floor, she looked toward where she thought the food tray was, wondering if the shadowy form had pushed it far enough for her to reach. Or was it just a cruel form of torture, leaving food she couldn't touch?

She moved, pulling her chain until it was tight, and then, lying facedown on the floor, she stretched her arms as far as she could and managed to grip the edges of what felt like a tray. She pulled it closer, and it scraped over the concrete floor. And then she sat up again and brought the tray onto her lap.

Her eyes had slowly begun adjusting to the darkness, but even so, she could barely see. She could smell, though, and she could taste. There was beef, she thought, and it felt tender and juicy when she touched it with her seeking fingers. There was a cup of water. There were mashed potatoes and gravy. There were vegetables, and she thought she smelled butter melting over them. Sadie didn't use butter, as a rule, but she was hungry enough to make an exception. This person, whoever he was, wasn't going to beat her easily. She would stay strong. Somehow, she would. And that meant she had to eat, even though she would rather throw his food into his face.

Not that she'd ever seen his face. Or *her* face, she thought grimly. She didn't even know if her abductor was a man or a woman. But she did know they were going to be sorry, either way.

Sadie shoveled the food into her mouth, and it was good, though she hated to admit it. Then she wondered if it was safe to return to the task of working on that eyebolt, or if her captor was still nearby, waiting to collect the empty tray. She hung on to the water, then shoved the tray across the floor, and it hit the wall beside the door, rattling and clanking. And then she waited.

Sure enough, the damned door opened within seconds. That sneaky bastard had been outside it, listening. Lurking like a freaking demon.

Sadie tried hard to see what lay beyond the door, but it was still black out there. She supposed that told her something. She saw no night sky, no stars, no moon. No fresh air wafted in. So the outside was not on the other side of her door. It must lead to someplace *inside,* then.

"Did you kill my friend? Kyle? Are you the one?" she demanded.

But the form only hunched to gather the tray and backed out again.

"Bastard!" she cried. She drained the cup of water, then hurled it at the door as it closed. But it only hit the door and clattered uselessly to the floor.

Setting her jaw, Sadie turned back to the cot, unsure whether she should move it and go back to work on the bolt, or whether the jerk was watching her somehow and would find out. She kept deciding to risk it and then deciding to wait a little while, just in case, unable to make a decision. Her brain didn't seem to be working right. No wonder, given the situation. Stress and fear must do that to the human mind, right? Rob it of its ability to function?

God, she was tired.

She sat on the edge of the cot and within two seconds was lying down instead. She hadn't really decided to, but her body didn't wait for her mind's permission. She lay on her back, letting one hand drop down between the cot and the wall, where she felt the eyebolt. Hell, she thought, she could lie down *and* work that bolt. He would never know she was doing it, even if he was still lurking beyond that door, watching her.

That, however, was the last clear thought to cross her mind before she found her eyes falling heavily, irresistibly closed.

Why am I so tired?

She slept. She only knew she slept because of those times when she would somehow become aware that she was sleeping, then jerk herself awake with a start and a feeling of panic. And then she would drift right off again.

At some point during her fitful rest she was aware of that dark form standing over her. She felt her shirtsleeve being pushed up, and her inner arm being swabbed with something cold and damp. And then there was a tiny stab of pain.

Opening her eyes, she tried to see what was happening. But she could only make out shadows in the darkness. That person, bending over her. A rubber band around her biceps being removed. A needle being slowly withdrawn from her flesh. A sterile adhesive strip being applied.

"Is that . . . my blood?" she murmured, seeing what looked like a small vial in the kidnapper's hand. "Why? Why are you . . . ?"

The dark form straightened. Sadie's vision was blurry, and it was so dark anyway. She wished she could see. It was frustrating. And she could barely keep her eyes open.

"You drugged the food?" she murmured. "God, you drugged the food, didn't you? Is that how you killed Kyle?"

There was no answer. The murderer pocketed the vial and turned toward the door.

"Please don't kill me," Sadie whispered.

But the kidnapper's only response to that was to leave the room. To leave her all alone in the darkness again. And she wondered if maybe he had already killed her. Maybe if she fell asleep right now, she would never wake up again.

And then she would never have the chance to see where things were going with Sam. She would never have the chance to go to college, or to become a veterinarian, like she planned. And her mother — God, her mother would be dead in six months with no one to take care of her.

She didn't want to die. She *really* didn't

want to die. She managed to tell the empty room so several times before she sank back into her drug-induced sleep, still wondering if she would ever awaken again.

"They'll be organizing volunteers to search in a couple of hours," Gabe said.

It was early morning, and they'd just arrived back at Carrie's place from their jaunt into Burlington and the independent lab there. She had yet to tell him what her secret theory was, but he had a notion that it had something to do with Sam. Of course, he changed his mind about that pretty much every ten minutes. First it seemed obvious and logical that Sam was his son, and then it seemed ludicrous. And maybe that had nothing to do with any of this. Or maybe it did. Hell, he didn't know.

He handed Carrie a cup of coffee and noticed how tired she looked, how overwrought. "You sure you want this? You probably ought to catch a little sleep, if you think you can."

"No, I couldn't sleep even if I wanted to."

"I doubt I could, either." He sat on the sofa beside her, took a sip from his own steaming mug. "At least Sam's getting a little rest."

"Yeah, he barely made it up the stairs.

Thanks for helping him, by the way."

"Anytime."

She tilted her head a little as she studied his face. "You really like him, don't you?"

"Does that surprise you?"

"No. He's a great kid. I don't see why anyone *wouldn't* like him. *Love* him. It's just that . . ."

"Just that what?"

She sipped again and shifted position a little. "A lot of the men I date, not that I date many — hardly any, really — but a few of them have sort of pretended to like Sam. You know, made these halfhearted, obvious attempts to befriend him, while being entirely transparent that they were only doing it to kind of . . . solidify their position with me."

"Was it as apparent to Sam as it was to you?"

"Oh, he caught on *way* before I did. The first time he pointed it out, I thought he was just being oversensitive, but he was right."

"He's too smart to fall for that kind of bull. And too honest not to resent it, I'll bet."

She nodded rapidly. "Yes, you've pegged him exactly." She sipped again. "But it's different with you. It's almost as if he can sense that you don't have any ulterior motive. You're not trying to hide your real reasons, you know? You just . . . like hanging out with him."

"I really do," he said, but inside, his guts resumed their guilty churning. He *did* have an ulterior motive. A big one.

"It means a lot to me." She held his gaze for a moment. "I think maybe *you're* starting to mean a lot to me, too."

He didn't know what to say. It was mutual. He could say that. That wouldn't be compounding his lie, because it was the truth. But it would be wrong to let this — this *thing* between them go any further without telling her the truth. All of it.

"That was stupid, wasn't it? We've only known each other a few days." She shook her head. "I'm really not one of those women who fall in love at the drop of a — not that I'm calling this love! I mean, it's something, it's definitely something, but not — I mean . . . God, I'm just making it worse, aren't I?" She lowered her head, embarrassed.

He reached out to hook a finger under her chin and tipped her head up a little. And when she met his eyes, he kissed her. He couldn't help it. He didn't intend it. It just happened.

He kissed her, and she kissed him back; then she twisted her arms around his waist and snuggled closer, nestling into the crook of his arm, curling her legs to one side, leaning her head on his shoulder. Everything in him went sort of warm and gooey.

"I'm glad you're here," she said.

"I am, too." And he was. Not because she was desperately in need of rescue. Not because she was a train wreck in need of repair. She was completely capable of getting by without his help. She'd done just fine, in spades, and raised a phenomenal son, to boot. She was amazing. He was in awe, and a little bit unsure of his footing.

He didn't really know how to relate to a woman who didn't need him. It was a new experience. And it was unsettling, because it seemed most likely to him that she would tell him to take a hike when she learned about his deception.

She hadn't been exactly honest with him, either. If Sam wasn't her biological offspring, that was. But then again, as far as she knew, that was none of his business.

"I have to tell you something, Carrie," he said softly.

"I have to tell you something first. I promised I would. It's about . . . it's about that missing baby from sixteen years ago."

Gabe sat up straighter, staring down at her. Was she about to confirm his suspicions? He realized he hoped she was. He really *wanted* Sam to be his son. He loved the kid.

So he watched her with hope in his eyes and his heart, and he waited.

"Kyle and Sadie were born within a few weeks of each other," she said.

He frowned. "So?"

"So I've been trying to figure out why someone would kidnap a child, take a blood sample and have it typed at a lab. And the only answer I can come up with is that missing baby. I think the killer is looking for it."

He blinked, and it felt as if the proverbial lightbulb had flashed on over his head. "For the reward," he said, nodding.

"A half million dollars is a lot of money. But to claim it, they would need to find the right child. So they're taking kids who were born during the right period of time — May or June, sixteen years ago."

"And then drawing their blood? But how would they know the baby's blood type?"

"They wouldn't have any trouble finding out the mother's. It's in the autopsy report, and for all I know it was in the papers, at the time, as well." She sighed, shook her head. "I don't know, maybe it's someone who also knows the father's type. Maybe it *is* the father." She rubbed her arms when she said that, and Gabe thought he knew why, though he wasn't supposed to. "When they found out Kyle wasn't the right child, they killed him. And now they've taken Sadie. And when they find out she's not the one, either . . ."

"Are you sure she's not?" Gabe asked.

Carrie looked at him sharply. "Of course I am."

"How?" He was hoping she would admit something. Tell him that she knew who the missing baby *wasn't,* because she knew who it *was:* her own Sam. She didn't, though.

"She looks just like her mother, for one thing. But that's not the point, Gabe. The point is that Sam could be the next one the killer targets. His birthday is in June."

"I see."

"No," she said. "No, you don't."

He looked down at her to see tears streaming down her face, and he tightened his arms around her. "You need to rest. You're barely keeping your eyes open."

"I have to call Bryan, tell him my theory."

"I imagine he's put it together himself by now, given that he was on his way to the lab to talk to Marcus."

"Still . . ."

"Rest," he said. "I'll call him. Just rest."

She didn't say another word. Gabe held her for a long time, stroking her arm and her hair. After a while he glanced down at her and realized that she had fallen asleep in his arms. It made him feel protective, even though she didn't need his protection.

Damn, he was afraid he really might be falling for this woman.

Just under two hours later, he was jarred awake by Sam thundering down the stairs. Gabe came awake fast, just in time to see the young man pulling a clean shirt over his tousled hair. As he did, Gabe glimpsed a lopsided birthmark on the boy's lean belly. Teardrop shaped, liver colored — and identical to the mark on Gabe's own skin. His hand went automatically to his abdomen, touching the spot just to the right below his navel.

Was there really any question now that Sam was his son? And the boy had been born at the right time; Carrie had confirmed that.

Even as he thought of her, Carrie sat up sleepily, stared at him and then frowned. "Gabe? Are you okay?"

He blinked the emotional storm of stunned revelation from his face and hoped the moisture in his eyes didn't show. "Yeah, just trying to wake up."

"I can't believe you guys fell asleep," Sam said. "Hell, I can't believe *I* did."

"We were all exhausted." Carrie sat up straighter, and smoothed her hair. "Besides, there was nothing we could do." She glanced at the grandfather clock that stood in the corner of the living room. "But maybe now there is. They'll probably start organizing searchers at the firehouse this morning. We should get ready and head down there."

Sam lowered his head. "A lot of good that did Kyle."

"I know, hon, but —"

"We can't do it that way, Mom. It doesn't make any sense to do it the same way again and expect different results, does it?"

Carrie got to her feet, and went to her son. She put her hands on his shoulders. "The results won't be the same. They *won't,* Sam, and I'll tell you why."

He looked her in the eyes, and Gabe could see the kid almost begging her to convince him that what she was saying was true. "Why?"

"Because Sadie is not Kyle." It wasn't enough. Carrie knew that and rushed on. "I loved Kyle. You know that, right? And I wouldn't say this to anyone else, but we both know he was no Einstein. And not only that, but he was kind of a . . .”

“A wuss,” Sam filled in.

She smiled slightly, lowering her head just a little. “I’m glad you said that and not me. But that’s where I was going, yes. Now, contrast that with Sadie.”

Sam’s gaze turned inward as he nodded slowly. “Sadie’s tougher than nails. She’s had to be.”

“Right about now, maybe that’s a good thing,” Carrie said. “You know how Gabe says things tend to happen for a reason?”

“That’s true. I do say that. And I’m thinking your mom’s right,” Gabe said. “Maybe this is the reason Sadie’s had the life she’s had. So she’d be tough enough to get through this.”

Sam nodded. “Maybe.”

“She’s smart, too,” Gabe added, getting up from his seat then.

Sam nodded harder. “She is. She’s smarter than just about anyone else I know.”

“Seems to me you found yourself a girl a lot like your mom, pal.”

“Don’t think I don’t know it,” Sam said. “Why do you think Mom likes her so much?”

Carrie made a face at him but gentled it with a soft smile.

Nodding, Sam drew a long, slow breath. "Okay, so we go and we search. But the thing is, if we find her body in the woods . . ."

"Kyle survived for six days," Gabe reminded him. "We're gonna find her before then. But you've got to believe it. Believe it like you believe in gravity, Sam."

Sam met Gabe's eyes. He looked so much like a man right then, and so much like Gabe himself, twenty-some-odd years ago, that Gabe's chest swelled with pride. Even though he'd no hand in raising him to be the amazing person he was, he was damn proud of him.

"I believe it." Sam said it with conviction.

"Good man." Gabe clapped him on the shoulder. "Let's get some food into us and head down to the firehouse. And while we're at it, let's keep our minds working on ideas for other things we can do."

"Let's get food on the way," Sam said. "It'll be faster."

A half hour later, they sat in a booth at the Cascade Diner, which was filled to near capacity. "Tourist season must be in full swing," Gabe said as the waitress refilled his cup.

"Not even close to the numbers we used

to get," the waitress said. "The past two years, business has been way down."

Carrie nodded and sighed. "I was hoping this year would be better, but with the kind of publicity we've been getting lately, the only people we'll be overrun with will be the press. Again." She rolled her eyes.

"I hear that," the waitress said. "But I guess they have to eat, too, and their tips are as good as anybody's."

"They don't need food. They feed on misery," Carrie muttered.

The waitress gave her a serious nod, refilling her cup, too. "I just hope we can quit providing their meals. Damn shame about the Becker boy. And now that poor Sadie Gray . . . I don't know what's happening around here."

She walked on to the next table, taking her coffee carafe with her.

"So these aren't tourists?" Gabe asked, looking around the diner with a fresh eye. He spotted Nathan Kelly, counting out change to pay for an oversize take-out bag. He guessed times *were* tough as he gave the man a friendly nod and the old fellow nodded back.

"A few are tourists," Carrie said. "Most are locals."

"All probably heading to the same place

we are."

The door swung open, and Chief Mac stuck his white-haired head inside. "Anyone here to help out with the search needs to be at the firehouse in ten minutes," he said.

"Any new clues, Chief?" someone called.

The chief met Carrie's eyes, and Gabe knew, from talking to Bryan by phone on the way to the diner, that he was working on the theory that whoever was taking these kids was after that missing baby and the reward that would come with finding it. But he wasn't about to divulge that bit of information to the general public.

Breaking eye contact, Chief Mac shook his head sadly. "No. But we have a judge's signature on a warrant allowing us to search any vacant buildings whose owner we can't reach."

"What about any whose owners say no?" Carrie asked.

"We need individual warrants for those. But we'll get 'em."

She lowered her head, muttering that it would take too long.

"It's a start, Mom," Sam told her. "It's a step forward, and that's better than we've had so far."

She smiled a little. "I think Gabe's positive attitude is rubbing off on you."

Then she pulled some bills from her wallet and laid them on the table. "You ready?"

Gabe took a last gulp of coffee and got to his feet. "Thanks for breakfast."

"You can get the next one," she told him.

"It's a date." He put a hand on her shoulder as they wove through the now-growing crowd of people hustling to pay their tabs and get out the door. The handful of tourists watched the activity, some looking worried, others puzzled. He was sure the waitress would fill in the blanks for anyone who didn't know what was going on.

They headed to the firehouse, where, as he had done before, Chief Mac took to the soapbox and gave his usual spiel. He repeated the news he'd told the crowd in the diner, and as the backpacks with maps, whistles and, sadly, copies of a brand-new poster with Sadie's smiling face on it, were handed out, Bryan sidled up to Carrie and nodded hello to Gabe.

"Anything new?" she asked softly.

"Besides what he just said?" he asked with a nod toward the chief. "Yeah. But keep it to yourself. We tried to find out who was behind that reward offer, and met a brick wall. Attorneys protecting his or her identity. Chief's working on a court order now."

"To make the lawyers tell you who it is?"

Carrie asked.

"Either that or force them to pull the reward offer altogether. But frankly, I'd like to know who's behind it, anyway. Just in case."

"Anything else?" she asked.

"Just what you already know. We're searching buildings now, with a strong focus on the ones that aren't open for the season yet. Based on Kyle's clean clothes, we figure he must have been held indoors somewhere."

"We should have done that before."

"We thought we were dealing with a runaway before," he reminded her.

"*I* never thought that," Sam said. "No one who *really* knew Kyle did. You guys should've listened."

"Sam."

"No, Carrie, he's right," Bryan said. "Sam, for the record, I'm sorry. I'm more sorry than I can ever tell you. And so is everyone on the force. But just so you know, we really were looking just as hard for him as we would have been if we'd known he'd been taken. Searching private property, though, that takes a warrant. And you can't get one of those without evidence."

"That doesn't make it suck any less."

"I know. I know."

Bryan nodded goodbye and went to the

front of the room, where the other cops were beginning to discuss who was going to lead which group. They were going to begin, the chief told them, in the area where Kyle had been found, then move in an ever-widening circle, with each group taking a pie-shaped wedge and working outward.

Gabe was afraid the killer wouldn't be stupid enough to have left Kyle's body near where he'd been holding him, though. He was antsy, as impatient with the process as Sam was, but without the excuse of youth.

"This is just awful, isn't it?"

Ambrose Peck had wormed his way through the crowd to latch onto them. "Good to see you again, Carrie," he said. "Though obviously I wish it were under any circumstances but these." He nodded to the others. "Sam, Gabe."

"Hi, Ambrose," Gabe said.

"Do you mind if I stick with you again today?" Ambrose asked.

"Of course we don't mind," Carrie said, with a look at Gabe that he read as *See? I'm being nice to him.* "Don't tell me you still haven't met anyone else in town, though."

"Oh, no. I *have,* actually — your boarder, as a matter of fact."

"You met Rose? Is she here?" Carrie

looked around.

"She was, but only long enough to leave a stack of these." He handed her a flyer. "I believe the firemen were putting one into each backpack."

Carrie opened the trifold sheet, and Gabe leaned in to read it over her shoulder. "She's organizing a candlelight vigil for Sadie," Carrie whispered. " 'Please bring your own candles.' " She sighed, shaking her head slowly as she handed the paper back to Ambrose. "She wanted to help, and searching the woods is a little beyond her physical ability. This is really sweet of her."

"Awfully sweet," Gabe agreed.

Sam lowered his head and, turning, walked away from them to stand in a relatively lonely spot amid the crowd.

"Oh, my. Did I say the wrong thing?" Ambrose asked.

"I think he's touched by Rose's gesture," Carrie told him. "And I don't think there's any *right* thing to say to him just now."

"No, I don't imagine there is." Ambrose shook his head slowly. "Such a nice girl, that Sadie. She was nothing but polite to me."

The buses were pulling to a stop in front. Gabe saw Carrie's troubled expression as she looked from the vehicles, to her son and back again. He moved a little nearer and kept his voice low. "Are you sure he's up for this?"

"He has to do something, Gabe, or he'll lose it. I just wish there were something more productive."

Gabe agreed, frustrated that they were basically going through the motions, while a young girl was fighting for her life. But maybe they would come up with a better idea while traipsing through the woods today. They had just reached the buses, catching Sam in their current along the way, when there was the sound of someone's beeper going off, followed by another. The chief and Bryan were both grabbing their pagers, Gabe realized with a quick sweeping glance. Something was up. Moments later the two of them headed over to a black-and-white SUV, trying not to look too obvious about it, but clearly in a hurry. As they pulled away, another pager went off.

Gabe slid his eyes toward the source and realized the beeping was coming from Carrie herself. She grasped her son's shoulder as she picked up her pager and read the screen. Then she went white. Before she could realize what was happening, Sam had snatched the tiny device from her hand and was staring at the message there.

When he looked up again, there was no life in his eyes. "No," he whispered. "No, no, no." Sam dropped the beeper, and it clattered to his feet on the pavement as he turned away, his head in his hands, muttering the same word over and over again.

Gabe bent to retrieve it, while Carrie lunged after her son. The text message on the screen, which had come from Bryan read, Body Found. Call ASAP.

12

"Get him into my bus," Gabe said. "Come on."

Carrie, who had a death grip on her trembling son, looked up at Gabe and felt a huge rush of gratitude that he was there. She'd never seen Sam look the way he looked right then. She didn't know how to help him, or even whether she could. Whether *anyone* could.

People milled closer, curious, while others just looked sympathetic as Gabe and Carrie managed to get Sam to the VW Bus. He moved like a puppet, like a life-size mannequin, just letting them manipulate his limbs in whatever way they needed. Carrie had no idea, until she closed the door on Sam and turned, that Ambrose was tagging along as if he were a part of the family. He was standing close behind her, his face taut with concern.

Nearby, Gabe met her eyes and provided

comfort without even trying.

She felt better having him there and wondered why it felt so much as if Gabe had become what Ambrose seemed to wish he could be. Part of the family. It seemed obvious that Gabe would stay with her and Sam as they faced what might be their most dire crisis yet. By contrast, it seemed mildly intrusive that Ambrose would consider it okay to do the same.

Ambrose circled around to the driver's side even as Gabe climbed into the back beside Sam, closing the door.

"Is he all right?" Ambrose asked. "Is there anything I can do?"

Carrie wanted to shove him away, because he was in her space, standing way too close — so close she could feel his breath as he asked his eager questions. Then again, there was a lot of noise and commotion around them, and he really did seem to want to help. But he didn't know about the chilling text message, and she was certain that the news of another body being found shouldn't be burning through the town grapevine just yet. "Sadie's his first serious girlfriend," she said. "I should have known this would be too much for him today." She gripped the car door.

"I thought perhaps it was whatever that

message was. The one on your beeper, just before he —"

"I'm a doctor, Ambrose. I can't even take a shower without getting beeped. It's normal." She opened the car door.

"So it was just a coincidence that the chief was paged at the same time, then?"

She turned her head, looked him in the eye this time and knew her lie was probably obvious. He so wanted to be included, to help, that it seemed mean to lie to him. "I don't know what that was about, but if the chief didn't tell anyone, there's probably a reason for that, don't you think?" He frowned, but nodded. "Ambrose, I really need to get my son home now and go check on the case I was just paged about. All right?"

"Oh. Of course, yes." He backed off a couple of steps, giving her room to get into the driver's seat. She did, then had to blow the horn a few times to get the crowd to clear as she inched through the parking lot. The VW had a manual transmission. She wasn't used to that, so there was a bit of grinding as she shifted from first gear into Second. As she drove, she kept glancing back at Sam. Gabe sat beside him, talking to him, but Sam looked almost catatonic. Of course he was. He'd seen the message.

Body found. He had to assume it was Sadie. But God, it couldn't be. It just couldn't be.

As Carrie drove, she pulled out her cell phone and called Bryan. As soon as he picked up, she said, "I got your page. Tell me, is —"

"They found a body," he told her.

"*That much* I got, and so did my son, unfortunately. Is it —"

"Jeez, Carrie, I'm sorry. No, no, it's not Sadie. It's male —"

"The body they found is male," she said loudly. "Do you hear me, Sam? It's not Sadie. It's a man's body."

Sam blinked twice and looked over at her.

"It's not Sadie," she said again, and finally it seemed to get through. Sam closed his eyes and sank back in his seat, lowering his head.

Relief washed through Carrie, as well. "All right, Bry, can you fill me in? Or do you want to do that when you meet me at the hospital morgue?"

"I'm gonna need to meet you in Burlington. At the scene."

"The scene?" Her brows drew together. "Where, exactly, is *the scene?*"

"Bloodworks," he said. "We haven't got a positive ID yet, but we think it may be Marcus Kenyon. I'm sorry, Carrie. I know you guys were friends. The Burlington cops knew from my visit there last night that the break-in looked to be connected to Kyle's death, so they figured we'd want to be here. And I knew you should be here, too."

She swallowed hard. "It's Marcus," she whispered, looking quickly at Gabe in the rearview mirror. "They think it's Marcus Kenyon."

He held her eyes and whispered, "Ah, hell."

Returning her attention to Bryan, Carrie said, "I can't believe this. I . . . I just talked to him last night."

"I know. Chief Mac is going to want details about that. No more holding anything back, Carrie. Not now."

"No, of course not." She looked at her watch. "I can be there in an hour. I've got to drop Sam off at home. So —"

"I'd rather go to Gabe's," Sam said softly. "If that's okay."

She covered the phone and looked in the rearview mirror at him. Then she glanced at Gabe, who nodded to let her know it was fine with him. "All right. Take me to get my car, and then you two can head over there."

Sam nodded and closed his eyes. "Thank God it's not her. Thank God."

"It's not going to be her, either, Sam.

Sadie's not going to die. I know it," Carrie said.

The usually neat-as-a-pin lab looked as if it had been used for football practice. It was far, far worse than it had been the night before, when they had discovered the break-in. Chairs were toppled, files scattered over the floor, a lamp lying on its side with the bulb shattered and the cord no more than a frayed three-inch stub.

"He's in here," Bryan said, holding the yellow crime scene tape down so she could step over it, and then leading Carrie carefully over papers and broken glass. "Don't touch anything. Watch where you step."

The Burlington cops and crime scene techs were already there, dusting, gathering, photographing. There were little flags with numbers on them all over the floor.

As she reached the end of a counter that was littered with equipment, Marcus's body came into view. He was lying on his side, next to a toppled chair. His hands were tied behind his back, his ankles bound with duct tape. A puddle of blood lay beneath his head.

"Is that Marcus Kenyon?" Bryan asked her.

Carrie nodded. "Yes." She closed her eyes

to block out the image of his face. "He has a wife. Two boys in college. Good God, what happened?"

"I have a feeling you might know more about that than we do." Bryan moved closer to her, slid a hand over her shoulder. "I'm sorry, Carrie."

"He was a decent man." She looked around the room. "What was the last test he ran?"

"I have no idea." He looked at the chief, then back at Carrie. "Could you tell, do you think, if you took a look around?"

"I doubt it. I'll look around, but if it was related to this — then I don't imagine anything obvious will be lying around in plain sight."

Just then someone came running with a pair of paper shoe covers and a set of latex gloves. Carrie donned them both and then carefully moved deeper into the lab.

She noted the wheel marks the chair's casters had left on the boring tan tiles of the floor. They crisscrossed it like a star map. She could see Marty in her mind's eye, pushing off from the desk with his feet and rolling across the floor to check on some piece of equipment, then back again.

"You need to tell us everything you know, Carrie," Bryan said when she'd finished her look around.

She nodded and joined the chief and Bryan, along with a pair of Burlington detectives, in the small office in the rear. She took off the shoe covers and gloves, sat down and started to tell her story, starting with her noticing that several things about Kyle's body didn't add up. "I went down to the morgue after Dr. Butcher finished Kyle's autopsy. I took some extra samples, even though I knew it wasn't exactly . . ."

"Legal?" Bryan supplied.

"I figure it never hurts to take extra samples, just in case anything goes wrong with the initial specimens. A mix-up at the lab or accidental contamination, anything that means the lab needs to redo any of the tests. This didn't seem any different to me."

"Except that it wasn't your job," one of the locals pointed out.

She shrugged. "I'm aware of that."

"What else?" Bryan asked, sounding as if he already knew.

Carrie cleared her throat. "I decided to run the toxicology screen through a private lab. I knew it wouldn't be admissible in court, but I thought that if you knew in advance what the state crime lab was going to find, it would speed up your investigation."

Chief Mac glared at her. "You took it upon yourself to do this? Without my knowledge or consent?"

"Yes, sir."

"And you didn't think that violated any laws, any ethical codes, any oath to which you've sworn?"

"Not precisely, no. Though I admit I was skating on the blurred edge of legality and medical ethics."

"I think that's putting it mildly." The chief's face was getting red, a sure sign he was good and pissed off.

"I met Marcus here at the lab, and we went inside, only to find that he'd had a break-in. The file under the name John Brown — clearly an alias — was missing."

"Marcus told us that much when he reported the break-in early this morning," the second detective said. "He said someone named John Brown had sent him a blood sample, and asked for a simple type and cross-match. Said it came through the mail and included cash in advance, and that the client's note requested that it be done immediately."

Carrie nodded. "He told you more than he told me."

"He also said he kept a second sample,

same reasons you stated," the detective went on.

"Yeah, and that sample he still had belonged to Kyle Becker," she said softly.

"You tested it already?"

"Marcus did. He knew I suspected a link, so he compared the samples I brought him with the frozen one he'd saved. They matched."

"He told me that, too," Bryan said. "Although he claimed the sample you brought him from the autopsy was just to double-check something — gave me a lot of scientific doublespeak."

"Marcus was a wiz at scientific double-speak," she said softly. She looked out the office door as Marcus's body was loaded onto a gurney and wheeled away. Then she turned to the chief. "I know Bryan told you my theory."

"Mmff," the chief grunted. "You think the kidnapper is after Shadow Falls' sixteen-year-old Baby Doe for the reward." He pursed his lips. "Frankly, I don't think there's any question about that now."

"So, what is this asshole doing?" Bryan asked aloud. "Kidnapping all the kids in town with birthdays that fit the Baby Doe scenario, then testing their blood to see if it matches? How, when we don't know the identity of Baby Doe's father?"

"Maybe this guy knows the father," Carrie whispered.

"Hell," the chief said. "Maybe this guy *is* the father. Maybe he wants his kid badly enough to find him by the process of elimination. You fail the blood test, you die."

"God, don't say that," Carrie whispered. She had to turn away to hide her face, and she pressed one hand to her stomach as it spasmed. All she could think of was Sam and that he might be next.

"It makes sense," Bryan said slowly. "A sixteen-year-old kid goes missing. Blood is drawn and tested here at this lab. Then the kid's found dead, the lab is broken into, and all traces of that test are removed. Skip forward, and another sixteen-year-old goes missing, one with a birthday the same month as the first victim. More blood comes here to be tested. And there's another break-in to remove the evidence."

The first detective nodded. "Only this time Marcus knew something was up. The guy probably didn't use the same name twice. He might have been Jim Smith this time. Who knows? But either way, he comes in person, maybe to save time. And Marcus is suspicious."

Bryan nodded and picked up the story.

"Maybe this time the kidnapper had to force Marcus to run his tests. But then what was he going to do? Leave Marcus alive to turn him in?"

"I think that's *exactly* what he did." Carrie got to her feet, and walked back into the lab, but only far enough to point. "See that statue over there? That stone angel? Look at the wing."

The cops looked. The tip of one wing was broken off, and there was a spattering of blood on the angel's skirt.

"I think Marcus slid his chair across the floor and tried to reach that phone right there. And I think he tipped the chair over and hit his head on the statue, breaking the wing and leaving that blood spatter. And then I think his brain swelled and he died."

"You saying you think this was an accident?" Detective Two asked skeptically.

"It's the obvious scenario. I wouldn't say for sure until the autopsy is done, but I always look at the obvious scenario first, before I make a single cut, and nine times out of ten, it's the one."

"Why would he leave Marcus alive?"

She shook her head slowly. "Maybe because the blood work didn't show him what he wanted to see." She swallowed hard. "And so now he's got to find another specimen to test."

"As soon as he gets rid of the current one," Bryan said. "Which means we're running out of time to find Sadie Gray."

Carrie returned to Shadow Falls — to Sam and Gabe at the cabin. She did so without pointing out to the police that Sam's birthday fit the Baby Doe profile, that he could be the next target, because she didn't want to believe it was possible. And she didn't feel she could tell them that much of the truth without telling them the rest. That he not only had the right birthday to fit, but he had the right DNA, too. Sam *was* Baby Doe. And she wasn't ready to tell anyone that until she had told *him.*

So she headed to Gabe's place to be with Sam. And when she pulled into the driveway and saw the two of them looking out the window at her, she felt warm all over. Despite the disasters around them, despite the fact that it felt as if the world and everything in it was in danger of crumbling to dust, she felt good when she saw those faces in the window.

She shut off the car and headed for the front door, which Gabe opened before she reached it. His arms closed around her like a protective shield that blocked out anything that could hurt her and soothed the pain from the things that already had. All the stress and all the tension and all the heartache seemed to dissipate, to fade, as soon as he held her against him. It was like magic. It was something she had never felt before.

"Are you okay?" he asked as he held her.

"I am now," she whispered, and she was surprised she had said it. But it was only the truth.

He held her a little tighter and rested his head against hers.

"It was Marcus?" he asked.

"Yeah." She stepped away from him, turning to search the room for Sam. He had retreated to the big chair near the window, gazing out, but not really seeing, she thought. But he was listening, she could tell. She moved a little farther into the room, not wanting to keep anything from him.

Or rather, anything more. She'd been keeping a pretty big thing from him for far too long now, she supposed.

"Someone broke into the lab. They either murdered Marcus or he died trying to get hold of the cops. But he's dead, and we don't know if it's related to the kidnappings here in town, but given that he typed Kyle's blood sample, I think it has to be."

Gabe nodded, met her worried eyes as she waited for a response from Sam that didn't come. Sighing, Carrie moved closer to her son and slid a hand to his shoulder. "We can go into town, join the next shift of volunteers, if you want. Or we can get a supply of posters and drive around putting them up."

He finally met her eyes — his so woefully tormented that she nearly gasped aloud. "I don't know what to do." Then he looked at Gabe. "What do you think we should do?"

Gabe drew a breath, pulled a chair in front of Sam's and sat down, leaning forward, elbows on his knees, hands clasped. "You shouldn't take action until you get your head straight about a matter. I know it sounds like New Age fluff, but everything that exists was a thought before it was a thing. And the thing usually follows the thought. So we need to get our thoughts about Sadie into line with the outcome we want here, and I think we'd better do it soon."

Sam didn't roll his eyes or wave a dismissive hand. He stared at Gabe as if drinking in every word. "How?" he asked softly.

"Sun's coming out," Gabe said. "Let's sit on the deck and look down at the water, and I'll see if I can show you what I mean."

So they moved outside, and Gabe started slowly, carefully, talking about the first day he'd met Sadie and what he had thought of her. He repeated turns of phrase he'd heard her use, funny things she had said, and managed to make them smile as they remembered. And then he talked about things he would like to do with her and Sam and Carrie when she got back — hiking up to the top of the falls, playing his new song for her to get her feedback, asking her advice on a gift for Carrie.

Pretty soon Carrie got the idea and joined in. Sadie had been dying to help rearrange the living room furniture, and Carrie had promised to let her be in charge of the design. In return, Carrie was going to help her pick out a dress for the upcoming Fall Formal at the high school.

In a short while Sam was adding things he was planning to do with Sadie, too. He talked about college, about her becoming a vet, about how much she loved animals. Together, they talked about everything *except* the fact that she was missing and in danger. They talked about her and fell into the growing expectation that she would soon be back with them, fulfilling all the plans they had made, plans they were still making in her absence.

And somehow they all felt better than before.

Sadie woke slowly, stunned that she had awoken at all after the latest dose of whatever drug the bastard had given her. She'd refused to eat all day long, knowing the food might be drugged, but by afternoon, or what she thought was afternoon — it was hard to tell in a state of constant darkness — she gave in to the urge to drink. Just drink.

But the water must have been drugged, as well, because it knocked her cold for hours.

Now she felt as if her head were stuffed with cotton, and her stomach was queasy. A drug hangover, she suspected, and she silently vowed not to eat another bite of food, or drink even a sip of water, no matter how long it took her to get out of there. She was still groggy, but not so much that she didn't know she was running out of time. If she couldn't eat or drink, she was going to get weaker. She would never be stronger than she was right now, and she had to escape while she still had the strength to do so. All she needed was a chance.

She scanned the room but saw only darkness and shadow. Every bit of light had been sucked away — from within, it seemed, as well as from without. And yet there was a spark of hope inside her as she tried to blink her way clear of the mists fogging her mind. That loose eyebolt she'd been playing with earlier — it was her only hope.

She sat up in the bed and called out to her abductor, "Hello? Are you there?"

But emptiness was all she heard.

Swallowing hard, she tried again to see into the shadows. God, if the shadowy figure was there, watching her from the dark corners, if she were seen, she would lose her only chance of escape.

And there was just no way to tell for sure if he were there or not. So she maneuvered her hand slowly along her side, and then thrust it down between the bed and the wall, feeling for the eyebolt, finding it, grasping it. And then, slowly, with as much strength as she had in one arm, she began pushing hard in one direction, then pulling hard in the other. All while trying fiercely not to move any other part of her, not to betray what she was doing to the shadowy, dangerous being who might be watching her.

She pushed, she pulled, and bit by bit, she felt the bolt give. A little more. And a little more. And still more.

And then that damned sound interrupted her, and she almost cursed out loud in frustration. She'd just begun making real progress. But the locks on her prison door were turning, and then the door was opening. The shadowy villain stepped inside, but not too close.

God, Sadie thought, this might be the end. He might be here to kill her. She could be out of time. Trying to feign sleep, she gripped the bolt harder, shoved and twisted with all her strength, and tried not to let the effort show on her face.

The form moved closer. No food tray this time. *Something* was gripped in its dark hand, however. Something small. Through slitted eyes she tried to make out what it was, and as the shape came up beside the bed, she saw its darker silhouette and realized her captor was carrying a needle.

Sadie remembered Carrie's remark about drugs as the possible cause of Kyle's death. Had that been what had killed him? Had she found needle tracks in his arm? If not, why would she have mentioned the possibility?

God, this maniac really *was* going to kill her!

The shape reached out, and Sadie's fear surged through her like a flash of lightning, giving her previously unimagined strength. She yanked hard, a knee-jerk reaction, and was stunned when the bolt came free.

The dark form's gloved hand gripped her left arm, the free one, and Sadie felt the tip of the needle sinking into her skin. In desperation, she twisted the chain around her right hand and swung at the bastard's head with everything she had in her.

Like a mace at the end of its chain, the eyebolt flew and slammed into the side of her attacker's head. Her captor dropped to the floor like a sack of bricks, and Sadie scrambled to her feet, yanked the partially filled needle from her arm, then jumped over the prone form on the floor, lunging toward the still-open door.

But a hand closed on her ankle, yanking so hard that she fell facedown on the floor. Already she could feel the effects of the drug, making her head swim. She had no idea how much she'd taken into her body, or what it was. She only knew there was still a little left in the syringe, because she shook it and could feel it there.

The killer began pulling her backward as she tried to claw her way across the floor to the door. Sadie shrieked at the top of her lungs. It wasn't a word, it was a primal growl of pure rage and the ancient, unstoppable drive toward self-preservation. Twisting around, she drove the needle into flesh

— a shoulder, she thought — and depressed the plunger by driving a fist into it.

The hold on her ankle faltered, and Sadie's leg sprang forward as if released from a rubber band. Pushing herself upright, she lunged once more and was through the door a second later.

Her vision swam, but everything was black as pitch anyway. She hit a wall, then turned, arms out in front of her until she felt emptiness, a stairway. She went up, arms still extended, and hit her head on something above her. Raising her hands overhead, she felt wood, and pushed against it.

It moved up and outward, a hatchway door. Dizzy, God she was so dizzy. She almost fell, but the energy of raw adrenaline drove her on, and she made her way to the top of the stairs and out into what turned out to be the night.

Blessed fresh air hit her face. She was outdoors, in the woods, stumbling forward, running full force, and she didn't look back. Not once. She kept on going, sure she was being pursued as her fogged mind slowly lost itself to whatever poison that bastard had shot into her body. She tried to keep running even when her feet no longer felt the impacts of her steps. She fell, got up, tried again, fell again, got up again. God, she couldn't stop. Not now. Not until she found a place to hide, or a place with people or — or something.

Footsteps were coming up behind her! Oh, God, he was after her. She'd been right! "Stay away!" she cried.

"Wait!" a man's voice shouted. "Wait, please!"

"Leave me alone!"

Once more she pulled herself upright, grabbing onto a sapling for support. Swaying on her feet, she ran, stumbling forward and breaking through a wall of brush into nothingness. There was no ground beneath her feet anymore, and she was falling rapidly through what seemed like endless darkness.

13

Six in the morning.

Carrie crossed the deck attached to the back of the rented log cabin and let the cold morning air chase her emotional exhaustion away. She wore her jeans from yesterday, warm socks and running shoes, and she'd borrowed one of Gabe's large hooded sweatshirts from the hook on the wall inside.

She hadn't planned to spend the entire day and then the night there. It had just turned out that way. She had let Bryan know where to reach her and had checked in with him often, but aside from learning that the anonymous person offering the reward had agreed, through a screen of lawyers, to publicly withdraw it, there had been no news.

And yet the day had been healing, somehow. Gabe and Sam had played guitar together, while she'd listened and offered advice on a lyric or two. They'd spent time on the dock down by the lake, just staring out at the water in silence. They'd cooked together in the kitchen, making more than anyone felt like eating and vowing to save the leftovers for when Sadie came back. They'd gone for a long walk, watched an old screwball comedy, and talked until they'd talked themselves out. None of them had forgotten about Sadie, not for one minute. On the contrary, she'd been the main topic of conversation and constantly on their minds.

They'd agreed, the three of them, to drive down the mountain just far enough to see the candlelight prayer vigil, but not to join in. It had felt sacred, somehow, to get out of the car on the dirt road that wound down the mountainside to stand, just the three of them, and look down at the mass of twinkling firefly-like candles below. There had to have been hundreds of them, lighting the night. Carrie said a silent thank-you to Rose as they looked on.

They watched the gathering for an hour, maybe a little more, until the tiny lights began blinking out one by one. And then they said their own silent prayers and headed back to the cabin.

Gabe's notion of positive thinking, positive living, being the fastest and best way to bring Sadie home safe and sound might be a little bit out there, but it had done Sam a world of good. His mood had improved. He seemed hopeful again. And eventually he'd even slept. He'd still been sleeping when Carrie crept out of the cabin for an early walk.

The water of the lake gleamed under the pink and orange sunrise as she stood on the dock, and the birds seemed to grow louder and more raucous as the sky grew brighter. It smelled like fall. Apples and a few decaying leaves and cold, frost-kissed air.

"Beautiful," Gabe said softly.

She didn't jump, wasn't startled by his voice coming from so close behind her. She'd hoped he would come out and join her. She'd stayed with Sam last night, in a room with twin beds in it, while Gabe had slept in the room he'd been using since he'd been there. She hadn't dared do otherwise. This was not the time for Sam to wake to the sounds of his mother making love — even to a man he liked as much as he liked Gabe.

And she'd also known that was what would happen if she left the room after Sam fell asleep. So she hadn't. Now, though . . .

"It is beautiful," she agreed softly, staring out at the lake. There were ducks floating serenely, and every once in a while a big fish jumped up to catch an insect, arcing and splashing as it disappeared again, leaving only the ever-widening rings in the water to mark its brief display.

"I was talking about you," Gabe said. His hands touched her shoulders, turned her to face him, and he moved in to kiss her. Their lips met and immediately parted, then met again. She shivered, and her arms curled around his neck. Her body pressed closer, and his did, too.

She rubbed against him, felt him, knew he wanted her and gently pulled her mouth free of his gentle suction. "Sam?" she asked.

"Still sleeping."

"Do you think . . . ?"

"I think he'll be fine," he said, and he kissed her again. Then he pulled her legs upward, anchoring them around his waist, and he carried her off the dock and into the sheltering trees along the lakeshore. "I can see the back door from here," he whispered. "But it's private, and it's fine." He dropped to his knees, still holding her, then fell forward, so that she landed on her back, his arms still around her. A huge pile of dried, fragrant maple leaves were their bed, and she felt tears burning in her eyes as he kissed her again.

"I feel something for you," he told her as he pulled off the hoodie she'd borrowed, and then the blouse beneath it. "This isn't just a . . . a fling."

"For me either." She took his shirt off, as well, struggling with the buttons because her hands were trembling. But once she got them undone and pushed the fabric down his shoulders, she was lost in staring at his broad chest, his flat belly, the dark hairs low on his abdomen making a trail that led lower.

She forced her eyes upward again, only to find his gaze on her breasts, plumped with extra cleavage thanks to the bra she wore. She hated to take it off, but he was way ahead of her, unhooking it already, pulling it away, staring at her chest as if he were looking at an undiscovered Rembrandt.

She caught her breath when he touched, squeezed and then kissed them. She closed her eyes and tipped her head back, and let him explore and taste all he wanted. And soon enough he was reaching for her jeans, unfastening the fly and shoving them down over her hips.

She helped him out of his own, pulled him on top of her and kissed him again as he nudged his way inside her. From then on, she didn't think or know anything at all.

There was just feeling. Delicious, sensual, beautiful feeling — like melding with him, body and soul. And the release she found in his arms was the closest thing she had ever felt to heaven.

Three hours later, Gabe was still trying to figure out what had made sex with Carrie so different from sex with anyone else ever. Because it *had* been different. It had been more intense, more natural, more . . . blissful than anything he'd felt before.

And yet he was still lying to her. And feeling worse about it every day, with every meeting of their eyes, every touch of her hand. Not only that, but he was dreading the moment when he had to tell her the truth, thinking up more and more reasons to delay it.

For now, all that was important was finding Sadie. He knew that. But for the life of him, it was tough to focus on anything besides Carrie right now.

They'd joined the morning gathering of volunteers at the firehouse and were even now hiking through the forest, poking into brush, calling Sadie's name and carrying those reusable plastic backpacks with the posters and whistles inside. Gabe kept Carrie and Sam close to him, in case they needed him, and wondered who he was kidding. *He* was the one who needed *them.*

Damn, his life had changed in the past few days more than it had in the previous twenty years. It was amazing.

Along with the other searchers, they moved slowly through the woods, Most of the volunteers seemed grim, dreading what they might find. Sam, though, seemed hopeful. Tired and stressed, worried still. But hopeful. Gabe thought he might have managed to ease the young man's mind a little bit yesterday. He hoped so. And while he wasn't sure that spending another day searching the forest was doing anyone any good, not with the memory of how they'd found Kyle Becker so fresh in everyone's mind, he knew that Sam had to be doing something. And this was the only thing he'd been able to think of.

With everything in him, Gabe wanted to take Sam aside and tell him that he was pretty sure he was his father. But he couldn't do that, not until he was completely sure. And *certainly* not until he had come clean with Carrie. And maybe not until this child killer was caught, because God knew, the revelation would make Gabe into the newest and by far the most interesting suspect. Time would be lost while the police focused on him, time Sadie needed if she were going to survive.

So his revelations would just have to wait. And yeah, he knew that was probably just another excuse, even if a good one, to put off the inevitable moment when Carrie stopped feeling anything for him but anger.

A few yards to his right, she stumbled on a root and fell forward, catching herself on a sapling. She was tired, as much as she denied it. He thought their lovemaking this morning had been as great a release for her as it had been for him, but as good as it had been, it couldn't make up for lack of sleep, or the tension and worry on her mind.

"Let's take a break," Gabe said, loudly enough so that Sam, on his left, and Ambrose, a few yards farther away, could hear him. "Five minutes, okay?"

Carrie sent him a grateful look and started toward him, flipping her backpack off her shoulders and digging around inside as she walked. She pulled out a bottle of water and sank onto a nearby stump to drink deeply.

Sam headed over, as well, and Ambrose trailed a few steps behind. But then Sam stopped walking and looked ahead to where a twisting stream cut a path through the trees. "Wait." He held up a hand then pointed. "What's that over there?"

Carrie rose from her tree stump, and Gabe turned to look. A colorful bundle lay on the ground near the edge of the stream, at the base of a high rocky drop-off. A bundle that didn't belong there.

Sam lunged toward it, even as Carrie said, "Sam, wait!" And then she was running after him.

Gabe took off, too, passing Carrie in his effort to catch up with Sam, and with every forward stride, he could see that the bundle on the ground more clearly resembled a human being. A girl. Sadie.

"Sadie!" Sam shouted. "God, Sadie!" And then he was on the ground, bending close to her face, touching her cheeks.

Gabe dropped to his knees beside them, his heart in his throat. Sadie's eyes were closed, her face was scraped and bruised, and her clothes were torn in places. "Easy, Sam," Gabe said. "Let me —"

"She's not moving! Gabe, she's not —"

"She's alive." Carrie's voice was firm and calm as she knelt between them, pushing them aside to get access. Gabe and Sam moved over to give her more room, as Ambrose, panting, stopped a couple of feet away.

Sam didn't take his eyes off Sadie as Carrie leaned in close, her fingers pressing against Sadie's neck, her eyes quickly sweeping the girl's body from head to toe.

"She's alive," Carrie repeated. "Sam, put your jacket over her. You, too, Gabe. Just don't move her head, or twist her neck or spine. Don't move her at all if you can help it. We don't know how bad this is."

Sam obeyed, shrugging quickly out of his jacket as Carrie took off her own, rolled it up and used it to elevate Sadie's feet. As he watched her, Gabe noticed a metal shackle clasped around one of Sadie's ankles, trailing a length of rusty chain.

Ambrose was pulling out his whistle to sound the alarm, but Carrie caught sight of him and held up a hand. "Don't do that. I'll use the phone. We don't need a big crowd out here, just a backboard." She pulled out her phone, punched in a number, then spoke to someone, filling them in.

Gabe tucked his jacket around Sadie as securely as he could without moving her, then sat back on his heels and looked around.

"Bryan says to be careful where we step," Carrie said when she disconnected. "It's a crime scene."

"I don't think so." Gabe looked up. "I think the crime scene is up there somewhere," he said, pointing.

Carrie followed his gaze up the more or less sheer face of the stone wall beside the stream, which shot straight up for about fifty feet before ending in dense forest.

"She must have fallen. She must have been running for her life," he said, and glanced at her shackle, shivering at the thought of her being chained like an animal before pushing the image away. "It was probably dark. She ran right over the edge."

"Or she was pushed," Ambrose put in, shaking his head sadly as he, too, gauged the distance Sadie had apparently fallen. Then he closed his eyes as if the thought were too much to bear and failed to suppress a shudder.

"The bruises and scrapes are consistent with a fall from that height." Carrie narrowed her eyes. "Yeah, look, there are some broken saplings sticking out halfway up. And is that a piece of her blouse, clinging to that briar right there?"

"Could be," Gabe said.

Carrie returned her attention to the girl, and Gabe watched, in awe of her expertise, as she moved her hands carefully over Sadie's body.

"She's got a broken arm, at the least," Carrie said. "Where are the EMTs, for God's sake?"

"You only called two minutes ago, hon." Gabe caught his breath when he realized he'd used the endearment, but he didn't think she was listening.

"Sadie. Sadie, c'mon, baby, open your eyes," Sam was saying. "C'mon, be okay. Please be okay."

Sadie's eyes moved behind her closed lids. Carrie saw it and met Sam's eyes, her own hopeful.

"That's it," Sam went on. "You're trying. I can see you're trying. Come on, Sadie, talk to me. Open your eyes and talk to me," he whispered.

Finally the thick lashes flitted open, then squeezed closed again, tightly, as if the light hurt her eyes.

"Sadie?" Sam asked.

"I got away," she whispered, and then her face relaxed into unconsciousness again.

Carrie and Gabe exchanged a glance. There was no question that someone had been holding her. Someone, Gabe thought, up there. He lifted his gaze to the top of the drop-off, and felt a dark anger uncoiling at the base of his spine and heating his entire body. "I'm going up there," he said.

The tone of his voice must have startled Carrie, because even as he rose, she gripped his forearm and pulled him back down. "I need you here."

"You're fine. The paramedics will be here any —"

"*We* need you here, Gabe." She said it again, including Sam, and maybe Sadie, as well, this time.

It got to him, reminded him who he was. Not an angry, vengeful vigilante. Not a violent human being. A caring, feeling, peaceful, man. And a better man for having met these two — these three — who surrounded him now.

And Sadie was alive, he reminded himself. Sadie was alive, thank God, and safe with the people who loved her.

A short while later Sadie was in a warm hospital bed, wearing a clean hospital gown and a cast on her right arm. Carrie leaned a little closer to her, running a hand through her hair and watching her eyes move rapidly beneath their closed lids.

"It's okay to wake up now," Carrie told her, as she'd been doing for a solid twenty minutes. "No one's going to hurt you. You're safe now, Sadie. You're safe."

Sadie's eyes opened, then widened, and she gasped and jerked in the bed, her gaze swinging wildly from side to side as she flung back the sheets, before she finally went still and seemed to focus on where she was. Blinking and confused, she met Carrie's eyes at last. "I'm in the hospital."

"Yeah, you are. And it's okay. You're all right, hon. You're safe. It's all over."

"I . . . got away." Sadie let her head fall back onto the pillows. "I got away. Oh, God, I got away. But then I fell and —"

"And that's where we found you. You're safe now," Carrie said gently. "How are you feeling?"

"Sleepy. Weak. My head's kind of . . . swimmy feeling." Sadie's eyes flashed wider. "I was drugged —"

"I know. You were injected with Benterol. It's okay, though, it's mostly out of your system by now. I promise, you're fine."

Sadie blinked as if it were taking her an inordinate amount of time to process the words. "My arm hurts."

"It's broken. It's the only thing that is, but you've got a nasty ankle sprain, and a whole lot of bumps and bruises from the fall, too."

Sadie rolled her eyes, shook her head very slightly on the pillows. "I thought you said I was fine."

That made Carrie smile and flooded her with relief. "Ahh, sarcasm. You really *are* okay. And you're *safe.*"

Sadie drew a deep breath and sighed. "I thought I was going to end up . . ."

"I know. But try not to think about that right now. Think about the fact that you got away, that you're going to be okay, that you're here and safe and relatively intact."

Sadie nodded as Carrie spoke, and her body seemed to relax a bit more in the bed. "Where's Sam?" she asked, looking toward the door.

"In the waiting room, pacing and impatient to talk to you. So are the police, for that matter."

"Sam. I want Sam," the girl said softly.

"I'll get him." Carrie turned and started to leave the room, but before she'd taken a single step away from Sadie's bedside, the girl reached out and grabbed her hand in a desperate hold.

Carrie looked at her again, saw the fear in her eyes and felt a huge lump rise in her throat, making it hard to speak and impossible to swallow. "I'm sorry, Sadie. I don't know what I was thinking. I can have someone send Sam in from right here." She depressed the call button, and when a nurse answered, she said, "It's Dr. Overton in room two-twenty. My son, Sam, is in the waiting room. I'd like you to send him in."

"The police are waiting, too, and they're

pushing, Carrie," the nurse replied.

"Tell the officers they're going to have to wait just a few more minutes."

Carrie released the button and turned to pour Sadie some water from the pitcher on the nightstand. She hadn't even finished filling the glass when Sam burst through the door, pausing only briefly just inside to stare at Sadie. His entire face was taut with fear as he entered, but then it relaxed in the most immense look of relief Carrie thought she had ever seen on a human being.

Sam moved to the bed, sliding his arms around Sadie and pulling her upright, holding her gently, rocking her, burying his face in her hair. Carrie backed away, intending to step into the hall and give them some privacy, but Bryan Kendall, in his uniform, and a bird-faced man in a dark blue suit, stood in the open doorway, blocking her path.

"Excuse me," she said. "We can talk out here."

"If she's awake, then it's not you we want to talk to, Doctor," said the suit.

Carrie blinked at him. He was a small man, with a wiry build, close-set, perfectly round eyes that shifted constantly and a beaky nose. Yup, he looked like a bird, all right. "You can talk to her in a couple of minutes," she said, holding his eyes and blocking his path into the room.

"Unless there's a medical reason, ma'am, we'll talk to her right now."

"Then there's a medical reason." She lowered her head and walked the rest of the way through the doorway, leaving the two cops no choice but to step aside or let her bump right into them. She held the doorknob in one hand, so she could pull it closed behind her.

"Do I need to speak to your superior?" the birdlike little man said.

Carrie frowned at him. "I've been working here for sixteen years. Good luck finding anyone to boss me around." Then she looked at Bryan. "Who is this pushy jerk, anyway?"

"He's FBI, Carrie."

She did a slow blink, then looked at the guy again. "Dr. Carrie Overton," she said, extending a hand.

"Special Agent Wesley Cooper." He shook her hand, his grip clammy and weak. Made her think he needed a good physical exam. But he was chirping again, so she listened up. "If the girl is well enough for one visitor, she's well enough for us," he said.

"*That* visitor is part of her therapy. A vital part. Give them ten minutes. Then you'll get your turn." She looked at Bryan. "Where's Pattie?"

"Who's Pattie?" Agent Cooper asked.

"Detox," Bryan said, ignoring Cooper's question to answer Carrie's instead. "It'll be a while."

"Then I'd like to stand in on any questioning, in lieu of a parent," Carrie said.

"I think that's a reasonable request," Bryan said, but he glanced at Agent Cooper, as if awaiting his consent.

Cooper looked at her with new interest. "You know the kid, huh?"

"Almost as well as I know my own."

"You need to understand that anything said in our conversation with her is not to be repeated."

"I'm a doctor. I know about confidentiality."

"Fine." Cooper put his hands into the pockets of his blue trousers and jingled the change in one of them. "I'm going to get a cup of coffee down the hall. We'll talk to the girl as soon as I get back."

He didn't ask if that was all right, just walked away with his polished black shoes tapping the hospital's tiled floor.

Carrie lifted her brows. "Used to getting his way, isn't he?"

"Probably because he usually does."

"So, what's going on?"

"We've pulled all the volunteers out of the woods and put officers in, instead, checking the vicinity of that cliff she fell from."

Bryan met her eyes, his serious. "Don't push Agent Cooper too hard, Carrie. He's a dick."

"Aren't they all?"

"You know better than that," he said. Then, more softly, "You look tired."

"I am. But I've got help." She nodded toward Gabe, who was in the waiting area, sitting patiently until she had time to fill him in. He'd been chatting up Ambrose the last time she'd seen him, but he was alone now.

"Go on, see him for a minute. It's fine." Then Bryan paused and tilted his head. "He's not . . . I mean, is he someone from your past, Carrie?"

She lifted her brows. "No, I only met him recently. Why?"

He shrugged. "I don't know, I just thought — he looks enough like Sammy to be — Well, I guess he's not."

Frowning, Carrie looked at Gabe with fresh eyes as she moved to the waiting room. He glanced up as she came toward him, caught her gaze and smiled slightly. His eyes crinkled a little at the corners, and deep dimples appeared in his cheeks.

Just like Sam.

She was so startled that she almost choked. He saw the way her expression changed, and his smile died. Rising to his feet, he met her halfway. "Carrie? What is it?"

This time she realized that there was something about his eyes. God, no wonder she'd found him so easy to trust right from the start. He looked like her son. He looked like Sam.

She pasted a smile over her sudden turmoil and lowered her eyes. "Nothing. She's awake and stable. No serious damage. But I'll still be a little while. The police want to question her, and I've convinced them to let me be in the room, since her mother can't."

"Oh, yes, her mother can."

Carrie and Gabe turned around simultaneously at the words. Patricia Gray was standing at the other end of the waiting room, wearing a pair of red polyester stretch pants under a hospital gown.

"She a patient?" Gabe asked.

"Sadie's mom. When they went to tell her the news, she was too drunk to stand up, so they took her in to the detox unit."

"Yeah, well, they took her out too soon."

The woman came closer, her gate uneven in the blue foam hospital-issue slippers, but surprisingly speedy. She looked like hell. Of course, she never looked well, being a chronic alcoholic, but the added strain of a missing daughter had taxed her obviously limited coping skills to their limits. She looked old enough to be Carrie's mother, though Carrie knew they were close to the same age. She had a puffy, pasty face, except for her cherry-red nose and cheeks, and she was skin and bone, except for the distended beer belly. Her hair looked as if she had cut it herself after finishing off a bottle of vodka, and was rat-gray in color and filthy to boot. She reeked, as alcoholics tended to, of the booze literally seeping out her pores with her perspiration. You would think they would understand how desperately their bodies wanted to get rid of it, Carrie thought vaguely. But they didn't tend to understand much, beyond their own excuses.

"I'm her mother," Pattie Gray said. "And I'm damn well gonna be with her for the questioning. Those goddamn cops got no reason to harass my little girl."

"Mrs. Gray," Carrie said, moving closer, reaching out to touch the woman's shoulder. "I know you've been through a lot, but you're in no condition to —"

"Get away from me!" The woman twisted away from Carrie as if her touch were contaminated. "Where's my daughter? I have the right to see her! Where is she?"

Carrie took two steps back, holding up both hands, and then Bryan stepped in, having heard the commotion from down the hall. Agent Cooper was right on his heels, complete with his cup of coffee.

"Where is she, I said!"

"Easy, ma'am." Bryan stepped into the woman's range of vision. "You're in no condition to see your daughter right now."

"I have a *right* —"

"Take her in," Carrie said softly, turning to Bryan. "Go on. It's all right. Sadie's seen her a lot worse than this."

"An' what's that s'posed to mean?" the woman slurred, leaning so close her breath made Carrie's hair wilt.

"It means —"

"It means," Gabe interrupted, one hand on Carrie's shoulder, "that after what your daughter's been through, she probably won't be shaken up by who's in the room during her questioning and who isn't."

Carrie glanced sideways at him, but she didn't smile or thank him. She was no longer sure about him or his motives, and she needed time to think her new suspicions through. In the meantime, she felt angry with him — perhaps unreasonably so. But she felt that way all the same.

"This way," she told the woman and, turning on her heel, left the waiting room. She didn't look back to see if the useless alcoholic was behind her. She didn't much care. She was going to be in the room during Sadie's police interview, and if they didn't like it, she would . . . she would . . . *explode.*

She stopped walking and lowered her head into her hands, trying to get a handle on the emotions roiling in the pit of her stomach. What was she thinking? That Gabe might be here for entirely different reasons than what he'd told her? That he'd been romancing her just to get closer to her son? That maybe Sam was in fact *his* son? And she was basing all that on what? A casual resemblance that she hadn't even noticed until Bryan had pointed it out to her?

No. No, she was basing it on something else entirely. She was basing it on the feeling in her gut when she'd first recognized that resemblance, the feeling of puzzle pieces snapping into place. The feeling of *knowing.* Just knowing. She had no doubt. She didn't know how she'd managed not to see it sooner.

"Carrie?"

Gabe stood close behind her.

"I'm fine," she said, without looking back. "I'm fine." And she was. Always had been and always would be. Sam loved her. He would still love her, even if he learned the truth about his birth. He wouldn't turn on her. And that was all that mattered. He was the *only* person in her life whose opinion mattered to her. Gabe was . . . Gabe was nothing to her.

She blinked and tried to silence the little voice in her head that whispered, *But he* is *something to Sam. He's his father. And whether you want to admit it or not, he's something to* you, *too.*

Lifting her chin, straightening her shoulders, she marched into Sadie's hospital room, leaving Gabe behind and probably confused. She didn't care. Let him be confused. He was the one who'd lied to her. Used her, all this time pretending to be feeling . . .

Oh, hell.

She tried to blink the moisture from her eyes, and the devastation and anger from her expression, as she reentered Sadie's room. Sam was sitting on the edge of the hospital bed, and the two teens were holding hands and talking softly, their eyes all tangled up in gazing at each other.

Carrie had never had that kind of a connection with anyone — until Gabe.

Stupid thought. She didn't *need* that kind of a connection.

"Sam, Sadie, this is Agent Cooper from the FBI," she said.

The two kids looked impressed and nodded hello.

"He and Bryan need to talk to Sadie now," Carrie went on, letting her own words distract her mind from the disastrous revelation that was still unfolding inside it. "Sam, I promise you can come back in as soon as they're done."

Sam started to get up as Bryan and Special Agent Cooper entered the room. Cooper had a hand on Pattie Gray's arm. The woman smiled as she saw her daughter and hurried across the room to the opposite side of the bed from Sam. "Baby!" she said. "Oh, my poor baby, I'm so glad you're all right. I'm so glad." She wrapped Sadie in her arms.

From her position, Carrie could see Sadie wrinkle her nose at the booze and cigarette stench that was her mother's signature scent. But she hugged the woman back all the same. "I'm fine, Mom. Everything's fine."

"I've been out of my mind with worry!" Pattie cried. "You don't know what I've been through, baby. You just don't know."

"I'm sorry," Sadie said.

Agent Cooper cleared his throat. "Actually, ma'am, it's what your daughter has been through that ought to be concerning you."

Pattie straightened and shot the agent a hateful glare. "Obviously *you* don't have kids."

"I do, actually. And when they go through a trauma, I don't make it all about me. But maybe that's just me."

Carrie suddenly regretted being less than pleasant to the man. He was decent — and insightful, to boot.

Agent Cooper shifted his gaze to Sadie. "We need to ask you some questions," he said, and his voice had altered. Softened. "I promise we're going to make this as painless as possible, Sadie, but we need your help to solve this thing. All right?"

"I want that animal caught and locked up for what he did to Kyle and what he put me through," she said. "But I'm not answering one question unless Sam and Doc can stay in the room. And I mean it."

Carrie nodded a little, impressed again by Sadie's steel spine. The girl was amazing.

The agent looked at Bryan, and Bryan shrugged. "It's your call, sir. But from what I know of this one, she means it."

"All right. Nothing she says leaves this room." With that, Cooper sent a stern look at Sadie's mother, who was clearly the agent's pick for the woman most likely to run her mouth. *"Nothing,"* he reiterated.

"I'm not deaf."

He nodded and returned his attention to Sadie. "Now, can you tell me what happened? Start at the beginning and just tell us in your own words. I might prompt you with a few questions here and there, but I'll try not to interrupt unless it's really necessary. Okay?"

Sadie nodded and sat up straighter in the bed. "Okay."

"Okay." The agent took a digital recorder from his pocket and turned it on. "Begin with when you left Dr. Overton's house. You were on your way to cheerleading practice, correct?"

Sadie nodded. Then she glanced at the recorder and said, "Yes. That's right. I was riding my bike. I got about a mile down the hill toward town and then something stung me — or that's what I thought at first. But it was a dart, and it knocked me out. I passed out. Then —"

"Just a sec now," the agent said. "We need to take it very slowly. Detail by detail. So this person shot you with a dart, you say?" Sadie nodded, then repeated her assent aloud. "Was there a vehicle nearby? Did you see anyone as you went down the road?"

"No. There was no one there. No vehicle . . . nothing."

"So someone was out of sight but managed to dart you. How do you think that could have happened?"

Sadie frowned, clearly searching her memory. "There were trees right up to the edge of the road. It was at that part where the big bend curves around to the right, just before the woods begin to thin out. You know the place I mean?" she asked, shooting a quick look at Sam.

"Yeah. I know," Sam said and looked at the agent. "It's the same spot where we found the bike."

"Good. That's very good. Did you see this person at all?"

"No."

"All right. Go on. What happened when you woke up?"

Sadie told her story. She told about being chained by her ankle to a wall in some kind of a basement room with no windows. She told about a person dressed all in black, right up to the ski mask, entering the room, feeding her meals she was convinced were drugged, returning with a hypodermic. She told about how she worked to loosen the chain from the wall, hit the person with it, then ran away. And she talked about escaping through a hatchway and running through the forest, all the while feeling pursued, and then falling a long ways before hitting the ground. She didn't know if the person chasing her had been male or female, though at one point she'd heard a man's voice calling out to her to wait. And all the while Bryan and the Fed made notes, asked questions, elicited memories, details. What the room looked like. What the meal consisted of. How tall the abductor had seemed to be. Whether he'd seemed fat or thin. Whether she'd noticed his shoes.

Sadie talked and talked, until she was too tired to talk anymore, and Carrie called the interview to a halt. "She needs to rest now. She's all in."

"I think we have everything we need." Agent Cooper shut off the recorder. "If you remember anything else, Sadie, you give me a call." He set a card on her nightstand. "Anything, even the most insignificant detail, could help. We need to get this person bef—"

His cell phone rang just then. He sent an apologetic look to Carrie. "Sorry. I should have turned it off."

"We dropped that regulation, Agent Cooper. The new phones don't interfere with pacemakers anymore. Go ahead and —"

And then *her* pager went off and Bryan's phone rang.

Before either of them answered, Cooper put a hand over his cell and said, "They found another body near where we found Sadie."

"God, not another kid," Carrie said.

"Not this time," Cooper said. "They think it might be our guy. Can you come with us, Dr. Overton? We might need your expertise out there."

"Of course," she told him. Then she looked at Sam. "Stay with her. And be careful, okay? Don't go anywhere with anyone."

"I'm sixteen, not six, Mom."

She smiled softly at him. "I know how old you are. I'm scared, that's all."

"I know. Gabe will stay with us, don't worry. Where is he anyway?"

"Still in the waiting room, I think." Carrie frowned, not liking Sam's notion one bit. She didn't want Gabe alone with her son. Not that she suspected he had anything to do with the abductions. He could be the best liar in the world, but she would have sensed it if he were a threat to her son. She was sure of that. He wouldn't hurt a fly. Not physically, at least.

But he might tell Sam who he was. And she had to be the one to tell him that. Right after she confronted Gabe himself about it.

Until then, she wanted to keep the two of them as far apart as humanly possible. "I'll need him out there with me. If that's okay."

Sam looked at her, and maybe he noticed something off about her tone. He knew her better than anyone, after all. But he let it slide. "Sure, Mom. We'll be fine."

"I'll keep an eye on them," Sadie's mother said.

"Thanks. That's very . . . reassuring. Thank you."

She gave her son a hug, then lavished one on Sadie, as well. "Be safe until I get back, both of you."

Then she left the room with Bryan and the agent flanking her, her heart in her throat as she prayed that this was the end of Shadow Falls' latest nightmare, and that the child killer was dead. Long live the children.

14

There was something wrong with Carrie.

Gabe didn't know what — or maybe he did. He could only think of two reasons why she might suddenly have turned so cold toward him. Either she'd found out who he really was and why he was in town, or she suspected him of having something to do with the kidnappings.

Or maybe both.

She barely spoke to him on the way to the little pull-off near the stream, where they parked the vehicles and started trudging through the woods again, following the streambed as it twisted amid the trees. It was an overcast morning, with dark clouds rolling in, slow but ever thicker, and blocking out the sun. The temperature was dropping rather than rising, and the air was heavy with pent-up rain. Gabe tried to engage Carrie in conversation, but she replied with one- or two-word responses that were little more than he might have elicited from a total stranger.

Okay, okay, he told himself. He would figure that out later. Talk to her when they were alone and could get to the bottom of this. For the moment, he had to focus on what was happening in the here and now.

And that became a whole lot easier when they passed the crime scene tape and the broken body came into view.

The man lay on his back, arched over a large boulder that was surrounded by scrub brush. He wasn't more than a dozen yards from where they had found Sadie, but the surrounding brush had hidden him from view. And of course, once they'd found Sadie, the police had pulled all searchers from the woods and taped off the area. The F.B.I. had taken time to organize their own team before going back in, thinking there was a murderous kidnapper in the vicinity. They'd insisted no one else get close — not even the local cops.

And maybe there was. It was just that he was dead.

"Do you know him?" Agent Cooper asked aloud, to no one in particular.

Carrie moved closer, but Gabe stayed where he was, just watching her, wishing he could read her mind, worried to hell and gone about what was happening to the easy, sexy energy that had flowed so readily between them up until now.

He couldn't see the man's face. But then Carrie pushed the brush aside and leaned in, before jumping back again with a sharp gasp. "Oh, God, it's Nate Kelly!"

Bryan tipped his head skyward and pressed a hand to his forehead.

"Who is Nate Kelly?" Agent Cooper asked. "How do you know him?"

"He's a local," Bryan said. "He owns Sugar Tree Lodge, a ski resort."

"But what could he have to do with any of this?" Carrie asked. "He's no kidnapper, and certainly no murderer."

Cooper tipped his head to one side. "Was the ski lodge in trouble? Financially?"

Sighing, she lowered her head. "It was. He was on the verge of being forced to sell out."

"Then he might have been after the reward for that missing baby, just as you people theorized. It certainly fits," Cooper said.

"No." Carrie shook her head emphatically. "No, he might have been unpleasant. Standoffish. A little odd, even, but not a killer."

"I don't know," Bryan said. "A half-million bucks has a strange effect on people."

"And we know he was in particular need of it," Gabe suggested. "I just heard someone the other day commenting on what a bad couple of years the ski business has had out here. No snow. Am I right?"

Carrie nodded. "Damn global warming."

"It's a natural cycle," Agent Cooper said.

She sent him a look that said he was not only ignorant but gullible, then shook it away. "I want to take a closer look at him."

The agent nodded, quickly retrieving a pair of latex gloves from the crime scene crew who were already there, taking photographs and measurements. Carrie pulled the gloves on and moved closer, bending over the body, touching, examining.

"Where is this Sugar Tree Lodge?" Agent Cooper asked.

Bryan lifted his head, looking around to orient himself. "The main lodge and the slopes can't be more than half a mile as the crow flies. Farther by road, though. He also has several private cabins, for guests who like more privacy."

Carrie looked up from the body. "Autopsy will say for sure, but I think he died of a broken neck, probably from a fall."

"He probably chased that poor kid right off the cliff," Agent Cooper said, looking up. "Someone was sure as hell looking out for her, huh?"

"She was looking out for herself," Carrie said softly. "Women have to, these days." Then she shook her head. "I'm just not sure he's been dead long enough to have fallen at the same time Sadie did."

"We don't know what time Sadie fell," Agent Cooper said. "Only that it was dark outside."

"Yeah, and it's been light for three or four hours now. I think he's been dead less than two."

"You're basing that on what, Doc? Feeling his forehead?"

She pursed her lips. "I'll get a more accurate reading when we get him to the morgue. He does have a head injury."

"Just like Sadie said he would," Bryan said. "Where she hit him with the bolt on the end of that chain."

"Or where *he* hit *himself* on the rocks," Carrie said. "It would be tough to imagine him *not* having a head wound after a landing like that."

Agent Cooper frowned at Bryan, and then they both looked at Gabe, as if he might understand why Carrie seemed to be looking for reasons to doubt this was the guy. But Gabe was as puzzled as any of them.

"All right, let's get him bagged and out of here." Agent Cooper pulled out a cell phone. "Now that we have a positive ID, I'll get a warrant to search that ski lodge of his and anything else he owns in the area."

"He already gave us permission to search his properties," Bryan said. "They were on our list for today."

"Probably intended to move the kid somewhere else and hide any evidence she'd ever been there before you got to it. But dying wasn't on his agenda," Cooper said. "Ten to one we'll find where the girl was held."

Gabe saw that Carrie still looked doubtful. "I just want to get that body temperature before we move him. The longer we wait, the larger the margin of error on time of death will be."

"Fine," Agent Cooper said. "Do you want to observe the autopsy again?"

Gabe stepped forward. "Maybe you could just read the report this time, Carrie? I think you need a little rest. You're damn near dead on your feet."

She nodded, sighed deeply. "Yeah. That's probably the best idea." She took the reading she needed, then let him take her arm to walk her back down through the woods, along the edge of the stream, toward the vehicles. And then she stopped along the way, and his heart jumped into his throat when she turned to face him and said, "So why don't we just get this out of the way here and now?"

"I can see something's wrong, so okay, shoot. What is it?" he asked, though he was pretty sure he already knew.

"When were you going to tell me, Gabe?"

He frowned. "Tell you what?"

"Don't insult my intelligence by keeping up the lie. Or is there more than one big thing you've been lying about? Oh, wait, actually, I already know there are at least two big lies, don't I? One is that the things you've been pretending to feel for me were ever anything other than an act to get closer to my son. And the other is the reason *why* you wanted to get closer to him. Isn't that right?"

He licked his lips, averted his eyes, searched his mind and came up with the lamest words possible. "I can explain."

"I should have seen it sooner. You're his father, aren't you, Gabe?"

He lowered his head. "If his birth mother was Livvy Dupree, then yeah. I think I just might be."

Carrie let her head drop forward. "I hoped it wasn't true. I hoped that you would tell me it was ridiculous. Damn you for letting me . . . for letting me believe in you. Trust you. With my son, for God's sake."

"I wanted to tell you . . . Dammit, Carrie, I didn't even know —"

"I don't want to talk about this." She turned away from him and resumed traipsing through the woods, her pace a reflection of her anger. "And I don't want to talk to you. Not ever, Gabe. Not ever."

He put a hand on her shoulder and spun her around to face him. "If he's mine, I have a right to see him. To get to know him. You can't deny me that. You can't deny *him* that. You know he'd want to know me, to know the truth. If you keep it from him, he'll never forgive —"

She smacked him, hard, right across the face. And Gabe staggered backward, stung and wounded.

"Don't you *dare* threaten to take my son from me, you son of a bitch!"

He stood there, holding his temper in a grip of pure iron. "I didn't. I wasn't threatening that. I just said —"

"What's your blood type?"

"A Positive," he said softly.

She swallowed hard, averted her eyes.

"What's his?"

When she didn't answer, he knew. "It's

the same, isn't it? What was hers? His mother's?"

"*I'm* his mother, you deceitful bastard."

"I meant Livvy's. You were the M.E. when she was murdered. You must know what hers was. It wasn't the same, was it? This means he's mine. This proves it, doesn't it, Carrie?"

"It proves nothing." She turned away and continued walking.

"Carrie, I know you're angry," he said, hurrying after her. "But you have to listen to me. Please, just hear me out. What I've started feeling for you, it's — I know what this looks like, but —"

"Get a ride back with one of the cops, okay, Gabe? We'll do a DNA swab and send it out. Until the results come back, I don't want to see or hear from you again."

"But —"

"There's nothing more to say."

"Won't you need a DNA swab from Sam, too? For comparison?"

She whirled on him. "If you breathe one word of this to Sam, I swear to God, I'll . . . I'll . . ."

"I won't. I *wouldn't.* Jeez, Carrie, will you let me get a word in here?"

She turned away again. "I'll get a sample from his toothbrush or something. It'll take a couple of weeks. Marcus is dead, so —"

"I didn't know it was Sam when I came out here," he said. "When I met you, I had no idea. I swear it."

"Right." She emerged from the forest into the parking area alongside the stream, where a brown wooden sign announced in white lettering that it was for anglers to park while fishing. She quickly unlocked her car with the remote and opened the door.

"Carrie!"

Gabe caught up, gripping her shoulders and turning her around to face him. He was stunned to see tears in her eyes. He knew he'd hurt her, that she was only lashing out because she was in pain and saw him as a threat to her son. He would have expected nothing less of a mother as devoted as she was.

She stared into his eyes but couldn't hold his gaze for long. She had to turn away. "That look in your eyes is so real, so hard not to believe. But I know that it's nothing more than a lie, Gabe. It never has been. And that hurts me more than I can make you understand."

"You've got it all wrong," he told her.

"Leave me alone, Gabe."

"Carrie, don't. Don't throw us away. What's been growing between us, it could be something special."

"Us? How can you say that, Gabe? There's no us. There never was. It was all a lie." She held up a hand as he began to interrupt. "No, you can't just say it was real and expect me to take that on faith, Gabe. You can't, not when the evidence says otherwise."

"You've got it backward, Carrie. Try believing what you wish were true, what it feels good to believe. And then you'll see evidence of *that.* Instead of seeing is believing, believing is seeing. Don't you get it?"

"I'm not a gullible idiot."

"Neither am I. And I know I screwed this up — badly. But it was a mistake. That's all. A mistake, Carrie. It wasn't vicious or deliberate or cruel. It was a huge bout of bad judgment, and I'm sorrier than I can tell you. Don't let my poorly thought-out choices ruin what could have been."

"You lied to me. And I believed you. I really, really *believed* in you. You *hurt* me. So now 'could have been' is all it will ever be. Goodbye, Gabe."

Then she got into her minivan and drove away.

"We got our guy."

Those were Bryan's first words when he

phoned the next morning. And Carrie found herself breathing a sigh of relief, even while doubting it could possibly be true. Nathan Kelly? A killer?

"Are you sure, Bry? It just doesn't seem —"

"We searched Nate's properties. One of the cabins — one that used to be someone's home a hundred years ago, that Nate had bought and renovated — was only a half mile from the cliff where we found him and Sadie. It had a rudimentary basement, more like a root cellar, really, with a hatchway."

She closed her eyes, swallowed hard. "Still . . ."

"That basement had a cot and a hole in the wall where we presume Sadie's chain was anchored. We found a broken hypodermic with traces of Benterol still inside. And we've collected hairs and other trace evidence that we fully expect will match samples from Kyle Becker and Sadie Gray."

"I see."

"Moreover, we spoke to Ambrose Peck. Apparently, he was giving Nate Kelly some financial advice. He said Nate was in a lot more trouble than we probably knew. Said the state was getting ready to put Sugar Tree up for auction over unpaid taxes."

"No."

"We verified it. Peck was dead on target. Nate was desperate, Carrie. The temptation of that half-million-dollar reward must have been more than he could resist."

She sighed, lowering her head and feeling a sense of relief wash over her like a warm, soothing bath. "Thank you for letting me know, Bryan. I really appreciate it." She licked her lips and said, "What about that anonymous person, the one who put up the reward? What ever came of that?"

"We still don't know who it was, but they did withdraw the reward, and their lawyers say now that they know it was a motive for kidnapping and murder, the person won't offer it again."

"But you still don't know who it was?"

"No. The lawyers are adamant about protecting their client's identity."

"I'd like to know why."

"You're borrowing trouble, Carrie. This is over. Our kids are safe again, and I hope to God this is the last trouble Shadow Falls sees for a long, long time. Fill Gabe in for me, will you?"

Gabe. God, if it hadn't been for Gabe, and what he knew, Carrie would have breathed a sigh of relief and closed the book on this entire segment of her life. But for her, it wasn't over at all. Not yet.

For her, the trouble was only just beginning. Because Gabriel Cain was her son's father. She didn't have any doubt about that, even without the DNA test results she would insist on waiting for. If he wanted to take her son from her, there wouldn't be one thing she could do to stop him.

"Carrie?" Bryan prompted.

"Yeah? Oh, yes, I'll tell him. Bye, Bryan."

"Bye."

She hung up the phone and stared at it for a long moment. Like a fool, she'd been waiting for it to ring all night long. And then, when it had finally complied, the wrong man's voice had come from the other end of the line. She hadn't heard from Gabe overnight. Apparently he had taken her request to be left alone to heart.

Men were so freaking clueless. Didn't he know that being left alone was the *last thing* she wanted? What she wanted was for him to *make her* believe what she so desperately wanted to believe. She needed a grand gesture. She needed him on his knees in apology, in remorse, with a tear or two in his eye. She needed a card filled with beautiful words. He was a wordsmith. Surely he could write something that would convince her. She needed flowers, and maybe some tiny, meaningful gift, and an explanation that would prove to her, beyond any doubt, that his feelings had been real.

She wanted his heartfelt promise that he would never take her son away from her. Because he loved her. Yes, that was it. She wanted him to love her. And say so. And prove it.

But she didn't want to have to ask for any of those things. He should know what she wanted and needed from him right now. He should *know.* A moron would know.

She hadn't gotten any of those things from him, though. He hadn't even bothered to call. And so she knew, as any other red-blooded woman would know, that the lack proved her most heartbreaking suspicions true. He didn't care for her, never had, probably wasn't even mildly attracted to her. He was just a good actor willing to do whatever he had to in order to find and claim his offspring.

She had lost Gabe. Hell, she'd never really had him. She had probably ensured that she would lose her career, too. Because when it came out that she had used her position as a doctor and forged signatures in order to commit an illegal adoption, her medical license would almost certainly be pulled.

But the only thing that truly mattered to her was that she was about to lose her son.

God, she didn't think she could bear it. Losing Sammy. It would be more than she could take.

"Mom?"

She looked up as Sam entered the kitchen, where she'd been baking cinnamon rolls when Bryan had called. She tried to paste a smile on her face, but she had no doubt the tear tracks were still visible.

Frowning, Sam moved closer and wrapped his arms around her, hugging her hard. "It's okay now, Mom. It's over. Sadie's safe."

"I know. I just got off the phone with Bryan." She frowned. "How do you know?"

"Sadie just called. Agent Cooper filled her in. And the chief is on TV right now, giving a press conference."

"Oh." She tried to hide the tears in her voice, but it was tough to fool Sam. He took a step back and looked down at her face. "How do you women stay so strong through all the hard stuff, and only break down after it's all said and done, anyway?"

She smiled in spite of the turmoil within. "It's in our genes," Carrie said. "If we break down during the crisis, the dingoes eat our babies. So things tend to hit us late. Why? Is Sadie having a hard day, too?"

"She can't stop crying. But she says she's happy. And that she knows now that she can handle anything that ever happens. But she still can't stop crying. It makes no sense at all."

"Makes perfect sense to me," she said.

"That must be because you're the same species."

"Could you sit down, Sam? I need to talk to you about something."

Sam sat at the kitchen table, helping himself to a cup of fresh coffee and one of the cinnamon buns she had just pulled out of the oven. She tended to cook when stressed. And then eat what she'd cooked. It wasn't her favorite habit. Sam took a bite, chewed and swallowed, watched his mother working up her nerve, then nodded firmly.

"You're finally going to tell me that I'm adopted, aren't you?"

Carrie's eyes widened, and she stared at him. "He told you?"

"Who?" Then he shook his head. "No one told me. I've known for years. We look nothing alike. Our blood types don't match. You won't talk about my father. I don't know any of your relatives." He licked his lips. "And you get so nervous every time anyone brings up the subject of that missing baby from sixteen years ago. I mean, you go white, Mom. I don't know, maybe it's not obvious to people who don't know you as well as I do. But to me, you might as well have bold-face print across your forehead."

She stared at him in disbelief.

"I'm Baby Doe, aren't I?"

Tears brimming, she nodded. "I was on a dark, deserted road, heading for here, where my first real job as a doctor was waiting. And I found this young girl on the side of the road, in labor. I delivered you right there."

He blinked slowly, nodding. "What was she like?"

"Pretty. And scared, and utterly alone. She said she was heading for Shadow Falls, too." Carrie shrugged. "I wish I could tell you more about her. But I can't. I went to find a phone to call for an ambulance to take the two of you to the hospital. This was before everyone had a cell phone. And when I came back, she was gone. She'd left you all bundled up in my jacket, with a note, asking me to raise you. See, during the labor, I'd told her I could never have kids of my own. And she seemed to think we were meant to meet on that road that night. She said when you want something badly enough, you can actually bring it into your life if you believe you can."

"Sounds like something Gabe would say," Sam muttered. He swallowed hard.

Carrie reached across the table to cover his hand with her own. "I loved you so much, so fast, that I knew I could never give you up. So I just let everyone in town believe you were mine by birth, and I started searching for her. I knew if I could find her, she would sign adoption papers and everything would be legal. But she was murdered before I had the chance. She was misidentified as Sarah Quinlan, with no family and no known love interest." Carrie drew a breath. "If I'd told the truth, I could have lost you, and that just wasn't a risk I was willing to take. So I forged names on the paperwork and filed for a birth certificate. And I've been terrified of the truth coming out ever since. I'm really sorry, Sam."

He nodded slowly. "And you have no idea who my father is?"

She blinked and lowered her head. She so didn't want to tell him. "I . . . I think I might. But I'd like to make sure before I tell you. Is that okay with you?"

"No. No, I think I've waited long enough. I love you, Mom, but you've been keeping way too many secrets from me for way too long now."

She looked at him with fear in her heart. "Are you mad at me?"

He made a face. "For saving me? Protecting me all this time? Keeping me from becoming a ward of the state? Being the best mother in this town, maybe in the entire state of Vermont? Yeah. I'm furious."

She blinked rapidly as tears spilled over from her eyes and onto her cheeks. "You're amazing, you know that?"

"I was raised well. So tell me, who is it you think might be my father?"

She lowered her head. "Gabe."

"Yes!" Sam shot to his feet, pumping his fist in the air. "I knew it. I just knew it! I mean, it makes sense. His VW Bus . . . its name is Livvy, after a woman he lived with once. He said he wanted to save her and couldn't. And he looks like me. And his dad's name is Sam and —"

"He told you that?" she asked sharply.

"Yeah. I promised to keep it to myself. But the name — how did that happen, anyway?"

"Livvy named you, in the note she left for me. She must have hoped it would help mend the rift between Gabe and his father someday."

"We both play guitar. And he even has a birthmark like mine. Does Gabe know? Have you told him?"

Carrie nodded. "He knows. It's why he

came here, to try to find you. I'm afraid it's also why he's been . . . pretending to have feelings for me."

Sam had been grinning, but his smile froze and died when she said that. "No, I don't think so. Gabe wouldn't do that, Mom."

"You'd be surprised what people will do to protect their own child. Look at what I've been doing all these years. I broke the law. That's not like me."

"Yeah, but still . . ."

"Nothing is for sure," Carrie said. "We're sending out DNA samples to make sure. I was going to steal your toothbrush and not tell you until I was sure, but since it's all out in the open now, I'll just take a mouth swab, with your permission."

He nodded. "Sure." He looked toward the door. "Mom, as much as I like him, if it turns out he was playing you to get close to me, I'll —"

"You'll forgive him and let it go," she said.

He didn't say he would, but he didn't argue, either.

"Gabe and I have some things to work out, too, Sam. We've got to discuss . . . a lot of legal matters. Because DNA notwithstanding, I'm really pretty sure about this. And I know you've waited a long time to get to know your father, but I'm wondering if you could manage to wait two more days. For me."

"What do you mean?" Sam asked.

Carrie sighed and thought about what was going to happen if word of the truth got out. The hordes of press that would descend on Shadow Falls — again. The publicity that would be focused on her and her son. The likelihood that she would be depicted as a kidnapper who'd stolen a baby and kept him from his rightful father, a beloved song-writer, and — if the whole truth were revealed — his grandfather, the adored country music legend, for all these years. She didn't want Sam exposed to any of the feeding frenzy that was about to ensue.

"I want you to do something for me, hon," Carrie said, getting out of her chair, putting a palm to his cheek and holding his eyes with hers. "And I know you're going to argue, but I really need you to give it some thought."

"I'd do anything for you, Mom. And if it means giving you and Gabe some time to sort this out, I will. Because I think he's really nuts about you."

She almost started crying again. But she sniffed, stiffened and took a breath to relax her clenched-up throat muscles.

"Yeah, and you're nuts about him, too, aren't you?" Sam asked.

She decided not to answer that. "I want you to go on that camping trip you had planned for this weekend."

He frowned at her. "Okay, then I have to retract my former statement. I'd do *almost* anything for you." He frowned and tilted his head to one side. "Mom, I don't want to leave Sadie."

"Sadie's fine. She's safe and well, and will probably be discharged in the morning. I've spoken to her, and she wants you to go. She even said she might come out and join you for the afternoon tomorrow, if it wouldn't interfere with your 'guy time.' "

"By tomorrow afternoon I'll be sick and tired of guy time," he said softly.

Carrie turned away to begin setting a few cinnamon buns, freshly iced and still warm, into a plastic container with an airtight lid. She was going to take them over to Rose to thank her for all she'd done to help during the crisis.

"I'll tell you what," Sam said. "I'll make a deal with you."

"What kind of a deal?" Carrie asked.

"I'll go, because it's only two nights and Sadie's already been trying to talk me into it, and because the guys and I want to dedicate the trip to Kyle's memory, like Gabe suggested. Kind of our own way of saying goodbye."

"Sounds like you'd already decided to go."

"My stuff's already packed and in the car. We're meeting at Alley's at one and heading up to the state park from there."

She rolled her eyes. "You couldn't have told me that when I was spending all that time trying to talk you into it?"

"No, because I was going to make you promise to do something for me in return."

"I'd do anything for you," she said, repeating his own words back to him. "Just ask."

"Try listening to what Gabe tells you," Sam said. "Try believing in him. Do whatever it takes to prove it to yourself, but really, really *try* believing him. Because even if he's not my father, Mom, I don't think he's a liar. I really don't. I think he's . . . one of a kind. I've never met anyone like him before. And I don't think you have, either."

She felt tears burning behind her eyes again. "It's true. I haven't."

"He's in tune, Mom. He's really onto something with this philosophy of his. So if it's six of one and a half dozen of the other, go with believing in him. Because I don't think you'll go wrong if you do."

"You really think so?"

He nodded. "I've seen the way he looks at you, Mom. And since you're one of a kind, too, and the best catch in town, it seems to me like it's meant to be."

"You think I'd be nuts to let him get away, don't you, Sam?"

He shook his head. "Nope. I think *he'd* be nuts to let *you* get away." He kissed her cheek. "I'm going to head over to the hospital to see Sadie. You coming later?"

"About an hour. I'm going to spend a little time with Rose first. And then I'll go to work and spend the first normal, routine day I've had in far too long." She handed him the plastic container of cinnamon buns. "Take these to Sadie. I've got more in the oven."

"You and Gabe get your shit together before I get back, would you?"

"I'll do my best." She hugged him. "God, I got lucky that night on the side of that road."

"So did I," Sam said, hugging her hard. "So did I."

15

Just before noon, Sam drove his pride and joy along what was commonly known as "Old Route Six." It used to be Shadow Falls' main drag but had been replaced by a wider, straighter strip of pavement. Most of the businesses had relocated to the section of new road that ran straight through the center of town. The buildings that had housed them before had been torn down, converted into homes or just left to the mercy of the elements, so Old Route Six had a ghost town look about it in places. Alley's was one of the few businesses that had stayed put and managed, somehow, to stay afloat, despite being off the beaten path. Probably partly because, unlike most ice-cream parlors, it stayed open year-round and served a limited but delicious selection of food, as well.

The location was a scenic one. A river flowed behind the building, and there were round redwood-stained picnic tables with umbrellas and benches set up alongside the place, where people liked to sit and enjoy a cold treat on a hot summer day.

Sam figured his friends were probably already waiting to meet him there, before heading out to the state park for their camping weekend. He'd had a great visit with Sadie and had confided everything his mom had told him that morning. He didn't have any doubt that he could trust Sadie to keep the news to herself.

She'd been surprised, excited and, predictably, worried about his mom. She'd actually threatened to punch Gabe in the nose if he hurt her. Sam smiled, shaking his head, as he recalled the fury in her eyes when she'd said it. He really did love that girl.

As he went to meet the guys, he told himself for the hundredth time that he had to keep what he knew private. His mom could get into a lot of trouble over it, and he didn't want to be the one to bring that raining down on her. But he could hardly contain himself.

And he couldn't help but wish that Kyle were there to discuss it with.

Sam was only about a mile away from Alley's when he spotted Rose standing beside her classic Ford wagon with the wood-grain side panels, looking up and down the road. When she saw him approaching, she waved her arms.

Frowning, he pulled over behind her and got out. "Hey, Rose."

"Oh, Sam, thank goodness you came along!" She was smiling in what appeared to be relief.

"What's going on? You having car trouble?"

"I'm afraid so. Your mother mentioned some ice-cream stand to me this morning, and I recklessly decided to come out for a treat. But Lord, if I'd known it was *so* out-of-the-way I would have opted for the drugstore in town."

He smiled. "It wouldn't be the same. Trust me. So what's up with your car?" He looked at it but didn't see anything obvious. No flat tires, no smoke rolling out from under the hood.

"It's behaving badly," she explained. "Could you take a look?"

He looked at his watch and then at the car. He could probably spare five or ten minutes to help out and still meet the guys on time. After all, Rose had made them that great dinner and then organized the candlelight vigil for Sadie. He owed her.

"Sure," he said, and he opened the driver's

door, saw the keys in the ignition, got in and started it up. Then he went around to the front and opened the hood. Leaning in, he listened, he looked, he even sniffed. But he didn't find anything the matter. "It's running fine now, Rose," he said. "What was it doing, exactly?"

"Oh, I don't know how to put it in mechanical terms." Her eyes sparkled when she smiled in that self-deprecating way. She reminded him of what Snow White would look like at retirement age. "But it was kind of . . . bucking. Like an unruly colt. And making odd noises."

"Odd noises?"

She tried to emulate the sound, and he had to bite his lip to keep from laughing out loud. He turned his face away to hide his reaction. "So you're saying that your car was trying to cough up a hairball?"

"Oh, Sam!" Rose waved a hand at him and smiled at his little joke.

He turned the car off and looked at the engine, then turned it back on and listened again. He even had her get in and drive it forward a few yards, to see if he could hear any signs of trouble. And then, when she stopped, he said, "I don't know what it could have been, Rose, but it's fine now."

She looked at the car as if it was not to be

trusted. "You know I trust your opinion, Sam, but honestly, I'm too old to get stranded and have to walk for help. Would you mind terribly driving me back?"

"But you didn't have your ice cream yet."

"I think my appetite has been spoiled. Honestly, I was afraid I'd be stuck out here forever."

He sighed. "You have a cell phone signal here, don't you?"

"Well, I might, but I wouldn't know." She held up her phone and showed him its blank face. "I forgot to plug it in last night, and it's utterly dead now."

Sam heaved a sigh. "All right, I'll take you back to the house. Come on. I'll have to help you in. Mom's always saying she needs a stepladder."

"Oh, we're taking your . . . car?"

He thought that much was obvious. "Rose, I don't dare leave it sitting on the side of the road. It's an expensive vehicle, and to me, it's just about priceless."

She looked at her old station wagon and then at his shiny red SUV, and then she smiled a little. "I guess you're right."

"Not that your car isn't pretty awesome, too," he said. "You know, I've seen people fix up old woody wagons like that, make hot rods out of them."

"Oh, I don't know that I'd go that far," she said. "But it gets me where I need to go just fine."

"Tell you what," Sam said. "Why don't you drive yours and I'll drive mine? I'll follow you, and that way, if you get into any trouble, I'll be right there. Okay?"

She shook her head. "No. No, I prefer to ride with you. I've had it with driving for today. It's too hard on my nerves."

He frowned but didn't say anything as he helped her into his SUV. Then he placed a quick call to Wes and Sonny to tell them not to wait for him, that he would meet them later at the park.

Gabe thought it best to give Carrie some time, so he gave her the entire night to reflect. And then he decided to give her the entire day. He didn't bother her with phone calls or even stop by the house to check on her. He could tell from the way she'd acted that she really didn't want anything to do with him, so he thought the best thing he could do would be to give her some space.

But it was driving him crazy.

He'd spent the morning at the cabin, flipping through the photos on his laptop and looking mostly at the ones of his own father, taken at various stages of his career. Gabe had saved every photo he'd ever found of the man, album covers, publicity shots, public service ads. There were shots of him when he was only a few years older than young Sam was now, just a lanky country boy with an acoustic guitar slung over his shoulder and a great big smile on his face. Not a clue in those dark eyes of his that he would soon become a country music legend. That he would achieve levels of fame reserved for an extremely select few. The Beatles. Johnny Cash. Elvis.

He hadn't known then what he would become. How *could* he have known?

The oldest photos were in black and white, but the later ones were in color. Gabe had collected them in spite of himself. Often he'd used the excuse that he was merely curious to see if there were any physical resemblances between himself and his father at different stages of their lives. Did his dad, at thirty, look the way Gabe had at thirty? How about at nineteen?

Now he was looking for a resemblance to Sam. Sam. God, what had possessed Carrie to take him, to raise him as her own? And by what stroke of serendipity had she chosen to name him Sam? That would have to be one hellishly huge coincidence, wouldn't it?

There was no doubt in his mind as he looked through the photos, though, that young Sam was of superstar Sammy Gold's bloodline. It was in everything from the solid, wide jawline to the dimples in the boy's cheeks. It was in the very noticeable curved bridge of his nose, which looked as if it had been broken in a bar fight but hadn't.

Gabe shared those traits with his father, and so did Sam. How had he missed them the first time he'd seen the kid?

How had Carrie?

As he looked away from the laptop, shaking his head, he felt awash in regret. The physical markers weren't the only things Gabe had passed on to his son. He'd given him more. A childhood without a father. A parent who acted as if his son didn't exist. Gabe had given young Sam those things, just like Sammy Gold had given them to Gabe. The only difference was that Gabe hadn't even known he had a son. Given the choice, he would have raised his son, loved him, taught him all he knew.

But Gabe hadn't been given the choice. It had been taken from him. And as angry as Carrie was, she had to know she was the one who'd taken it. He had as much right to be angry as she did. More.

And yet he wasn't. Couldn't be. God, if he'd had to handpick a mother for his son, he couldn't have chosen better than Carrie. She adored Sam. How could he be angry when she'd raised his boy so damn well?

He shut the laptop down, and decided he had let her cool off long enough. It was getting on toward dinnertime. She should be home. He wasn't going to call first, because that would make it too easy for her to hang up on him. He was just going to go over there and sit her down and make her talk to him. He didn't intend to give her a choice. He had the right to know his son, and she had no right to keep the truth from the boy. Or from him.

At 6:00 p.m. Gabe found himself standing outside Carrie Overton's front door with a heat-preserving take-out bag in his left hand and a big fat bottle of hard lemonade in his right. His righteous indignation had taken a backseat to common sense. You caught more flies with honey and all that. And there was the small matter of his attraction to her. More than attraction. He liked the woman. More than liked. Hell, maybe if he could just get that through to her . . .

She opened the door, and looked from him to the bottle to the take-out bag, then back to him again. "I figured you'd bring a lawyer, not dinner."

He stood there and let his eyes drink in the sight of her. All her long, curly red hair was spilling loose tonight. She was wearing yoga pants and a tiny, tight-fitting T-shirt, with thick cushy socks. She was dressed for comfort, and yet she was sexy as hell.

"It was either this or flowers and chocolate. And frankly, I thought a solid meal would do us both more good."

She stepped aside to let him in. "Flowers and candy are overrated anyway."

"Yeah, and so are lawyers." He walked inside, all the way through to the kitchen, and set the bag on the table. "The fire department was having a chicken barbecue," he said. "I could smell it for two miles before I got there."

She leaned in the kitchen doorway, watching him as he got plates from the cupboard and unpacked the large white bag. He felt nervous, as if *he* were the one who'd been keeping secrets and telling lies for sixteen years, when he'd only been doing so for a week. He took out cardboard containers holding tiny salt potatoes and corn on the cob, all locally grown.

"So is this some kind of a bribe?" she asked.

He looked up. “No. It’s some kind of a meal.” He slid huge brown-skinned chicken pieces onto the two dinner plates, yanked a handful of paper towels from the roll and sat down. “You gonna eat?”

She crossed her arms over her chest and stared at him. “What are you doing, Gabe?”

“Having dinner.”

“You know what I mean. Why are you . . . being friendly? What are you up to?”

Gabe sighed, lowering his head. “Look, what’s the point in fighting? We are where we are, so we can deal with it like reasonable people or like total jerks. But nothing will change the basic truth. We’ll still be where we are.” He lifted his head. “We have some talking to do, Carrie. There’s no way around it. I figured, why not do it over a nice dinner? That’s all.”

She nodded slowly, pushing herself away from the wall. “I expected you to be furious. To march in here demanding your rights.”

“Well, I’m not. That’s not who I am. If you’ve been paying attention at all, you should already know that.”

“Oh, I’ve been paying attention. I just thought maybe I was seeing what you wanted me to see and not who you really are.”

"Well, you were seeing *me.* I don't play games. I know it seems like that's what was going on, but I'm telling you, I don't do that shit. This just got . . . it got away from me."

Studying him, at first warily and then with growing interest in her eyes, she sat down at the table and started eating.

"Should we save some for Sam?" he asked.

She averted her eyes a little. "I talked him into going camping after all. He left before noon."

He met her eyes. "You wanted to keep him away from me until we'd hashed this out."

She nodded but had the sense to look guilty about it. "I told him the truth myself. I didn't want you blurting it out to him until I'd had a chance to explain."

"I wouldn't have done that, Carrie."

She met his eyes, held them, and in a moment her brows bent closer. "I really don't think you would have, would you?" He shook his head, and she went on. "Still, I thought if word got out there would be another media circus. So I told him everything and asked him to give me this weekend to try to work things out. I just didn't want him here if all hell broke loose again."

"I don't see any reason why it should," he said.

She frowned and picked at her chicken. "So you want to talk this out, huh?"

"I don't think we have a choice. Do you?"

Sighing, she lowered her head. "No, so . . . Okay. We'll talk. Tell me about you and Sam's birth mother."

"I was going to ask *you* to tell *me* about her," he said.

She shook her head, her red curls bouncing. He wanted to touch them but held back.

"I barely know anything about her," she said. "Besides, this was your idea. You go first." Sitting back in her chair, she ate some chicken, and despite the conversation's seriousness, seemed to appreciate the flavor. How could she not? Gabe wondered. It was mouthwateringly good.

He finished chewing, then wiped his mouth with a paper towel and reached for the bottle of hard lemonade. "All right, I'll go first." He twisted off the cap and filled their glasses. "Livvy was a mess. A train wreck. And I tend to be . . . drawn to train wrecks."

Carrie lifted her brows.

"Until I met you, I mean. I've been pretty shocked at the chemistry between us from the very beginning, Carrie. I have to be honest about that. You're far from my type."

"You're the polar opposite of mine."

He smiled. "I met Livvy one summer when I was camping on a deserted patch of shoreline on the Gulf of Mexico. I was strumming my guitar beside a little campfire, and she just came walking along the beach and stopped to say hello."

"She just saw some stranger living out of his van on the beach and stopped to say hello?"

He shrugged. "Actually, she was looking to score some drugs, and she wasn't too fussy about what kind. I had a bottle of wine and offered to share it. And she wound up staying the night. When she didn't leave, I started thinking maybe I could . . . save her. Fix her."

Carrie frowned. "Did she ask you to?"

"No. No, it was my own knight-in-shining-armor complex kicking in. I know it's a flaw. But knowing it and beating it are two different things. She told me she'd been in a psych ward in Galveston just before I met her — she'd made a suicide attempt. I just . . . I wanted to save her. So I found a little beach house for rent, and we moved in there together. White sand, green water, summer sun. It was beautiful. And for a while, so were we."

"I imagine you were. So she stayed off

drugs while she was with you?"

He nodded slowly, his mind seeing her pretty face, her slightly dull eyes, her far too thin frame. "But she was drinking all the time, so I don't imagine there's too much difference."

"Substance abuse is substance abuse," Carrie said. "And an addict is an addict."

He nodded. "I wanted to save her. She didn't want to be saved."

"They rarely do. When did you figure it out?" she asked.

"She stayed with me through that summer and fall, and into the winter. Then one day — in January, it was — she left to run some errands and just never came back. I had no idea she was pregnant. And until a few weeks ago, no idea she'd died only a few months after I'd last seen her." He looked at Carrie, searched her face. "That's it. That's all of it. Though I'd like to know what happened to her between the time she left me and the time she died. I'd like to know a lot of things."

"Did you love her?" Carrie asked softly.

He sighed. "I think I loved the idea of who she could be. I think I had an image of her clean and sober and healthy and happy. But she wasn't any of those things. In hindsight, I started to realize she'd probably been using the entire time we were together. She was a pessimist. She was a fatalist, actually. So no, I was in love with a fantasy of who she could have become. I didn't love who she really was. To tell the truth, I didn't even like her all that much. And I think that's really sad. That I was so focused on who I thought she could become that I didn't even notice who she was until she was gone."

Carrie nodded. "I'm afraid I can't tell you much about her, either," she said. "But I can tell you what I know."

"That would mean a lot to me."

She nodded. "I'm not a rule breaker. I'm so by the book, my nickname at the hospital is Anal Annie."

He chuckled, and she sent him a look that made him put a lid on it.

"I was on my way to my first real job as a doctor, here in Shadow Falls, when I came upon a car on the side of the road, and a very pregnant, very distressed woman standing beside it," she began.

And she went on to tell him the story of the night she'd met Livvy Dupree, alone and about to give birth, along the side of a deserted road. She told him about her own defective fallopian tubes, a secret only her own ob-gyn knew. The doctor she went to see in the next town assumed Sam was adopted and had never probed further. Why would she?

Carrie said that Livvy had left her a note, a note she had kept all this time, because it was the only real evidence she had that Livvy had wanted Carrie to raise her son. She told Gabe that she'd intended to track the girl down again, get her to sign papers making Sam hers by private, legal adoption, but that before she ever found her, Livvy's body was on a table in Carrie's morgue, misidentified — though she didn't know it at the time — as Sarah Quinlan.

Carrie had been forced to make note of the signs of a recent pregnancy when she'd performed the autopsy, but she'd tried to bury the information, glossing over it lightly, and when asked, she had insisted to the police that it was entirely believable that the girl had given the baby up for private adoption. Since there was no sign of a potential father, the case of the missing baby remained little more than a curiosity. A loose thread left dangling and forgotten.

Eventually Carrie finished her story by telling Gabe that she'd forged the paperwork to obtain a birth certificate, using the name of a midwife she'd worked with during her residency. The woman had specialized in home births and had retired to the Bahamas just before Carrie left town. No one had ever had cause to double-check. Why would they?

Gabe took it all in and found himself absurdly glad he'd decided to reserve judgment until he'd heard the entire story. He believed her, with no reason to doubt any part of what she'd said.

"Given all you've told me," he said when she'd finished, "I don't see how you could have done anything differently. Not without the risk of losing Sam. And I'm glad you didn't lose him, Carrie. You've done a beautiful job raising him."

"Thank you for that." She sighed. "I only learned that the dead girl wasn't really Sarah Quinlan a few weeks ago, when the rest of the world learned it, too. Then there was the reward, and the tabloids, and I've . . . I've just been living in fear ever since, worried that someone, somehow, would find out and try to take Sam away from me."

"He's old enough that his preferences would have to be taken into consideration, though," Gabe said.

"They might be. But they might not. Besides, for all I knew, he would be so angry with me for lying to him all these years that he wouldn't *want* to go on living here."

"You know better than that. He adores you."

She blinked back the moisture that had suddenly gathered in her eyes. "You're trying to comfort me, when you're the one who's been denied your son all this time."

"You really think he is? My son?"

She looked across the table at him. "Of course I do. And so do you. God, he looks just like you. I don't need DNA results to tell me that. I mean, we'll get them anyway. I took a swab from him this morning, in fact. But still . . . I don't think there's any doubt."

Gabe felt his lips curve slightly upward in pride as his chest swelled with the validation of what he'd already known in his heart to be true. Sam was his son. Even Carrie admitted it.

"What made you choose the name?" Gabe asked.

"Livvy. It was in her note. She didn't say why, just asked me to name him Sam. It was the only thing she asked of me, so naturally I honored the request."

He nodded slowly. "She knew about my . . . history."

"The superstar father who pretends you don't exist and writes enough checks to let him keep on pretending?"

"Yeah. She used to tell me to go find him, confront him, demand some answers. She thought we could find some way to build a relationship, I guess. I thought she was dead wrong, of course, but . . . I don't know. Maybe naming my son after my father was her way of trying to . . . plant a seed."

"A seed of healing. I can see that."

"She really wasn't all bad," he said. "She was messed up, but the girl had a heart bigger than the moon."

Carrie nodded. "See? You really *did* see her for who she was, and you *did* like her. And I know there was goodness in her, too. There had to be. Sam is too incredible to have come from anything less. Frankly, you must have seen something in her worth saving, or you wouldn't have tried so hard."

"I'll never regret it for a minute," he said. "She gave me Sam. Even if it took me this long to find him . . ." He broke off there, seeing the tears rising in Carrie's eyes.

She licked her dry lips, blinked against the moisture. "I could lose my license over this. But that doesn't mean a damn thing if I lose my son."

"You're not going to lose him," Gabe said. "But he's my son, too. I have rights, Carrie. If anything happened to you, I wouldn't have a leg to stand on without a huge court case and a lot of noise. Carrie, he's my *son.* Tell me you're not going to try to deny me the chance to be his father."

They sat facing each other across the table. He saw anger and fear warring for top spot in her eyes. He was frustrated and fast running out of patience. He'd been more than fair.

He looked at her, at her eyes and the way they sparked with the intensity of her emotions. He looked at the fullness of her lips and the way they trembled just a little. He looked at the rise and fall of her chest beneath those folded arms. He knew she wanted him, liked him, maybe more. Why was she being so damned stubborn?

None of Gabe's explanations, none of his answers, had told Carrie the one thing that was stuck in her craw like a two-inch thorn. And he ought to know what it was she needed to hear him say. She needed him to tell her that his feelings for her had nothing to do with Sam. That he wasn't just using her to get closer to his son, or trying to grease the wheels of an impending custody battle.

In fact, he probably did know that was what she needed to hear from him. That he was refusing to say it told her more than words could that his feelings for her were nothing. Less than nothing. An act. A big lie. And if he were lying to her about that, she couldn't trust him about anything else, could she? His promise that he would never want to take Sam away from her? Or that he would never want to come between the two of them? What did those words mean, coming from a man who would seduce her just to get to her son? A man who would try to make her fall for him? God, she'd been a fool. A blind, naive fool. Because she had fallen in love with this man, and what she wanted was to hear him tell her that he loved her, too. She was an idiot.

The phone started ringing before she thought of anything to say to him. She felt defeated, beaten, wounded and abused. "Excuse me," she managed, and she knew her voice sounded cold as ice.

He took a bite of chicken as she got up to answer. Bastard hadn't even lost his appetite over any of this. She couldn't have eaten another mouthful if she'd had to.

She picked up the cordless phone. "Hello?"

"Hey, Doc. It's Wes Haskins. Is Sam there?"

She blinked three times in quick succession. "No, Wes, he's camping out at the state park for the weekend. Actually, I thought you were going with him."

"I was. I mean, I am. I'm there now. Using the pay phone at the ranger station. No signal up here in the wilderness." He chuckled softly.

She wasn't laughing. "I don't understand. Why isn't he with you?"

"Oh, you didn't know? We were supposed to meet at Alley's, but he called and said for us to go on ahead, that he'd meet up with us later at the park. I just wondered if he had an ETA, 'cause we really thought he'd be here by now."

"He's not here," she said softly, and her eyes shifted to Gabe, sitting at the table. He read the look in them, frowned and got to his feet. "Last I saw of him, he was leaving the hospital and heading out to Alley's to meet you all. What exactly did Sam say when he called, Wes?"

"Said he needed to give a hand to a friend in trouble. Couldn't say no to a sweet little old lady."

"A sweet little old lady?" Again, Carrie met Gabe's eyes. "Thanks for calling, Wes. If you see him or hear from him, have him call me immediately. *Immediately,* do you understand?"

"Sure. But, Doc, they found out who the

kidnapper was, right? Mean old Mr. Kelly. I always knew he was an SOB. I mean, all that's over, right?"

"I hope so. Right now, though, I'm not so sure."

She put the phone down and shifted her gaze to the window, gazing across the driveway at the garage. Then she walked to the door.

Gabe was on her heels. "What's going on? Where's Sam?"

"He told the guys he had to help out a little old lady in trouble, and that he'd meet them at the park. That had to be around noon. But he never got there." She opened the door and stepped out onto the deck. Then she went down the stairs and walked steadily toward the garage. "Something's wrong. Rose's car isn't here," she said.

"Come on. *Rose?* You think *Rose* has done something to Sam? I thought you *liked* her."

"She paid me in cash. Did I tell you she paid me in cash?"

"What is that supposed to mean?" He put a hand on her shoulder. "Carrie, the case is over. No one's out there kidnapping innocent kids anymore. Nate Kelly was a monster, but he's dead. Your nerves must still be raw from all that's happened, and . . .

Carrie?"

She pulled free of his hand and crossed the driveway, then went up the stairs to the garage apartment. Taking the key she kept hidden under the shade of the outdoor light, she unlocked the door and went inside.

"I think you're overreacting," Gabe said.

"I don't really care what you think. I'm his mother. I know something's wrong."

"You should try calling him on his cell."

"Wes said he'd tried. No answer." Stepping inside, she gazed around the place, with the rock in the pit of her stomach growing heavier all the time. She walked into the bedroom, saw some books on the neatly made bed, some kind of scrapbook and . . .

"What the hell is she doing with this?" she asked, moving closer, flipping open the high school yearbook. "Good God, this is our school!" She turned pages rapidly, stopping at the group photo of her son's class. Several faces were circled in red ink, and two of them had Xs through the circles. Kyle and Sadie. Sam's face, though, had been circled, then circled again.

"Oh, my God," she breathed.

Gabe gasped from behind her, and he quickly flipped open the other book, a scrapbook filled with clippings from tabloid trash sheets and legitimate press sources alike — all about the sixteen-year-old murder and the mystery of the missing baby.

"Holy shit," he muttered. "I can't believe this. Who the hell is this woman, anyway?"

Carrie tucked the books under her arm and raced out of the apartment, across the driveway and back into her house. She grabbed her phone and hit the preprogrammed number for the hospital, then waited for someone at the nurses' station to pick up. By the third ring she was pacing rapidly, adrenaline surging so fast it was making her skin tingle. Finally someone answered, and she cut the woman off before she finished her well-practiced greeting.

"This is Carrie Overton. Has my son been in to see Sadie Gray?"

"Oh, hi, Dr. Overton. Yes, Sam was in today — oh, but you remember that. You were here, too. I think he left around lunchtime. Someone said he was going camping."

"What about after that?"

"No, Doctor. And Sadie's actually going home tonight instead of tomorrow, so he probably won't be back. Is anything wrong?"

Carrie lowered her head and pinched the bridge of her nose hard, squeezing her eyes tightly. "I think there might be." And then she hung up and dialed Bryan's home number, while Gabe paced to the windows, looking outside as if expecting to see Sam's giant red SUV come bouncing into the driveway at any moment. But Carrie had a sick feeling in the pit of her stomach that he wouldn't see anything of the sort.

Bryan picked up on the second ring, and she blurted her darkest fears without preamble.

"It wasn't Nate Kelly, Bryan. He wasn't the one."

"Carrie?" he asked. "What are you talking about?" Then, "You sound odd. Are you okay?"

A sob caught in her throat. Gabe came up behind her and put a hand on her shoulder. She forced the words out, words every parent secretly believed they would never have to utter. The last words she had ever imagined she would hear herself say.

"Bryan, Sam is gone. My son is missing."

And then she sank slowly to the floor, as if saying those words had taken the last ounce of strength she possessed. She felt Gabe pry the phone from her trembling, frozen grip, heard him speaking as if from a great distance, giving Bryan the details. But all she could see was an endless black hole opening up before her and sucking her inside.

"He's gone," she whispered. "Oh, God, he's gone, he's gone, he's gone. My baby's gone."

16

Gabe felt more helpless than he had ever felt in his life as he paced and waited for the police to arrive.

It was only ten minutes, maybe less, but it seemed like hours before Bryan Kendall showed up at the door. He had obviously been off duty when he'd taken Carrie's call, and he hadn't spent the extra time to put on a uniform. He arrived in street clothes, jeans and a sweater in deference to the chill in the air on a September night in Shadow Falls.

Carrie was shaking, pale, weepy, as she met him at the front door. She offered no greeting, just burst into rapid-fire speech. "I don't know what to do, Bryan. I don't know what to do. He was supposed to be camping, but —"

"Easy. Just tell me what happened. Start at the beginning. You said Sam was going camping this weekend."

She nodded. "Wes said he never showed up. He never showed up, and he didn't come home, either, and it had to be Rose. It had to be!"

She was on the edge of panic, Gabe thought, and he slid an arm around her shoulders, jumping in to try to clarify. "Sam was supposed to meet his friends at Alley's around noon. But one of them — Wes something —"

"Wesley Haskins?" Bryan asked.

Gabe looked at Carrie, who nodded jerkily and wiped her nose with a wad of tissues she had crumpled in her hand. "Tell him about Rose. Rose did this!"

"I'm getting to that, Carrie." Gabe went on. "Wes phoned here looking for Sam. Said he'd had a call from Sam telling them to go ahead to the park, that he'd meet them there later. Sam told him that he had to help a sweet little old lady in trouble."

"Sweet little old lady, my ass. I'll *kill* her if she's hurt my son!"

Bryan frowned at her, then turned back to Gabe for clarification. "Rose is the woman who's staying in the garage apartment," he said. "Her car is gone, and when we went up there, we found a high school yearbook with three faces circled, Kyle's, Sadie's and Sam's. Kyle and Sadie had Xs drawn through them."

"Shit," Bryan muttered. And then he said it again in dawning disbelief.

"There were clippings, too," Carrie blurted. "Clippings about the missing baby and the reward."

"Okay, okay." Bryan put a hand on her shoulder. "Look, the cavalry is here," he said, nodding toward the window, through which Gabe saw other police cars pulling to a stop. "Let me get them moving. I called Cooper, and he's on his way back. I've already put out an APB on Sam's car, and, honey, you know that thing is going to be easy to spot. It's practically one of a kind. What was this Rose driving?"

"An old station wagon," Carrie said.

"Ford, seventy-four or seventy-five," Gabe filled in. "I never saw it, but Sam told me about it. Brown, with wood-grain sides."

"You don't know the plate number by any chance, do you?"

"No." Gabe looked at Carrie, but she, too, answered in the negative.

"They were Vermont plates, though," she said. "I did notice that much."

"What's this Rose's last name?" Bryan asked.

Carrie frowned and lowered her head. "McQueen, or so she told me. And she paid me in cash, said she'd left her checkbook at home or something. God, why wasn't I suspicious of her then?"

"Because who would be suspicious of a sweet little old lady?" Gabe asked. "It still seems pretty hard to believe, if you ask me."

Bryan nodded. "I'm still not sure this isn't more than a misunderstanding. Sam is probably out somewhere and just forgot to call, or —"

As quick as a cobra striking, Carrie had him by the front of his shirt and was right up in his face. "My son is *missing,* Bryan, and *that woman* has him. Don't you *dare* write this off as an irresponsible teenager's latest stunt, because that's not what it is. It wasn't with Kyle and it's not with Sam."

"Hey, hey, c'mon, Carrie, it's me. You know I'm taking this seriously. I *like* Sam."

He held her gaze for one long moment, then looked down at her hand on the front of his shirt.

Swallowing hard, Carrie relaxed her grip and backed off. Bryan headed out the door and down the steps to speak with the cops in the driveway below. She watched as several of them headed over to the garage apartment, no doubt to search it for clues. Gabe saw Bryan Kendall get on his cell phone and knew everything humanly possible would be done to find Sam.

He just hoped to God it would be enough.

Carrie looked at him, her eyes red and wet and all but lifeless. "I should tell him the rest of it," she said. "That Sam is the missing baby from the tabloids, that I've been keeping that secret all this time. That you're probably his father."

"And how would that help?" he asked.

"I don't know. I just . . . I don't know what to do."

"Lean on me, Carrie," he said. "Let's put our differences aside — although as far as I'm concerned, we don't have any, but I know in your mind we do. So put them aside for right now and let's try our best to help each other through this. We'll get him back. But we need to be strong, sharp, alert. We have to do all the right things, not make any mistakes now. And we're more likely to mess up if we give in to panic and fear and grief."

She met his eyes.

"Just forget everything else except this," he said softly. "You're his mother. I'm his father. We both love him, and we'll both do anything we have to do to get him back. Nothing else matters right now."

She lifted her chin a little higher, nodded hard. "Okay."

"Good."

Footsteps on the front deck made them both turn just as the door opened and Bryan came back inside. "We sent a car out to Alley's when you first called, and they've already called in. There's a car matching the description of Rose's station wagon parked along Old Route Six, a mile from the ice-cream place. We're heading out there now."

"We're going, too," Gabe said. He closed a hand around hers as he asked, "Just a car? No . . . people?"

"Just a car," Bryan said. "Come on, you can ride with me."

"We'll drive. That way we can take off if we need to," Gabe said. "You ready, Carrie?"

She nodded, a quick, jerky movement, then turned, looking blankly around the kitchen. "I need my phone. In case he calls. It's in my bag. Where's my bag?"

"I'll get it." Gabe knew where the bag was. It was on a hook by the door, where it always was. Her confusion told him more than anything how hard this was hitting her. Not that he'd needed any evidence of that. He knew she loved Sam enough to die for him. He'd never doubted that at all.

■ ■ ■ ■

Rose's station wagon sat on the side of the road. Nothing was wrong with it — nothing readily apparent, at least. The keys were gone, and she'd left nothing inside it to tell the tale of where she was. Bryan's police issue SUV was pulled up behind the station wagon. The other police vehicle sat just ahead of it, lights flashing. Gabe had pulled his VW Bus to a stop behind Bryan's SUV, and they had stayed in the vehicle, listening through the open window to the cops talking. He glanced at Carrie now. She still had that dazed look in her eyes. She hadn't spoken a word the entire trip.

"Are you okay?"

She shook her head.

He wished to God there was something he could do to erase the fear from her eyes, but there wasn't. She was in hell, and he wasn't far behind.

Bryan leaned in the window. "It's registered to a Maxwell Walters from Burlington. We're trying to contact him now. Meanwhile, I need a physical description of Rose McQueen."

He looked at Gabe as he said it, probably thinking he was more capable of a coherent answer than Carrie at that point. Gabe could only shake his head. "I've never seen the woman."

"Carrie?" Bryan prompted.

"Sweet," she said. "Bright smile. Even white teeth. Snowy-white hair. A couple of inches shorter than me, so . . . five two, five three. Maybe a hundred and forty or forty-five pounds."

"That's really good, Carrie. How old?"

She shrugged. "Mid-to-late-sixties."

Bryan narrowed his eyes. "It's less and less likely this is another abduction," he said. "How's a little old lady going to dart and then move a sixteen-year-old? An unconscious one, at that. Deadweight."

"Bryan —" Carrie began, but he kept on talking.

"Sadie hit this person upside the head with an iron eyebolt before she made her escape," he said. "When did you last see Rose?"

"This morning. I took her some cinnamon buns."

"Did you see any sign of a head injury?"

"No." Carrie clearly didn't like admitting it. "But it could have been hidden by her hair."

"Maybe she was an accomplice," Gabe suggested. "I mean, she would almost have to be working with someone else, if she did this. How do we know she wasn't working with Nate Kelly?"

"We're not ruling anything out." But Bryan clearly thought they were reaching. Still, even he couldn't ignore the existence of that yearbook and all those news clippings.

Carrie stared straight ahead, not meeting Bryan's eyes, and deliberately not looking too closely at the station wagon. "They've searched the entire car? There's no sign of . . ."

"No sign of anything, hon," Bryan said. "Not a struggle, not a body, no blood, no weapons, nothing like that."

She nodded, then refocused, turning her head to scan the gently rolling meadow along the roadside, and the creek beyond. "We should look out there."

"Right now we're looking for Sam's Expedition. Tire tracks suggest someone in a large truck or SUV pulled over near this car, then left again."

"You should get fingerprints, run them, see if Rose is wanted for anything else," Gabe suggested.

Bryan looked irritated. "We're way ahead of you on that. We have a team out at the apartment gathering evidence, and they'll be here next. We'll know pretty much right away, once we get the prints back to the station, whether there were any matches. We'll have all that before the night is out."

"I want my son back before the night is out," Carrie muttered.

"I know you do, Carrie. I know you do."

"Kendall!" one of the cops shouted. He was leaning against his vehicle, a radio mike in his hand. "We've got a location on the Expedition!"

"Where?" Bryan shouted back.

"The pull-off by the top of the falls."

"All right." Bryan turned back toward Gabe, but Gabe was already putting the VW into Reverse. He backed up ten feet, then pulled a U-turn and pressed his foot to the accelerator.

Moments later, a police vehicle came screaming up behind him, lights flashing, and then it passed him as if he were standing still. Bryan, in his SUV, trying to beat him and Carrie to the scene. Which didn't bode well. Gabe wondered if the cop expected to find something bad, something Carrie would be better off not seeing.

When he looked at Carrie's stricken face, he knew she was wondering the same thing.

"Try not to expect the worst," he said. "It'll only make it more likely to happen."

She shot him a sideways glance. "Is that part of your *we create our own reality* philosophy?"

"Yeah. It is."

"So tell me, Yoda, what did I do to create this? What did Kyle do to create what happened to him? What did Sammy do to get himself kidnapped, huh? Tell me that. You think anyone *wanted* any of this?"

"I never said you get what you want. I said you get what you expect. What you fear, what you focus on. Shouting 'I want that' at something is the same as shouting 'I don't want that.' You're creating it by your attention to it. Period."

"It's bullshit."

"You think?"

"I *know.* I didn't create my son being taken from me. My secret coming out."

"No, but you feared it. For sixteen years you've been worrying about that secret coming out. About losing Sam. You can't pay that much attention to something and not draw it straight to you."

"So if I lose him now, it's my fault? Is that what you're saying?"

"Of course not, Carrie. You didn't know." He licked his lips, knew it wasn't the time to say it, then said it anyway. "But now you do, so don't you think you'd better start thinking about getting him back? Focusing on that? Creating that?"

She stared at him. "I think I hate you right now."

"No you don't," he said. "But if it makes you feel better, go ahead and think it. It's better than feeling powerless."

Gabe turned, following the now-distant cop car onto a dirt track that writhed up a mountainside. And then, near what seemed to be the very precipice, he spotted it: the giant red, shiny SUV parked in the pull-off that overlooked the gorgeous, if slightly ominous — especially now — Shadow Falls. Every cell in him filled with dread, and he glanced at Carrie. "I'm sorry. Even I'm having trouble expecting the best right now. But I'm trying, Carrie. I'm trying. Sam is fine. He's fine, and he's coming home, and — what the hell is that?" He pointed. Something — no, some*one* — had just staggered out of the woods and collapsed in the grass by the parking area.

"It's Rose!" Carrie wrenched her door open before Gabe had even brought the van to a full stop. She was lunging out of the car and running for the woman, who had dropped down onto all fours, her head down, her snowy hair littered with brambles and leaves.

"What have you done with him!" Carrie demanded, even as Gabe and Bryan both surged after her. Gabe didn't know what Bryan was thinking, but his own dread stemmed from the worry that she might do the older woman bodily harm.

"What have you done with my son, you lying, scheming bitch!"

Gabe couldn't catch Carrie, but Bryan managed to lunge into her path just as she reached for the other woman. He caught her shoulders and held her off, as Gabe came running up behind.

"That's her!" Carrie shouted, fighting to get past the police officer. "That's Rose McQueen!"

Gabe looked past them at the woman on the ground, a sickening feeling rising in his stomach as the woman lifted her head slowly. There was a gash in her forehead, trickling blood. Her clothes were torn, her face scratched, and he thought she might have a black eye. But even with all that, there was no way he could fail to recognize her.

"Gabriel . . ." She lifted a hand toward him as he shook free of his stunned paralysis, moved forward and bent to help her. He was still reeling with shock.

"Where is my son, Rose? Where is he?"

Carrie cried, still fighting against Bryan Kendall's death grip on her.

"Her name's not Rose McQueen," Gabe said softly. His hands were on the older woman's frail shoulders, and he was helping her up. She'd made it onto her knees, but she was shaking and crying and clinging to him. "It's Roseanna," he went on. "Rose-anna Cain."

The frail woman wrapped her arms around his waist and laid her head against his chest. Gabe kept his hands on her shoulders, not hugging her back, but not quite cruel enough to push her away. He felt the others' eyes on him and turned to see Bryan staring at him. Carrie had stopped her struggling and gone still, her eyes filled with disbelief and confusion as she, too, stared at him.

"Cain?" she whispered.

Gabe nodded. "She's my mother."

17

Sammy opened his eyes, his brain foggy and his mind dull. But he knew something was very, *very* wrong, and he knew that he couldn't afford to stay asleep.

There was a sense of motion, and he realized he was lying on his back inside a moving vehicle. The surface beneath him was hard, though. More like a floor than a seat. And the ride was rough. It was completely dark, and he smelled something pretty pungent. Not exhaust, though.

He tried to move his hands to feel around himself as a suspicion took shape in the mists of his mind, and he found his hands tied together. He lifted them as one and touched the ceiling of his prison, only a foot above him.

His suspicion had been right. He was in the trunk of a car. The kidnapper had him. The same one who'd killed Kyle. The same one who'd taken Sadie. It hadn't been grumpy old Nate Kelly after all. Sam's breath came faster, and his heart began to pound in his chest, but he gave himself a mental shake. Sadie had gotten away. If she could do it, so could he.

He wasn't gagged, but he didn't think yelling would do him a hell of a lot of good right now. Who would hear him besides the killer driving the car? And why tip that bastard off that he was awake?

He had to think. And the first thing he tried to think about was how he had wound up here. He remembered stopping to help Rose, and that she'd asked him to take her up to the falls before taking her home. Just for a few minutes, she'd said. She didn't want to leave town without seeing the waterfall, but she was afraid to traverse such a winding, remote route all alone, especially now that her car was acting up.

He remembered thinking it wasn't all that much to ask. He remembered thinking how she had organized that candlelight vigil for Sadie, and that he ought to show her how much he appreciated that. So he drove her up there, even though he was going to be even later meeting his friends than he'd intended.

Rose had been thrilled, though. And she'd promised not to linger long. They got out of

The Beast and walked over to the path that began at the edge of the pull-off. Sam had promised her that it wasn't far to the best view, then led her over the meandering trail some fifty yards through the woods to the spot where the trees parted like curtains on a stage. There was a steep drop at the edge, but the town had erected a low barricade to keep people from walking over the edge in the dark. The view from this spot was just awesome, because you were standing practically on top of the falls' very crest. Below, and forty-five degrees to the left, the waterfall shot out from its rocky riverbed and tumbled some ninety feet to the frothy, violent pool below before rushing onward once more. As they stood there admiring the cascade, Rose said there was something she had been wanting to talk to him about.

And then he heard a sickening, smacking sound that made him jump, and Rose crumpled to the ground right beside him. Just like that. One heartbeat and bam. He saw a black crowbar lying beside her, felt a presence, but before he could even turn the rest of the way around to look, a pair of arms encircled him from behind and a wet rag was smashed into his face. It stank, and a single word floated into his mind.

Chloroform.

■ ■ ■ ■

"I was out cold, I think," Rose said, "after he hit me with — whatever it was he hit me with."

Her voice was trembling, and Gabe felt as if he were bleeding inside. His mother was sitting in the backseat of Bryan Kendall's SUV, holding a cold pack from the cop's first aid kit to her cheek, recounting the tale of how she'd had car trouble and asked Sam to drive her home, with a brief detour up here to see the falls.

Gabe didn't believe a word of her story, but he needed to hear it to the end. Give her enough rope to hang herself. Eventually, he was sure, she would. Not that he thought she'd had a thing to do with the abduction of two — now three, he thought with a shudder — teens. Much less the murder of one of them. But he knew her too well to think she wasn't here for a reason — or, more accurately, five hundred thousand reasons.

"I managed to get to my feet," Rose went on. "And I realized I could hear someone moving, so I ran back along the trail, the way we'd come. I glimpsed someone walking, with Sam flung over his shoulder."

"Oh, God," Carrie whispered. "Was he . . . ?"

"I don't know. He wasn't moving. Wasn't . . . conscious." Rose's eyes pleaded with Carrie's as they filled with tears. "God, I never meant for this to happen. You have to believe me." Her desperate gaze moved from Carrie's face to Gabe's.

"Just finish the story, Mother."

She sniffled, and Bryan handed her a tissue. "I ran after them. I saw the man putting Sammy into the trunk of a car, and I just — I didn't know what to do. I shouted at him to stop. I ran as fast as I could at him. I don't even know what I thought I was going to do! But he slammed the trunk and turned, and then he came right up to me and . . . Oh, God, I was so scared. I was petrified. I started to back away. And that's when he punched me. He actually *punched* me, hard, right in the face." She moved the cold pack away, shaking her head slowly and wincing at the movement.

"You said it was a man who hit you and took Sam," Bryan said. "Can you tell me what he looked like?"

She shook her head. "He wore a black ski mask."

"Then how do you know it was a man?"

She frowned. "I don't know how. I just

do. Maybe from how easily he carried Sammy. Maybe from how hard he could hit." She grimaced and lowered her head, eyes blinking rapidly as tears filled them.

"What about his hands, his clothes?" Bryan prompted.

She frowned hard, shaking her head, blowing her nose as gently as she could. "I don't know, I don't know. I think he wore gloves." She nodded. "Yes, gloves. Black ones. I don't remember his clothes. That black ski mask held my attention."

"All right then, what about the car?"

She tilted her head to one side. "It was silver. An ordinary-looking silver car."

"New or old?" Bryan asked.

"It seemed like a fairly new model."

"Was there anything about it that you noticed? A logo? A bumper sticker? A dent?"

She blinked, frowned, and it seemed to Gabe that everyone held their breath as they awaited her answer. When she only sighed and shook her head, the disappointment was palpable.

"All right," Bryan said. "Now, we're going to have to know why you lied about your name when you came here — when you rented the apartment from Carrie."

She lifted her eyes, and her expression was all innocence. "I didn't want my son to know I was here . . . not until I was ready. Gabe and I . . . we're somewhat estranged. I knew he was coming here, and I just thought this would be a beautiful place, a beautiful time, to try to patch things up with him. But then, when I got here, I got scared he'd send me packing. So I gave a false name, so he wouldn't find out I was in town until I was ready. I was working up my courage, but mostly thinking about chucking the whole idea and heading home without ever seeing him or letting him know I had even been here."

Bryan studied her, nodding, and looking for all the world, Gabe thought, as if he believed her. Gabe knew better. She was lying through her perfect, expensive, white teeth.

"And the yearbook we found among your things?" Bryan asked. "Why were the faces of all the victims circled?"

She seemed to search inwardly for an answer. "I guess I got caught up in that missing baby story like everyone else. Those were my guesses for who it could be. I —" She closed her eyes. "I . . . I'm going to faint."

A siren blurted briefly to announce the ambulance that came trundling up the dirt road and into the pull-off. Several official police vehicles came behind it.

Bryan spoke firmly to Rose. “You need to go to the hospital and get checked out. You’ve got some pretty nasty injuries. I’ll be by later to talk to you some more. I don’t want you leaving town, Mrs. Cain.”

“It’s Miss,” she corrected.

Bryan nodded at her and turned to Gabe. “You can go with her if you want.”

Gabe met Carrie’s eyes, and saw that they were filled with anger. At him or at his mother? Maybe both of them.

“We don’t need the ambulance,” Gabe said. “Carrie and I will drive her in.”

Bryan spoke up quickly. “I don’t think that’s —”

“I’m a doctor,” Carrie said. “She couldn’t be safer.”

“Yeah, and I couldn’t be more likely to lose my badge.”

“She’s my mother,” Gabe said. “I’m not going to let anything happen to her.”

“It’s all right,” said “Rose.” “I’ll ride with them.” And she started limping toward the VW Bus.

Chloroform. Yeah, that was what Sam smelled now in the trunk of the car. He brought his bound hands to his face to try to wipe it clean, realizing that traces of the stuff had probably clung to his lips, his face. He didn't need to be inhaling that shit and getting woozy again. He spat on his hands and scrubbed at his face some more, then tried to wipe his hands on the carpeted floor of the trunk.

In the process, he discovered that his hands were bound with duct tape, not rope, so he brought them back up to his mouth and, locating an edge, started working on the tape with his teeth.

His ankles were bound, too, he realized, but if he could get his hands free, they would be no problem.

Okay, so he would get himself free; that was step one. And he would stay alive; that was step two. And then, step three, he would get away. Alive. He *would.*

God, his mother must be going ballistic by now. There was no doubt in Sam's mind that she would know he was missing in short order. She was too protective not to check up on him and learn that he had never made it to the park. He wondered how long he had been unconscious. He wondered if poor Rose was okay, and he hoped to God the bastard hadn't killed her when he'd hit her with that crowbar. Damn, he was in a mess.

But if there was one thing Sam knew about, it was cars. Maybe he could find the trunk release and get himself free. Maybe.

It might just be his only chance. He didn't know what kind of car he was in. Still, there was a good chance he could get out. He tore at the duct tape with his teeth while he ran through the next step in his mind, his eyes straining in the dark, trying to see. If there was an inside trunk release, it could be a T-handle attached to a short length of cable, or it might be a button. It would probably be brightly or at least lightly colored, to make it stand out. He got his wrists free, then struggled to reach his ankles and began tearing the tape from them, as well.

Finally unbound, he felt around the inside of the trunk, almost giving up, until something yellow caught his dark-adapted eye. He reached for it. A T-shaped yellow handle. That had to be the release!

They hit a bump, and he was jarred so forcefully he let go. The vehicle continued to bounce over rough terrain, and it was moving slower than before.

Sam quickly located the T-handle again, and this time he managed to hold on long enough to give it a solid yank.

The trunk popped loose, and he grabbed the edge of the lid before it rose too far and gave him away. Twisting onto his side, he peered out. He didn't see pavement or road stripes or other vehicles. He saw darkness — night had fallen. He saw the red glow of the car's taillights. He saw what looked like grass and weeds rolling away behind them, rather than blacktop or gravel.

They weren't even on a road.

He drew a breath and prepared himself to dive out of the car and run for his life. But just when he began to move, about to do just that, the car braked hard, rocking to an abrupt stop and hurling him to the front of the trunk, where he hit hard.

He heard the driver's door slam, and before he could even think of what to do, the trunk lid rose high, and a human shape, just a shade darker than the night around it, stood staring in at him.

"You're smart. Like me. I guess that's one more piece of the puzzle, isn't it, Sam?"

"I don't know what you're talking about." Sam narrowed his eyes, straining to see the man's face in the darkness. The taillights no longer glowed. He must have shut the car off.

There was something familiar about his voice.

"It doesn't matter," the man said. "We're here. Come on, climb out."

Seeing no point in arguing, Sam climbed out of the trunk and stood facing the man.

And then, finally, his eyes adjusted enough to let him see the man's face.

Blinking in shock, he said, "Ambrose?"

"Come on. Come with me and quit trying to delay the inevitable."

Those words sent a chill through Sam that he hadn't felt before. He was more afraid now than ever. Because this *was* Ambrose. Just not the Ambrose he knew. No awkward, almost shy attitude. This guy was confident, cocky, aggressive. Dangerous. He gripped Sam's upper arm, jerking him forward and leading him around the car.

Just ahead stood a small hunting cabin. It was too dark to tell much, other than that it was built of logs and its roof was sagging noticeably. As his captor tugged him toward it, Sam said, "Ambrose, I don't understand what's happening here. What do you want with me?"

"Isn't it obvious, Sam?" Ambrose said. "I'm your father."

"You want to tell me the truth, now, Mother?" Gabe asked.

Rose — Roseanna, Carrie corrected inwardly — held the ice pack to her face and said nothing. The woman was sitting in the backseat of the VW Bus while Gabe drove and Carrie sat in the passenger seat beside him.

Now she turned in her seat to face the older woman. "Come on, tell us. And don't hold anything back. Sam is my life, and you might do well to remember that I'm the doctor who'll be taking care of you in the E.R."

Gabe glanced at her with stark surprise on his face. "Easy, Carrie."

"Shut up, Gabe. She got my son kidnapped, at the very least. Frankly, I'm not sure she wasn't involved. And neither of you seem to be too familiar with honesty."

"I've told you the truth, Carrie. And he's my son, too."

"He is?" Rose leaned forward in her seat. "I *knew* it. I just knew it was Sam. It had to be. He looks just like you did, Gabe. Those dimples, the birthmark, those eyes."

"Stop talking about my son!" Carrie barked. She climbed out of her seat and into the back to sit beside Roseanna and saw Gabe tense, saw him watching in the rearview mirror. "The only thing I want to hear coming from that lying mouth of yours is what the hell you know about this that you didn't tell the police."

Roseanna nodded hard. "I know it looks bad. I do. I just . . . When I read that Livvy

— the woman Gabe once lived with — had been dead for sixteen years, and that she'd had a child right before she'd been murdered . . . I just had to know if that child was Gabe's. The timing fit so perfectly. Don't you see? I *had* to know. He's my *grandson,* Carrie."

"What brought you to this town? What brought you to Sam?"

"I hired a private investigator. I used a false name. I paid him — *a lot* — and I might as well tell you, I'm the one who offered the reward, as well."

"The reward that got Kyle killed, you mean," Carrie asked her.

"We don't know for sure the reward was the motive, Carrie," Gabe reminded her. "We do know now that it wasn't Nate Kelly."

"We only know it wasn't him alone," Carrie said. "His time of death fits."

"It might not have been him at all," Gabe insisted. "And we have no idea what Sam's abductor's motive is, seeing as the reward's been withdrawn. Even if it was the money in the beginning, there was no way my mother could have known *that* would happen."

Carrie ignored him. "What did this P.I. find out for you?"

The old woman sighed. "That there were only a handful of sixteen-year-olds with May or June birthdays in this town. I managed to get my hands on a copy of the school yearbook, and I knew as soon as I saw Sam that he was Gabe's son." She lowered her head, her face crumpling as she wept openly. "God, please let him be all right."

"He'd better be."

"I only wanted to spend some time with him," she muttered through her tears. "I wasn't even going to tell him. I just wanted to spend some time —" she sniffled "— with my grandson. You told me, Carrie, that he was meeting his friends at that ice-cream place and going camping for the weekend, and I just wanted a chance to see him before he left. I thought I might have to leave before he got back. So I went out there, and I waited for him, and I told him I had car trouble. I asked him to take me up to the falls. And now . . ." She choked back a sob, then lifted her head again.

"I knew Kyle wasn't Gabe's boy as soon as I saw him. He looks nothing like either Gabe or Livvy. So that left Sadie or Sammy. And even though I felt right to my toes that Sam was the one, I wasn't sure. At least not until I saw Sadie's mother — she looks just like her."

"She looks like her minus years of alcohol ravaging her health," Carrie said softly. Incredibly, she found herself starting to believe the woman.

"I couldn't tell the police all of that — not without giving away your secret, Carrie. And despite what you might think of me, I didn't come here to ruin your life or your career. I only wanted to get to know my grandson, not to challenge you for him. At least, not once I saw what a good mother you were." She sighed. "I was stunned to find you in town, too, Gabe."

"I knew you hadn't come just to see me," Gabe said. "At least that explains why you had the yearbook, with the faces circled."

"All the prospects were circled, then crossed off as I ruled them out."

Carrie looked into the front seat, met Gabe's eyes in the mirror. "And you honestly didn't know she was the one who'd offered that reward? Or that she was here in town?"

"I swear, I didn't know. I'd have sent her packing if I had. And that reward — hell, I thought she was trying to collect it, not pay it out."

"I didn't know it might become a possible motive for a killer," Rose said slowly. "I withdrew it as soon as I found out. God, I've messed everything up so badly that I don't know how I'll ever make it right."

Carrie shook her head. "If you're not telling me everything, I swear to God, Rose . . ."

"It's everything. I swear. Except that I've been deliberately avoiding running into Gabe ever since I realized he was here."

Gabe was turning the car, pulling into the hospital parking lot, maneuvering slowly toward the E.R. entrance. "I still don't understand what your motives were, Mom," Gabe said. "If you were the one offering the reward, then you weren't after the money. So what *were* you after? The notoriety? The fame?"

Roseanna lowered her head as the car came to a stop at the E.R. doors. "I don't expect you to believe me, Gabe. But I wanted to know my grandson. I wanted . . . to have the kind of relationship with him that I never had with you. And . . . and I guess that when I realized you had been denied your own son, denied even knowing you had one all these years, I saw my own actions in a different light."

"As much as I dislike the deal you made with my birth father," Gabe said, "he wasn't denied the chance to know me. You can't take the blame for that."

"No, Gabe. You don't underssssstann . . ."

Carrie frowned at the woman, first because of what she'd said, and then because of the odd slur in her voice as she'd said it. She saw that Roseanna's mouth was slack on one side and shouted, "Gabe, forget this! We need to get her inside *now!*"

She dived out of the bus and ran to the E.R. doors, pushing them open and shouting, "I've got a head injury with a possible bleed! I need a gurney and an O.R., STAT! Someone page a neurologist. This patient is stroking out. Move!"

Then she turned to run back outside again, only to see Gabe, his mother's unconscious body in his arms, on the other side of the doorway. "What happened to her?" he asked.

"I think there's a bleed in her brain." A nurse wheeled up a stretcher, and he lowered his mother onto it. "Pressure might be building up under her skull," Carrie went on, following as the gurney was rolled into a treatment room. "We need to get her into surgery immediately to relieve the pressure and stop the bleeding." She turned to the nurse. "You get hold of a neurologist?"

"Chelsea's on the phone with Dr. Kramer. They're getting an O.R. ready upstairs.

CT is ready for her now. I'll take her."

"I'll be right down."

"Will she live?" Gabe asked, as the nurse began to wheel his mother away.

Carrie blinked at the woman, unable to take her eyes off the darkening bruise from the killer's blow to her face. "I don't know," she said. "I'm sorry, Gabe. I'll do all I can. I didn't mean what I said — you know I'd never hurt her."

"I know — it's just — what *is that?*"

"Hold up," Carrie told the nurse. She bent closer. "It's . . . it's an imprint. She said he punched her in the face, didn't she?"

"Yeah. The bastard was wearing a ring."

"A ring with a figure eight embossed on it." Carrie lifted her head and met Gabe's eyes. "Ambrose," she whispered.

He nodded. "Go, take care of her. I'll get hold of Bryan."

She nodded, dipping into her pocket and tossing him her cell phone. "The number's in there." Then she raced down the hall after the gurney.

18

Ambrose led Sam into the tumbledown cabin and closed the door behind him, plunging them into inky blackness. Sam heard locks turning, then fading footsteps as the man, who seemed a stranger to him now, stomped away from him through the darkness. A second later there was a flare of light as Ambrose struck a match. It glowed orange on his face, then grew brighter as he held it to the wick of an old kerosene lantern.

Then Ambrose paused, gave his head a shake and said, "Sit down. I'll show you."

He brought the lantern to a rickety table, set it in the center, then looked around the room and found a chair Sam wasn't sure would support his weight. "Sit," Ambrose said again.

Sam looked at him, then at the door.

Ambrose pulled a gun from inside his jacket. He didn't point it at him, but the sight of it made Sam's heart pound harder.

"Sit," he said once more.

Sam sat.

Ambrose reached into his jacket again and pulled out a rolled-up newspaper, then unrolled it and laid it on the table. The headline was about the missing baby from sixteen years ago. "See?"

"See what?"

"The obvious. It's you, don't you get it?"

Sam did, but pretended not to. "No, I don't."

"Okay, well, I'll clarify. At the beginning, before I came here, I was thinking about the reward. I'd find the missing child and get proof he or she was the one they were looking for, and then I'd collect the money. It was almost too much to resist, you know? But then I realized that reward was only put there to get my attention."

"To get your attention?"

"Yes. They had to make sure I would notice it, would look into it a little bit."

"They?" Sam frowned. "Who are 'they'?"

Ambrose looked bewildered for a moment, then looked at the tabloid again. "I knew her. Your birth mother. Olivia."

"Look, I think you've got me confused with someone else."

"I'm not confused!" Ambrose snatched

the newspaper away, throwing it onto the floor, and got to his feet. "Why did you take off the tape? I didn't tell you to do that, did I?"

"No. I'm sorry. It was really uncomfortable."

"Well, I can't have that. I won't stand for disobedience. Do you understand?"

"Okay. Okay, I —"

"You will do as I say. You'll do as you're told from now on, or there will be repercussions!"

"All right."

"I know you're the one. I'm certain now. That's why I dispensed with that suffocating ski mask. Don't you see? You're the only sixteen-year-old in this town who was born at the right time, besides those other two."

"Kyle and Sadie, you mean?"

Ambrose closed his eyes. "But I ran their blood. It wasn't my type."

"Maybe it was the mother's type."

Ambrose's eyes flashed. "It would be *my* type. I know that."

"How do you know that?" Sam asked.

Ambrose lashed out and backhanded him right across the face, knocking Sam out of the chair and onto the floor. "Because I do," he said. "I *know*."

Sam didn't move as Ambrose paced away,

locating a backpack in a dusty corner. He must have stashed it there earlier. God knew he'd had time. It was after dark. Sam guessed he'd been taken between one-thirty and two this afternoon. "I know because Livvy's blood type was in the autopsy report, which was posted online by the *National Insider.* Kyle's and Sadie's blood wasn't her type, either. So that only leaves you."

Sam said, "Unless the kid isn't *in* Shadow Falls anymore at all. Did you ever think of that? This missing kid could be anywhere in the country. In the world for that matter. Are you going to kidnap every kid ever born in May or June sixteen years ago?"

"He's here. I know he's here. I *feel* it. It has to be you."

Sam didn't respond. It seemed safest not to say anything. This guy was completely nuts. And then he caught himself responding anyway. "Why did you kill Kyle? If you're just trying to find your kid, why kill Kyle just because he wasn't the right one?"

Ambrose stared down at Sam, and his face softened as he reached out his hand and waited for Sam to reach back. When Sam didn't, he lowered his own with a sigh. "I didn't mean to kill him."

"My mother said you injected him with

enough Benterol to kill a horse," Sam said. "How was that not supposed to kill him?"

"I misread the label." He lowered his head. "I only wanted to keep him out long enough to take him into the woods and leave him there to be found by the searchers."

Sam remembered Ambrose being the one to find Kyle's body. He remembered how far off the planned grid Ambrose had wandered, how far ahead of them he'd been. But he also remembered his reaction. He'd been sick, horrified. It hadn't seemed fake.

"He wasn't supposed to die," Ambrose said, and Sam thought there was a tear in his eye as he said it. "Neither was Nathan, but he saw the girl when she got away. And he saw me, too, running after her. He tried to reach her first, called out to her. Then he saw her fall, and he stood there, on the edge of that steep cliff, looking down at her. He had to die. He saw me. There was nothing I could do. I pushed him over and left them both." He closed his eyes, shook his head slowly and pushed a hand across his brow. "I was so relieved that Sadie survived the fall."

And that was when Sam saw the roll of duct tape in the man's left hand and the needle in his right.

"Listen, if that stuff killed Kyle, it'll kill me, too."

"No. No, it won't. I checked the label more carefully this time. It's point one zero cc's, not ten. It'll be fine. I just didn't see the decimal point."

"Just tie me up again," Sam said. "Just tie me up again and I won't try to get loose. I promise."

"I don't think that's going to be good enough, Sam. You're too smart." Ambrose smiled. "Just like your father."

Sam rose from the floor, backing slowly away and racking his brain to think of something, anything, to distract the man. And then something came to him. He prayed he was as good an actor as his drama club director kept saying he was, then grabbed his chest and started sucking in noisy breaths, one after another. He fell onto his knees and kept panting.

Frowning, Ambrose moved closer. "What — what's wrong? Sam, what's wrong?"

"A-a-asthma!" Sam stammered. "Need my in-in-in-haler!"

"Where is it?"

"H-h-home!" Reaching up a hand, Sam clutched Ambrose's shirt and whispered, "Don't let me d-d-die . . . Fa-Father."

And then he rolled his eyes back in his

head and fell backward onto the floor, refusing to wake up, even when Ambrose bent over him, shaking him. The man didn't inject him with anything. He didn't bind him again. He didn't threaten him. He held him in his arms, rocking him back and forth, and weeping. "I won't let you die, son. I won't let you die."

Batshit crazy, Sam thought. The guy was completely and totally batshit crazy.

His mother was in critical condition and awaiting brain surgery. Gabe could hardly believe she was at death's door. Suddenly she opened her eyes.

He sat by her bedside, glad she had come around and he would have a moment to talk to her before the operation.

"Oh, Gabe," she whispered. "I'm so glad you're here. I've messed up — badly."

"Yeah, you have. But I believe your heart was in the right place. I just . . . I need to know if there's anything else you haven't told me. Anything you've remembered . . . about the man who took Sammy. Any hint he gave as to where he might be going. Anything at all."

She shook her head. "No, there's nothing. But I do have something I need to say before . . . before the operation."

"All right."

She closed her eyes. "You'll hate me for this. But I don't think that's going to matter so much. The thing is, you've hated him your entire life, when there was never really a reason."

"What do you mean?"

Roseanna licked her lips and met Gabe's eyes. "Where is Carrie?"

"She had to leave. She made sure there were plenty of people here to take care of you, but she had to go with the police, Mom. She had to go find her son. Our son."

"My grandson." She inhaled nasally and closed her eyes. "Your father doesn't even know you exist, Gabriel."

Gabe frowned hard. "I don't understand. He's been sending money all these years to keep you quiet —"

"No, not him. His handlers. His attorney. His people, the ones he pays to take care of things for him. They never told him about you, Gabe. Part of our arrangement was that I would never tell him, either. If I did, the payments would stop."

"I don't understand. What are you saying?"

She had tears streaming down her cheeks now. "I never told him about you. His handlers didn't, either. They didn't pay me just to keep the public from knowing, but to keep Sammy Gold from knowing. He never knew about you, Gabe."

Gabe's heart seemed to crack in his chest. "He never even knew I'd been born? Mom, why?"

"I think they knew the kind of man he is. All that stuff about family and honor and doing the right thing — that's who he is, Gabe. It's not a part of his act. It's for real. If he'd known about you, he would have insisted on being a part of your life. He would have confessed the affair to his wife, maybe ending his marriage, and for sure tarnishing the family-man image and doing irreparable damage to his career. Fans are . . . well, they can be terribly unforgiving, you know."

"He doesn't know?" Gabe kept saying it over and over in his mind, still not quite sure it was for real.

"He doesn't know," she said. "He's never known."

"You didn't tell him. You kept my father from me for money? All those years?"

"I'm so sorry, Gabe. I'm so very sorry. I'd take it back if I could. I . . . I'm dying, Gabe. I'm dying."

"You're not dying. Carrie says this can be fixed. It's —"

"It's cancer. It's inoperable. They said six months — three months ago. And it's really getting bad now. The pain. The weakness. It's hitting me harder than before, and it'll get a lot worse for me from here on in. Until the end."

He stared at her, unbelieving. His mother . . . dying.

"Why didn't you tell me?"

"I didn't want your pity. But then this story about Livvy and her missing baby broke, and it just seemed to me to be a final chance to do the right thing. Find your son for you. To make up for robbing you of your father. And I did — I did — but then I lost him again."

"Sam's going to be all right, Mom."

"I'd give every penny I ever had to make sure of that, Gabe. I swear I would. But I know it's probably too little, too late."

The door opened and the pretty blonde nurse who stepped in said, "We're ready to take you to surgery now, Ms. Cain."

His mother nodded. "I'm ready to go." She looked at Gabe, looked at him hard. "I love you. No matter what you think, I love you. I always have, in my own selfish way."

The nurse tapped his shoulder. "You'll have to step out of the way."

He did, and then the nurse pulled the bed

straight out the door and headed down the hall to the elevators. Gabe followed and watched the doors close on his mother, then lunged and caught them before they shut all the way.

"I love you, too, Mom," he told her.

He wasn't even sure if he meant it. But he knew himself well enough to know he would regret not saying it if she died on the table. And he knew she needed to hear it. It cost him nothing to give her those words. It would cost him everything not to. So he told what might have been a lie. And he saw the relief in his mother's eyes as he stepped back and let the doors close.

He lowered his head, pinched his nose with his fingers, closed his eyes.

Someone clapped him on the shoulder. "She's in good hands," a man said.

Lifting his head, Gabe turned to see Bryan Kendall standing behind him, along with another uniformed officer. "We were looking for Carrie."

Gabe sniffed hard and tried to push his way through the overwhelming fog of emotion that had taken over his brain. "I thought she was with you."

Carrie was on her way to the little B and B where Ambrose Peck had been staying.

She'd phoned Bryan about the mark on Rose's face and the ring Ambrose had been wearing, and he'd said he would head out there to meet her and see what he could learn.

She knew the owner, Barbie Law, a woman in her mid-fifties with a heart as big as all outdoors and a love for gossip that was almost as huge. Barbie would feel terrible about what had happened to Sam, even while being thrilled to be at the center of it all. The after-hours visit from the police wouldn't bother her at all and would, in fact, only add drama to the story when she retold it to anyone who would listen. She would probably make them tea and serve cookies.

Mentally preparing herself not to let Barbie's tendencies get to her, Carrie jumped when the phone rang and pulled her car off to the side before answering.

Ambrose Peck's name was on the screen.

Her heart in her throat, Carrie stopped the car and answered the phone, schooling her voice to be utterly calm. *Don't let him know you know he's the one,* she thought. *Do let him know you're upset. He would expect you to be upset. He knows Sam is missing.*

She drew a breath and hit the answer button. "Hello?"

"Carrie, it's Ambrose. I need your help. Are you alone?"

"Yes, Ambrose. I'm alone. What — what's wrong? Where are you?"

"I'm with Sam. He needs you, Carrie. He's . . . well, he's sick."

She felt her heart go cold and instantly dropped her act. When she spoke again, the words emerged in a tone gone dangerously low. "What do you mean, *he's sick?*"

"His asthma," Ambrose said. "I didn't know. He's . . . he's having an attack. He says he needs his inhaler — and —"

"Just tell me where you are. I'll come." She had no idea what the hell was going on. Her son didn't have asthma, so what the — Wait a minute. Sam had seen enough asthma attacks to know how to fake one. They were noisy and dramatic, and always got everyone's attention and brought everything to a halt. Maybe he was faking.

"I have an extra inhaler in my bag," she said. "Along with his pills. If it's severe, he might need something stronger. He could die without help. Ambrose, you don't want him to die."

"No, no, I don't want that. But you have to come alone. If you don't —"

"I will. I'll come alone. Where are you?"

"There's a road through the state forest that leads to a fire tower," he said. "Do you know it?"

"Yes. We just call it Tower Road."

"There's a hunting cabin about halfway up. Barely discernible dirt track. A gate at the front with a faded No Trespassing sign. We're there. You really do need to come alone. Don't call anyone — especially the police. Just bring his medicine. And then you have to leave again. Do you understand?"

"I'm not a stupid woman, Ambrose."

"I never thought you were."

"I'll be there just as fast as I can," she promised, the car already in motion.

"Here's what we know," Bryan said as he led Gabe out of the hospital and into the cool night air so they could speak without the possibility of anyone overhearing them. "We got Peck's credit card info from Barbie Law at the B and B and ran a background check on him. And the thing is, Ambrose Peck is seriously ill. He's been in and out of psych wards since he was in his teens, and he has a history of going off his meds as soon as he feels better. He also has a history of stalking — gets obsessed with a woman, invents a relationship that never happened, then can't figure out why she pretends not to know him. That's what got him fired from his last job, which actually was as a financial advisor."

"And I was so eager to give him the benefit of the doubt." Gabe felt his heart flip-flop in his chest. "So do you think he has Sam?"

"I do. He was helping Nate Kelly, giving him financial advice, and somehow he got access to one of the cabins. I suspect Nate found out and Ambrose had to kill him. I don't know. I haven't put it all together yet, but I think we're close."

"And what about Carrie? Where the hell is she?" Gabe asked, looking up at the night sky helplessly.

"I don't know. She never showed up at the B and B, so I just figured she got held up here."

"I'm getting worried," Gabe said. "She's not answering her cell or her home phone, and she's not here. I don't know what to think."

"But you're thinking something. I can see you are." Bryan studied him and Gabe thought the guy was a good cop and apparently a decent human being, as well.

"If she's not here, she's out looking for Sam. But where?"

Just then his phone rang. Gabe damn near jumped out of his skin, but he picked it up fast, not even looking at the name on the call ID. "Carrie?"

"Yeah. It's me, but if you're with anyone, you need to pretend it's not. Understand?"

He frowned, glancing up at Bryan, shaking his head side to side. "Bill. Sorry, I was hoping you were someone else."

"So you're not alone?"

"No."

"I don't have time to wait for you to get that way, so I'll keep it simple. There's a hunting shack three miles up Tower Road. You'll know it by the gate and the No Trespassing sign at the end of the overgrown path that used to be a driveway. He told me to come alone, and I don't dare tell the cops. I'm almost there now. Get here as soon as you can, but be quiet and be careful."

"Um, I know you're in a hurry, Bill, but I'd really prefer you wait for my input on this."

"No can do. Get a map and get up here." She hung up, just like that. Bryan was watching him way too closely, Gabe realized. And his mother was having brain surgery.

"Bill, things here are a little crazy right

now," he said into the dead phone. "I'll get back to you in a couple of days." He folded his cell phone, and dropped it into his pocket. Then he looked at Bryan. "Look, you should be finding out all you can about this Ambrose Peck and hunting for any sign of his car. I need to stay here. My mother is having brain surgery. I can't leave, not even to go looking for Carrie."

Bryan nodded slowly. "I understand. All right, I'm heading back to the station. If Carrie calls, let me know. If we don't hear from her within the hour, I'm putting out an APB on her car, too."

"Good. Thanks for updating me, Kendall."

"You're welcome."

Bryan got into his car, and Gabe turned to head back toward the hospital doors, but only until Bryan's car was out of sight. As soon as the cop was gone, Gabe ran to his Volkswagen, got in and turned on the GPS system, programming a course for Tower Road in Shadow Falls.

The little machine told him it was "Planning Route" while he drummed his fingers impatiently, but finally the screen filled itself with a colorful backlit map. ETA: thirty minutes, the machine told him. And that was thirty minutes too damned long. Gabe started the engine and hit the gas.

19

Carrie turned the cell phone's ringer off and then hid it in the crotch of a crabapple tree outside the cabin where her son was being held prisoner. She saw the glowing light inside and hurried closer, walking as softly and as quickly as she could. In her hand, she clutched the inhaler she kept in her medical bag for emergencies, even though she was sure her son didn't need it, and the bag itself hung from her arm. She had left her car out at the road, a good thirty yards away, to make it easier for Gabe to find her and harder for Ambrose to know exactly when she was coming.

But he would know anyway. She was sure of it.

God, she was still stunned by the knowledge that Rose was Sam's grandmother. Gabe's mother. A woman who had used her own son to extort money from a superstar. Gabe had told her how strained his relationship with his mother was. And she knew that finding her here in town had been a shock to him, too. She'd been hard on him. Too hard, maybe.

Rose had tried to fight off a murderer and taken a serious injury in the process, all in an effort to save Sam. Carrie found herself believing the older woman's story. Believing *her.*

Why, then, was it so hard for her to believe Gabe? He'd told her once, before she'd learned the truth about him, that his feelings for her had been real. She'd been waiting for him to tell her again. To prove it to her. But maybe she should have listened to the wisdom of her son and just believed him. Just *decided* to believe him. It was what she wanted to be true, what she hoped was true. Why not just decide to believe it?

Such a radical notion. But it was feeling more and more like a valid one. Even to her.

But none of that mattered now. All that mattered right now was getting Sam back safe and sound.

She crept closer, edging around to one side of the cabin to peer through a dirty window. Inside, she saw Sam lying on the floor, some wadded-up bundle — a shirt, perhaps — under his head for a pillow. His eyes were closed. Ambrose was pacing — and holding a gun in his hand.

Backing away from the window, Carrie went to the cabin's only door and hoped to God Ambrose didn't intend to just shoot her once he had what he wanted.

She tapped on the door, then jumped backward when she heard him moving toward it. He opened it just a crack, looked left and right, then opened it farther. "Come inside. Quick!"

Carrie darted into the cabin, her eyes on her son. "Sam? Sam, honey, are you okay?" He didn't answer, and she turned accusing eyes on Ambrose. "What did you do to him?"

"Nothing. You brought the inhaler?"

"Did you give him anything? Did you drug him the way you did poor Kyle?"

"I didn't give him anything. It's his asthma, I tell you. Give him the inhaler and let's get on with this."

She almost blurted that an inhaler didn't work very well when the asthmatic was unconscious, but she bit the words back. Ambrose didn't need to know that, and Sam didn't need the inhaler, anyway. If something *was* truly wrong with him, it wasn't asthma. Trembling, Carrie knelt beside Sam, holding the inhaler near enough to his lips to make it look convincing and depressing it, so it released a short sharp puff of medication.

As Carrie bent over him, blocking his face from Ambrose's view, Sam opened his eyes slightly, winked at her and closed them again. Thinking fast, she backed away. "It's this dust! He's allergic. And it's a deadly allergy, Ambrose. It could kill him. We need to get him out of this filthy cabin."

"He's not going anywhere until I'm ready."

"Then he'll die," she said softly. "Why did you take him, Ambrose? Why did you take my son?"

"My son," he said. "He's my son. Not yours."

"And this is how you treat your son? You take him to a place that could kill him?"

Ambrose frowned, pursed his lips, paced a few steps one way, then a few steps the other. Finally he turned. "All right, we'll take him outside for a little while. But don't try anything, Carrie. I'm warning you."

"I wouldn't risk his life for anything in the entire world, Ambrose. I think you know that."

He held her eyes, searching them. Carrie went on, hoping the power of suggestion would be as effective on him as she had seen it be on certain patients. "You can see that I'm telling the truth by looking into my eyes. So look, and see. I mean it."

Ambrose stared for a long moment, and then, finally, he bent and scooped Sam up in his arms. Sam did a great job of pretending to be deadweight as Ambrose carried him out into the darkness of a night in the forest. A tiny patch of star-dotted sky was all that was visible between the fragrant limbs of the overhanging pines. Ambrose laid Sam down in the grass, then straightened, looking around. "Where's your car?" he asked.

"I left it by the road. I didn't think it would make it up here." Then, with an idea taking root in her mind, she added, "I'll be lucky if it's still there when I go back for it. I was so distracted, I left the keys inside." Then she knelt beside Sam again and set her medical bag on the ground beside her. She took out her stethoscope and made a show of listening to his breathing.

"He needs water. He's terribly dehydrated." Turning her head toward Ambrose, who hunkered beside her, she said, "Do you have any water here?"

"Some bottles. Inside."

"Would you get him one?"

"Do you think I'm an idiot, Carrie?"

She shot him a look as she took hold of Sam's hand where he couldn't see. "What do you think he's going to do, Ambrose? Suddenly recover from an asthma attack and —" she squeezed Sam's hand, *hard,* so he would understand that she was telling him exactly what to do "— make a run for it while you're gone? Go to my car and take off in search of help?"

She saw Sam's face tense, and he shook his head so slightly it was nearly imperceptible.

"He wouldn't leave me here with you, for one thing," she said. "Even if he knew you were going kill me no matter what." *Squeeze.* "He's just a kid. He'd never realize that his escaping would be my only chance." *Squeeze.* "Besides, he can't even walk. Look how blue his skin is. He's oxygen deprived. And if you really believed he was your son, you'd be doing something about it instead of worrying about protecting your own interests."

"You're trying to trick me, Carrie."

"Fine. I'll go get the water. But don't even pretend to think you could be related to Sam. You're evil, and he's nothing like you. My son knows enough to *always* do the right thing. *Always.* No matter what."

She rose to her feet and strode toward the

cabin, her heart beating a thousand miles an hour as she prayed Sam would do the right thing when she created an opportunity for him. He was an athlete. He was young and strong, and he could outrun damn near every kid on his soccer team, not to mention he could drive like a pro. He could do this. He could get away.

She opened the cabin door and spoke loudly to absolutely no one. "Who the hell are *you,* this maniac's accomplice?" And then she threw herself inside as if being jerked by some unseen hand, and slammed the door behind her.

Immediately she went for the lantern, blowing out the flame. Then she hurled it through the only unbroken window, shattering the glass.

Barely a second passed before Ambrose was slamming through the cabin door, peering inside. He struck a match and held it high, looking around the room. And then he saw her standing there, and his eyes widened as she brought the iron frying pan around in a home run swing.

Quicker than she'd expected him to, he ducked, dropped the match and tackled her with his head and shoulders to her midsection. His momentum carried her backward until they smashed into the wall, the impact forcing the air from her lungs.

She brought her hands up and clawed his face, his neck, yanked his hair. He backed off, tugging free of her and swinging a fist to her face. It connected, and then he turned, lunging for the door. She leaped onto his back, linking her arms around his neck and squeezing for all she was worth. She had to hold him off, had to give Sammy time to get away. She told herself he was running even now, heading for the road, for her car. He could make it. He *would* make it.

Ambrose growled and backed up hard until he smashed her into the stovepipe that thrust up through the ceiling. It clattered to the floor, and she felt soot raining down on her as she reached behind her to clasp a length of the broken pipe. She brought it around in a two-handed roundhouse, but only managed to hit him in the shoulder.

Ambrose swung at her with his other arm. His fist connected, and her head snapped back, hitting the cast-iron woodstove as she fell to the floor.

She saw stars, even though she was indoors. And her final thought was of Sammy. Please, she prayed, let him have had enough time.

■ ■ ■ ■

Gabe was pushing the VW Bus harder than he had ever pushed *any* vehicle, up the twisting cow path that his GPS told him was Tower Road. The curves were so snake-like and sudden that the bus kept losing its footing and skidding around them, as if the loose gravel were standing water.

He was terrified at the thought of Carrie facing down that madman alone. The fear of losing her was as big as his fear of losing the son he'd only just found. He refused to consider the possibility that he would lose either one of them.

He couldn't. He *wouldn't.*

And so he pressed harder on the gas, then nearly lost control when he saw headlights bounding toward him. At the last minute he recognized Carrie's minivan. She apparently recognized the bus, too, because she skidded to a halt in a cloud of dust and got out.

Except it wasn't her.

"Sam!" Gabe wrenched his door open and got out, too, running to the boy. He wrapped his arms around Sam, hugging him hard. "Thank God, thank God!"

"No." Sam was twisting against his embrace. "Gabe, let go! We've gotta go back for Mom!"

Gabe dropped his arms. "Ambrose has her?"

"Yeah, and I'm afraid he'll kill her when he figures out I'm gone. The guy's completely insane, Gabe." He pulled free and raced around to the passenger side of the bus. "Get in. Come on!"

Gabe yanked his phone from his pocket and tossed it to Sam as he climbed back behind the wheel. "Call Bryan."

"We can't wait for the police," Sam said, but he was dialing as he said it.

"I know. Just call anyway."

Nodding hard, Sam continued hitting numbers. Then he pointed. "It's around the next bend. Stop here. We'll cut through the woods."

"Okay." Gabe pulled over and got out. "You stay here. Wait for the cops. I'll go get her."

"Yeah, right." Sam was out of the car as soon as it came to a halt, speaking rapidly into the phone as he ran. "Hunting cabin off Tower Road. Ambrose Peck has my mom and a gun. Hurry!" Then he pocketed the phone and ran ahead of Gabe into the woods.

"We've got to save my mom, Gabe. I know she's done some things she maybe shouldn't have, but . . ." His voice tightened, as if his throat were closing up. "I love her."

"So do I," Gabe said, and then he realized he'd said it and blinked in stunned shock. "Hell, so do I."

"Shh. There's the cabin."

Sam parted some branches, and they looked toward the cabin. Light was flickering through the open windows, and everything was quiet.

"Livvy and I met in the hospital when we were both very sick," Ambrose was saying as he paced. "It was love at first sight."

Carrie had shaken off her stupor to find herself bound to a rickety chair with what felt like duct tape holding her wrists and ankles. But she hadn't been gagged, so to buy herself some time, she'd started talking, asking Ambrose about why he thought he was Sam's father.

"Was it a mental hospital?" she asked.

He shot her a hateful look. "I am *not* insane. And she was only there for a suicide attempt. Signed herself in to keep herself alive."

"This was the one in Galveston?" she asked.

"How do you know that?" he demanded. "You knew her, didn't you? Sam *is* her son, isn't he?"

"Sam is *my* son," she said. "And even if he wasn't, he wouldn't be yours. Not if your only contact with Livvy was in that hospital. Because that was well over a year before he was born."

"It was not!"

"Yeah, it was. Think about it, Ambrose. Think really hard."

"You're wrong. He's mine. I know he is."

"He's not yours, Ambrose. He's mine. Mine . . . and Gabe's."

He shot her an expression that was nothing short of stunned. Good. It was keeping him distracted. "I was under the impression you and Gabe had only just met."

"That's what we wanted people to think. Until I was ready to tell Sam, I mean."

He lowered his head and was silent for a long moment. And then he lifted it again, his eyes ablaze with something she hadn't seen in them before. "I know what you're trying to do. Keep me here until the help *my son* has gone for arrives. But it's not going to work."

"I was only trying to clarify the situation for you, Ambrose. You're on a path of destruction — destruction of everyone you encounter, and of yourself, in the end — all in search of a child that cannot possibly be yours."

He blinked at her. "Even if that were true, and it's not, but even if it were, I have to kill you. You know that, right?"

She could hardly believe he'd looked right into her eyes and told her he was going to kill her. It was the most frightening thing she had ever experienced, because she could tell he meant it.

"You don't have to kill me. You don't have to do anything you don't want to do. You have a choice, Ambrose."

"You know who I am."

"So do the police, by now. Killing me just gives them more to charge you with. Look, why don't you run right now? Go to Mexico or South America or somewhere without an extradition policy and —"

He brought the gun up, pointed it at her head, thumbed back the hammer. "I'm sorry, Carrie. I actually kind of liked you."

"Ambrose, this doesn't make any sense."

"My son chose you over me. It makes perfect sense. Goodbye, Carrie."

The door crashed open. Ambrose turned involuntarily in that direction even as the gun went off, and Carrie saw Gabe jerk backward, then catch himself and surge forward again. He tackled Ambrose, and the gun went flying. As the two men wrestled on the floor, Sam ran in, moving quickly to her side, and freeing her hands and feet.

She stood up and pushed him toward the door. "Get out. Get out now!"

Then she let go of him, her eyes glued to the men still fighting on the floor. As they rolled briefly apart, she saw the spreading red stain on Gabe's shirt, and her heart turned into a machine that pumped raw fury through her veins.

Ambrose scrambled for the gun, and Carrie heard a roar like that of an angry lioness, then realized she was the one who'd made the sound. She lunged, kicking the gun aside, then kicked again, this time connecting with the side of Ambrose's head.

He rolled away, then pushed himself up onto hands and knees, but she strode after him, delivering a kick to his belly that lifted him off the floor, and when he landed facedown and tried to push himself up again, she grabbed the chair that had held her and swung it over her head and down onto his. It splintered to bits.

He stayed down that time.

She picked up the gun and hurled it out through the open door, then realized Sam was still there. "Get help, baby," she told him. "Get help for Gabe."

"It's already on the way, Mom."

Nodding, she dropped to her knees beside Gabe, tearing open his shirt and looking at the pulsing wound in his abdomen. She ripped a section off the shirt, then tore it into two pieces, which she wadded up before pressing one to the entry wound in his abdomen and the other to the exit wound in his back.

Gabe reached up to take her bloody hand. "You okay?"

"I'm fine." She managed to drag her gaze from the wound to meet his eyes. Sam was kneeling beside them, too. He'd found the shirt he'd been using as a pillow earlier, and put it underneath Gabe's feet, to elevate them and prevent him from going into shock. Trying not to cry, Carrie asked Gabe, "Why did you go and get yourself shot like that?"

"Seemed like the thing to do at the time."

"That's so much bull," Sam said. "It's because he loves you, Mom. He said so on the way here."

She blinked rapidly, her gaze jumping from Sam's to Gabe's again. "You did? You said that?"

But his eyes had fallen closed just as sirens started screaming their way.

Sam leaned close and spoke near Gabe's

ear. "I know you're my dad. So you better be okay, Gabe. You've got a lot of time to make up for."

Carrie saw Gabe's eyes twitch at those words and decided to believe he had heard them. And that they would help.

20

"Ambrose Peck did spend some time with Livvy Dupree in that psych center in Galveston," Bryan explained. "Fixated on her, even though he only knew her for a week or less. His scrambled brain ignored the fact that a pregnancy takes nine months, not eighteen. When he saw the headlines, he believed they were placed there to get his attention by some higher power. And the rest of the tale spun out in his mixed-up mind from there. Somehow he got one thing right when he finally fixated on Sam as Livvy's son."

"Where is Ambrose now?" Carrie asked.

"He's been transferred to a psych ward for the time being. He's unfit to stand trial the way things stand. He's admitted to killing Kyle Becker, though he insists the murder wasn't intentional. He also admits to killing Nate Kelly, and that one he said was deliberate."

Carrie stood in her doorway, dressed to the nines and eagerly anticipating a special night out. But Bryan's visit was welcome, all the same. "He really is ill. And Kyle's still dead. I just — there's just no sense to be made of any of this, is there, Bryan?"

"I can't see any. But at least it's over. Truly over, this time. And the kids of this town are safe again."

"Thanks for the news, Bryan. I appreciate you keeping us posted."

"You're welcome."

He headed back to his car and pulled away just as the VW Bus arrived. Gabe got out, favoring his left side only a little. He was still sore but otherwise fully recovered from the bullet that had passed cleanly through him.

He stood beside the bus, smiling at Carrie, waiting.

She'd asked him a dozen times since that night how he felt about her. But he kept putting her off, telling her it had to wait, first until he got out of the hospital, then until he was fully healed. And then until this special night. It had been two weeks. Two grueling weeks.

But he loved her. She had taken Gabe's own philosophy to heart and simply decided to believe that he loved her. And tonight, she thought, he was going to tell her so.

He'd had a lot to deal with, she knew that. His mother had been transferred to a hospice center in the Hamptons, very high-end. He hadn't made peace with the life she'd forced on him, but he wasn't moping about it, either. It was in the past, he said. And maybe before she died they would even become close again. Gabe was certainly making an effort.

Carrie descended the stairs and hurried toward the bus, where Gabe waited, holding her door.

"You look gorgeous, as always." His eyes said he meant it.

"Thank you. Are you ready to tell me yet what this is all about?"

"Yeah. I'm taking you to meet the rest of my family."

She frowned at him, both puzzled and excited. "Am I overdressed?" she asked, looking down at the little black sequined dress, the high heels, the shoulder wrap.

"You're beautiful and perfect. And your chariot awaits." He indicated the door, and she got in, trying to stop smiling so much.

An hour later Carrie sat in the reserved box seat beside Gabe, the man she adored but hadn't yet told so. When they'd arrived at the venue, the marquee out front had announced that Sammy Gold was playing to a sold-out crowd for one night only.

"I had no idea," she'd told Gabe breathlessly, leaning close. "And these seats!"

"It was the least he could do for the son he never knew he had," Gabe said. "Relax, enjoy."

"I can't believe you talked to him and didn't tell me about it."

"I've actually been talking to him quite a bit. He helped me plan this night, as a matter of fact. But I didn't want to ruin the surprise, so I had to keep it to myself. And it wasn't easy, keeping it quiet that he was going to be playing only two hours from home." Gabe looked into her eyes. "It was killing me not to share it all with you, but I'll fill you in. Later, though."

She blinked, because that meant something. Didn't it? That he wanted to share what was happening between him and his long-lost father with her?

No time to think. The lights went down, the spotlight came up, and the crowd roared as Sammy Gold took to the stage. He wore black jeans and a Western shirt with rhinestone stars on the shoulders, and he began playing one of his most beloved tunes. It was hard to hear above the wild applause, but eventually the noise died down and Carrie was able to enjoy her favorite artist playing one of her favorite songs.

When he finished, he took the microphone from its stand and looked out over the crowd, his face a road map of the life he'd lived. He held up his hands for silence and said, "This next number is a very special one, a brand-new song written by the son I never knew I had — and since it's gonna be hittin' the tabloids next week, I may as well break the news myself right here and now. It turns out that I am the proud father of the award-winning songwriter Mr. Gabriel Cain. Stand up, Gabe, so the folks can take a gander at you."

There was a gasp, a lot of muttering, a smattering of applause that grew louder, as Gabe rose to his feet and the spotlight picked him out. He gave a shy wave, then sat back down.

"And here to help me perform it," Sammy Gold went on, "is my grandson, Sam Overton."

"Sam?" Carrie whispered, with a quick look at Gabe.

He nodded, smiled. "Just watch."

She did, returning her attention to the stage as her Sammy stepped out from behind the curtains and shyly took up a position beside his grandfather.

"Say hello to the audience, Sam," the living legend said.

Sam gave a confident wave and leaned closer to the microphone before him. "I'm pretty much a classic rock guy, but I guess I'll have to learn to adjust. Turns out, country music runs in the family."

Laughter broke out, and then Sam the elder struck the opening chords of a song and Sam the younger joined in.

"You are the woman
I've waited my whole life to find.
You're the one who makes me want to
leave
My wanderin' ways behind.
You're the one who's had my heart,
Holdin' it for me to claim
And now I'm here, to take it back,
If you'll just take my name.
Carrie, sweet Carrie
You're the girl I want to marry
Damn far-sight from ordinary
Won't you say you'll be my wife?
Carrie, marry me."

As the final chord echoed throughout the arena, Sammy Gold pointed at the spotlight and led it with his forefinger until it fell on Carrie, sitting dumbstruck in her seat in the balcony.

Grinning, the living legend boomed, "In case you didn't get it, little lady, that was a proposal. Uh, from my son, that is. What do you say?"

She turned to stare at Gabe in shock, even as he dropped from his chair and down onto one knee in front of her. It was a moment before she could tear her tear-filled eyes from his long enough to realize there was a ring in his hand. The audience had fallen stone silent.

"You wrote that song . . . for me?"

"I did."

"You really *did* say you loved me that night, in the woods, didn't you?" she whispered.

"I did. And I'll say it again and again. I love you, Carrie. You're the only woman in the universe I would have wanted raising my son — our son — all this time. I'll die being grateful for that — and for that alone, if you say no. But I'm hoping you'll say yes and give me even more to be grateful for. Say you'll marry me, please?"

Tears streaming now, she smiled through them and managed to blurt the words, "Yes, Gabe. Yes, I'll marry you."

The crowd roared, every single member of the audience rising to their feet as the thunderous applause grew louder.

"Well, now," Sammy Gold drawled. "I guess I just got me a little more family to love." He hit the strings again and launched into a happy song as Gabe rose and folded Carrie into his arms for the kiss to end all kisses.

Right then and there, Carrie decided to believe that she would always be this happy. And she was right.

We hope you have enjoyed this Large Print book. Other Thorndike, Wheeler, Kennebec and Chivers Press Large Print books are available at your library or directly from the publishers.

For information about current and upcoming titles, please call or write, without obligation, to:

Publisher
Thorndike Press
295 Kennedy Memorial Drive
Waterville, ME 04901
Tel. (800) 223-1244

or visit our Web site at:

http://gale.cengage.com/thorndike

OR

Chivers Large Print
published by AudioGO Ltd
St James House, The Square
Lower Bristol Road
Bath BA2 3SB
England
Tel. +44(0) 800 136919
www.audiogo.co.uk

All our Large Print titles are designed for easy reading, and all our books are made to last.